For Moran —

THE FOREVER GAME

Life-Saving Technology Can Be Deadly

To the future of humanity, the ultimate forever game.

JEFFREY JAMES

HIGGINS

Black Rose Writing | Texas

The author grants the final approval for this literary material.

First printing

This is a work of fiction. Names, characters, businesses, places, events, and incidents are either the products of the author's imagination or used in a fictitious manner. Any resemblance to actual persons, living or dead, or actual events is purely coincidental.

ISBN: 978-1-68513-379-5
LIBRARY OF CONGRESS CONTROL NUMBER: 2023949145
PUBLISHED BY BLACK ROSE WRITING
www.blackrosewriting.com

Printed in the United States of America
Suggested Retail Price (SRP) $24.95

Credit for Author Photo: Rowland Scherman, Rowland Scherman Photography, https://www.rowlandscherman.com/

The Forever Game is printed in Garamond Premier Pro

*As a planet-friendly publisher, Black Rose Writing does its best to eliminate unnecessary waste to reduce paper usage and energy costs, while never compromising the reading experience. As a result, the final word count vs. page count may not meet common expectations.

For Amir Farahat Abdelmalek, my brother-in-law and friend.
You were creative, generous, and loving. You left us far too soon,
but you'll never be forgotten. I miss you. Rest in peace.

THE
FOREVER
GAME

CHAPTER ONE

DEA Special Agent Adam Locke stared out the naval ship's open hull door and across the dark Caribbean at Haiti, a sliver of terra firma on the horizon, but the cloudy night obscured the island and hid predators above and below the surface of the rolling sea. His target lived there, in the shadows, and from his lair, he spread poison and death around the world.

"It's dark as fuck," Brian Moore said. Adam's assistant team leader had whispered, even though the ship lay miles offshore.

"Good," Adam said. "Let's hope it stays that way."

Adam had planned to launch their mission under the cover of a new moon, and the clouds were an unexpected benefit. Darkness aided both monsters and the men who hunted them.

Adam grasped the bulkhead's coaming and leaned out the ship's port beam, fifteen feet above the waterline. A cargo net hung from clamps and almost reached the water. A three-foot chop roiled the sea, hopefully enough to deter lookouts who usually buzzed around in motorboats like green flies feasting on a carcass.

The USS Minuteman, a San Antonio-class amphibious transport dock, had departed Norfolk three days before to deliver Adam's FAST team of twelve special agents to Côteaux, a small commune on Haiti's Southern claw—the home of Jean Laguerre.

Laguerre controlled a massive transnational criminal organization and had been a DEA high-value target for years. He imported Colombian cocaine and Mexican heroin into the US, but worse, he used his smuggling routes to traffic young girls, condemning hundreds of women to the flesh trade. Until recently, Laguerre had used the corrupt Haitian government as protection from American law enforcement, but then he had made the fatal mistake of transporting materials for Hezbollah across the US border. Narco-terrorism was the nexus between law enforcement and the military, and the justification DEA needed to access naval assets.

"Agent Locke?" an unfamiliar voice called out.

Adam turned back to the passageway bathed in red light, as a sailor stepped off a ladder.

"I'm Locke."

"Phone call for you, sir. It's patched through from the DEA Command Center. They told me to tell you it's Ms. Hope."

Effie? Why was his girlfriend calling when he was deployed on an operation? She knew better than that.

"Take a message. We're about to launch."

"Aye, aye, sir." The sailor climbed the ladder.

"It could be an emergency," Brian said. "Want us to hold?"

"The mission comes first," Adam said. A knot formed in his stomach. "We're on a timeline, and we must follow protocol. I'll call when we're safely back aboard."

Adam faced away so Brian couldn't see the worry on his face. Effie had not been feeling well, and he didn't want to ignore her—but rules were rules. Shit. They needed to wrap up this mission so he could get home to her.

Adam pivoted on the rubber mat, already wet with salty dew, and swung his leg through the door. He stretched his leg along the gray hull to the life net, which was constructed of rough-hewn rope and designed as an evacuation ladder. He hooked it with his toe, then grabbed the thick rope with his gloved hand.

His Colt M4 carbine bounced against his chest as he moved. He wore a ballistic vest with SAPE plates in the front and back to prevent rifle rounds from penetrating. Eight Velcro pouches attached to his MOLLE cover contained a radio, smoke grenade, GPS, ten thirty-round magazines of 5.56mm ammunition, medical kit, and a Glock 22 .40-caliber handgun.

Adam glanced at the black water. This far off the coast, the ocean floor lay forty fathoms below. His gear weighed fifty-two pounds, a light combat load, but if he fell into the sea, he would go straight to the bottom, despite two tactical inflatables attached to his utility belt. And then there were the sharks. Those silent beasts had terrified him since he roamed the beaches of Cape Cod as a child.

He released the bulkhead, grasped the net with both hands, and shifted his weight onto it. He swung onto the ship's hull. His arms strained under the weight of his gear, and he squeezed the rope tighter.

Water splashed against the hull twenty feet below. He crouched and found the next horizontal strand with his boot toe. He transferred his weight into it and descended.

The low hum of an engine drew his attention to two Naval Special Warfare RHIBs—rigid-hull, inflatable boats with twin 470-hp engines—maneuvering toward the ship from their staging area. The RHIB's boat teams, each manned by three Special Warfare Combat Craft Crewmen, would deliver Adam's team to a remote cove five kilometers from Laguerre's residence.

Adam paused ten feet above the water as the first RHIB moved beneath him. Its rubber sides ground against the steel hull, and a childhood memory flashed in his mind of playing on an inflatable raft off Nauset Beach.

The RHIB's engines purred as it rose and fell with each wave. The thirty-six-foot boat had a cockpit near the bow and mounted fifty-caliber machine guns fore and aft. A radar and communications array jutted above the cockpit and offered the latest classified technology.

The boat team leader waved him down, and Adam took a deep breath. He needed to land near the stern, where eight members of his Alpha team would stand against padded backrests. The last two members of his team would join eight agents on loan from Bravo Team in the second RHIB.

Adam had to time his drop perfectly or risk being crushed between the boat and the Minuteman's hull. He climbed down two more rungs and waited.

The RHIB dipped into the trough of a wave, then rose again.

Adam stepped off the net and released it. He plummeted into space.

The boat crested a swell as Adam's boots collided with the deck. A crewman grabbed his shoulders and steadied him as they dropped into another trough.

Easy.

Effie waited for him at home in their bed. She had not sounded well the last time they spoke, and dread had tinged her voice when she mentioned her abdominal pain. Had she made it to her doctor yet? The long absences required by DEA were hardest when things happened at home. He should be with her right now, not floating beside a naval ship in the Caribbean.

Adam lowered his AN/PVS-15, dual-tube night vision, off his helmet, and it clicked into place. He turned the dial, and through goggles known as "nods," the world glowed green. He looked up at Brian, who peeked out the hull door. Adam waved him down. They had to hurry to their target, find Laguerre, then return to the ship before the sea came alive with commercial fishermen and compromised the mission. If they missed him, Laguerre would go underground.

They had one shot to cut off the head of the snake.

CHAPTER TWO

Adam crouched on the beach and pointed his M-4 carbine at the rear wall of Laguerre's compound while the rest of his team disembarked from the second RHIB and plodded ashore. Alpha Team's eight agents would make the entry, while eight members of Bravo Team would cover the perimeter and two Alpha agents would hold the beachhead. The forest was quiet at night, except for the lapping of waves behind them and the occasional chirping insect or croaking frog.

His men moved into a semicircle and lay prone, their weapons pointing out. They had practiced this assault dozens of times on the Lunga Reservoir beside the DEA Academy in Quantico, Virginia.

Intelligence from Adam's human source indicated Laguerre would be home with two or three bodyguards and possibly a girlfriend from his harem. Video from a DEA overflight had confirmed three vehicles in the circular driveway in front of the residence, including Laguerre's Escalade.

Adam scanned the wall. No cameras. That was sloppy of Laguerre. The protection money he paid to Haitian officials had given him a false sense of security. He must feel untouchable.

The commune of Côteaux lay on the southern coast, 250 miles west of Port-au-Prince. The island of Hispaniola was shaped like a lobster claw, and its southern pincer had been strangled by poverty and disease. Far from the power of the central government, it had become a perfect haven for

Laguerre. Most of the commune's nineteen thousand residents lived in two-room hovels with mud walls, thatched roofs, and shuttered windows—but Laguerre lived in luxury. His domicile lay halfway between Côteaux and Roche-à-Bateaux, in the Côteaux Arrondissement. His two-story, eight-bedroom residence had concrete construction, a tiled roof, and a satellite dish. A Haitian palace.

Unfortunately, it also came with armed guards and ten-foot exterior walls topped with concertina wire.

Laguerre's residence faced the only road, Route Departmentale Twenty-Five, which paralleled the coast. According to satellite imagery, which Adam had meticulously studied, Laguerre kept his armed guards at his main gate by the road. His backyard extended to a dock on the sea where a forty-foot yacht floated in darkness. The walls kept his property safe, but an approach by water appeared unguarded.

Two members of Bravo team moved up the beach, then followed the west side of the walled compound toward the front, and two others mirrored them on the eastern side. Pairs of agents positioned themselves on the southeast and southwest corners of the compound and stayed behind cover. The last two Alpha members remained on the beach and covered the rear.

Adam released the foregrip of his M4 and keyed the microphone attached to his ballistic vest.

"Alpha Six, Alpha One," he said.

"Six, go," Special Agent Dean Rafferty responded.

"Breacher team up."

Rafferty, Alpha team's demolitions specialist, crept forward with Brian at his hip. Rafferty aimed at the door while Brian scanned the top of the wall.

Adam watched Bravo team focus outward, ignoring the breach team. Human nature made it difficult to look at nothing when something exciting was happening behind you, yet every agent aimed his muzzle at his individual area of responsibility. True professionals. Adam smiled.

Rafferty shrugged off his pack and knelt beside the wooden door. Brian stepped aside and trained his carbine on it. He grasped the door handle and jiggled it. The door remained closed. Brian looked at Rafferty and shook his head.

Rafferty unbuckled a flap on his pack, dug inside, and carefully removed a linear breaching charge. The device comprised three tightly coiled detonation cords wrapped in electrical tape, with a small square of C-4 high explosives in the center for insurance. Rafferty affixed a blasting cap to the exposed pigtail of detonation cord and attached two leads. Rafferty had built a replica door in Quantico, based on surveillance video footage a source had taken from a passing boat. It should be enough to breach the thick door.

Rafferty unraveled double-sided tape, ran it down the hinged side of the door and affixed the charge. He held the initiator and spool of wire as he backed down the wall. Brian walked with him, keeping his barrel pointed at the rear door. They stopped twenty feet away, and Rafferty looked across the beach in Adam's direction.

"Alpha One, Alpha Six."

"One," Adam said.

"Primed and ready."

"Standby. Entry team, Alpha One. Form up on me." Adam stood and shifted to the opposite side, twenty feet from the door.

His team moved from the beach into their positions around him. They formed a staggered column, each pointing a carbine to an alternating side. As team leader, he would be near the back of the stack. He wanted to be first through the door, but those days were over. He needed space to manage his team, like a coach on the sideline.

Adam reached his AN/PRC-163 radio strapped into a pouch on his left side and turned the knob from his VHF/UHF tactical channel to the SATCOM link. He needed to reach his intelligence cell on the USS Minuteman to see if they had any intelligence updates from their telephone intercepts, their confidential source, or the quick reaction force's advance team. Laguerre had at least 130 armed men in the Côteaux Arrondissement, and if DEA's infiltration had been compromised, Adam needed to know. They could still signal the RHIBs and retreat. He waited for the radio to beep in his headset, and when it did, he transmitted.

"Delta Base, Alpha One."

Nothing.

"Delta Base, Delta Base, this is Alpha One. Come in."

Static.

"Shit."

Brian glanced at him.

"Delta Base. Do you copy?"

Silence.

Adam shook his head. Why did technology always fail at the worst time? A dog barked in the distance. Adam listened. No sound from Laguerre's residence.

DEA seldom acted without host country permission, and missions like this were rare, but the attorney general himself had signed off on Operation Lobster Boil. The Haitian government did not know they were there, which meant the Haitian National Police would not help. That agency had been far too corrupted to trust with this mission. DEA's FAST Charlie and Delta teams had surreptitiously infiltrated Haiti under the cover of a State Department-funded training mission, and they waited in three vans, halfway to Les Cayes, but it would take their quick-reaction force at least thirty minutes to arrive.

Half an hour was an eternity in a gunfight.

Having to make these decisions was what it meant to be a leader. He switched back to the tactical channel.

"Alpha Six, Alpha One."

"Alpha Six." Rafferty's voice sounded tight.

"Execute."

CHAPTER THREE

The explosion rocked the night. The pressure wave passed through Adam before the sound of the detonating breaching charge reached his ears. The door shattered and flew off its frame. His entry team, led by Special Agent Amir Boutros, hit the doorway as wood chips fluttered to the ground.

Boutros stepped across the threshold and broke left into a courtyard. The number two man went right and three and four covered the middle as the rest of the team flowed into the yard. Two-story stucco walls rose above yellowed grass. Wooden shutters stood open to allow the cool October air to infiltrate the structure. Green beams of infrared lasers flashed over each window as the team moved to the French doors at the rear of the house. Adam's breath fogged his goggles, and he pursed his lips to angle his breath down and away. He reached the structure and leaned against the wall.

The last man in the line knelt and covered the windows while the team stacked to the left of the entrance. Brian and Rafferty hustled through the yard and set up opposite them. Rafferty removed another breaching charge and watched Brian. Brian grabbed the door handle and turned it.

Open.

A light illuminated an upstairs bedroom and the entire yard glowed in Adam's night vision. They needed to hurry.

Brian held a flash-bang beside his face. Amir nodded. Brian flung the door open and tossed the grenade.

One, two, three, four . . . Adam closed his eyes.

Boom.

Adam opened his eyes as Boutros stepped through the door. Adam shuffled forward, and the stack flowed into the house. The team split, half moving through the kitchen and half through the dining room.

Crack, crack, crack.

Gunshots from outside. Adam tensed.

"Alpha One, Bravo Three," a radio call cackled in Adam's headset. "Contact side A, front gate. Target down."

Shit. The perimeter team had taken out a bad guy. A shooting overseas would draw much scrutiny from DEA Headquarters, the Department of Justice, and the Inspector General. Adam shook the thought away. Second-guessing now could get them killed.

"Bravo Three, Alpha One. Copy." Adam moved through the dining room into a foyer and aimed at a spiral staircase leading to the open second-floor hallway while his team cleared the rest of the first floor.

"Ki moun ki la?" a man's voice called from somewhere in the darkness upstairs.

Adam tightened his fingers on his carbine's grip and shouted. *"Lapolis."* Police.

A heavyset man wearing a white cotton shirt and jeans moved to the railing carrying an Uzi submachine gun.

Adam aimed his laser at the man's chest. "Police, drop the gun!"

The chandelier flooded the foyer with light, and Adam's view turned to a green blur. He flipped up his nods as the Uzi barked. Rounds ricocheted off the marble floor inches from him.

Adam squinted and pulled his trigger twice. The man ducked and poked his Uzi between the banister slats.

Adam lowered his aim and fired again, this time with a sustained burst.

Wood splintered, and the man screamed. The Uzi slipped over the side and crashed onto the marble. The man collapsed backward into the upstairs hallway—out of sight.

"Team, Alpha One. Target down, second-floor hallway."

"Alpha One, Alpha Two," Brian broadcast. "First floor clear. Coming in."

Brian appeared at Adam's side with his weapon trained on the upstairs hallway.

The man Adam had shot groaned. Blood pooled on the lip of the balcony, then dripped over the side and splattered onto the white marble.

"We're up," Brian said. "Ready."

"Bang the second floor," Adam said.

"Bang out." Brian threw a flash grenade, and it arced in the air and disappeared near where the downed man had fallen. Another Alpha team member threw a second flashbang onto the far side of the hallway.

Adam crouched on the balls of his feet. Ready. Get aggressive.

Bang . . . bang.

Adam moved, keeping his muzzle centered on the top of the stairs. Beside him, Brian covered the end of the hall. Adam paused and peeked over the last step, with only his helmet visible. He glanced left and right in a maneuver known as a quick peek. Four doors were closed on the right and four more on the left, all probably bedrooms. A bathroom stood open down the hallway.

Adam waited to feel a bump, a physical signal the team was ready. Brian nudged his leg, and Adam climbed to the top. He focused his carbine on the open bathroom door. Four agents moved past him and down the hallway. Adam didn't have to check behind him to know Brian had covered the opposing side of the corridor while the team searched.

The bodyguard lay in a pool of dark arterial blood in the hallway. His glassy eyes stared at nothing. An agent knelt beside him, rolled the body over, and handcuffed him. They handcuffed everyone. Even dead men.

In front of Adam, the leading agents stopped at the first door. The second man bumped the first, then sidestepped to have a clear shot. The first man turned the knob and threw the door open as the second charged into the room and broke left. The first agent followed and turned right.

The moment they entered, the second pair cleared a room on the opposite side of the hall. Adam remained in the hallway, covering the unsecure area. Behind him, doors opened, and boots thumped on the floor as his team swarmed into other rooms.

"Clear, coming out," the first agent called. Agents one and two exited the bedroom and moved to the next.

Bang, bang, bang.

Adam glanced behind him toward the shots fired, then quickly refocused on the hallway in front of him. His men would handle the violent confrontation, and Adam needed to cover his area of responsibility.

"Contact, B-C side," a voice crackled in Adam's headset. "Target down. Bodyguard in the closet with a shotgun."

"Alpha One copies."

Agents moved past Adam and searched the remaining bedrooms. Two posted on either side of the bathroom door. Adam lowered his weapon.

Both agents entered. Shower rings scraped on a metal rod.

"Clear, coming out."

Adam turned and hurried toward the rear bedroom where the shots had been fired. Had they killed Laguerre?

CHAPTER FOUR

A young, shirtless man sprawled over a shoe rack in the walk-in closet. A trickle of blood dripped out of a tiny hole in his forehead, and the back of his head was gone. Blood, white bone chips, and gray brain matter stuck to the wall. Another small hole had punctured the plaster near the blood spray pattern. A miss. Adam would have to remind his team to aim at the center of mass.

Adam entered the closet for a better look, and the metallic scent of blood and feces assaulted his sinuses. A shotgun protruded from underneath the body. Adam leaned in close and inspected the man's face.

The man was not Laguerre.

Adam keyed his mike and broadcast on the tactical channel, for the entry and perimeter teams only. "All, Alpha One. Negative jackpot. Repeat, negative jackpot."

"Alpha One, Alpha Two," Brian responded. "Good copy. What's the plan?"

"Perimeter team maintain position. I want a secondary search, then a quick SSE. We exfil in five mikes." SSE stood for Sensitive Site Exploitation. They needed to seize ledgers, address books, computers, telephones, or anything else that contained evidence of crimes.

"Copy."

Adam exited the closet and joined the agents involved in the shooting. They looked up with wide eyes.

"Who took the shot?"

"Me," Special Agent Jamal Davis said. An artery visibly thumped in his neck.

"What happened?"

"We cleared the room and Andy yanked the closet open. That fucker was holding a Mossberg. I double tapped him, and he went down."

Adam searched Jamal's eyes. Shootings were traumatic.

"Great job. He didn't get a shot off."

Jamal expelled a breath and nodded.

"You saved somebody's life," Adam said. He turned to Andrew. "You too. Textbook clearing. I want you to stay out of this room and let someone else document it, just to be safe. Go downstairs and search again."

"Yes, sir," Jamal said.

Adam moved down the hall and found Brian giving assignments. He waited for him to finish. Agents spread out to conduct a secondary search for Laguerre, then an SSE. Each agent carried plastic envelopes in their kit to secure anything of evidentiary value. Laguerre ruled a massive international organization and the DEA wanted to dismantle it. Had they been in the US, the search would take hours, but here, they had to get out fast.

Adam looked through towering foyer windows at the cars in the driveway, then turned to Brian.

"Laguerre's Escalade is here."

"We searched everything," Brian said.

"Clock's ticking. Where's the master bedroom?"

"Last door on the left."

"Come with me."

Adam stood in the doorway to the master bedroom and took in the entire scene. Bedding looked rumpled, as if it had been remade in haste. The closet door stood open, and clothes had fallen on the floor where his men had searched. The bureau and bed lay askew where agents had looked behind and under them, and the bathroom door was ajar.

Adam had always been able to think like a crook. If he had awoken to an unexpected raid, where would he hide? The house was grandiose, by Haitian standards, but did not contain a safe room. Assuming Laguerre had been sleeping when the explosive charge breached the outer wall's door, he would only have had a few minutes to hide.

"What would I do?"

Adam stepped into the room with Brian on his heels. He moved to the bathroom. Someone had ripped the shower curtain off and the cabinet door under the sink stood open. His men had done a good job with the initial search.

"Room's empty," Brian said.

Adam grunted and brushed past him. He stood in the middle of the room. A MacBook Air laptop was open on an antique writer's desk with a green leather surface.

"Take the laptop and any papers inside the desk," Adam said.

"On it." Brian pulled a DEA evidence envelope out of a MOLLE pouch attached to his vest.

Adam stood beside a nightstand and stared at the bed.

"The explosion wakes him. He hears his bodyguard yelling in the hallway. Where does he go?"

The bed, bureau, closet, and bathroom had been searched. The other bedrooms were smaller, but similar. Adam looked down at the unevenly made bedspread.

Why make the bed? He must have wanted them to think he wasn't here.

Adam looked at the nightstand. A clump of dust lay near a small brass clock. He froze. He forced himself not to look up.

"We're done here," Adam said. "Come with me."

"But I haven't finished bagging—"

"I said we're done." Adam stared hard at him and nodded toward the hallway.

Adam walked out, and Brian followed. In the hallway, Adam put his fingers to his lips. He moved around Brian and looked at the bedroom ceiling without entering the room. The ceiling was paneled with thick wood.

The residence had a gabled roof with red tiles, which meant a space existed between roof and ceiling.

Adam shouldered his carbine and pointed up. Brian moved to the opposite side of the door, ready.

Adam leaned into the room, muzzle first, and aimed at the ceiling above the bed.

"Jean Laguerre," Adam said. "This is the DEA. *Lapolis.* Come down now or I'll shoot."

Nothing.

"We know you're up there."

A panel moved with a loud scrape, and dust drifted off the ceiling. Adam lowered his finger onto his trigger.

Two bare feet appeared, then a naked Laguerre dangled from the ceiling. He dropped onto the nightstand and raised his hands above his head.

CHAPTER FIVE

A ramp lowered in the USS Minuteman's stern, now that stealth was no longer necessary, and both RHIBs motored into the dock inside the ship. The boat crews tied off to the railings along the perimeter, and Adam climbed a metal ladder onto a walkway.

Adam pointed at Laguerre. "Take him into the holding berth and photograph him to document his physical condition. I don't want him claiming we abused him."

"On it, boss," Brian said. He climbed onto the walkway.

"How's Jamal doing?" Adam whispered. "He say anything on the way back?"

"He's fine. Adrenaline's still pumping. It was a righteous shoot."

Adam nodded. "Closets are tough. I don't want the stress to make him go on tilt."

"You and your poker terminology. Didn't your parents teach you gambling was bad?"

What parents? "Poker isn't gambling. It's a game of skill."

Brian laughed. "That's why I'll never play with you again." He hurried off to deal with Laguerre.

Adam's body hummed. Getting shot at and coming close to dying left him with an adrenaline-driven, insatiable quest for life, a desire to swing from a chandelier or draw a saber and sail the high seas. After a gunfight, he always had a giddiness, a lust for sex. His life has almost ended, and he wanted to experience every moment of whatever time he had left.

He needed to call Effie.

His men helped a handcuffed Laguerre off the RHIB and onto the dry dock. Two agents carried boxes of seized documents, cellular telephones, and hard drives. Adam wished they had searched more, but they had needed to leave before Laguerre's henchmen arrived. Eighteen agents were barely enough for a raid and an insufficient number to withstand an assault.

"Clean up here," Adam said. "I'll call HQ."

"They gonna be okay with this?"

"Who knows? All three shootings were textbook."

Shootings were rare in DEA and in law enforcement in general. Only a small percentage of law enforcement officers ever fired their guns outside a range, and only a fraction of them had been involved in multiple shootings. Now, Adam had to justify life-and-death decisions made in milliseconds to bureaucrats on the twelfth floor of DEA Headquarters. Luckily, Doug Barnstable had been promoted to deputy section chief of the FAST tactical teams. Doug had been an exemplary agent and had only left FAST because his aging knees could no longer take the strain. Doug would support them.

The starboard hatch cracked open, and a sailor entered wearing a blue camouflage navy working uniform. He looked around the dock, then made his way to Adam.

"Excuse me, Sir. Who's Agent Adam Locke?"

"I am."

"We have an urgent call for you, topside, Sir. I was ordered to get you as soon as you came aboard."

Did the DEA already know about the shooting?

Adam followed the sailor up a ladder to the communications room. Another sailor offered him a headset. Adam unclipped his helmet, pulled off his Pelletier headset, and set them on a metal console. He took the headset.

"This is Adam Locke."

"Adam, it's Doug," the deputy section chief said.

"Hey, Doug. We just came aboard. It was about to call you and—"

"Everyone safe?"

"Yes, Sir. No friendlies injured, and we have jackpot, but three suspects are KIA."

"Crap. Okay, we'll deal with that later. Congrats on getting our man."

"Thanks, my guys did well, they—"

"Listen, Adam, I need you to assign your backup to orchestrate transporting your prisoner to CONUS."

"I'm handling it. I—"

"There's a problem."

Adam's chest tightened. "Problem?"

"There's no easy way to say this . . . your girlfriend had a medical emergency. She—"

Adam's body turned to ice. "Effie? When? What happened?"

"The Comms Center received a call from George Washington Hospital. Your girlfriend collapsed and was admitted. It sounds serious. I think you should get back here right away. The air wing is sending a helo to pick you up in two hours."

A fog of panic and guilt clouded Adam's vision. He touched the Rolex Sea-Dweller on his wrist, a gift from Effie. "What's wrong? What did they say?"

Doug expelled a long breath. "I'm sorry. They think it's cancer."

CHAPTER SIX

Dr. Fang Jin followed Dr. Sarah Smith down a dirt path coated with broken shells and pebbles. Powerful waves crashed against boulders at the base of the cliff beside the trail. The air smelled of salt, sand, and freedom. A seagull cawed as it floated on the Atlantic breeze, and Fang clutched her white lab coat around her throat as she watched it. To the east, Martha's Vineyard looked like a black smudge on the horizon.

"I'll never get used to the natural beauty here," Sarah said.

"*Shì de,* yes, exquisite," Fang said.

She watched Sarah, whose blond hair and blue eyes glistened in the November sun. Sarah looked like a movie star. A carefree spirit, uncontrolled by an all-powerful state.

Born in China, Fang had spent the past six years earning her PhD from California Institute of Technology. She had anticipated culture shock, but she had not expected the lure of a free society. New England valued individualism too, especially on Cuttyhunk, a two-and-a-half-mile-long island off the coast of Cape Cod.

"We should head back," Sarah said. "They don't want us leaving the property."

Fang knew the regulation, but she needed to talk to Sarah away from prying eyes—away from the cameras and security officers. "I cannot stay in my computer lab all day. I love disappearing into my work . . . into the data. But I need time outside. We are so isolated here."

"I think that's the point," Sarah said. "Bryce, I mean Mr. Hastings, moved us here to get away from everybody. I couldn't believe it when I heard Forever Technology was relocating to this little island."

"What harm is there in taking a walk?" Fang asked.

"I don't think they want us talking to the locals. We might let something slip."

"Like what?"

"Our work," Sarah said. "They don't want anyone to know what we're doing."

"You mean Black Diamond?"

Sarah stared at her. "We're not supposed to talk about that outside the lab. I didn't know they read you onto the project."

Be careful.

"They did not. I just support it, but what I have heard makes me uncomfortable."

Sarah bit her lip and seemed to be thinking. Fang held her breath and waited.

"Me too," Sarah finally said. "I want to say something, but they'd fire me, and I have a daughter to support."

Fang's body electrified. "Say something about what?"

"I, uh, you know, like maybe we're going too far. Like maybe we should consult someone first."

"Who?"

"An ethics board, the government, someone. I don't know. Our work has implications."

"Like what?"

Sarah's face hardened. "We shouldn't be talking about the project out here."

"Sorry, you are right." Fang nodded. "I just enjoy having someone to confide in."

Sarah smiled and continued walking.

The island had been the first place occupied by Europeans in New England. It only had thirty year-round residents, but the population swelled to five hundred during the summer tourist season. Most homes were clustered in the Town of Gosnold on the northern end of the island, but a handful of residents—people who thought Gosnold was too populated—had moved into conservation land that covered much of the island.

Something scurried through the thick underbrush along the footpath, and a flash of adrenaline shocked Fang's body. She stopped and stared. Nothing grew above waist-high on this part of the island because icy winter winds raged off the ocean.

"What is it?" Sarah asked.

"Something is in there."

"This island has all kinds of wildlife," Sarah said. "Jim saw a coyote. It must have swum across the strait from Woods Hole."

"Life finds a way," Fang said.

"Ha."

"I guess we are here for the same reason," Fang said.

"We are?"

"Forever Technology. Is it not our mission to find a way?"

Sarah nodded but said nothing. She continued along the path. Had Fang said too much? She should step lightly, nurture their relationship. Fang needed to understand things and having a friend would not hurt either. She had never felt so alone.

"Maybe we should turn around," Sarah said.

Don't push. "You are correct. I cannot get in trouble. I am new here."

They walked back through the wildlife preserve toward Forever Technology's laboratory, which was nestled in the woods on Cuttyhunk's eastern shore. Construction of the lab had recently completed, just before Forever Technology's CEO, Bryce Hastings, had moved the tech company from Silicon Valley. The main laboratory remained in Palo Alto, but Bryce's private project had relocated to Cuttyhunk.

Another noise emanated from the bushes. Fang stopped. The yellow flare of a wild chrysanthemum caught her eye among the dying shrubbery. She stared at it, transfixed. The chrysanthemum was the official city flower of Beijing, and the subject of many poems. It signified autumn and the ninth moon, unlike in Europe where chrysanthemums symbolized death. It reminded her of home. She remembered playing with her sister and mother in the fields behind their home on the outskirts of Qinhuangdao, in the Hebei Province, a coastal area near Beijing.

Fang looked up the pathway, but Sarah had rounded the bend and moved out of sight. Fang wanted to pick the flower. She needed a reminder of home, a symbol of what China meant to her—something more than the Communist Party. She had enough of that in her life already.

"Sarah?"

Nothing.

No sense in pushing her. Not now. Fang would get the answers she sought soon enough. She tightened her lab coat and picked her way through the thorny bushes toward the flower.

Something skittered near her feet, and she stopped. She had seen snakes and rodents and all types of slithery things since arriving on Cuttyhunk two months before. She shivered, but she wanted that beautiful flower. Fang pushed farther into the underbrush, hoping the deer ticks had vanished for the season. She reached for the flower, drew its stem toward her, and plucked it. She caressed its velvety petals. Fang pictured her mother and sister laughing, and her eyes welled. Everything Fang was doing, she did for them.

Sarah screamed.

Or had a seagull cawed? Those damn birds sounded so human. Fang looked up but could not see the path through the brush. She pocketed the chrysanthemum in her coat and pushed through the shrubs, taking less care than before. She reached the trail and brushed herself off.

"Sarah?"

No answer.

Fang walked toward the lab. Waves crashed below. She rounded the corner, but Sarah wasn't there.

A seagull, that's all. Just a bird.

Fang made her way along the path, her eyes darting to the brush. Silly to be afraid. With the summer tourists gone, few people remained on the island, and residents seldom walked on this part of the eastern shore.

She reached a bend in the trail and stopped. Sarah's scarf lay on the ground. Fang's spine tingled. She whirled around, but there was no one behind her. She turned in a circle, searching.

"Sarah?"

To her right, a small cutaway led to the cliff. Fang glanced behind her again, then walked to the precipice. The bluff was majestic with sand dunes, massive boulders, and yellow grass. Heights terrified her, but she peered over the edge. The Atlantic crashed against the shore ninety feet below.

Her stomach turned to stone.

Sarah's body lay motionless on the rocks. The surf washed over her, and the water turned crimson.

CHAPTER SEVEN

Effie Hope's cancer was a death sentence. Six weeks of blood tests, MRIs, and biopsies had made that obvious. Six weeks of oncologists, radiologists, and surgeons, all wearing the same solemn expression. Six weeks of hell.

Adam watched Effie's chest rise and fall as she slept in bed beside him. His eyes burned. Fatigue overwhelmed him as he dangled at the end of an emotional rope. How to describe the terror of waiting for lab results and hearing the telephone ring? Or the chilling moment when the examination room door opened, and the oncologist explained how the cancer had spread. The memory brought back the odor of hospital disinfectants and cramped his stomach.

Effie had stacked books high on her nightstand. As an author, she read every night, even through her sickness. She wrote literary fiction, and her novels were beautiful, full of imagery and reflection—not Adam's cup of tea—but beautiful. Real art. She had landed a new publisher and teetered on the edge of breaking out.

Then cancer struck.

Things that had been important to him six weeks ago had become meaningless. He had discarded old priorities without a second thought, so he could focus on Effie. Half his life threatened to disappear and leave him in ruins. He had asked her to marry him a dozen times over their years together, but she had always declined. Her love for him could not overcome her aversion to marriage. He had hoped to wear her down, but now, that might never happen.

His heart ached. Who knew that was more than a literary expression? His heart wanted to burst, and his soul had withdrawn deep inside and threatened to disappear. What would happen if she died? The helplessness, the desperation, the horror. How long could he keep going?

His cell phone rang. He tiptoed out of the room and answered.

"How's Effie?" Doug Barnstable asked.

"Not good."

"I doubt there's anything I can do, but I want to offer. If you need—"

"Thanks, Doug. I appreciate it."

"I'm calling because I opened your resignation letter. Talk to me. What's going on?"

Adam's heart thumped in his chest. It had taken him years to become a special agent. He had passed a polygraph, physical assessment, medical exam, psychological test, and panel interview, then spent over a year waiting for DEA to offer him a position. He had accepted a spot in a DEA Basic Agent class and poured everything into his training at DEA's Academy in Quantico. Adam had graduated at the top of his class and then worked fifteen-hour days making cases in New York City before being selected for DEA FAST, the agency's foreign tactical teams.

Now he had to give it up.

"It's Effie," he said. "We haven't lost hope yet. She's fighting, but it looks bad. Really bad. She needs me."

Doug exhaled into the phone. "I'm so sorry, and I get it. I do. But you don't need to resign."

"I hate to fold my hand early, but I've burned all of my annual leave, and I'm almost out of sick time."

"There's a voluntary leave donation program. You can ask people to transfer hours to you."

Adam had considered it. "I don't know how long we'll have to fight the cancer. The longer the better, because that means she's alive—" A lump caught in Adam's throat.

"I understand, but giving up your career won't help her."

"She needs me. I don't want to force her to go to appointments alone. I want to be there, physically and emotionally."

"If my Maria was sick, I'd like to think I'd respond the same way, but you're the best agent I have, and I know what this job means to you. How can I talk you into staying?"

"There's no choice. I need to be closer to home. If she recovers—I mean *when* she recovers—she'll require care. I want to spend what time I have left with her. However long that is."

"I know this is none of my business, but how will you cover expenses?"

Adam's back knotted. He had accepted a job as a security consultant at a tech company—a position his brother had offered him. It was employment far below his experience and talent and the last place he wanted to work, but what choice did he have? He had not told Effie yet, because he wanted to commit first and remove the option of her talking him out of it. He would tell her today.

"Effie and I have been staying at her mother's old house in Falmouth, Massachusetts. I took a job on Cuttyhunk Island. It's an hour's boat ride from Cape Cod."

"Doing what?"

"Security."

"Jesus."

A bump came from the bedroom.

"I think Effie's awake. Gotta go."

"Call if you need anything. And Adam?"

"Yes?"

"If you try to return to DEA after a year, you'll have to repeat the academy, and age thirty-seven is the cutoff, so you only have a few years left."

Adam thanked Doug and hung up. He stared out the living room windows at the Vineyard Sound. Waves lapped the rocky Falmouth shore. It was a gorgeous setting, more calming than the urban view they had in Washington, DC. They had always wanted to return to New England, and now that his job no longer tied him to the nation's capital, there was no reason to stay. Her mother's house had been vacant for almost a year after she passed away, and it provided a simple solution. Adam would do anything to make Effie more comfortable.

He cracked the door and inched it open. Effie sat in bed listening to a sports show on her phone. She followed college and professional football like an analyst, yet she loved literature. He smiled at the dichotomy.

"Who were you talking to?" she asked.

"Doug. I gave notice."

She adjusted the scarf covering her bald head. It had colorful patterns common in hospitals, as if splashes of orange and red would hide reality. "You can't resign. I won't be responsible for ruining your personal and professional lives."

Adam sat on the bed. "You aren't ruining anything. You're sick and I'm doing what's necessary to care for you."

A tear rolled down her cheek. "I'll never forgive myself."

"It's my choice, not yours. I can't work in some foreign land tramping over sand dunes while you're home going through hell. I'd be miserable, and you'd be alone. We'd both lose. At least this way, I'm here to support you when you're foggy from the pain and meds. I'll be here to help you make the right choices and to keep your medical team vigilant."

Effie bit her lip.

Adam rubbed her leg. "We will beat this together."

"I'm trying." Her voice cracked.

"You're stronger and braver than anyone I know."

Her tears flowed, and her body shook. Adam hugged her tight as she sobbed. He waited until she stopped, then he sat back and dabbed her eyes with a tissue.

"Thank you," she said.

"It's just a tissue."

She smiled. "I meant, thank you for standing by me."

"You're my favorite person."

"You haven't worked in weeks. Don't you miss the excitement?"

"No," he lied.

"Investigating narco-terrorism is who you are. You're a sheepdog. You need to protect people. It's in your blood."

"That's why I resigned. To protect *you.*"

"You can't turn your back on law enforcement."

"I can't turn my back on you."

"I don't want you to give up your life."

"You're my life," Adam said.

She took his hand. "It's not right."

He squeezed her hand.

"We've exhausted our savings," she said, "and my book royalties aren't enough to pay our bills. I may not finish my latest novel by deadline. How will we survive?"

Adam inhaled. "I took a job. Here, on the Cape."

She stiffened. "Where?"

"I took the position my brother offered. Maybe Tommy's decision to chase a paycheck was more pragmatic than my dedication to duty."

Effie rubbed the bridge of her nose. "You said you'd never work with him."

"Things changed."

"Oh, Adam." She shook her head. "A security job? Really?"

A sour taste filled Adam's mouth, and he had difficulty swallowing. "I'll make it work."

CHAPTER EIGHT

Edna Cooper chewed on a stick of Trident bubblegum as she flipped open her notepad in Bryce Hasting's office and prepared to interview one of the five richest men in the world. Tech CEOs were an odd bunch. What would Bryce Hastings be like? Did he own a monkey?

"Cooper . . . Cooper," Bryce said, as he scratched his chin. His emerald-green eyes penetrated her soul. "Didn't you used to work for the New York Times?"

"A long time ago. A lifetime ago. Thank you for seeing me."

Bryce wore a white shirt—so crisp it looked like it had just come out of the box—with black slacks and a black jacket. A day's growth of stubble covered his jaw, and based on the meticulous way he had dressed, he had probably chosen not to shave. It imparted a rugged masculinity.

It had been ages since she had brushed elbows with the masters of the universe, a decade since her fall from grace. Edna had once been a household name, the "people's journalist" who graced the front pages of national magazines—the most sought-after reporter in the country. But that was before she had pushed too far and the powers that be had destroyed her. Now, she was a reporter at the Cape Cod Post, a third-rate regional daily newspaper, a publication barely clinging to life.

"When my people set this up with the Post," Bryce said, "I never thought I'd have a celebrity interviewing me."

"I'm more infamous than famous," she said.

"Yes, I remember now. Something about false allegations . . . about the vice president, right? That adultery thing?"

"My source was right. They paid witnesses to lie."

She fondled the large ceramic balls hanging from her necklace. She had always liked big, flashy jewelry, even when she had rubbed elbows with New York's fashionista. Somehow, garish fake jewelry appeared kitschy, a bold statement that bucked fashion trends and expectations. Besides, they matched her giant hoop earrings.

"Well, it's a tough business," Bryce said. "Let's get to it, shall we? I have little time, and I'll need to cut this short."

Edna perched on a leather seat, and its chrome frame squeaked beneath her. She had always sat like that, balanced on the edge, like a cheetah ready to pounce. She clicked her Fisher Space retractable astronaut pen and felt a glimmer of her former self.

"I won't bother asking you to go into detail about what Forever Technology does," she said. "I've read everything I could find about your research using artificial intelligence to prolong life, and I can give readers background, but I need quotes. In a sentence, what's your mission?"

"To improve the human condition."

Edna smiled. "Okay, how about a little more? Explain to the people of Massachusetts why your work matters."

"The human mind remains sharp, well after our bodies begin to decline. At Forever Technology, we are using artificial intelligence to mend people, relieve their mortal coil. Life ends when our organs fail, but we believe artificial intelligence, in the form of nanotechnology, can extend human life. Nanoparticles will deliver treatment through the bloodstream and attack disease, even repair damage at the cellular level. Robots made of gelatin and sugar will dissolve after delivering medicine or making repairs. I predict we will increase the average lifespan to over a hundred and fifty years."

"That's quite a claim."

"Artificial intelligence will change everything."

"Are you talking about bionic men?"

"We call it transhuman, but you're not that far off. AI can identify and fix problems automatically, without our current limitations. Or human error."

Edna clicker her pen absently. "Your success in this field is well documented, but your move to Massachusetts was unexpected. Why did you uproot from Silicon Valley?"

"We didn't leave. Our primary laboratories remain in Palo Alto, as does our server complex, corporate offices, and ninety percent of our personnel. I simply moved my headquarters team and key researchers to the east coast."

"Did you move for tax reasons?"

Bryce laughed. "If we wanted to escape California's tax burden, we wouldn't have moved to Massachusetts. Texas would have made more sense. Or Florida. Besides, Forever Technology is happy to pay our fair share. I've based our entire mission on helping people."

"Then why move? You put a continent between you and the world's tech hub. Cuttyhunk must be inconvenient."

Bryce glanced at his watch. "I've always been an unconventional thinker, and Forever Technology expresses that. Living and working in Silicon Valley's tech culture stifled my creativity. I needed a change."

Edna squinted. "That doesn't satisfy me. Someone burglarized your headquarters two years ago and your server farm was hacked a short time later. Did you—"

"We repelled the hack. They never accessed our data."

"There has been wild speculation that you're close to a breakthrough. Did you move here for added security to—"

Bryce smirked. "Rumors of a breakthrough are just that—rumors. But we lead the way in life-extending technology, and we are always forging new ground."

"That's my question. Did you come here to avoid industrial espionage or to drop out of the spotlight?"

"Moving my office to a small New England community is not the way to avoid the spotlight. Your presence here is evidence of that."

Edna finished writing his quote and clicked her pen twice. "Why Cuttyhunk?"

"It's beautiful and remote, and the people are wonderful. This place allows me to think and feel safe while I envision our future."

"So, it *is* about security."

"Privacy, certainly. Cuttyhunk is far from the prying eyes in Silicon Valley."

"Aren't the locals interested in what you're doing?"

"Sure, but when the season ended, the population dropped from five hundred to thirty. This is an insular community, and New Englanders know how to keep to themselves."

"But aren't residents curious?"

"They're busy taking care of their families and living their lives."

"Have you hired locals to work here?"

"I've chosen to keep the integrity of my team. The people on Cuttyhunk are industrious, and they already have jobs. There's a schoolteacher, a carpenter, and plumber, but most people eke out a living by cleaning houses or selling fish or doing whatever they can to make a buck. They don't have time to worry about us."

"But they must want to know what you're up to here."

"What I'm 'up to' is making their lives better by improving everyone's health and wellness. AI may sound complicated, and when I lapse into techno speak, people's eyes roll back in their heads, but they will love our innovations."

"Aren't you afraid of leaks?"

"I've forbidden my people from mingling. My employees use our private ferry to commute to Forever's housing complex on Martha's Vineyard."

Bryce looked at his watch again. Edna did not have much time left, and she still had to address local issues her editor had insisted she cover. "People have criticized you for coming to a tiny New England town. Won't Forever technology's presence raise real estate prices and the cost of living?"

"We're not trying to gentrify the island. We're here to better the world."

"Sewage and power are perennial problems in Cuttyhunk. Are residents concerned that a facility like yours will drain their resources?"

Bryce scowled. "Battery power and storage are among the biggest challenges we face when creating AI technology. AI uses incredible amounts of energy, and we had to get special permission to tap into underwater cables that support Martha's Vineyard. The existence of fiber-optic cables was one of the reasons I chose Cuttyhunk."

"So Forever Technology won't drain Cuttyhunk's existing resources?" she asked.

"Cuttyhunk uses generators for power, augmented with a solar panel field, but that only helps when it's sunny. I'm proud to announce that Forever Technology has donated a significant amount of money to improve the island's infrastructure. It's our way of being good neighbors."

"I'm sure that didn't hurt getting building approvals."

Bryce's eyes narrowed. "The income we generate will explode Gosnold's tax revenue, and we have our own generators, sewage retrieval, and wells, so we don't impinge on the town's resources. Or rely on them. Relocating Forever Technology here was a win-win."

The interview had taken a confrontational tone, and the smile lines had disappeared from Bryce's face. The name Edna meant "pleasant," a word never used to describe her personality. She knew people didn't like her, but not only did she not care, their criticism validated her. People were shit. Always had been, always would be.

"Some warn about the dangers of artificial intelligence," she said. "What happens to jobs when robots do everything."

"That Luddite argument started with opposition to the loom. Technology makes products cheaper. In our case, it will make people live longer and healthier lives. It will transform the world."

"But what—"

Bryce stood. "I'm sorry, but that's all the time I have. Thank you for coming."

CHAPTER NINE

Fang's pulse raced as she knocked on Felix Suggs's door. Was she doing the right thing? She needed to know what happened to Sarah Smith, but was asking questions smart? Was she risking approaching Forever Technology's chief of security, because she had cared for Sarah, or because her best chance of getting inside the Black Diamond project had died on those rocks beneath the cliff?

"Come," Suggs said. He sounded like a grunting guerrilla.

Suggs did not look up as she entered. She stopped opposite his desk and waited. He glanced at her, then returned his attention to a document in front of him.

"Yes, Dr. Jin?"

"I need to speak with Mr. Hastings."

Suggs put his pen down and stared at her. His eyes were black and hooded like a serpent's. "What seems to be the problem?"

She did not possess official standing to inquire about Sarah's work, and if she lied, Suggs would know the moment he spoke with Bryce Hastings. But she needed access to Black Diamond, and Bryce could make that happen. She was running out of time and needed to be bold.

"I have a question about my data," she said.

He stared for an eternity before he spoke. "Talk to your project chief. Mr. Hastings is a busy man. He doesn't have time to crunch numbers. That's why you make the big bucks."

"No, it is not that. I . . ."

"What?"

"I ran analytics on our compression model to improve the download time. I pulled the files from last week and—"

"You did what?" Alarm flashed across his face, like heat lightning.

"I examined the recent beta testing data and compared the numbers. I thought if I could—"

"Who told you to retrieve that data?"

Fang was accustomed to having men question her competence, as if having a woman in a STEM field was an oddity. She was not a unicorn, but one misstep, and she would give them the rope they needed to get rid of her. She had gone into the secure data files for a different reason, but Suggs didn't know that. She needed to go on the offensive.

"No one has to tell me how to do my job," Fang said. "Not you. Not anyone. I have been given a task, and I am trying to achieve my goals in the most efficient way."

Suggs pushed back in his chair. He rolled his tongue across his teeth and his cheek bulged. A vulgar habit. "What's the problem?"

"The reports included additional files. Experimental data. I thought someone had misfiled information, but then I noticed the numbers were backward. The times do not make sense."

Suggs mouth formed a rigid line. "And?"

"I realized it was not a download. Someone had *uploaded* new numbers."

"What's your point?"

"If we are trying to upload into a simulation model, I need to reconfigure the data, and how I do that depends on the target receiver. I did not know anyone else was involved with this part of the project. I am confused."

Suggs tapped his pen on the desk. "We build redundancy into the system. We have dozens of scientists here, and sometimes, we let them experiment with each other's work and play with the numbers."

"I am used to a collaborative environment," Fang said, "but that makes little sense. If you want effective systems integration, I need to work directly with the upload team."

"I'll pass that along to Mr. Hastings."

Fang nodded, more out of habit than understanding. She turned to go, then stopped. She needed the information and could not let him stand in her way, no matter how tough he acted. The Chinese government had granted her admission to Tsinghua University, despite her poor upbringing. They had allowed her to immigrate to the United States to get her master's degree, then her doctorate in computation and neural systems. They had awarded her grants to pay for tuition, housing, and living expenses. Their support had allowed her to achieve her breakthrough research in neurophotonics, a new method of mapping brain circuits. But that support had come with stipulations. Things she preferred not to dwell on. Things that had come back to haunt her.

"Is the upload part of Black Diamond?" Her veins thumped in her temples. She hoped Suggs did not notice.

He raised his eyebrows. "You're not read on to Black Diamond."

"That is my point. I should be. Sarah Smith was on that project, no?"

Suggs's eyes widened, and she thought he would jump out of his chair. He balled his hands into fists, stood, and leaned his knuckles on the desk.

"Who told you that?"

"Sarah did. Before she died. Now, I want to see Mr. Hastings. I cannot do my job if I am kept in the dark."

"These jobs are difficult to come by," Suggs said. "You're playing a dangerous game."

Fang's head swam. If they fired her, what would happen to her mother and sister? "Will you tell Mr. Hastings I am coming, or should I make a surprise?"

Suggs ground his teeth so hard she heard it. A drop of sweat ran down her back.

Suggs expelled a long breath. "God dammit. I'll let him know you're on the way."

CHAPTER TEN

Adam drove from Falmouth to New Bedford and boarded a passenger ferry for the quick voyage to Cuttyhunk. New Bedford had been a whaling hub, then an industrial town, and now its sluggish economy survived on fishing and textiles. The pier was a mishmash of pulleys and taught metal lines, and it smelled of diesel fumes and saltwater. Adam handed his ticket to a woman and climbed down the gangplank onto the two-tiered boat. Ropes creaked as the ferry strained against the dock.

He could have made the crossing from Falmouth to Cuttyhunk on his brother's forty-two-foot Cantius yacht, but Adam could not stomach having Tommy lord his new toy over him. Tommy had been bragging about that damn yacht since he transferred from Silicon Valley. It was bad enough having to ask him for a job but listening to Tommy flaunt his success and wealth was too much to bear. Adam had chosen a life of service and adventure. He had earned little money as a DEA agent, but he had made the world a better place.

Adam sauntered through the ferry's cabin, where a dozen passengers carried canvas bags stuffed with canned meats, laundry detergent, and other essentials they would need during an endless Massachusetts winter. Men and women with rough, wind-wrinkled skin greeted each other with the familiarity of old neighbors but maintained their rugged New England reservedness. These were hearty people. Solitary. People who chose to live on a remote island, cut off from society.

He could not stop watching their hands, assessing potential threats, and discerning motives. Adam may have resigned from DEA, but he could not shed survival habits ingrained during a decade of law enforcement. He saw a different world than civilians—a world populated with criminals. A world of savagery. A world where evil flowed freely, and wolves stalked clueless sheep. He saw things others didn't, as if he existed in another dimension and could look directly into the hearts of men.

The horn blared, and the captain eased the ferry away from the dock. Within minutes, the diesel engine chugged rhythmically, and the bow sliced across Buzzards Bay. Adam leaned over the side and listened to the foamy crinkle of the wake slosh against the hull. The ferry slogged through the cool water, and the brisk air revived him.

Should he have accepted a menial job working for his brother? Tommy could be an asshole. No, that wasn't fair. Tommy had offered, and the position paid well. Too well. What the hell was happening on a small island with a few dozen residents that required a tech billionaire to pay two-hundred grand a year for a security consultant?

Forty-five minutes later, Cuttyhunk appeared on the horizon, a thin black line growing as they bounced over the waves.

A metal buoy clanged as it rocked in the ferry's wake, and the town of Gosnold came into focus. A cluster of white and gray clapboard homes perched on a hill facing the bay. Like Haiti, the island resembled a lobster claw, with a protected bay between the pincers.

The ferry docked in front of the old Coast Guard station, and Adam shuffled down the ramp with the other passengers. Tommy stood on the dock wearing khaki pants, a blue Oxford shirt, and scarf. Seriously, a scarf? What a dick.

"Welcome to Fantasy Island," Tommy said. He always talked like he had aces in the hole.

Adam shook his hand. "Morning, Tommy."

"I go by 'Thomas' now."

"You're a pretentious ass."

Tommy smirked. "I don't know why you insisted on taking that damn ferry. My yacht could have had you here in twenty minutes."

It had taken five seconds for Tommy to mention his yacht.

"I didn't want to impose," Adam said. "Thanks again for arranging this for me."

"It was easy. They respect me, and I vouched for you. Think of Forever as your incubator. Make seed money here, then pivot and fly out of the nest on your own."

"I'm still not sure what I'll be doing."

"I'll give you a quick tour of the facility, then you'll meet the CEO, Bryce Hastings, and his chief of security, Felix Suggs. Suggs is a piece of work."

"Meaning?"

"You'll see."

Adam would owe Tommy an enormous favor for this job, and even if Adam's background made him overqualified for a security job, he could not shake the feeling Tommy saw hiring Adam as charity. He sighed.

"You don't look happy, Bro," Tommy said. "Aren't you excited about the job?"

"It's not that. I'm grateful. Effie's medical bills have been piling up, and I've run through my savings. I need something, and the salary here is more than what I earned at DEA. It's just . . ." Adam took a deep breath. "It's not hunting terrorists and drug traffickers."

"Listen, sport." Tommy popped a toothpick into his mouth and twirled it with his tongue. "This is an enormous opportunity for you. I know you miss gallivanting around the globe shooting bad guys, but Forever Technology is going to change the world. Bryce is a visionary. What we're doing here will reshape life as we know it."

"How?"

"You'll see."

"That doesn't tell me anything."

"Artificial intelligence is the future, and Bryce will lead us there."

"I appreciate the job offer, and I won't embarrass you. It's just difficult becoming a glorified security guard on a two-mile island."

"It's two and a half miles, and there's more to the job than that."

Adam followed Tommy across the wooden dock. A seagull snatched something off the sand. They climbed into a golf cart with the Forever Technology logo painted on the side. Tommy annoyed him, the way brothers usually do, but being with him satisfied Adam's desire to protect him. As children, they had bounced around foster homes but somehow managed to stay together. Adam had always felt more like a father than a brother.

Adam inspected the cart. "We're meeting on the links?"

"Cuttyhunk isn't big enough to have a miniature golf course. Most people drive golf carts here, especially tourists during the season. People have cars, but they're a pain in the ass to get on and off the island. You're in Mayberry now."

They drove south, and Tommy gestured at the dozen wooden homes on the hill. "That's the booming metropolis of Gosnold." They passed a small home with corkboard, harpoons, and fish netting adorning the windows, like a kitschy seafood restaurant. Another home had a rusting anchor and upended rowboat killing grass in the yard. Gray clapboard homes faced the water but looked unoccupied, post-apocalyptic. The hum of crickets filled the air.

They followed the road along the east side of the island and after a few hundred yards, it turned into a dirt path, barely wide enough to allow two carts to pass. Not that traffic was a problem. Scrub brush grew high enough to obscure the view of the ocean, but every few seconds, waves crashed somewhere below. The sound was simultaneously powerful and soothing.

The brush opened on the left and a sign read, "Forever Technology." Beyond it, a paved driveway led toward the ocean. Tommy turned and Adam held on. The cart whined across the pavement for thirty seconds, then they rounded a corner and stopped in front of a massive, three-story, circular building. Expansive windows lined the entire first floor, affording a view of the Atlantic Ocean. In contrast, the second and third floors were metallic-blue steel with tinted windows that reflected the sky, ocean, and woods. The contemporary structure—both beautiful and ominous—looked like it had been airlifted out of an industrial park and dropped into an eighteenth-century whaling village.

Tommy parked in a tiny lot beside a handful of golf carts and two Chevrolet Suburban SUVs with limo tint. Adam stepped out and stared at the building.

"Welcome to Forever Technology," Tommy said.

Above them, an enclosed bridgeway led from the second story to another structure beside it. They had constructed that obsidian square monolith without windows and surrounded it with a steel wall, topped with concertina wire.

"I'm surprised the Town of Gosnold allowed them to build a lab like this," Adam said. "It doesn't fit the town's decor."

"Gosnold doesn't have strict zoning laws. Bryce offered to attach a colonial facade, but the town selectmen said it wasn't necessary. The woods conceal the building from the road, and townsfolk won't have reason to visit. The five million dollars Bryce donated to upgrade the island's energy system didn't hurt."

"Nice to be a billionaire."

"We're all going to be rich. Stick with me and your financial problems are over."

"What's inside that windowless structure?" Adam asked.

"That facility is why you're here."

The Silicon Valley architecture looked out of place, and the security seemed unwarranted. What were they doing?

"You haven't given me much information," Adam said. "What do you research here?"

"The Black Diamond project. You'll get a full briefing."

"I feel like I'm pulling teeth. What exactly am I supposed to do as a security consultant?"

"Bryce will explain everything when you meet him, and Suggs will give you your assignment."

"Why the mystery? They can't have many security problems. The island is populated by fishermen, and nothing ever happens here."

"There's more to it than that."

"Meaning?"

Tommy's face clouded, and he looked down at his loafers. "A scientist died."

"What? Someone was killed?"

"Sarah Smith."

"When?"

"Last week."

"I didn't hear about that."

"They kept it quiet. The chief medical examiner ruled it an accident, but deaths don't help Forever Technology's image, and they aren't good for tourism. It was in everyone's interest to put a lid on it."

"Everyone except the scientist."

"Bryce got paranoid after that. It's why he agreed to bring you onboard."

"How did she die?"

"She was out walking and fell off the cliff. It happens." Tommy scowled.

"You sound skeptical."

"Come on, we're going to be late."

Tommy turned toward the main building, but Adam grabbed his arm. When Tommy faced him, his eyes glistened.

"Tommy, what aren't you telling me?"

Tommy stuck his hands in his pockets and turned away from the building. "Sarah's death was suspicious, but there's something else." He lowered his voice. "I didn't ask you here just to help you make a buck. I have concerns. I'm glad you're here with me."

"What kind of concerns?"

"When you're done with your meetings, meet me down at the dock. We can talk on my yacht. It's important."

"What do you need to tell me?"

"Not here. Just keep your head down and your ears open."

CHAPTER ELEVEN

Fang rode an exterior glass elevator to Bryce Hastings' penthouse office on the third floor. She gazed through the transparent walls across the Atlantic Ocean to Martha's Vineyard. In the distance, a sailing yacht heeled to starboard under the pull of a bulbous spinnaker. The massive red sails reminded her of junks off the coastal city of Qinhuangdao.

The elevator doors opened behind her, and she entered the anteroom to the CEO's office. Concrete walls were adorned with photographs of constellations, their galaxies concentrated like colorful clouds of gas.

"Good morning, Dr. Jin," the young man said from behind the receptionist's desk.

She started. "Oh, good morning." How did he know her name? She had only met Bryce Hastings once, during her final interview, and that had been in Silicon Valley at Forever Technology's primary facility.

The receptionist pressed a button on his desk, then touched his earpiece. He glanced at her. "Mr. Hastings is ready for you. You may go in." He pushed another button, and two frosted-glass doors slid open. The soothing sounds of Vivaldi's Four Seasons leaked out of the office.

Fang's pulse quickened, and not just because she had forced this meeting. Bryce Hastings was a billionaire and an international celebrity. For a decade, he had been a visionary and intellectual giant, who turned science-fiction into reality. The world knew the benefits of artificial intelligence, but

Bryce had used his foresight, daring, and charisma to push in new directions. Reinvesting billions from his previous exits into Forever Technology had not hurt either.

She entered the office, where Bryce stood behind his desk, a black-lacquered tabletop holding only a MacBook desktop computer and a crystal globe. He placed a coffee mug emblazoned with NASA's logo on his desk and came around to greet her. He wore black slacks, black jacket, and a white Oxford shirt. A shark tooth pendant hung from a black leather cord. His trademark look. She had never seen him in anything else.

"Dr. Jin, it's a pleasure to see you again. I've been meaning to check in to see how your move to Massachusetts went."

"Uneventful," she said.

He clasped her hand between his and shook it. He flashed impossibly white teeth, and his coffee-brown eyes filled with warmth. Bryce was in his early forties, with a few gray strands dusting his brown hair, but only at the temples. She wondered, not for the first time, why he had remained single.

"Glad to hear it," he said. He guided her into a leather-backed chrome chair. "I was so pleased you agreed to leave Silicon Valley. Cuttyhunk is where the magic will happen."

"Magic?"

"That's what people call phenomenon they don't understand. This is where we will change the human experience, and you're a big part of that. Your analysis impresses me. No, not just that, your aggression, your willingness to try new things—to improvise. That's what first attracted me to your work, and why I needed you on my team."

Fang's cheeks warmed. He made her feel like the most important person in the world. This man, who had been on the cover of Time Magazine—a man who golfed with presidents—treated her like visiting royalty.

"It is an honor to be here, sir."

"Call me Bryce. We're family now."

Her ears burned from the open expression of affection—an American trait alien to Chinese culture. She averted her eyes and stared out his windows at the ocean. Whitecaps danced on the surface, foaming, then disappearing. The invisible currents below were powerful.

She turned back to Bryce, and a thin smile cracked his face.

"Felix tells me you have questions about our work," he said. The time for small talk had ended.

"I, uh, I found data that does not make sense to me."

"The uploads." He never beat around the bush.

"I did not realize we began that phase of the project. I still have not perfected the power mapping technique. I assumed we would wait until we had a less clunky representation of the brain. Our modeling still has bugs."

Bryce stood and walked to the window. He gazed at the water. "I don't create cutting-edge technology by waiting for bugs to be fixed. Perfection is unattainable."

She stared at her hands in her lap and hunched her shoulders. Her throat felt thick, the way it had as a child when her father had lectured her about her failings. How did Bryce make her feel like she needed to impress him?

"I'm sorry."

Bryce faced her. "Don't be sorry. It's your job to make the mapping function as planned. I want you deep in the weeds. You and the other four hundred scientists I've employed are the real brains behind our work. I don't have the bandwidth for it, and even if I could crunch the numbers, I need to stay focused on the future."

"Your vision is the reason I joined Forever Technology. Since I was a child, I have wanted to use artificial intelligence to make people healthier and prolong their lives."

"Because of your brother?" he said.

She flinched. How did he know about Bojing? She had told no one in America about losing her brother to Lupus.

"You know?"

"We don't hire just anyone," he said. "We conduct extensive backgrounds. I lost my mother to disease when I was young. I understand how life-changing a loss like that can be, and I need people fully committed to our mission. You have excelled in every stage of your career, despite your youth, but sometimes, people are motivated by the wrong reasons. Before I allow people into my inner sanctum, I must know what drives them. Your brother's death must have been a horrific experience, but instead of letting it crush you, you internalized your pain and sorrow, and used it to fuel your career. I respect that."

He had done it again. He had taken her to a dark moment, then made her . . . what? Proud? He trusted her. This was her moment. Time to take a chance.

"I want to be the vanguard," she said. "I do not want to sound ungrateful, but if we have begun phase two, I need to be part of it."

Bryce drummed his fingers on the desk. "We compartmentalize here. Allowing people to focus helps them reach their goals quicker. It also creates an element of safety. If one person knows the entire operation, that person can become a liability."

"No, I—"

Bryce raised a hand and chuckled. "I'm not calling your motivations into question. Many people are interested in our work here, and the more specialized your area, the less of a target you become."

Fang fondled the Jade pendant on her necklace, a gift from her mother. She would not have another opportunity to expand her access to Black Diamond. She could not fail. She had no choice but to push.

"Sarah told me about Black Diamond." She kept her face impassive and waited. If he questioned her about details, her bluff would fail.

The smile slid off Bryce's face. "Dr. Smith should not have done that."

"She was my friend."

He came around and leaned against his desk—inches from her. "I'm sorry for your loss. That accident was horrible. We lost a member of our family."

A lump formed in her throat. "Yes."

"Dr. Smith was a brilliant researcher. I didn't know how to replace her." He wrapped his knuckle on the desk. "Until now." He pressed a button on his desktop. "Dale, get Dr. Perlman in here."

"Yes, sir," Dale responded.

Bryce returned his focus to her. "Dr. Shlomo Perlman leads the Black Diamond program. Here's what we'll do. I'll clear you for Black Diamond, and you'll work with his team."

Fang's chest swelled, and the weight lifted off her. "Thank you, I—"

"I'm breaking my own rules," he said, "but you may be my secret weapon. Help me bring this project across the finish line. Help me change the world."

JEFFREY JAMES HIGGINS | 49

CHAPTER TWELVE

Tommy placed his palm on a biometric reader and swiveled so Adam could not see him enter his code into the keypad. So much for family trust. The light above the door turned from red to green. Forever Technology's front doors opened with a whoosh, and Adam followed Tommy into a spacious lobby of glass and chrome.

"Good morning, Mr. Locke," the security guard greeted Tommy. He wore a white shirt, black pants, and a navy blue blazer with Forever Technology's logo embroidered on it. He looked like he could bench-press a Toyota.

"Morning, Ivan. This is my brother, Adam. He's joining our corporate family."

The guard scanned Adam's hands. "Welcome to Forever."

"Thank you," Adam said. He extended his hand, but the guard made no move to take it.

"Ivan doesn't shake hands," Tommy said. "Something to do with tactics. Isn't that right, Ivan?"

"Yes, Mr. Locke."

Adam lowered his hand.

"This is reception," Tommy said, and led Adam to the front desk. Beyond tall windows, waves rolled toward the island.

Tommy spoke to the receptionist, a woman in her sixties with her hair pulled into a tight bun. She handed him a laminated identification card, and he gave it to Adam. "Keep this visible at all times."

Adam clipped it onto his shirt.

Tommy led him into the center of the room. "Behind that glass wall is our visitors' conference room. We do multimedia presentations for investors and the press." He pointed at a gallery of photographs on the wall beside the conference room. "Those are Forever Technology's groundbreaking inventions."

Adam glanced at photographs of robots and machinery. "Impressive."

"The future is now. In the back, we have an employee lounge and cafeteria. Help yourself to food and beverages, especially coffee, which is available twenty-four hours a day. You'll need the caffeine, trust me."

"It's like a Buck Rogers' movie with a spectacular view."

"Best part of leaving California. People call Cali the prettiest state in the country, but palm trees and incessant sun make me uneasy. Plus, it's nice to be back home in New England. How are you and Effie doing in her folks' old house?"

"Haven't had time to enjoy it."

"Of course not. She any better?"

"No."

"That sucks. Sorry." Tommy frowned and scratched his head. "Anyway, there are three subterranean levels beneath us, under both this building and the annex."

"The annex is that square building next door?"

"Black Diamond. It's the future."

"Which you won't tell me about?"

"I'll leave that for Bryce. Felix Suggs is our security chief. He's a hard-nosed little bastard, but you'll get used to him. Just don't cross him. He used to work in West Africa, and I've heard stories."

"Stories?" Adam raised his eyebrows.

Tommy glanced back at the security guard. "Later. Upstairs on the second floor, we have offices for our thirty-one scientists who work on-site. That floor also houses our servers, employee lounge, and research library.

The third floor contains the primary labs for genetic research, nanotechnology, and other research."

"Do I sit in the lobby with a baseball bat?"

"Bryce has led the way in the artificial intelligence movement. He's trying things that nobody else will touch. Well, not in the West. The world wants to know what we're doing, which is why we moved."

"I know nothing about AI technology," Adam said. "I can dismantle a transnational criminal organization in my sleep, but other than emailing or surfing the internet, I don't understand computers."

"Doesn't matter. I brought you here because I trust you, not for your coding skills. Besides, you don't have to understand the technology. Only a handful of people in the world really do. You just have to keep it from falling into the wrong hands."

Tommy looked at his watch. "Shit. We're late. I'll introduce you to Suggs later. Come on, let's talk to the big man."

Their footsteps echoed off the marble floor as they moved across the lobby and entered the glass elevator.

"Why so showy?" Adam asked.

"Bryce understands the value of perception. Sometimes, what people see matters more than what's real."

The elevator rose, and the doors opened. "Good morning, Mr. Locke," the receptionist said.

"Morning, Dale. My brother is here to meet Mr. Bryce."

The doors to Bryce's office slid open and a gorgeous Asian woman walked out wearing a white lab coat. She beamed.

"Ah, Fang," Tommy said. "Let me introduce my brother. Adam, this is Dr. Jin."

"Mr. Locke," she said.

"Adam, please. It's a pleasure."

"Dr. Jin has been mapping the human brain," Tommy said.

She raised her eyebrows and glanced at Tommy.

"It's okay," Tommy said. "Adam is coming onboard to thwart industrial espionage. He'll have full access."

"Excuse me," Dale said. "Mr. Hastings is flying to Washington in fifteen minutes."

"I won't keep you," Fang said. She turned and left.

"Flying?" Adam whispered as they entered the CEO's office.

"Bryce owns a seaplane. Several of them."

Bryce stood in front of his desk and smiled like a politician. "You must be Adam."

"Nice to meet you," Adam said. "Tommy has been close-lipped about what you're doing here."

"Out of necessity, I'm afraid," Bryce said. "Many AI tech firms have targeted us, and a few governments as well. That's why you're here. Sit."

Adam slid into a chair opposite the desk. "The technology is over my head, but I'll do what I can to keep it safe."

"I hired you because of your familial connection to Tommy," Bryce said. "I don't know who to trust these days. Things have been tough. Tell me, what do you know about artificial intelligence?

"Not much."

"I'll keep it simple. There are four kinds of artificial intelligence. Reactive AI is known as machine learning. It does not actually learn but uses algorithms to make predictions. Limited memory AI, or deep learning, uses historical data inputs to solve problems, similar to the human process. These are artificial neural networks. Tracking?"

"So far."

"AGI, artificial general intelligence, is even closer to the human mind. It learns from data, like limited memory AI, but it also has a basic understanding of emotions. This is known as theory of mind thinking."

"Computers feel things?"

"No, but AGI understands the human response. Actually, I may have said 'no' too quickly. It depends on what 'feels' means, but that's a discussion for another time."

A speaker beeped on the wall. "You depart in ten minutes, Mr. Hastings," Dale's voice crackled out of the speaker. "They gassed your aircraft, and it's ready."

"Sorry, gents, but I'll have to keep this brief. The fourth type of AI is super intelligence. In theory, this stage of AI creates an artificial human brain with superior capabilities. Those are the basic categories."

"What exactly are you researching here?" Adam asked.

"Before I brief you on our projects, let me add a final level of artificial intelligence, which few people talk about, and that's what happens after we hit the technological singularity."

"What's that?"

"The singularity is the point when an artificial brain continues to learn at a rate beyond human capability and becomes self-aware. After that, growth will become exponential and reach far beyond human understanding. The artificial brain will achieve things we're incapable of doing and move above us on the food chain. We will no longer be the alpha life form."

"Come on," Tommy said. "That's an argument against progress."

"On the contrary. The singularity is a certainty. It's why some philosophers are discussing governmental restrictions on AI, ways to put these smart bots into boxes so we maintain control."

"I know nothing about that," Adam said, "but I've been in law enforcement long enough to know that criminals always find a way out of a box. And they're usually not the smartest people in the room."

"That's our fear," Bryce said, "assuming the AI we create wants to become the dominant life form."

"You've referred to it as a 'life form' twice," Adam said.

"That's also conversation for another time. I'm certain we don't have time to discuss the meaning of life."

"Five minutes, Mr. Hastings," the intercom squawked.

Bryce grabbed a leather satchel from the floor and pulled his coat off a rack. "Sorry, to run. In a nutshell, Forever Technology's mission is to overcome human frailty by improving health and extending life-spans. We're creating the stuff of science fiction, but that's how all great breakthroughs have occurred. When the human body, or what we call the biological substrate, fails to function, we have death. Our goal is to use AI in a myriad of ways to prevent that death."

"The fountain of youth?" Adam asked.

"Exactly. We can cure the human substrate using AI."

"How?"

"Several ways. We engineer synthetic organs using stem cells. We 3D-print organs. We implant AI into organs to monitor, control, and repair them. By using nanotechnology, we can attack cancers and other diseases by introducing AI-driven robots into the bloodstream. We—"

"Cancer?" Adam asked, now alert.

"Conceptually, yes. Nanotechnology will allow us to locate, identify, and destroy an invading disease. We—" Bryce hesitated. "I'm very sorry. I forgot about your wife. Is she—"

"Girlfriend."

"Excuse me?" Bryce said.

"We're not married."

"Oh, well, either way, I should have chosen my words more carefully. I'm usually more sensitive than that. I lost my mother to cancer at an early age."

"Then you understand."

"It's what motivated me to start this company," Bryce said. "We're still several iterations away from curing cancer, but it will happen. Soon."

Adam nodded. "I hope so."

"We all do. In the future, curing cancer won't even be the goal. With CRISPR and CPF1, we—"

"CRISPR? Adam asked.

Bryce glanced at his watch. "Gene editing. We'll be able to edit out genetically driven diseases and add improvements to the human body. We will make people stronger, smarter, healthier. The possibilities are limitless. Besides fixing and improving the human substrate, we're also looking into mapping and digitizing neural activity."

"Meaning?"

"We're identifying synaptic connections to read brain processes. Once we do that, we'll be able to download the data and preserve it. With AI, our model brain will continue to learn and function. Quantum computing provides the necessary computing speed, and a combination of cloud-based heuristics and blockchain data storage has solved security and space problems. We have some other advanced projects, but that's the gist of it. Based on our AI, life will change."

"Depending on how you define life," Adam said.

"You commented on my use of the term 'life' earlier. That wasn't an accident. Our brains are what make us human. Our bodies can deteriorate, but if our brains remain intact, we're fundamentally human. I give you Stephen Hawkins as an example."

"But what about the soul?"

"Ah, yes. The religious question."

"Not necessarily religion," Tommy interjected. "The soul could describe consciousness existing outside the body, which is also a secular concept."

"Unfortunately, we don't have time to dive down the rabbit hole of consciousness," Bryce said.

"Before you go, I have to ask," Adam said. "What is Black Diamond?"

"I'm afraid I'm out of time. Tommy will have Felix get you set up. Welcome aboard."

CHAPTER THIRTEEN

A cacophony of clacking keyboards, ringing telephones, and muffled conversations filled the Cape Cod Post's newsroom. It did not radiate the same frenetic pace of the national magazines where Edna Cooper had previously worked, but it still hummed with journalistic energy. And desperation.

The Post's undersized staff were overworked and underpaid. Many of the younger reporters dreamed of working at the New York Times or other mainstream powerhouses, and for them, the Post was a stepping-stone, a vehicle for advancement.

For Edna, the newspaper was a lifeboat.

She leaned back and stared at the hand-painted seashells that decorated her desk. They were as garish as her jewelry, but the pallet of turquoise, burnt oranges, lilac, and robin's egg soothed her—almost as much as hunting for the shells on Barnstable's Sandy Neck Beach. She straightened her turtleneck sweater, one of a dozen she owned, and moved with purpose across the newsroom floor.

Harry Willard, the long-time news editor, ran his fingers through his thinning gray hair as he sat at his desk talking to someone on the telephone. He caught Edna's eye through the glass and waved her into his office. He pointed to a chair and held up a finger to tell her to wait.

"Yes, ma'am, I plan to send a reporter," he said into the phone. "We're on it." He hung up and leaned back.

"Morning, Harry," Edna said.

"I need you to cover the Woods Hole Antique Festival tomorrow."

"Jesus, that's a bullshit assignment."

"I just hung up with the queen bee," he said, referring to Mildred Worth, the paper's owner. "She specifically requested we cover it. I think she's redecorating her beach house in Hyannis."

"Send one of the kids."

"I'm giving it to you. They know nothing about antiques, and they're all about fifty years younger than the average festival customer. They won't get those people to open up the same way as someone from their generation, er, someone more seasoned."

"Did you just call me old?"

"Experienced."

"I should sue you for ageism."

Harry rubbed his temples. "Just give me something Mildred will like."

"I'm onto a story. Something big."

Harry smirked. "I've heard this before. Cape Cod is not New York. You've got to stop looking for the next Pentagon Papers. It's not what we're here to report."

"There's a problem at Forever Technology. Why does a tech billionaire move his headquarters out of Silicon Valley?"

"Do not, I repeat, *do not* piss off the wealthiest man in Massachusetts with unsubstantiated conspiracy theories."

"I'm not afraid of Bryce Hastings."

"You should be. Anyone with a shred of common sense would step lightly around him. If you make him angry enough, he'll dump ten million dollars into our competition and run us out of business."

"You're telling me to bury a story when—"

"There is no story."

Edna removed her glasses and wiped them on her sweater without thinking. She squinted and felt the wrinkles around her eyes deepen. "It makes no sense that Forever Technology is on Cuttyhunk. What if Dr. Sarah Smith discovered something? What if someone pushed her and—"

"Right there! That's the kind of unsubstantiated statement that will have us all looking for jobs."

"But—"

"I can't have you accusing Bryce Hastings of murder so you can write your way back onto a national publication."

"But we're a newspaper. It's our job to—"

"Don't tell me my job," Harry said. "You find a shred of evidence of wrongdoing, and we'll run a story. But you better be careful, or you'll end up working for a weekly out in Western Mass."

CHAPTER FOURTEEN

Felix Suggs's office was as cold and hard as the man. His desk was a slab of black polymer, barren, except for three interlocking computer monitors. The gray walls held not a single picture, but the stark decor revealed the man. The only decoration was a shark's jaw mounted on the wall behind him with its jagged teeth pointed at Adam.

"Great white?" Adam asked.

"Bull Shark in the Gulf of Mexico. Killed him with a bangstick. He came at me while I was diving a wreck. Thought I was a goner. Ever think you were about to die?"

"I had a few operations when it could have gone either way, but I never stopped long enough to consider it. Not until after."

"You weren't scared in combat?" Suggs asked.

"When the bullets are flying, anyone who isn't afraid is either suicidal or a lunatic. But I never thought about dying. I stayed focused on the threat. In combat, there's a real possibility you won't exist a few minutes later. You could be done. Game over."

Suggs nodded with understanding.

"Before life taught me the difference between fantasy and reality," Adam said, "I thought the more training I had, the less likely I'd be to die. I thought if I could be a better shot, more tactical, cleverer, I would increase my chance of survival. Now, I know that's fantasy. When mortars and rockets explode, it doesn't matter if you're Rambo. If you're on the X, you're dead."

"PTSD?" Suggs asked.

"No."

Adam had not experienced PTSD or nightmares after he shot Laguerre's bodyguard, not in the way people talked about it. Maybe it didn't bother him because the man had needed killing. But he thought about the expression on the man's face. What would that bodyguard be doing now if Adam hadn't ended his life? Was the man looking down on Adam and judging? More likely, he was looking up. Not that Adam believed in that kind of thing.

Suggs scowled with the same tough-guy expression Adam had seen on drug traffickers, terrorists, and other hardened criminals who relied on violence to assert their immoral and indefensible ideas.

"Feeling okay?" Adam asked. "You look like you're in pain."

"That supposed to be funny?"

"That depends," Adam said.

"On what?"

"On your sense of humor."

Suggs stared a hole through him. The office was windowless, sullen. Like the man. It was as quiet as a tomb. The computer hummed.

"We gonna have a problem?" Suggs asked.

"Hope not."

Suggs came around his desk. He was massive through the chest and shoulders, and his biceps strained the fabric of his jacket. He wore a black turtleneck beneath it, which made his bald head look like a turtle. Or a penis. His slacks hung loose, which meant he had spent his time working on beach muscles in the gym instead of improving core strength and functional fitness.

"You work for me, you know."

"Happy to be here."

Someone knocked on the door.

"Come."

Tommy stuck his head inside. "Hey bro, meet me on the dock at lunch. I've got to take care of something, then I'm headed to my boat. We can grab a sandwich on the water. I want to talk to you about that thing I mentioned earlier."

"Sure thing. I'll walk."

"Take a golf cart to save time," Tommy said. "We have a long day ahead of us."

Tommy left and Adam turned back to Suggs. "Bryce gave me a fifteen-minute briefing on your work here," Adam said. "I'm not sure how I can help. What do you want me to do?"

Suggs looked like he'd eaten a bad clam. He leaned against his desk. "I'm responsible for the security of Forever Technology's facilities here and on the West Coast. That means protecting our infrastructure, personnel, and research."

"From whom?"

Suggs smirked. "From the world. Our company is worth fifty billion dollars, and that's based on today's market value and not on technology we've yet to reveal. We're leading the field of artificial intelligence in bioengineering. That makes us a target of competing tech companies and foreign governments—enemies and allies. We even have to worry about the US government, which is constantly investigating us for everything from tax evasion to anti-trust violations."

"Fun job."

"It's almost impossible. Between threats of increased regulation, corporate espionage, and theft, we're always on the run."

"Which is why Bryce moved to Cuttyhunk?"

"Yes."

Adam appreciated Suggs's no-bullshit response. Maybe he had misjudged him. "Makes sense."

"You worked for DEA for nine years . . . until your girlfriend's disease."

Hearing Suggs mention Effie pissed him off, but Suggs was correct, and he had a right to know.

"Almost ten years."

"They investigated your shootings in Afghanistan and Haiti."

Adam nodded. "Standard post-shoot investigations by the Office of Professional Responsibility and the Office of Inspections. They ruled both were justified."

"You won't have that level of excitement here, but don't let the boredom lull you into a false sense of security. There are fortunes behind the bad actors who want to steal our products, and that buys a lot of evil. Stay on your toes."

"I'll read the table and keep my cards covered, which brings us back to my original question. 'Stay on my toes' doing what?"

"Digital penetration is our biggest threat, but I've got a room full of tech geeks on the first floor who are monitoring our firewalls. For now, I'm going to have you assist with physical security."

Adam exhaled. "I'm an excellent investigator. I can help you find the people targeting us."

"I'm sure you can, and that's where you'll end up. To be honest, I didn't ask for you. Bryce hired you because he's concerned, and Tommy is maybe the only person he trusts. Besides me. When Tommy said you left DEA, Bryce figured you could help. I'm willing to find a role for you, but for now, help me secure the grounds and facilities. Make sure our scientists are safe commuting from our corporate housing on Martha's Vineyard."

"They're not staying on Cuttyhunk?"

"We didn't want them socializing with locals, and this place overflows with tourists in the summer. We could never vet everyone our team met."

"But Martha's Vineyard offers the same vulnerabilities."

"We house them in a gated community with its own cafeteria. We don't confine them to quarters, but we tell them to be careful. I spend a significant amount of time monitoring them to make sure our sheep don't stray."

"Monitoring?" Adam asked.

"More on that later. For now, inspect our physical security and make sure locals aren't getting close."

"What if I catch someone snooping around? Do I call the cops?"

"There aren't any police on this island," Suggs said. "Not one. Years ago, their senior selectman was a law enforcement officer, but he's gone now. Just before we arrived, they had a retired cop covering the island, but he aged out, per Massachusetts law. Now they have to call Martha's Vineyard for a law enforcement response."

"What about doctors, firefighters?"

"Volunteer fire department, and a doctor visits once a week for sick calls."

So, this was the job. A security guard. Almost a decade of federal investigations, and Adam was going to be chasing lobstermen away from the building. He sighed.

"Problem?"

"This job won't exactly challenge me."

"Impress me and I'll move you up."

A red light flashed on Sugg's computer, and he hurried back around the desk. "Shit, I need to deal with this. Come back at one o'clock and I'll give you a tour of the facilities."

"What's wrong?"

"One o'clock."

CHAPTER FIFTEEN

Dr. Shlomo Perlman led Fang through the second-floor walkway between the main building and the Annex. He tapped the red tip of his white cane in front of him like a metronome. How had Shlomo become the top researcher at Black Diamond while being legally blind? The man impressed her.

"It's a long walk to schlepp equipment," he said. "I'll show you around . . . in a manner of speaking."

"I am excited to join your team," Fang said.

At Bryce's direction, Suggs had given her access to the new facility, but he had not looked happy about it. Fang bridled with excitement, and not just because she was about to discover the secrets of Black Diamond, but because the project represented the tip of the spear in the high-tech AI revolution.

Fang's brain-mapping techniques had moved decades beyond what the scientific community realized. She had identified, mapped, and coded neural interactions in the brain to a point where she could read digital signatures and re-create human thoughts. In the early stages, researchers had inserted electrodes into patients' brains during surgery, and by recording electric impulses, they crudely reconstructed what the patient saw. Achieving the next level gave her the capability to read those neural connections and re-create thought. Memory would come next. When a patient accessed a memory, reexperiencing feelings and images, she could capture it. There were still dark areas, places where the brain remained a mystery. For example, she could not monitor a person's brain and decipher memory unless the patient actively remembered it.

Forever Technology's breakthrough had allowed them to re-create much of the human mind, which created significant opportunities. If they could download the unique process by which a brain interpreted reality, they could, in essence, download a person's mind. A digital version of a person.

Bryce often talked about extending human life by repairing the biological substrate, but even that solution left bodies vulnerable to accident, unseen diseases, or sudden trauma. Downloading a mind onto a server could theoretically extend life beyond the death of the body.

That had been her dream.

The second capability came from her mapping of the brain. By identifying synaptic interfaces and tying them to specific emotions and rational thought, she could digitize the functionality of the human brain. By doing that, she could duplicate those processes into a digital mind and create artificial intelligence that mirrored an individual's biological processes. A robot mind that thought like a human.

Exactly like a human.

They stopped at an elevator at the end of the hallway. Shlomo placed his hand on a biometric scan, then lifted his glasses and leaned forward into the optical reader. The frame around the door changed from red to green, and the elevator opened. He pressed a button for P-2. The annex was shorter than the primary structure but had several subterranean levels.

"We've been uploading your work into Lazarus on sub-level three," Shlomo said.

"Lazarus?"

"That's what we call our artificial mind," Shlomo said. "Project Lazarus."

"I wish I had known you advanced to this stage," she said. "There are many details and nuances involved with understanding neural connections."

"We're not plumbers here," he said, "and you're not giving yourself enough credit. You're a *mensch*. Your analysis has been brilliant, and the download process relatively seamless. But I'm still glad you're here. I want to accelerate the process to the next level."

"Next level?" she asked.

Shlomo smirked. "Of course, my dear. There is always a next level."

They walked down a long sterile hallway under blue light. She glanced through glass doors on either side as they passed. Technicians wearing white coats, goggles, surgical slippers, and hairnets, moved between computers and servers. Robotic heads sat on tables—a futuristic morgue.

"What is done in these labs?" she asked.

"We have a dozen projects running simultaneously, all with the same goal. Black Diamond has one overarching mission."

"And that is?"

"Why it's eternal life, my dear."

She stopped short. "Excuse me?"

He must have heard her stop or sensed it. He turned to face her. "You didn't think we were just backing up data here, did you? We're not cloud computing. What did you think would happen when we were able to fully map the brain? We're not just downloading synaptic interfaces. We're downloading consciousness."

"Not consciousness," she said. "We are mapping a brain's process for capturing memory . . . for learning."

"That too. But when you download an actual person, what do you have? A person's mind is their essence. Their personality, their opinions, their memories—what they truly are. And once you have that, why stop at a digital backup?"

Fang's head swam. Shlomo was talking about fantasy, theoretical possibilities debated by philosophers. But he spoke as if it was real. Today.

"You are actually doing this?" she asked.

"For over a year."

She bit her lip. "But no one knows about this. What about the government? What about—"

"Nobody knows. If they did, there would be questions. Concerns. People would want to stop us. Stop science."

"But maybe—"

"You can't avoid the future," he said. "The cat is out of the bag."

"There are moral and ethical considerations."

"People always have concerns, my dear. And what do you think comes next? Would you want to have your consciousness in storage on a server, waiting for some scientist to access it? No, you would want to live. Live forever. Once we capture the data, we connect them to Apep and—"

"What's Apep?" she asked.

"The synthetic processor inside Lazarus that mimics and directs Lazarus's neural pathways. It's the cryptographic device that connects through the cloud to the exabytes of data, and it's the engine that processes the data you collect. It's the key to locate and unlock the data from Forever's server farms, which solved our massive storage problem. Cloud-based heuristics and systems were the key. After that, it's simple to transfer Lazarus into a synthetic organism. We have several Lazarus frames, but only one functioning Apep. We're still tinkering with the earlier models to bring them up to speed."

"You mean cybernetic bot?"

"Of course. Why would we embed an artificially intelligent mind into a biological substrate? It makes no sense after we spent all this effort avoiding those physical human vulnerabilities."

"You are talking about taking a person's mind, a real person, and uploading their mind into a cyborg."

"Welcome to Black Diamond."

CHAPTER SIXTEEN

Adam motored a golf cart up Forever Technology's serpentine driveway, then turned onto West Road and headed into town. A weathered gray pickup truck rolled past him. Adam waved, but the old man behind the wheel scowled.

Adam continued down Gosnold County Road past the Avalon Inn and turned down a narrow road that ran by Town Hall. A closed sign hung on the gate in front of the town's only market, and an engine repair store appeared closed, as if Cuttyhunk had begun its winter hibernation. The tidal estuary lay on his left, and the marina stretched out before him. Beyond the public restroom, a single-story clapboard building ran down the center of the dock and contained anglers' shops and food shacks—all closed for the season.

Adam parked the cart, leaving the key in the ignition, and walked past the fishing platform. He strode across the dock, his feet thumping on the wooden planks, as if he walked across a drum. The fishing boats had departed for the day, and only two sailboats remained tied to cleats. More pleasure craft bobbed on moorings in the bay.

Tommy's yacht floated at the end of the dock. Adam understood why Tommy had bragged about it. The boat sported sleek lines, classic and contemporary, and tinted glass enclosed a two-story cabin amidships. The yacht gleamed, shiny and new. It reeked of money.

"Maybe I will let Tommy pick me up for work," Adam said.

The sun shone bright, and crisp morning air cooled Adam's face. November in New England felt clean, invigorating, and unpredictable. Adam continued down the dock as Tommy emerged from the cabin.

Tommy spotted Adam and waved. He flashed a smile full of white teeth. How much had that dental work cost?

Adam's cell phone buzzed, and he dug it out of his pocket. Effie. Adam's heart jumped. Was something wrong?

"Hey baby, are you alright?"

"Hi, Rufus," she said. Rufus had been the name of her childhood dog and she had called Adam that after she heard police officers referred to as sheepdogs. She sounded tired.

"I didn't expect a call. You scared me."

"Sorry. I wanted to see how your first day is going."

"Interesting. Getting a feel for the players."

"Maybe this is your chance to reconnect with Tommy. Make things right."

An image of a five-year-old Tommy flashed in his mind. They had shuttled between a dozen foster homes before landing with Gin and Alex, the parents who stuck with them. Adam had acted like Tommy's father for so many years, it was hard for them to be friends as adults. Or maybe they had just grown into different people.

"What's your pain number this morning?" he asked. Doctors always asked patients to rate their discomfort on a scale of one to ten, and Adam had adopted the practice. He inquired daily, but always knew the answer before she said it.

"Four," she said.

"That's not too bad. It—"

"I'm on two milligrams of Dilaudid."

"Shit."

"I'll be fine. What's interesting about your job?"

The yacht's engine coughed and then purred to life. Tommy smiled behind the wheel, then he climbed down onto the deck and grabbed the stern line.

"It's *all* interesting," Adam told Effie. "I'll fill you in when—"

The yacht exploded in a fireball.

CHAPTER SEVENTEEN

Adam ducked and dropped his phone as he raised his hands for protection. A wave of overpressure moved through him, and a mushroom cloud rose high into the air. Fire stung Adam's face.

Flames engulfed Tommy's body. He flailed in the stern, shrieking like an inhuman specter. Black smoke rose from the hole where the cabin once stood.

Adam exploded out of his crouch like a sprinter and dashed toward the yacht. His heart raced as adrenaline pumped into his system. He pushed off his toes and swung his arms as he focused on the edge of the dock and timed his jump.

Tommy spun in a circle and banged against the railing. His hair was on fire, and his screams reached the high pitch of a terrified child.

Adam shortened his final stride as he approached the end of the dock then pushed off. He leapt into the air and landed on the smoldering deck. He stumbled but maintained his momentum. He lunged for Tommy.

Flames danced across Tommy's blackened skin.

Adam lowered his shoulder and crashed into Tommy as he stumbled across the deck. He contacted Tommy around the waist, a perfect open field tackle, and lifted him into the air. Adam's hands burned as they slammed into the starboard railing.

They toppled overboard into the bay.

Adam closed his mouth as the icy water extinguished Tommy with the sizzle. Tommy twisted in his arms, and they sank beneath the surface.

Tommy thrashed and jerked like a drowning victim. Adam coiled and pushed for the surface, but Tommy grabbed his face, scratching and pulling. Adam had not taken a full breath and his lungs burned from lack of oxygen.

Instead of pushing away, Adam pulled Tommy into him and threw his arm around his neck, securing a headlock. He bent Tommy backward as his brother pawed at his face.

Adam scissor-kicked for the surface.

One stroke, two, three. They broke the surface. Adam gasped and pulled Tommy's head above the water. He had stopped moving.

Adam sidestroked to the dock, forgoing the burning yacht. He reached it and grasped a cleat with his hand, careful to keep Tommy's head above water.

"Oh my God, oh my God," a middle-aged woman screamed on the dock. "What happened?"

"Help us," Adam said.

"I'll call 911."

"Help me lift him out of the water."

Tommy's eyelids had burned off and his eyeballs had turned to soupy goo. Skin sloughed off his neck and face and floated beside him, like peeling wallpaper.

Adam hoisted himself up with one arm and leaned on the dock. He kept a grip on Tommy, who grew heavier as water saturated his clothing and his feet began to sink.

"Give me a hand," Adam said.

The woman backed away with the phone to her ear. "I can't. It's too horrible."

"Son of a bitch."

Adam aligned Tommy's body with the dock, straining with one hand, and climbed up onto the wooden planks. He reached over with both hands and lifted Tommy. Adam struggled, then got a foot beneath him and pushed with his legs until Tommy lay beside him on the dock.

Adam gulped air. "Did you call?"

"They're coming," she said. "They'll send the chopper."

"How long?"

"Thirty minutes."

"Is there a doctor on the island?"

"I don't think so. Sally knows first-aid, I'll have her bring the truck."

"And blankets and bandages, if she has them."

Adam rolled Tommy onto his side and tilted his head. Water gushed out of his mouth and nose. Adam pounded his back with an open slap, then lowered him onto his back. Tommy's clothing was gone, except for his boxer shorts and socks. He looked barbecued.

Adam knelt beside Tommy's head and grasped him under the jaw with both hands. Tommy's skin came off like he was shedding. Adam opened Tommy's mouth and tilted his head. He hovered his ear over Tommy's nose and mouth and listened while he watched his chest for respirations.

Tommy stopped breathing.

CHAPTER EIGHTEEN

Adam slumped on the dock and gawked at the crisp white sheet covering his brother's body. It had taken thirty minutes for the medevac helicopter to arrive, and by then, Tommy had been long dead. Adam's arms hung at his sides, his energy depleted from performing chest compressions, which he had continued until the first EMTs had arrived and told him to stop. Adam had known his efforts were hopeless, but he had not been able to stop trying.

Tommy was dead.

Despite Tommy's shallow and narcissistic behavior, he had always impressed Adam. Tommy had displayed a gift for computation at Yale University, and Adam had assumed he would become a mathematician or a scientist—until Tommy pivoted to business. Adam had never possessed a gift for mathematics, and their now-deceased foster parents had always seen his move into law enforcement as a disappointment, a decay into a blue-collar existence. Maybe their disapproval had made Adam work harder and take more chances to prove his career had meaning. Maybe he had been trying to impress them. Or Tommy. Maybe he had needed to prove something to himself.

"Let's go back to earlier in the day," Massachusetts State Police Sergeant Keisha Gunn said. Her speech was seasoned with the rhythmic notes of Trinidad. She was young, black, and sinewy, and she moved with the grace of a dancer. She was flawless, except for a thin scar that started below her left eye and ran to her jaw. Somehow, it made her more alluring.

The dearth of law enforcement officers on Cuttyhunk had necessitated a State Police response from Troop D at the Oak Bluffs State Police Barracks on Martha's Vineyard. They arrived on a boat, twenty minutes after the rescue flight and had treated the dock as a crime scene from the beginning.

"Like I told you," Adam said, "Tommy invited me for lunch on his yacht."

"Did he say why?"

"He mentioned something about a scientist's death last week. Tommy thought it was suspicious. He said he had concerns."

"Concerns?"

"Yes."

"He used that word?"

"Yes."

"I'm looking for more," Gunn said.

Adam sighed. "Sorry, this is hard."

Gunn nodded but stayed silent.

"Tommy seemed uneasy. He wanted to talk, away from Forever Technology."

"What made him uneasy?"

"I was meeting him to find out."

Gunn cracked her knuckles and looked back at the dock, which had been charred by the burning yacht. Cuttyhunk's volunteer fire department had arrived ten minutes after the fire breached the boat's hull and sank it. Only the antenna affixed to the yacht's radar array poked above the surface. The air still smelled like a house fire—toxic and dangerous.

"Do you know anyone who wanted to harm your brother?"

"You think it wasn't an accident?"

"We'll know once we recover the yacht and forensics can determine what caused the explosion."

Gunn had explained that Gosnold was part of Dukes County, and the District Attorney's Office in Barnstable investigated homicides. While

Tommy's death could have been an accident, the circumstances were suspicious, which was why the Barnstable DA had asked her to respond from the Cape and Islands State Police Detective Unit.

"But it could be homicide?" Adam asked.

"It's an unnatural death. We must rule out foul play."

"You think it's suspicious, right?"

"The victim's, uh, your brother's statements to you about Sarah Smith, combined with an explosion, make it suspicious. Two accidental deaths on Cuttyhunk in just over a month is extremely odd."

Adam nodded. He could still hear the pain in Effie's voice when he had called to tell her what happened. He would have preferred to do it in person, but she had heard the explosion when he dropped the phone, and he had needed to assure her he was okay. Plus, he wouldn't return home for hours, and she was bound to hear about the accident. Or murder. Or whatever the hell had happened.

"If it's murder, I guess I'm a suspect."

"It's not a homicide . . . yet."

"But if it is, I'm sure you'll look at the family."

Gunn did not blink. "Should we investigate the family?"

"I told you I was a federal agent, so I know how it works. Tommy's my brother, and I was here when it happened, which means I'm a suspect. I want to cooperate and help you clear me as soon as possible, so you can find out who did this."

"If *anyone* is responsible. Accidents happen."

The sun flashed off yellow police tape that stretched from a public restroom to the marina's shops, blocking the dock. Beyond it, a dozen townspeople watched like mourners at a funeral. Death seldom visited Cuttyhunk.

"Will you interview the people at Forever Technology?"

"That's up to Derek Adams. He's the DA in Barnstable, and he runs our homicide investigations. Assuming that's what we have."

She seemed serious and determined, but she had perfect white teeth, and her smile could probably light up a room. Cops outside big cities did not handle many serious crimes, but Gunn had intelligence behind her eyes. And hunger.

"Tommy was worried," Adam said. "He needed to tell me something, and he couldn't do it at Forever Technology."

"We don't know if his death is related to what he wanted to tell you."

"We don't that it's not. You don't find this suspicious?"

"From one cop to another, yeah, it's suspicious as hell. But the decision isn't mine."

"He was my brother."

"I won't brush this off. If someone killed your brother, I'll find them. Until then, don't leave the state."

CHAPTER NINETEEN

The shiny gold dolphin on Fang's necklace slid across her skin, as if it danced through the surf. And a statue of jumping dolphins decorated her desk. She had always loved aquatic creatures and the sea. Among the sound of crashing waves and the odor of decaying fish—she was at home.

She clicked an icon on her desktop and opened a secure digital tunnel into the cloud-based mainframe that held her data. She scrolled through a series of folders and found the file Shlomo had uploaded into Lazarus. Her input was represented as ones and zeros, a coded copy of synaptic connections in Test Subject-3208's brain and a digital record of the subject's response to stimuli. It was a road map for how TS-3208 thought, a recreation of the subject's thoughts as he or she watched a video screen and answered questions.

All the subjects took the same tests in windowless rooms to control external stimuli. Limiting variables allowed Fang to pinpoint connections made in response to specific questions. If a terrifying image flashed on a screen, the subject's brain flooded with chemicals and sent a series of signals to the body. Fight or flight. In response to a complicated question that required intellectual analysis, a distinct set of synaptic connections occurred.

After years of experimentation, piggybacking on the research of scientists more brilliant than her, Fang had constructed a reliable model of the brain. When that model was fed into a computer driven by artificial intelligence, the result was a replica of the subject's thought process—a digital shadow of the mind.

A knock came from the door, and Shlomo Perlman opened it. "Are you in?"

"Yes, Dr. Perlman."

"You heard about Thomas Locke?" he asked.

"What about Thomas?" Fang asked.

Shlomo sat down and tucked his cane against his leg. He sipped from a coffee mug with "Your God is my Algorithm" written on its side. Fang could never tell what Shlomo was thinking. The dark glasses didn't help, but he wore the same thoughtful expression in response to good news or bad, as if every setback had a silver lining, and every victory concealed unexpected defeat. He should have been a philosopher instead of a scientist.

"There was an accident," he said.

Her pulse quickened, her nerves still raw from Sarah's death. "Accident?"

"A fire," Shlomo said. "On his yacht. He's dead."

The room tilted, and Fang seized her desk for support. Thomas had been kind to her. He had convinced her to move from Palo Alto and had promised her that Bryce was the champion they all needed and craved. He had greeted her when she arrived on Cuttyhunk and introduced her to the staff. None of that had been his job. She had assumed he wanted to get into her pants, from the way he had leered when he thought she wasn't looking, but he had also been a friend.

Now he was gone.

First Sarah and now Thomas. Her only allies in the company. Both dead. Was that a coincidence?

"When?" she asked.

"Today at the dock."

"I do not understand. How?"

"Apparently, he was on his boat when it exploded."

"A bomb?"

Shlomo sipped his coffee. "I assume it's too early to tell. The police have a forensic team combing the marina. I saw divers in the water."

"Looking for other victims?"

"Or evidence. This kind of thing doesn't happen in a little New England town. Especially Gosnold."

"Thomas was murdered," Fang said.

Shlomo narrowed his eyes. "Be careful, my dear. Don't be a *yenta*. It's not wise to cast unwarranted accusations."

"Someone killed Sarah and now this."

"Let's not jump to conclusions. Sarah's death was an accident."

"Bái mù. You don't understand. How could Sarah fall off that cliff?"

Shlomo rubbed the stubble on his chin. "It happens. Maybe she walked to the edge for a better view. She looked down, got vertigo, and fell. It's possible."

"Someone pushed her."

Shlomo clutched his mug with both hands. "Who?"

Heat rose in Fang's cheeks, and she willed herself not to cry. "I don't know. I thought I heard something. Movement in bushes."

"My dear, I submit this to you; unsubstantiated claims will put a target on your back."

"A target?"

"Figuratively, of course. An accidental death is awful, and two are worse, but murder would have serious ramifications for this company. Investors don't want to be associated with crime, and murder draws media like flies to shit. If you run around claiming employees of Forever Technology were murdered, I'm afraid they'll find a way to silence you."

"And what? Kill me too?"

"They'll transfer you back to Palo Alto then dismiss you quietly once the crisis is over."

"Huǒyǎn xiéshén."

"What's that?"

"Evil spirits." Fang rubbed the dolphin hanging from her neck—an old habit. "You are a man of reason. You think it is a coincidence? Two violent deaths in one month?"

"Time will tell. Perhaps it's best we leave the detecting to the police and focus on our research. Science has been my refuge through many rough patches. Science never falls to the vagaries of politics or greed or anger. It requires reason and objectivity. It's what kept me sane in Moscow before the Soviet Union fell, and it's what will keep us focused now. I suggest you spend your time in her company. Science has served me well."

Fang nodded. Science, computer engineering, and advanced mathematics had attracted her because those disciplines were black and white. They had few gray areas, little ambiguity. Questions had answers. You were right or wrong and there was no reason to second guess. She loved its starkness. She had craved its purity compared to the constant propaganda, disinformation, and warped ideology she had lived with in China.

Maybe Shlomo was right. "Thank you for your wisdom," Fang said. A tear caressed her cheek.

Shlomo nodded. "I'll leave you to your work." He turned and the tapping of his cane echoed like a metronome until her airtight door closed and she was alone with her thoughts.

What had she gotten herself into? She wanted to help humanity and change the world, yet she was a cog in a machine exploring untested theories—technology that could alter everything. Once the genie escaped the bottle, it would be impossible to put back. History had shown her that. But was fear of the unknown worth giving up on progress that could benefit everyone? What would be the unintended consequences of her research?

Now, two of her colleagues were dead. People she had liked. Had she played a role in their deaths?

CHAPTER TWENTY

Adam left his golf cart parked behind the police tape at the marina and hiked up the road toward Forever Technology. Being in motion always sharpened his mind, and he needed to process what had happened.

Tommy's death invaded his consciousness, its horror impossible to ignore. Every time his mind wandered, Tommy's face appeared behind his eyes and the crushing weight of loss slowed his pace. He tried to remember Tommy's voice, but the timber of his brother's words had already begun to disappear from his memory. Was life a mere flicker in time and then nothing? When everyone Tommy had known had died, would anything be left to prove he had lived?

Adam stumbled absently into the entrance of Forever Technology and bumped into a woman coming out. He grabbed her to prevent her from falling.

"Excuse me," Fang said.

"I'm sorry. I wasn't paying attention. Dr. Jin, isn't it?"

She looked up with glassy eyes. "I heard about your brother."

"Yes." The horror of death weighed him down.

"He was kind to me," she said.

Adam stared at his shoes. Fang had known him. Adam had forgotten that Tommy had lived with his own circle of friends and colleagues. Adam had not been close to his brother, but there must have been others who cared for him, who saw Tommy differently. Tommy, the boss. Tommy, the finance guy. Adam had spent little time with his brother since they had shared a childhood bedroom. Now, the opportunity to reconnect had vanished forever.

Adam looked up and found Fang watching him. Somehow, it comforted him to know she also had a Tommy-sized hole in her life. Death was a human condition they all had to confront.

"Were you close?" he asked.

"We, uh, he was one of the first people I met at the company. He welcomed me here."

"I'm sure Tommy touched many lives."

"I . . . yes. He did. I need to get some air."

Fang walked across the parking lot to a trailhead and disappeared into the woods.

CHAPTER TWENTY-ONE

Adam hesitated at his bedroom door with his hand on the knob. Knowing Effie had cancer was like swimming in the ocean and then feeling something brush against his leg. He waited for the inevitable, knowing his worst nightmare could strike at any moment. Terror had settled deep in his bones, and he needed it to stop.

Caring for Effie brought unending sorrow, unending fear, unending love. Never knowing what each day would bring—breathing problems, pain, some new form of agony. Each time, he would die with her, a little at a time. He cared for her, loved her, suffered each moment, every setback, until her pain became a presence of its own—a part of him.

Dread hovered above him, ready to pounce. Eternally.

Adam had rushed home to be with Effie. The cancer had left her on an emotional tightrope, and the hormones they forced her to take had poured gasoline onto the fire. Tommy's death had made her distraught, and he needed to be with her. Her father had abandoned Effie, and Adam would not be the second man to leave her, no matter how hard things became. Not now. Not ever.

He entered the room quietly to avoid waking her, but she sat in bed writing in a notebook.

"I have to meet the police at Tommy's, er, Svetlana's house," Adam said. "I want to be there when they interview her. For support."

"I wish I could go with you," Effie said. "I called, but she didn't pick up, so I sent a text. Tell her I'm here for her, and she's welcome to stay with us."

That surprised him. Effie had never liked Svetlana. She had called Svetlana narcissistic and vain, which Adam had assumed was competition between attractive women, but Effie also had a point. Svetlana could be fiercely self-involved. Tommy had married her for her looks, and in Adam's experience, exceptional beauty often accompanied personality problems.

"I'll offer," he said. "Helping Svetlana is the least I can do for Tommy."

"She certainly won't want for money," Effie said, an icy wind carrying her words.

"I know you think she married Tommy for his money—"

"And he married her for her body."

It felt wrong to talk about them this way, after what happened. "Her money won't fix her sadness."

Effie stayed quiet.

CHAPTER TWENTY-TWO

Adam waited beside Sergeant Keisha Gunn's car while she spoke with Svetlana Volkov about Tommy's death. As a professional courtesy, Gunn had given Adam a ride on a State Police boat to Martha's Vineyard, but she had insisted he stay outside until she interviewed Svetlana. Adam understood. He could still become a suspect.

The front door opened, and two hulking state troopers exited. What did they feed those guys? Every trooper he had seen was big enough to start with the New England Patriots. Gunn exited behind them. She paused in the door and handed a card to Svetlana then walked toward Adam. She gave him a thumbs up as she continued past him to her car.

Adam watched the police drive away before he hiked up the long driveway. Svetlana held the door open for him. She wore a white sweater and tight Capri pants that showed her figure. She had pulled her chestnut hair into a French braid, but a stray lock had fallen over her crystal-blue eyes.

"You and Tommy never got along," Svetlana said as a greeting.

Adam stopped on the stoop. His chest ached with the rawness of Tommy's death. "I always protected him. Especially when we were younger."

"He thought you didn't respect him."

Another thing Adam would never be able to set straight. Why had he waited to reconnect with Tommy? "I respected him, on some level. I chose a life fighting for my ideals. Tommy had the brains, but instead of pursuing research, he pivoted and used his skills to lure investors. I guess I thought he sold out."

"Money is survival."

"Don't get me wrong," Adam said. "I love capitalism, but Tommy's early passion was science. After he switched to business, he seemed more drawn to whatever made money."

"He was enthusiastic about science *and* making money. The investments he attracted to Forever made their research possible."

"I may have judged him for not using his giant brain for science."

"Scientists don't always use their talents to save the world," she said. "Sometimes, they create monsters."

"I know."

"Your brother was excellent at his job."

"He was always driven. Once he decided he wanted to be rich, he made it happen. Part of me envied the way he saw things in black and white. He knew what he wanted, and he took it without the moral consternation I suffer."

Svetlana's eyes narrowed. "He wasn't always certain. You may have idealized him as a child, but your precious brother had his flaws."

Tommy inhaled the sea air. "What did the police say?"

"They're investigating the explosion, and it should take a few days to determine the cause. They asked if Tommy had enemies."

"I'm worried his job had something to do with his death."

"You don't think it's an accident?" Svetlana asked.

Adam shook his head. "No."

"Do the police agree?"

"Not yet."

"You're an agent, will—"

"Not anymore."

"What can you do?"

That was the question. "Tommy was my brother. I need to find the truth."

"And you think Forever Technology is involved?"

"I don't know, but if they are, it'll be trouble. Taking on a billion-dollar corporation will cause problems."

"Losing your job?"

"I'm more worried about protecting Effie. Protecting you. But I have to discover what happened. I won't stop until I do."

Svetlana took his hand. Her skin was soft as satin. "You're all I have left. I don't want to lose you too." She squeezed his hand. It felt vaguely inappropriate. But she was grieving. And scared.

"I'll find out who killed him. I promise."

Fang paced her office, her chest tightening as the walls closed in on her. Sarah, the woman who would have revealed Forever's secrets to her, was dead. And now, Tommy Locke—Bryce's right-hand man—was gone too.

Fang needed to get away and clear her head. Crying in public was unacceptable because demonstrations of emotion showed weakness.

But her tears were coming.

Fang grabbed a tissue off her desk and crumpled it. Shlomo had left to give her privacy. That was something. She opened her door and hurried down the hall. Her heels clicked on the tile, and it echoed like a snare drum. She wore Jimmy Choo's, low enough to function in her computer lab but stylish enough for her to retain a sense of femininity. She stared down the long hallway at red lights illuminating the elevated walkway to the annex. Shlomo had assigned her a workspace in Black Diamond. He had given her a tour—but he had not shown her everything.

The only thing Sarah and Tommy had in common was Black Diamond—Forever Technology's crown jewel. Sarah had driven research while Tommy found investors to fund the future. *Had found,* she corrected herself. Tommy had also been Bryce's confidant, and they had collaborated for almost a decade. Bryce had trusted him most.

Fang had only recently arrived in Cuttyhunk, but she had been with Forever Technology for a year and knew every aspect of the brain mapping program. If something connected to her program could motivate murder, she would find it. Digital mapping and recreating the human mind had enormous potential, both to change human life and for financial ascendancy. People always wanted what others had. If Sarah and Tommy's deaths were related to Black Diamond, then the answer lay inside the Annex.

She proceeded down the stainless-steel hallway past the black tinted glass covering a surveillance camera. Bryce had approved her access, so why did she feel nervous? She placed her hand onto the biometric reader and slid her fingers between the guideposts. She leaned forward and pressed her eye into an optical reader. A red light glowed inside, which forced her to blink. The machine beeped, and the door opened with a whoosh.

The hallway connected to the second floor, but the most innovative work happened in the subterranean levels. Shlomo's team operated on level P-2, which he had shown her, but there was another level below them. She entered the elevator, which also required a biometric scan, and pressed the button for P-2. Beneath the button for P3 was an unmarked selector with a key slot beside it. Was there a fourth subterranean level?

What was going on down there?

She exited on P-2 and passed two scientists, Jim Wilson and David something. She nodded and continued toward her workspace. This level had a common area in the center, where robotics and other machinery sat atop stainless-steel tables. Four hallways branched off the common area, each with its own group of laboratories.

She crossed the center, but instead of turning down the hallway to her lab, she walked to the other side and down a hallway she had not explored. Black Diamond employed a combination of computer scientists, neurologists, microbiologists, and mechanical engineers. Researchers in white coats orbited around tables covered with computers. Many appeared distracted and spoke in hushed tones. Everyone must have heard about Tommy by now, and these were scientists, intellectuals, big brains who lived inside their own heads, theorizing, computing, analyzing. The average IQ in these labs was well above one-fifty, but some had emotional IQs far below normal. Two deaths in a short time would not sit well with socially inept and introverted personalities who had trouble making sense of human behavior on a good day. How would they process the sudden, violent deaths of two colleagues?

She passed a group of older men puttering around the mechanical arm, but no one looked up. She entered the wing on the far side and peered through glass windows at laboratories on both sides of the hallway. In one room, two women strung wires between an external server and a black box on a wheeled trolley. Yellow, red, blue, and green wires looked like spaghetti.

What were they doing?

Fang continued and other labs offered similar tableaus. She reached the end and stopped. What had she expected to find, a treasure chest with a sign over it saying, "must murder for entry?"

Fang retraced her steps, crossed the center lobby, and entered the elevator. She pressed the button for P-3. The elevator descended and stopped. She exited, but another security door blocked the hallway. She placed her hand on the biometrics and the laser scanned her eye. The door did not open.

"Level restricted," the British accent of a computer-generated voice crackled from a speaker.

Fang cupped her hands on the window and looked through the glass door at a long hallway—dark and empty. The lights were on motion sensors, and no-one had activated them yet. What happened on this level?

She stared at the restricted sign over the door at the end. Below it, a second steel door had another biometric access panel. That was strange.

Fang finally had access to Black Diamond and understood their efforts to download consciousness, yet some areas remained off-limits.

Forever Technology still held secrets. Things she needed to uncover.

CHAPTER TWENTY-THREE

Edna stood on the stoop of the late Thomas Locke's mansion and summoned her most compassionate smile for Svetlana Volkov. Empathy had never been Edna's strength. She had always lacked charisma, that indefinable quality that could make people want to be around her. Just the opposite. Since childhood, Edna had repelled men and women, even their family pets. She had long ago abandoned trying to earn people's affection. In a sense, her lack of charisma had made her an aggressive reporter. She did not care who she pissed off. She wanted the truth. Needed the truth. And if someone didn't like it, tough nuggets.

The door opened halfway, and a waif of a woman peeked out. She had silky hair, ruby red lips, and arctic-blue eyes set on a porcelain canvas. She wore a silk blouse and a tight pencil skirt that extended past her knees. It had to be Givenchy or Armani Priví. Svetlana looked like every rich wife in Westchester County and every Manhattanite who had sneered at Edna when they thought she wasn't looking.

"Svetlana Volkov?" Edna asked.

"Yes?"

"Edna Cooper, Cape Cod Post."

"What the fuck do you want?"

Whoa. This dainty creature had fangs. How unexpected. Edna wanted to be conciliatory, but Svetlana had been the aggressor, and Edna's natural defense was always a full blitz.

"I'm covering your husband's death," Edna said. "I'm looking for answers."

"No comment."

"I'm sorry for your loss, but I'm trying to find out what happened."

"His boat caught fire, and he died."

"It exploded," Edna said. "The police have not ruled on cause yet. It may not have been an accident."

Svetlana narrowed her eyes. "Is this what you do? Traffic in gossip?"

"It was the second death on Cuttyhunk this fall."

"We're done here," Svetlana said. She started to close the door.

"Both victims worked for Forever Technology. Do you think the company is involved?"

The door stopped, then Svetlana peered through the crack, her face bathed in shadows. "What are you saying?"

"I'm not saying anything. I'm asking if you think your husband's job had anything to do with his death."

"I wouldn't know."

"Did he have enemies at work?"

"Everyone loved Tommy."

"That's not what I asked."

Svetlana opened the door wider. "Everyone has enemies, Mrs.?"

"*Ms.* Cooper. Edna Cooper. Who were your husband's adversaries?"

"Tommy . . ." she bit her lip. "He helped run one of the biggest artificial intelligence companies in the world. People were jealous."

"Jealous enough to murder?"

"The police aren't calling it murder."

"Not yet," Edna said. "Who at Forever Technology had a problem with your husband?"

"I don't know. There was the usual gossip, inter-office rivalry, that kind of thing, but Tommy didn't discuss it much."

"What did he talk about?"

A thin smile cracked Svetlana's face. "You're a bit of an insensitive bitch, aren't you?"

Edna had heard that before. And much worse. She laughed. "I'm doing my job. People have a right to know."

"About what my husband told me in the privacy of our home?"

"What was Thomas working—"

"Tommy."

"Excuse me?"

"I called him Tommy. If you want me to tell you about my husband, at least get his name right."

"What was *Tommy* working on recently?"

"None of your fucking business."

"Do you think he was murdered?"

"If he was, you should ask Bryce Hastings about it."

Edna's spine tingled. "Why Mr. Hastings?"

"It's your job to find out. Not mine. If you want to write about my husband, talk to Bryce Hastings."

Svetlana shut the door, and the bolt locked with a thunk. Edna strained to hear Svetlana walk away but heard nothing. She stared into the peephole and smiled, then walked back to her fifteen-year-old Volvo.

She had her quote. Edna jotted it into her notebook, "Ask Bryce Hastings about it." Edna reached into the pocket of her sweater and removed her audio recorder. Massachusetts law prohibited recording someone without first obtaining consent, but people clammed up when recorders came out, and Edna would not allow a source to lie about what she had said. Failing to record an interview had destroyed her career and she would not make the same mistake a second time.

Never again.

Edna started her car and smiled. Her instincts had been right. Something was wrong at Forever Technology.

CHAPTER TWENTY-FOUR

The elevator opened on the third floor of Forever Technology, and Adam rushed past Dale's reception desk toward Tommy's old office.

"Sir?" Dale asked. "May I help you?"

Adam continued down the hall. It was time to act—make a blind raise.

"You can't go in there," Dale said.

Adam reached the end of the hall, and Tommy's frosted-glass doors opened automatically. He entered the massive corner office. Tommy's thick-glass desk stood in front of floor-to-ceiling windows. Outside, brown scrub grass swayed in the wind, and the ocean churned in the distance.

Adam hesitated at the sight of Tommy's empty leather chair. It was a symbol of his brother's loss, like a riderless horse with backward stirrups. Adam moved to a black-lacquered file cabinet and jiggled the handle. Locked.

Dale appeared in the doorway. "Mr. Locke, you can't be in here."

Adam ignored him and moved around the desk to a series of cupboards. He threw them open, revealing stacks of manuals, scientific journals, marketing textbooks, and sales guides. The next cabinet contained pens, pads, loose-leaf binders, and other office supplies.

"Dammit," Adam said. "What was my brother working on?"

"Sir, all work product is need-to-know only. I'm sorry I—"

"He was my brother."

"Nobody is allowed in the executive offices without express permission."

"Tommy's right to privacy sank with his yacht," Adam said.

"I've called security. I—"

Felix Suggs burst into the room, panting. A sheen of sweat coated his bald head. "What the hell are you doing, Locke?"

"I want to know what my brother was into that got him killed."

"Whoa, whoa, slow down," Suggs said. "I'm sorry about the accident, but—"

"Don't give me that shit about an accident. I was there. I know a bomb when I see one."

Suggs started to say something, then stopped. His breathing had slowed to normal, and he adjusted his blazer by pulling its lapels. "Listen, Locke. You were a Fed, so you know jumping to conclusions can be dangerous. Wait and see what the police find before we tear apart offices searching for phantoms."

Adam stared hard at Suggs. The security chief was right, of course. Emotion drove Adam, but that realization did not stop him from wanting to punch Suggs in the nose. "You arrived in Cuttyhunk a few months ago, and two of your senior people are dead. You think that's a coincidence?"

"Unlikely," Suggs said. "It's my job to keep Forever employees safe, and it seems I'm not doing a competent job."

Suggs's self-admonishment took some of the wind out of Adam's sails. "If you admit it's suspicious, help me find motive."

Suggs rubbed his face in his hands. He paced the room. "If we get a shred of evidence that shows his death was murder, I'll let you run wild, but until then, I won't expose this company's secrets. And I won't fuel conspiracy theories that scare away investors."

"You think I give a shit about your investors?" Adam asked.

"You should. Your brother devoted a decade of his life to this company. The things we're creating are important. Consequential. You're angry and looking for vengeance, a way to make sense of this, but it's my job to protect this company and its people. I won't let you destroy them for some irrational quest for vengeance."

Adam balled his fists, and a red cloud colored the edges of his vision. He rolled his shoulders to release the tension building in his neck. Lashing out at Suggs would not help him, and it might get him tossed out of the company, which would eliminate any chance of investigating Tommy's murder.

"You moved from Silicon Valley to one of the smallest and safest little towns in New England," Adam said. "They don't even have a police officer on the island, for crying out loud. I don't believe in crazy conspiracy theories, but I'd be a fool to ignore the almost impossible coincidence. Someone killed my brother, and I'll find out who's responsible."

Suggs crossed his arms, and his chin hardened. "I'd fire you for insubordination, but Bryce wants you, so I can't. But as long as you're employed here, you'll do what I tell you. I'm ordering you to leave this office and let the police do their jobs. If somebody killed your brother, I want to find them as badly as you do."

"Not even close."

CHAPTER TWENTY-FIVE

Adam scooped his vibrating phone off the bed stand and glanced at Effie, who lay on her side facing away from him. She had been in pain all night—a dreadful night. Lack of sleep made her symptoms worse and created a vicious cycle that could spiral down into another emergency room visit. She needed restorative sleep to fight the cancer.

He leaned close and listened. She snored. Thank God.

His phone vibrated again. He tiptoed out of the bedroom and hurried downstairs as he answered.

"I need your help," Doug Barnstable said.

"Good morning to you too."

"Uh, sorry. How are you holding up?"

"Things are great. My girlfriend is dying, someone murdered my brother, the CEO is stonewalling me, and the State Police have me on their suspect list."

"That's too much for anyone to handle alone."

"I'm out on a limb," Adam said. "Tommy's death was the second on Cuttyhunk in a month. Another scientist fell off a cliff. My spidey sense is tingling."

"Want me to call the State Police? Wanda Benson is the special agent in charge of DEA's New England Division. I'm sure she has influence with the Staties."

"The detective who caught the case is Sergeant Keisha Gunn. Seems like a straight shooter."

"Maybe the SAC can offer support, push them to look into Forever Technology."

"It might cause problems if the State Police feel like we're interfering," Adam said. "Let's see what Gunn does first."

"Roger that."

Adam cracked open the back door and walked onto his patio. The early morning sun glistened off the placid Vineyard Sound like a million diamonds. "You need my help with something?"

"Dastigar Shinwari is at it again."

"That asshole."

"He popped up on our radar in Quetta. He met with a couple members of the Taliban Shura in a mosque. One of your old sources overheard him chatting with their money man. It looks like he's made a deal, twelve million to transport heroin from his Nangarhar lab to a freighter in Karachi."

"We knew the Taliban would control trafficking once they took over Afghanistan."

"Shinwari is our biggest narco-terrorism target in the region. This is our chance to—"

"I resigned," Adam said. "I mucked my hand, and I'm out."

"You have more narco-terrorism cases under your belt than anyone in the world, and you know Shinwari's organization. Come back and help us nail him."

"I can't. I'm dealing with Tommy's death investigation." Saying the words made his chest ache. "If I'm not here, I'm afraid Forever Technology will steamroll the locals and have the fire ruled an accident."

"I can reach out to my contacts up there, get the Cape Cod or New Bedford offices involved. Low key. I'm sure they have solid relationships with the Staties."

"Maybe . . . if it's unofficial."

"Meanwhile, I want you on Shinwari. You hunted him for years, and we have a real shot to get him. I know you want back in. Police work is in your blood."

"Effie needs me."

Doug exhaled into the phone. "Yeah, I know, brother."

"I'd help if I could, but I made my choice. Besides, you have excellent agents working for you."

"How about you and Effie come back to DC? I'll look the other way if you need to cut out during the day and check on her."

"We're both from Massachusetts," Adam said. "Effie needs the comfort of being home. She never liked the District."

"You can't stay away forever."

Adam looked back at the house. Their bedroom was dark, which meant Effie was still asleep. "I need to be here right now."

"If you wait too long, it'll be hard to return. Think about the future."

"My future is lying upstairs in bed fighting for her life."

"How can I help?"

"Funny you should ask," Adam said. "I need a favor."

CHAPTER TWENTY-SIX

Edna Cooper pushed up her glasses with the end of her astronaut pen, then unwrapped two sticks of Trident bubblegum and popped them into her mouth. Why did they make them so small? She climbed out of her faded-blue Volvo and walked up the driveway to Adam Locke's residence. The two-story Cape-Cod-style house had weathered gray clapboard with wooden shingles frayed at the ends. The rhythmic chugging of a fishing boat carried across the Vineyard Sound.

A neighbor's dog barked as she approached. She reached for the doorbell and the door swung open.

Adam stood there wearing blue jeans and a gray tee shirt with the Boston Red Sox logo on the front. "Good morning," he said. "May I help you?"

"Edna Cooper, Cape Cod Post. I'd like to ask you a few questions."

The smile slid off Adam's face. "Who gave you my address?"

"Falmouth is a small town. It wasn't hard to track you down. May I come in?"

"You should have called."

"I like to interview people face-to-face. Maybe I'm old-fashioned."

His jaw hardened. "This is my home."

"Then I'm in the right place."

Adam stepped onto the front porch. He towered over her but did nothing threatening. He closed the door, using his hand to prevent it from banging shut. "My girlfriend is sleeping."

"We can talk out here."

"Come with me," he said.

She followed him around the house and into the backyard. A rock protruded off the beach and into the Sound. A group of seagulls leaned into the wind. The air smelled of salt and seaweed.

He stopped beside a brick barbecue pit. "I don't think I should comment. Not while the case is being investigated."

"But you were there when it happened, right?"

"Yes."

"I'm more interested in whatever you can tell me about Forever Technology," Edna said. "Sergeant Gunn told me you're an employee, but the only thing I found online about you was your testimony in the trial of a narco-terrorist."

"I recently left DEA."

"Forever Technology made you an offer you couldn't refuse?"

Adam did not smile. "My girlfriend has medical problems. I resigned to care for her."

That jolted Edna. She had suffered through her father's Alzheimer's. "I'm sorry, I didn't know. Did you choose Forever Technology because of your brother?"

"What exactly are you writing?"

"Nothing yet. I'm trying to understand what a massive tech company is doing on Cape Cod."

"Then you should talk to Bryce Hastings. Not me."

"I did. Your brother was the second suspicious death since Forever Technology set up shop on Cuttyhunk."

"Is this on the record?"

"Yes."

"No comment."

A familiar aggression bubbled inside Edna, firing her engines. The truth was out there, and this man stood in her way. He had no obligation to speak to her, but she could make things unpleasant for him. He was new to the company and probably had less loyalty to Forever than other employees—especially after his brother's accident. She needed him to help her.

"Don't you want to sort this out?" she asked.

"Sort what out?"

"What happened to your brother and Dr. Smith? What drove Forever Technology to flee Palo Alto and set up shop on a sliver of rock in the Atlantic."

"You think I have those answers?"

"You know more than I do. Give me something. Help me shine a light on the truth."

Adam looked out to sea. He flexed his hands and rolled his shoulders, then turned to her. "Off the record, if something's going on with that damn company, I hope you find it, but I'm stumbling around in the dark the same as you."

"On background then."

"I just started there."

"What are they working on?"

"Artificial intelligence."

"I've read the PR materials," Edna said. "Why did they really move to Cuttyhunk?"

"It's a reasonable question. I asked too. I think they wanted a secure location. Intellectual property theft is a serious threat to any innovative tech company."

"What's so valuable they have to hide on an island."

"That's what I'd like to know."

CHAPTER TWENTY-SEVEN

Fang entered the Annex's break room and dropped a tea bag into a mug with a cartoon dolphin logo. The tapping of Dr. Shlomo Perlman's cane resonated through the hall. She turned as he entered the room.

"Dr. Jin?" he asked. He held his cane in one hand and a thick file in the other.

"I needed caffeine."

"I saw you in the restricted area," Shlomo said.

"Saw?"

"My language is habitual. It hasn't recognized my infirmities. Not after decades of blindness. I get a notification whenever Project Lazarus is accessed."

"And?" Fang's body chilled. She had known someone would notice her snooping on the lower levels.

"Do I need to be concerned? What were you doing down there?"

Don't lie. He'll know. "Feeding my curiosity. I wanted to see the project. You shocked me with the news your team has started uploading my data. I do not want another surprise."

His tongue darted across cracked lips, like a nursing home patient. "Why do you want to know?"

"I am worried about . . . philosophical issues, medical and scientific decisions with long-term ramifications."

Shlomo smiled. "Yes."

"This technology can change the way humans live from this point forward." Using ethical issues to explain her snooping wasn't difficult because she worried about how AI would affect the world.

"Don't you want to be able to fix broken bodies?" Shlomo asked. "Be able to grow new organs and limbs? Heal the infirm?"

"Bioengineering won't stop at fixing deformities. People will want enhancements. Stronger bodies, smarter brains."

Shlomo moved across the room, tapping the floor. *Tick, tick, tick.* He settled into a chair and leaned the cane against his leg. "Why shouldn't people improve themselves? Want better vision, enhance your eyes. Want better sex, grow a bigger *schlong*. If parents wish their child to excel at basketball, why not genetically enhance his stem cells and grow him to be eight feet tall?"

"The moral and ethical questions range beyond that. When we download a subject's processes, their thoughts and memories, are we downloading them or something else?"

"Like shadows on Plato's cave?"

"Are synaptic connections their essence? If that is what we are doing, then we need to step with care. Can a person exist in their minds and inside a computer at the same time?"

Shlomo smiled. "Like an evil twin?"

"I am serious. Is the digitized version of their mind conscious? Have we created another being—a unique life?"

"You think I'm playing God."

"Are you?"

"We can extend lives for years. Theoretically, forever."

"That comes with additional ethical concerns," Fang said. "Who gets to live forever? Do we make our technology available to everyone?"

"Would everyone want to live forever? I know people who would consider that a hellish sentence."

"What happens to the earth when people do not die?" she asked. "And we will give long lives to both angels and devils."

"You mean, how do we deal with a Joseph Stalin for an eternity?" Shlomo asked.

"*Duì.* Exactly. This technology will change the nature of our existence. Who gets to decide? Should we be making these decisions in a bunker on an island?"

"If we share our technology, others will steal it, or the government will try to control it . . . or seize it."

"Maybe the government should take it," she said.

"Don't be a *putz*. We can't trust politicians and bureaucrats with Forever Technology. When have they ever made the world better?"

"Will Mr. Bryce be better? Nobody elected him."

"Hitler was elected."

"You know what I am saying."

"Your questions are important," Shlomo said, "and I see why Bryce hired you, but we don't have an institutional review board like at a university. We don't answer to anyone. Scientists and philosophers have debated the issues surrounding AI for many, many years. We—" Shlomo cocked his head toward the door. "We'll have to continue this later. Here comes Old Spice, and Mr. Italian shoes."

"Excuse me?"

The break room door opened, and Suggs entered with Dr. Wilson. The faint odor of cologne tingled her nose, and she glanced down at the doctor's feet. He wore brown leather Gucci shoes. Fang smiled.

"Dr. Perlman, Dr. Jin," Suggs said.

"The room is all yours," Shlomo said. "We were just leaving."

Fang touched Shlomo's arm and whispered, "But my questions about the project?"

"My dear, it's been decided," Shlomo said. "We're moving forward because it's the right thing to do. And because we can."

CHAPTER TWENTY-EIGHT

The wind blew across the grassy airfield on Cuttyhunk's eastern shore and carried the scent of marram grass and sand. It always brought Adam back to his childhood. Suggs stood beside him with his arms crossed as Bryce's plane made a wide turn and slowed on its final approach.

The Icon A5 amphibious aircraft's engine quieted as it glided over the grass airfield. Cuttyhunk Island had a helicopter pad and two private airfields, and Bryce had secured this bumpy field for Forever Technology's exclusive use.

Suggs kept his eyes on the plane. "Stop asking questions about your brother's accident. And Dr. Smith's."

"Stop calling them accidents."

Suggs swung around fast, his face close. His breath reeked of garlic and coffee. "The medical examiner ruled on Dr. Smith's death."

"People make mistakes."

Suggs's eyes flared. "And you're making one now. Bryce may be putting up with you out of loyalty to your dead brother, but push me hard enough and I'll find a way to get rid of you. Do your job or I'll find someone else to do it. Are we clear?"

Adam bit his tongue.

Suggs led him to the end of the airfield, at the end of a small rise, and they stood beside what looked like a petrified stingray. A windsock fluttered atop a pole next to the landing strip.

The Icon A5 touched down, bounced hard on the uneven earth, then settled on its wheels. The two-seater was white with orange wingtips and had a propeller behind the tinted cockpit. It slowed, then turned around at the end of the strip, positioned to take off again. Its engine cut off, and the propeller rotated to a stop. Bryce cracked open the aircraft's canopy and climbed out. He wore black slacks with a black jacket and dark aviator sunglasses. He ran his fingers through his hair and approached them. His shoulders slumped with fatigue.

"My God, Adam," Bryce said. "I'm sorry I couldn't return sooner."

"There have been developments," Suggs said. He cocked his head at Adam.

"Tommy was murdered," Adam said. "He—"

Bryce's eyes widened. "What? They told me it was a boating accident."

"There's no evidence of a crime," Suggs said.

"I saw it with my own goddamn eyes," Adam said.

"Hold on," Bryce said. "Are the police calling it a homicide?"

"No, they're not," Suggs said.

Heat rose from Adam's chest and warmed his cheeks. Effie lay dying in their bed, and he had lost his only brother. He wanted to punch something. He stepped close to Bryce. "What did my brother know that got him killed?"

"Hold on Adam," Bryce said, raising his palms in surrender. "Let's not jump to conclusions. Is there any evidence we're dealing with foul play?"

"I didn't see Dr. Smith fall off the cliff," Adam said, "but I watched Tommy's brand-new yacht blow up. I'm not buying a gas leak."

"Nothing but conjecture," Suggs said. "That's all you're—"

"Time to show your cards," Adam interrupted. "What was Tommy working on that would motivate someone to kill him?"

Bryce let out a long breath and stretched his back. "Shit," he said. "I can't believe this is happening."

"It happened," Adam said, "and it will not stop until you tell me what's going on. I need to—"

"That's enough," Suggs said. "Bryce, Adam is too close to this. It's my job to handle security at this company, and he's a liability. This kind of inquisition—"

Bryce held up his hand. "Stop it. We just lost a valued member of our company. I lost a friend. Emotions are high, and we need to take a moment to decide our next steps."

"While we're sitting around having a meeting, the killer is getting farther away," Adam said, "Unless he's been here all along."

"What the fuck do you mean by that?" Suggs asked.

"You know exactly what I mean."

"Enough," Bryce said. "Adam, I understand how you feel—"

"Do you?"

"Tommy was with me from the beginning. He was family—not a blood relation—but I chose him, and we were together every day. I know you didn't get along, but Tommy had flair. Real talent. Forever Technology would still be a pipe dream, something I scrawled on a barroom napkin if not for him. I feel his loss as much as any man alive. I promise we'll get answers."

"You can start by briefing me on everything Tommy was doing," Adam said.

"That's sensitive," Suggs said, "and we can't disclose—"

"Sensitive information is what I need," Adam said. "If Tommy was killed because of his work, then it was something important, something that would justify murder. I need to see everything he touched over the last six months."

"I'll give you whatever you need," Bryce said, "but we must be careful. Anything we tell the police can damage our reputation and delay our work. We're treading water, surrounded by sharks, and we're hemorrhaging blood. Powerful, dangerous people want to steal what we've produced and stop us from getting there first."

"Getting where?"

Bryce exchanged a look with Suggs. "To the event horizon," Bryce said.

"The what?"

"The moment when what it means to be human changes forever."

CHAPTER TWENTY-NINE

Adam sat across from Svetlana on the patio at the Atlantic, a trendy restaurant on Martha's Vineyard. Across the beach, waves crashed onto the shore. Svetlana looked thinner than usual, her Russian cheekbones more prominent than before.

"You need to eat something," Adam said.

"The thought of food makes me want to vomit," she said. "And not in a 'stay fit' kind of way."

"When was the last time you had a meal?"

"I can't believe he's gone."

Adam pushed fried scallops around his plate with a fork. "I keep expecting to wake up from a dream."

"You mean a nightmare."

"I'll find out who did this," Adam said. "But it takes time. I've worked on complex federal racketeering cases and transnational conspiracies, and I know crimes don't get solved overnight."

"Forever Technology did this," Svetlana said.

"If Tommy's death was work-related, serious players are involved. If we assume that's the case, then a rival company or foreign government would have had to gain something by killing him."

"Yes, but—"

"Hold on," Adam said, "Let me finish. If their risk-reward calculation made killing Tommy rational, then they had to infiltrate an island with fewer than thirty full-time residents, sneak onto his boat, and plant a bomb or sabotage it without killing anyone else."

"Why not—"

"And assuming we're looking at a conspiracy, the killer would have made the same calculation for Dr. Smith, then established surveillance, followed her into the conservation land, and killed her without Dr. Jin witnessing it. In both cases the killer, or killers, would have had to escape undetected."

"That's possible?" she asked.

"Improbable, but not impossible. But that's not the problem."

"It was a problem for Tommy," Svetlana said. "And for me."

"I'm not trying to be insensitive. Tommy's death tore a hole in my heart too. I'm trying to think clinically and evaluate the situation. We need to establish a thesis so we're not spinning our wheels."

"What's wrong with the scenario you described?" Svetlana asked.

"If it's a rival government or company, what changed by killing Tommy and Sarah?"

"My husband is dead, Dr. Smith's brains are scattered on the beach, and I'm about to lose my mind. That's what changed."

"And I've lost my brother."

Fire flared behind Svetlana's eyes. She had always exhibited a temper. Over cocktails, Tommy had confided in him that Svetlana had been abused by her uncle. Maybe her defensiveness had come from that assault. Betrayal by a family member had to leave deep scars.

"We can't let them get away with it," she said.

"If someone wants to steal Forever's research, how does killing a scientist and a financier accomplish that? Maybe their intent was to hamper Forever's progress by taking out key personnel. Or was it something I'm not seeing?"

"Nothing's been stolen?" she asked.

"Not that I know about." Adam slammed his hand on the table. "Dammit."

"What?"

"Maybe Suggs was right. He said rumors about a murder conspiracy would damage their company more than their competition ever could. Bryce insinuated the same thing."

"None of this makes sense," Svetlana said. "Who would kill two people just to create negative publicity?"

"I don't know. I'm thinking out loud."

Svetlana shut her eyes and massaged her temples.

"I'm sorry," Adam said. "Maybe I shouldn't discuss this with you."

"Take me home, please."

"You haven't eaten."

Svetlana reached across the table and grabbed a French fry off his plate. She popped it into her mouth and glared at him. "There. Now I've eaten. Let's go."

Svetlana had the habit of taking food off other people's plates. At first, he had thought it was her way of dieting, of keeping her dancer's body, but he had been wrong. She was cheap. Once, Effie had eaten one of Svetlana's shrimp, and when the bill had come, Svetlana charged her for it. Seriously.

He led her into the parking lot, and they entered a Mercedes G-Class SUV Bryce had lent him. She stared out the window and remained silent as he drove. At least she wasn't crying. He pulled into her driveway and shells and gravel crunched beneath his wheels.

He parked and faced her. "I'm worried about you."

"I don't know what's happening. I can't think. Everything's cloudy."

"You don't need to decide anything now," Adam said. "Effie and I will help. I'll assist you with the insurance, police reports, press. Whatever you need."

"Will you come inside and stay for a while?" She said it like a child, full of innocence and vulnerability.

"Maybe it's better if you sleep. Effie offered to have you stay at the house with us."

"With you?"

"She thought it might help if you had family around."

"I'd like that," Svetlana said, "but I can't be away from home right now. This was Tommy's house. *Our* house. I feel him here with me."

"I understand," Adam said, a little relieved. Caring for Effie, starting a new job, and investigating Tommy's death was all he could handle. Taking care of Svetlana would leave less time to solve the murders, and the longer it took, the more likely the killer would escape.

Svetlana glanced at the house and then back at him. "Come in. Just for a bit. The thought of being alone scares me. I don't know what's wrong with me."

"I don't think you're in danger," Adam said it to calm her, but was that true? Was she a target too?

"I'm not worried about a killer," she said. "I'm scared of myself. Scared how I'll survive without Tommy."

"You caught a bad flop," Adam said, "but you still have a tall stack in front of you. And you have us."

"I'm not afraid of going broke. I'm terrified of being alone."

"I'd stay, but it's going to be dark soon. Forever lent me a Boston Whaler to come over here, but—"

"What's a Whaler?" she asked.

"It's a fifteen-foot motorboat with a fifty horsepower Mercury engine. I'll use it to motor back to Falmouth, but I want to avoid the water after the sun goes down. Old fears . . ."

"I promise to let you go soon."

Adam followed her inside. The house was cool and dark, and Svetlana had been right—it felt empty. Spooky. He sensed Tommy's presence too.

"Can I get you something to drink?" she asked.

"I don't think that's a good idea," he said, but a drink sounded good. What could it hurt? "Okay. I'll take a beer."

She smiled for the first time and disappeared into the kitchen.

Adam flopped onto the couch and closed his eyes. Where to go from here? Bryce had promised to divulge the projects Tommy had been involved with—their most precious secrets—but would he share everything? Federal prosecutors used two techniques to stymie the defense. First was to disclose as little as possible and fight every request in suppression hearings. The other strategy was to dump everything they had, and then some, into a discovery motion. The sheer volume of data, evidence, witness statements, photos, and other forensics would bury the defense and make it difficult for them to identify critical information—like hiding a diamond in a wheelbarrow full of glass.

What's taking her so long?

Adam leaned forward and looked down the hall. No sound came from the kitchen. He leaned back and rubbed his eyes.

What would Bryce give him? Even if Adam received everything as promised, he was not fluent in the scientific jargon surrounding the world of artificial intelligence. He would need someone to translate it, analyze the data, and guide him to what mattered. Who could do that?

Svetlana came into the room wearing a robe. The edge of something black and silky poked from beneath it. She held a Sam Adams Oktoberfest in one hand and a cocktail glass with a brown liquid in the other, probably a Manhattan.

"I hope you don't mind," she said, "I wanted to get comfortable."

"No, uh—"

"I don't know how I'll fall asleep tonight." She handed him the lager and slid onto the couch beside him. She curled her leg beneath her like a cat.

Was it inappropriate to be alone with her? Should he leave? This was her house, and she had every right to get comfortable, but how would this look if someone walked in? Maybe he was being paranoid. Narcissistic. Did he think so highly of himself that he assumed Svetlana was flirting?

Stop it.

"To family," Svetlana said. She clinked her cocktail against his bottle.

"Family," he said. He took a swig of the beer. "Effie and I will support you through this. You're not alone."

"You've always been kind to me. You're so strong."

She shifted in her seat and her long leg slipped out from under her robe. Her skin was smooth and toned. A cascade of guilt washed over him. How could he be attracted to his brother's widow? How could he drink with another woman while Effie lay home sick in bed? What was wrong with him to think Svetlana was even interested? His guilt morphed into self-hatred.

"I should get going," he said.

She downed half her Manhattan and set it on the table. She untied the sash of her robe and shrugged it off her shoulders. Underneath, she wore a black translucent nightie.

He froze, unable to speak.

She placed her hand on his knee and slid her fingers up his thigh.

CHAPTER THIRTY

Forever Technology was into some creepy Sci-Fi shit. Edna reached for her coffee and knocked the Styrofoam cup over. Cold liquid sloshed across her desk and dripped onto her keyboard.

"Shit."

She pushed her chair back and yanked tissues out of a box to clean the mess. A fluorescent light hummed on the ceiling above her desk, but the rest of the newsroom remained dark. Not much happened on Cape Cod at eleven o'clock at night, at least not enough to require a night shift of reporters.

Edna mopped up the coffee and sighed. "Why did you move to Cuttyhunk, Mr. Hastings?"

She removed her glasses and let them hang from the chain around her neck. Edna had been researching Forever Technology and its eccentric CEO for hours, and her eyes burned.

Bryce Hastings was an interesting character. He grew up in the United Kingdom, the son of a wealthy British barrister and an American mother. He had studied philosophy at Cambridge, and according to an interview in a British gossip column, had added a degree in computer science once he discovered philosophers could not make money in the twenty-first century.

Bryce had entered the industry at the beginning of the artificial intelligence revolution and realized it would change the future. He had bounced around start-up companies in Silicon Valley, never staying for more than a year or two. According to an interview in the LA Times, Bryce recognized how AI could accelerate man's ability to research and create computer models. AI could grow organs, identify disease, and prolong life. Bryce formed The Happiness Institute, then a medical research facility, before he met Tommy Locke, an MBA drawn to Palo Alto—a land where money flowed like water. Tommy hitched himself to Bryce's star and a year later, Forever Technology was born.

Edna stood up and stretched. Something clanked in the hallway. She stared into the dark. Being alone in a newsroom always put her on edge.

Forever Technology had originally sought to quantify the workings of the human brain to recalibrate and access memory in damaged tissue. Then the company's focus moved into using AI to regenerate tissue and other bioengineering solutions. Mapping brain processes was at the forefront of Forever Technology's research, but it integrated AI into all forms of healing. In a Time Magazine article, Bryce had claimed his company would provide disease-free living within ten years. That had been five years ago. He did not lack confidence. Or charisma. His actual power came from the intersection of his philosophy roots with his tech specialty. He was brilliant, visionary, and bold.

A natural leader.

"What are you hiding?"

CHAPTER THIRTY-ONE

West End Road narrowed, and Adam's golf cart lumbered over uneven ground toward Bryce's residence near the southern tip of Cuttyhunk. Unlike his employees who commuted to Martha's Vineyard or New Bedford, Bryce had wanted to stay close to his company. Was his desire rooted in dedication, pragmatism, or paranoia?

The embarrassing scene on Svetlana's couch replayed on a continuous loop in his mind. When she had touched his thigh, he had leapt off the couch like a teenage virgin. He had spilled his beer and stammered an apology as he fled her house. Real macho. Their next meeting would be awkward.

The wind rustled through bare bushes, and waves pounded the eastern shore below the cliffs. The path dipped, and he turned right at a fork leading up a hill. He pulled into a driveway and stopped in front of Bryce's residence. The house had floor-to-ceiling windows and sat atop a hill with views of the entire island. From his perch, Adam gazed over the southern end of the island, which curled like a scorpion's tail. An old lighthouse rose above Gosnold Island in the middle of West End Pond, far below him.

Bryce opened his front door and flashed a smile. He wore a thick wool sweater and blue jeans. It was hard not to be drawn in by his charisma. He had a politician's ability to make Adam feel important.

"Thanks for coming," Bryce said.

"Every moment we wait decreases our chances of solving Tommy's death."

A cloud passed over Bryce's face. Was he upset about Tommy or Adam's insistence on investigating?

"Let's talk," Bryce said. He led Adam inside. "Can I get you a coffee? Something stronger?"

"Nothing, thank you. I'm meeting Sergeant Gunn in a few minutes."

"Are you a suspect?"

"Why would you ask that?"

"You were present when it happened."

"If I had wanted to kill my brother, I wouldn't detonate a bomb when I was twenty yards away."

Bryce poured himself a coffee. "Tommy told me you two never got along."

"That was childhood stuff. We had a natural competition."

"Who was winning?" Bryce asked.

"Depends on how you keep score. We took different paths."

"Yet you both ended up here."

The wind howled and rattled the windows. Adam stared into Bryce's eyes but could not tell what he was thinking. "What is so secret you had to move here to protect it?"

"I'm headed to my archery range," Bryce said. "Ever use a bow?"

"I grew up with guns."

"What kind?"

Was he stalling? "I had BB guns as a child, then hunted with the Remington 300 in high school. DEA issued me a Remington 870 shotgun and a Glock 22. When I joined the FAST teams, I carried a Colt M4 with an H&K grenade launcher. I also qualified on the Mk 46 and Mk 48 machine guns. They even issued us 7.62 mm REPRS to give us extra power to reach out and touch someone."

"Archery has always been meditative for me," Bryce said. "I guess you can say we're operating on opposite ends of the weaponry spectrum. The Stone Age meets the twenty-first century."

Adam followed Bryce out the back door and across a large wooden deck. An empty scotch glass sat on the glass table beside an ashtray overflowing with cigar butts. Bryce continued down a path surrounded by thorny shrubs. He stopped in a clearing hidden from the road. Two archery targets had been set up ninety yards away. Beyond it, a narrow trail led down the hill.

Bryce walked to a metal shed and plugged a code into a security box. The door popped open, and they entered. Three sets of foul weather gear hung from a coatrack, and a dozen bows suspended from hooks. Quivers filled with arrows leaned against a workbench covered with tools.

"You take this seriously," Adam said.

"I made the Cambridge University Archery Club, and I flirted with joining the British Olympic team."

"You were that good?"

"So I was told. I was the top-ranked bowman in outdoor, indoor, and field competitions. The problem was that to reach world-class status in any sport, or any endeavor, one has to spend tens of thousands of hours doing nothing else. I knew I could make the Olympics, and I appreciated the discipline and joy that being the best would bring me, but I wasn't willing to sacrifice the time required to earn it. Instead, I spent years studying business and the philosophy and science behind artificial intelligence. I'm comfortable with my decision."

"Yet, we're standing in your archery shed."

"Grab a bow. The concentration and the body control needed to hit targets at a distance necessitates blocking out the rest of the world. Spending an hour on an archery range is like meditation. It's rehabilitative."

Adam strolled along the rack. Six bows had futuristic exoskeletons with wheels, pulleys, and multiple strings. "These look complicated, like I need a PhD to operate them."

"Compound bows require less strength and offer greater distance and accuracy."

Another half dozen smaller bows hung on the far wall. Each had a simple polymer frame and a single string. "Now, these look like the bows I shot at camp when I was a kid," Adam said.

"They're recursive bows. Much harder to draw and shoot and without the range. Some competitions require them."

Adam took a compound bow off the wall. It was light for its size. Bryce selected a recursive bow and slung a quiver of arrows over his shoulder. He led Adam out onto the range.

Bryce demonstrated how to stand sideways to the target. "Don't grip the bow too tight or you'll shake." He handed an arrow to Adam. "Point it at the ground and nock the bowstring. Make sure you seat the arrow."

"Got it."

Bryce held Adam's other hand and positioned his index finger above the feather and two fingers beneath it. "Draw the bowstring back until your index finger touches your cheek and try to keep the arrowhead on the target."

The man-sized targets looked like postage stamps in the distance. Adam could make out concentric circles of yellow, red, blue, black, and white. He focused on the tip of the arrow and the target turned fuzzy behind it. It was similar to aiming the front sight of his M4 at a target, except the exertion of holding the compound bow made the arrow oscillate.

"Aim above the target from this range," Bryce said. "The arrow travels 350 feet-per-second but will drop in flight."

"It's hard to keep it steady."

"Relax your fingers and let the release surprise you or you'll affect the trajectory. And keep your bow pointed downrange, like your follow-through throwing a baseball."

Adam released his grip on the arrow and the string snapped forward. The arrow flew.

Crunch.

The release stung his fingers, and the bow twisted in his hand as it vibrated. He lowered it and looked down range. The arrow stuck in the ground at the base of the target. A miss.

"Shit."

"That's not too bad for your first time," Bryce said.

"A miss is a miss. I'm a marksman with handguns and carbines."

Bryce slid an arrow out of the quiver and nocked it. He raised the bow, drew the bowstring back, and released it—all in an instant.

Thwack.

Adam shielded his eyes with his palm. Bryce had hit the ten-ring. Dead center. "Impressive."

"It's harder with a moving target."

"Interesting, but I'm hunting a different kind of target. Why would someone kill my brother? What are you doing here that would justify murder?"

"Our advancements in artificial general intelligence put us ahead of the competition. You already know about our use of AI to identify disease and bioengineer organs. That's groundbreaking work and has serious market value, but our other research makes us truly unique."

"Tommy mentioned the brain mapping."

"That's the first step, and we've had more success than we've admitted to the public."

"How much success?"

"We're close to a fully functional model of the synaptic connections inside a human mind. Our research and experiments have identified over seventy percent of the connections."

"Meaning?"

"We can recreate a human mind. We can download a replica of a human mind in a digital format. My team hasn't perfected the process, but we can analyze the data and interpret thoughts from digital signatures. To a lesser extent, we can recreate stored memory, although we're in the early stages. This technology will transform lives for people with dementia or other cognitive failings."

"You can tell a person's thoughts by monitoring their brain waves?" Adam asked.

"To a degree, but our most important research is the creation of a digital mind with a similar process. We're close to achieving a cloned brain. It's stunning tech and a giant breakthrough in AI."

"Tommy worked on this?" Adam asked.

Bryce stared over the brush. Dark clouds blew out of the east, approaching Martha's Vineyard. The northeaster would hit them soon.

"Tommy had a sharp mind and a scientific background, but he was not a scientist. He used his skills to attract investors. It's tricky business to get people excited about our research without giving away too much."

"If your technology is as transformative as you say, I understand why you're worried about other companies trying to steal it."

"Not just other tech companies. Governments want it. The national security applications are profound. Governments could use our AI models to manipulate and control populations. "

"Would they kill to get it?"

"People kill for a few dollars, a loaf of bread. This is the most valuable product on earth. Life-altering technology. I'm surrounded by enemies, and I don't know who I can trust."

Adam looked at Bryce, unable to read his eyes. "Neither do I."

CHAPTER THIRTY-TWO

Adam floated in a Boston Whaler, three hundred yards off Cuttyhunk. The swells were enormous, because Martha's Vineyard lay to the north and nothing protected Cuttyhunk from the frigid Atlantic waters. He lifted Bushnell binoculars to his eyes, braced against the hull, and focused on Forever Technology's long pier. The seventy-four-foot Princess Y-Class yacht they used to ferry employees to Martha's Vineyard idled alongside the wharf.

Despite growing up on Cape Cod, Adam had always feared the water. Maybe his phobia had started when something had brushed his leg while he was snorkeling in the frigid waters off Nauset Beach, then hours later, a swimmer had been mauled by a shark in the same area. Or maybe his terror came from watching Peter Benchley's *Jaws* on television. Whatever had done it, his trepidation usually tethered him to the beach.

A line of Forever's employees descended a newly constructed wooden stairway along the face of the cliff. Adam could not identify faces at this distance, but Fang's diminutive frame was easy to pick out among the other scientists.

Would Fang cooperate? That unknown outcome had made Adam decide to approach her away from Forever Technology. He could have taken the yacht to Martha's Vineyard and waited for her to disembark, but if she was not on that shuttle run—the ferry ran eight times a day—then he would have wasted precious hours.

At least a dozen employees boarded the ferry, and Adam waited for it to get far offshore before he followed at a safe distance. No one should be watching, but he had recruited enough sources to understand the importance of secrecy. The yacht made twenty-five knots, and Adam opened his throttle to keep pace. The hull of his flat-bottomed boat smashed into oncoming swells, and he absorbed each impact with his legs. By the time the yacht entered Menemsha Creek and docked along Boathouse Road, on the Vineyard Sound side of the island, his entire body ached.

Adam tied off to the quay and hurried down the dock, but he did not run to avoid drawing attention to himself. A Forever shuttle bus pulled away from the Marina just as Adam reached the Mercedes SUV Bryce had lent him. The shuttle headed for Forever's new residential subdivision. When Adam had driven by before, he had seen a guard shack, gates, and surveillance cameras. The purpose of the private complex was to separate Forever Technology's employees from the Vineyard population, not keep them as prisoners, though the distinction blurred the more Adam learned about the company.

He drove through the fishing village of Menemsha and into a residential area of Chilmark. He caught up with the shuttle bus as it approached the wooded Mill Brook area.

As part of DEA's FAST team, Adam had received specialized training in close target reconnaissance. Creating a hide from which to conduct surveillance was critical in long-term criminal investigations. The DEA constructed stings, infiltrated criminal groups, and used dozens of other passive and proactive techniques to identify suspects and collect evidence. Adam had done close target reconnaissance, known as CTRs, on both foreign and domestic targets. Here, he would not need to spend hours low crawling through woods and then burrowing into a shrub. This was a tract of residential houses, full of scientists and mathematicians, with a rent-a-cop at the front gate.

Getting into Fang's neighborhood was easy, assuming nothing unexpected happened. The hard part would be soliciting her cooperation.

According to Adam's research, Fang was a Chinese national with a resident alien card, and she owed her financial success, professional reputation, and pending American citizenship to Forever Technology. Getting her to divulge the information he needed would not be easy. Luckily, Adam had flipped many high-ranking members of criminal organizations and terror groups—people for whom cooperation often meant death if they were caught. Information about Fang was scarce online, which meant Suggs or a tech geek at Forever had cleansed their employees' public profiles. Competitors involved in industrial espionage often sought weak links to exploit employees through blackmail, bribery, or intimidation. If Suggs had cleaned their public profiles, he did it to protect them as much as the company.

The shuttle bus turned off Wequobsque Road into the private community of Island Gables. Adam continued past the entrance to Forever Technology's housing community. He continued for a mile until the road wrapped around to the east. He stopped on the southern end of the neighborhood where a wooden fence marked the property boundary.

In a perfect world, Adam would have had someone drop him off to establish surveillance, then he'd call for extraction when finished. But in this, he was alone.

He parked where the shoulder was wider and edged his vehicle against the trees. If the police drove down the street, they'd probably run his license plate but not tow it. He got out to insure no cars were coming then jogged across the pavement.

No cameras were visible along the fence. If he tripped an alarm and Suggs caught him sneaking into the property, Adam would give him some excuse about wanting to check on the employees to see if anyone was acting suspiciously. He would not mention Fang's name or divulge his real reason for coming.

He hopped the fence and made his way through conservation land, which comprised pitch pines, white oaks, and catbrier. They had not cleared the land in years. Adam carved his way through a hundred yards of vegetation until he reached a four-foot brick wall. He crouched and peeked over it. He could have worn a hood or blacked out his face, but that would have made his presence harder to explain to the police, Suggs, or Fang. He looked across a manicured backyard at a two-story white colonial.

Forever Technology owned every residence in the new development, but Doug Barnstable had identified Fang's address. Doug had been hesitant to help at first, but he had been willing to bend the rules to help Adam find Tommy's murderer. It hadn't hurt that Adam had first politely listened to another of Doug's "return to DEA" speeches. Adam opened Google Maps on his phone. Fang's residence was one of six houses along the boundary. Adam tapped the satellite view and compared the terrain to the image.

Fang's house was two doors down.

He pocketed his phone so the screen light would not reveal him in the twilight. He moved through the trees for fifty yards, then returned to the wall. Adam studied the four-bedroom colonial house. He checked the Google Earth image again. It matched. He flicked to Google Maps and confirmed he was behind the correct house. Would Fang appreciate his attempt to contact her in private or would she perceive his uninvited appearance at her house as a threat?

The kitchen light came on. Fang entered the hallway and disappeared into the dining room. He glanced at the adjacent backyards—both empty.

Now or never.

Adam braced his hands on top of the wall and vaulted into the backyard. He hurried across, scanning for a dog door or chew toys.

A light went on inside Fang's neighbor's house, as Forever Technology employees returned home, and a yellow glow illuminated their back porch. Adam stopped and bladed himself against the side of Fang's house—careful not to scrape against the siding.

Adam crept through the side yard, skirting freshly planted shrubbery, and peeked around the corner. Half of the residences had lights on, but the street was deserted. He brushed off his clothes, knocking dried leaves and twigs from the fabric, and sauntered up Fang's front path in case any neighbors were watching.

He knocked.

Translucent white curtains moved behind a rectangular window beside the door. Fang's face peered out at him. He made eye contact, smiled, and waved.

"Yes?" she asked from behind the closed door.

"It's Adam. Adam Locke, the new security consultant at Forever Technology."

She did not open the door. Smart lady. Her paranoia must run deep. As a Chinese national, what emotions stirred inside her when confronted with a security official?

She cracked the door and looked at him. Fang wore a knee-length, gray dress, the same one he had seen beneath her lab coat at work. She was barely five feet tall, and he towered over her. He pasted on his best smile, hoping to disarm her. It had worked in the past. Most of the time.

"Can I help you, Mr. Locke?"

"Sorry to bother you at home. I have a sensitive matter to discuss, and I think it's best we talk away from the office."

Her eyes narrowed. "A professional matter or a *personal* one?"

"I guess it's both. It's about my brother. I need your help."

She glanced up and down the street then opened the door. "Let's talk in the living room."

He followed her down the short hallway and into a sparsely decorated room with a couch, two chairs, and a coffee table. The furniture looked brand new, as if he would be the first person to sit on it.

"I'm sorry about this," he said. "I don't want to invade your privacy, but I'm trying to determine what happened to Tommy, and I need someone who understands the technology."

Her forehead wrinkled. "I know nothing about your brother's accident, and—"

"He was murdered."

Her hands covered her mouth, and her eyes grew distant. She recovered and placed her hands in her lap, one on top of the other. "The police determined that?"

"They haven't officially ruled yet, but I was there, and I saw what happened. His yacht exploded. Until a couple months ago, I was a federal agent, and I've experienced my share of combat. I recognize high explosives."

"But could a gas leak, or fuel—"

"I heard you were friends with Sarah Smith."

She clenched her hand into a fist, but her face remained impassive. "I knew Sarah, but I don't know if you could call us friends."

"You've been with Forever for a while," Adam said, "so I won't beat around the bush. I think you've figured out two violent deaths this close together can't be coincidence. I'm looking for whatever Tommy and Sarah had in common that made them targets. I'll need help to decipher the techno-speak."

"You should speak with Mr. Hastings. He was very close to Thomas. He knows far more about his work."

"The truth is, I don't trust him. Forever Technology's work product is worth a fortune, and they may have killed Tommy and Sarah for it. I don't know if whoever did it is trying to steal research or protect it."

"Why come to me?" Fang asked.

"I spoke to Tommy before he died, and he told me they staffed Forever with bright young minds. He mentioned you."

Fang's eyes moistened, and she stiffened her jaw, trying to hold back tears. "He said that about me? I barely knew him. He was always friendly, but I didn't know he felt that way."

"Whether the threat is internal or external, you're all in danger until I bring the killer to justice."

"Aren't the police investigating?"

"Bryce has invested millions to make Cuttyhunk hospitable for his company. Don't you find it odd that a little New England fishing village welcomed a Silicon Valley tech company?"

Fang averted her eyes. "Bryce wanted privacy."

"He got it. That money buys a lot of goodwill, and even if the cops are honest, the politicians who control them are often not. That's been my experience all over the world."

"You should talk to Felix Suggs. He has access to everything."

"I'm talking to you."

"I don't know."

"I'm not asking you to do anything illegal or anything that will get you fired. I just need someone to interpret what I find. The science is a mystery to me. I need a guide."

"I don't want to get into trouble."

"I won't let anything happen to you," Adam said. "Every minute you wait, the killer becomes harder to identify."

"I—"

"Please. Help me."

CHAPTER THIRTY-THREE

Fang stared at Adam. In her heart, she knew he was right. Sarah had not fallen off the cliff by herself. Someone had helped her over the edge. Fang told that to the police, and they had promised they were looking into it.

She stood and moved to the window. The sun had hidden behind the trees and cast the neighborhood into darkness. What if Forever Technology had influenced the police? Could a powerful politician make the police back off? That happened all the time in China. And how would she know if the case had been compromised?

Her life was already complicated enough.

Her eyes darted to the phone. She wanted to call Suggs, tell him what Adam had said, and affirm her loyalty to the company. She needed her job, and not just for a paycheck. Her mother's and sister's lives hung in the balance. How had she become beholden to so many people?

An image of Sarah's face appeared behind her eyes. Fang had been cultivating Sarah as a source to uncover the depth of Forever Technology's research, but Sarah had become more than that. She had been a friend. And Fang did not have many of those. Not in Cuttyhunk or in Palo Alto. Not anywhere. If someone had killed Sarah, Fang had a moral obligation to help. She could not ignore her murder. Adam believed someone may be trying to steal Forever's product. Her work. If that were true, wouldn't she be helping her company by helping Adam find the killer?

"God damn it," Adam said. He slammed his fist against the wall.

Fang flinched.

"I'm sorry," he said. "Tommy was my only brother, and someone took him from me."

"He was always kind to me."

"Then help me. Tell me who killed him."

Fang shook her head slowly. "I don't know."

"You know something."

"I cared for Sarah. She and Tommy were . . . close."

Adam raised an eyebrow. "Meaning?"

Fang avoided his gaze. "Sarah hinted about a sexual relationship. I do not know what happened to your brother, but I think the same person killed Sarah."

"Then help me."

Maybe she should assist him. Maybe he could get her the information she needed. She bit her lip. "Something is happening here. Something big. The research, what we are doing, it is historic. Everyone will want it."

"Who?"

"Corporations, CIA . . . everyone."

Adam's brow furrowed. "What exactly are you doing there?"

"The extension of life. The end of illness. What we are developing has unprecedented commercial value. Our project will become the most valuable commodity on earth."

"That sounds like hyperbolic marketing copy from someone who helped create it."

Fang shook her head. "You do not understand. We will offer what only religions and cults have been able to promise. It is the fountain of youth, the treasure humanity has been seeking since the beginning of time."

"I'm not following," Adam said. "What are you offering?"

Fang smiled. "Eternal life."

CHAPTER THIRTY-FOUR

Adam showed his pass to Ivan, the burly security guard at the entrance to Forever Technology, then crossed the lobby to Keisha Gunn. She sat in a chair under the watchful eye of the receptionist. Gunn wore tan slacks, pink blouse, and a mocha jacket—tailored clothing that clung to the contours of her athletic body.

She spotted him and stood.

"Thanks for coming," he said. "Sorry I'm late. It's an effort to boat across the sound."

"I wanted another look at the facility. Maybe you can show me around."

"I'll need Felix Suggs to grant you access. They run this place like a government SCIF," he said, referring to a Sensitive Compartmentalized Information Facility. Adam had spent many hours in those controlled environments reading classified reports and satellite imagery.

"It helps to see where victims worked."

"Victims? You're ready to rule Tommy's death a homicide?"

"Officially, we're still evaluating the circumstances. Unofficially, I don't believe it was an accident."

"And Dr. Smith?"

"I don't know."

"Follow me." Adam led her into the glass-walled conference room off the lobby. He sat facing the door, forcing Gunn into a chair with her back to the entrance. Over a decade in law enforcement had instilled in him the need to keep his eyes on the door, and a wave of sympathy for her discomfort passed through him.

Gunn did not speak. Adam suppressed the urge to talk first, having used the same technique with dozens of suspects over the years. Her investigation would clear him, but he didn't want to fall for a common interrogator's trick. They sat in silence for thirty seconds, before he cracked a smile.

She smiled too, an expression that came from somewhere deep, somewhere authentic.

"I guess I'll begin," she said.

"Please."

"It will take time to raise the Galileo."

"I hadn't realized Tommy named his boat that," he said. "I never had a chance to get onboard." It was pure Tommy to name his yacht after a great mind and historic innovator who changed the world. Tommy never lacked ego.

"It's an involved process, as I'm sure you can imagine, but our divers have been all over it to search for additional victims and determine the cause of the explosion."

"And?"

"Nothing conclusive, but there are troubling signs."

Adam leaned forward.

"One of the lines leading from the gas tank to the engine had been disconnected—"

"Disconnected?"

"Someone unscrewed a flange on the fuel line, and rubber melted over the pipe and the engine compartment."

"What kind of rubber?" Adam asked.

"It appears someone tampered with the pipe and fed the gas into a rubber vessel. It—"

"A bad repair or sabotage?" He should not interrupt, but he couldn't stop himself. This could be the lead he needed to prove his brother was murdered.

"This stays between us, right?" she said.

Adam looked at the security camera on the ceiling. Had Suggs rigged the room for audio too? He could ask Gunn to step outside, but if anyone were listening, they would think Adam was hiding something. "I'll keep this between us. I appreciate the professional courtesy."

"Your prior career as a special agent has nothing to do with it. You're Mr. Locke's closest living family member, and you deserve to know where the investigation is headed."

Prior career. The phrase hung in the air like a dark cloud. But she was right. He no longer carried a badge, no longer fought for the rule of law. What did that make him? A security guard? Consultant sounded better, but the distinction was semantic.

"Either way, I appreciate it," he said. "Where's the investigation focused?"

"Our forensic team believes somebody severed the line, captured fuel vapors in a balloon until it expanded and filled the engine compartment."

"If they wanted to create a gas leak, why not just punch a hole in the line?"

"Diesel fuel is not very flammable in liquid form. The perpetrator used the balloon to avoid the decidable odor of fuel and create a massive buildup of combustible gas. We were lucky the boat sank before the fire destroyed the evidence. If that's what happened. It's just a theory."

He had been right. His stomach hardened. "How was the explosion initiated?"

"Someone removed the shield covering the spark plugs. That allowed a spark from the ignition to ignite the gas. That part is more speculative. The detonation could also have been triggered remotely by a cell phone or other device, and we just haven't found the receiver yet. They could also have used a fuse."

The image of Tommy standing in the cockpit flashed in Adam's mind. Tommy had started the motor, then waved at him before moving into the stern.

"There was a delay," Adam said.

"What?"

"At least ten seconds from the time Tommy turned the ignition until the yacht exploded."

Gunn played with her barn-red fingernails. "That makes the ignition theory less plausible, and fuse more likely."

Adam had used detonator cord to initiate explosions many times, and he had also witnessed cell phones strapped to IEDs in Afghanistan. DEA had trained him in demolitions, but his tactical experience focused on using the minimum high explosives required to breach gates, doors, and walls. Blowing up a quarter-million-dollar yacht had not been part of his training scenarios.

"So that's it," he said. "Homicide."

"Not officially, but I think so." She dug into her purse and popped a red candy into her mouth. "Want one?"

"What is it?"

"Hot balls. They're made with scorpion peppers. Very popular in Trinidad."

"I'll pass. Is Forever Technology involved?"

"That's what I'm trying to determine," Gunn said. "I've had the forensic report for less than a day."

"You came all the way out here to tell me this?"

"I try to make these kinds of notifications face-to-face, especially with family. But that's not the only reason I'm here."

The way she said it sounded ominous, and Adam's stomach clenched into a fist. What cards did she have in the hole? "You have a lead?"

"When I'm running an investigation into any violent crime, I do two things. First, I re-create the victim's pattern of life over the weeks leading up to the attack. Second, I identify everyone in the victim's circle of friends, family, and acquaintances. An effective investigative tool for both is to analyze the victim's telephone toll records."

Adam nodded. He had used similar techniques when identifying members of transnational criminal groups. "Go on."

"Your brother did not have a home telephone, and he used a personal cell phone for almost everything. I tried to run his office phone, but it seems Forever Technology issues their employees prepaid cell phones at this facility, which makes it difficult to identify who used which phone. All they have is a block of phones purchased for the company's use on Cuttyhunk, and they won't give it to me."

"Get a search warrant."

"My request is too broad for a warrant, because it involves every Forever employee on the island."

"I'm sure Suggs can get Tommy's assigned phone numbers for you. They probably used prepaids to prevent competitors from analyzing phone usage."

"Perhaps," Gunn said. "But that also inhibits official investigations."

"I'll ask Suggs for you."

"I'm getting a Grand Jury subpoena and once I have the number, I'll get a warrant."

"Grand jury? You *are* treating this as a homicide."

"The reason I wanted to speak to you in person," Gunn said, "is because of what I found in your brother's personal call records."

Adam's chest fluttered. Where was she going with this? It did not sound good. He waited.

"Whose number is (202) 555-6478?" she asked.

Effie's number.

Adam cringed as if he had been gut-punched. "That belongs to my girlfriend, Effie Hope."

"Yes, it does. And do you know why your brother would call her?"

An icy chill traveled up Adam's spine, his every sense of alert. Effie had rarely talked to his brother, only a handful of times at awkward gatherings when Tommy had traveled to DC for business. She had known Adam and Tommy had a fraternal dislike for each other, and that had cooled any chance she had of developing a relationship with him. Adam had to be careful. Gunn knew more than she was saying, and if Effie was connected to this, he didn't want to get her in trouble. His loyalty lay with the law, but Effie owned his heart.

"When did they speak?" he asked.

"That wasn't my question," Gunn said. "I asked if you knew why your brother called her. I have toll records showing numerous calls between

Thomas Locke's cell phone and hers, but that doesn't mean she was on the other end."

"How many calls?"

"You still haven't answered the question."

"I don't know if they spoke," Adam said. "Maybe they did. They knew each other. They were family."

"For the record, you never used Ms. Hope's cellular phone, the 6478 number, to speak to your brother?"

"I don't like the tone your questions have taken."

"My tone is irrelevant. I'm investigating a homicide and your girlfriend and brother talked frequently, often late at night. I want to know why. Or did you make those calls?"

"I think I should talk to an attorney," Adam said.

My God, Effie, what have you done?

CHAPTER THIRTY-FIVE

Adam drove with his fingers wrapped tight on the wheel. Why had Tommy called Effie and why hadn't she mentioned it? An affair? Ridiculous. Or was it? He shook away the thought. Should he confront her about the calls? Could she handle more emotional conflict? Stress inhibited her immune system, and she could not afford that.

He turned onto his street, and his heart skipped a beat. An ambulance blocked the driveway and the front door stood open. He screeched to a stop and leapt from his car. Adrenaline dumped into his system as he raced across the lawn.

An EMT wearing a blue uniform backed through the doorway, and Adam jumped out of his path. Two paramedics struggled to maneuver a gurney across the threshold. Effie inhaled oxygen through a nasal cannula. Her face had gone pale, and her eyes radiated concern.

"Effie, what happened?" Adam's voice sounded tight. He bounced on his toes to dissipate his energy.

She saw him, and relief seemed to wash over her. "I'm okay. Don't worry."

"What's wrong?"

"I had trouble breathing, and I called 9-1-1, but I'm better now. I just got scared."

The EMT's strained to roll her down the gravel path to the driveway. Adam jogged alongside and held Effie's hand.

"Where are you taking her?" He asked a heavyset paramedic.

"Falmouth Hospital," the medic replied.

"I'll ride with you."

"It's a little tight in back, and insurance prohibits—"

"I'm riding with her," Adam said.

"I'm fine," Effie said. "Follow in your car so we don't have to call a taxi to come home."

"Is she stable?" Adam asked the EMT.

"Her breathing is tacky and shallow," he said, "but her oh-two level is ninety-six, so she's getting enough oxygen."

"I'll follow you."

Adam waited for them to load Effie inside, and then he dashed to his car and fell in behind the ambulance. His chest hurt. Dread created physical tightness, a psychological chokehold. Mental fog. The past couple of months had become a blur of diagnostic tests, lab results, and grim results. The worst had been Effie's chemotherapy infusions, given through a subcutaneous port implanted in her chest. Her pain, fatigue, and hair loss had crushed him.

He remembered all the stupid fights, the political arguments— disagreements he dove into headfirst when he thought they had all the time in the world. All lost time.

The ambulance stopped in front of the Emergency Center doors. Adam parked in the visitor lot and jogged after them as they rolled Effie inside. He hurried to admitting while they took Effie into the triage. Adam balled his fists as he answered an administrator's questions needed to admit Effie and satisfy the insurance company's requirements. Pausing to fill out paperwork in an emergency room was the ultimate expression of bureaucracy. It could have been run by the federal government.

A nurse assessed Effie's vitals and Adam answered questions about her grocery list of medications while a young Pakistani doctor evaluated her.

The doctor administered an ultrasound, then ordered chest X-rays and an MRI. His competence relaxed Adam.

An orderly took Effie down to radiology, and Adam paced the halls, waiting. They had decorated the walls with pictures of animals and landscapes, and the odor of antiseptic hung in the air. The intercom blared, and a nurse called a code for someone else in the wing. Adam wandered past doors with radiology symbols, medicine carts, and gurneys. Impatient doctors hurried past, followed by nurses whose faces wore the weight of fatigue. The hospital was always hectic. Falmouth was a small town, but with an average age of sixty-one, medical ailments kept the staff busy. During the summer, tourists swelled the population and drunken accidents filled the emergency room.

Adam reached the end of the hallway and turned back. He wanted to be there when she returned but standing alone in a room waiting for the love of his life was unbearable. How many hours had he spent sitting on plastic chairs reading medical instructions and wanting it all to stop?

She had to beat the cancer.

Adam passed a family lounge, where a handful of men and women—friends and spouses of patients—paced the cold floor wearing expressions of horror and shock, like survivors after a terrorist attack.

Adam returned to the room and pulled back the curtain. No Effie. How long would this take? His phone rang, and Doug Barnstable's name displayed on the caller ID. One persistent SOB.

Adam sighed and answered. "Not a good time, Doug."

"Sorry to bother you. I'll keep it short. I had an epiphany this morning."

"You realized you should have been a ballet dancer?"

"Funny, asshole. I had an idea. Why don't you come back as a contractor? I can make a few calls and get one of the bigger corporations to hire you. Once you're onboard, we can contract you to assist with the Dastigar Shinwari case. You could—"

"We've been through this, Doug. I need to stay home with Effie."

"You could make your own hours. Meet sources in Boston. Write reports from home. You wouldn't have to move to DC."

Adam stared out the window at the foliage. Maple and oak leaves glowed in death. Soon they would wither and fall onto the cold ground. The cycle of life. What Doug suggested interested him. Contracting could work. He would make decent money, more than he had as an agent, and he could quit when the project ended. Maybe. No, he was fooling himself. They would pull him into a complex conspiracy investigation that would last for years.

"I know what will happen," Adam said. "I can't work a case from home. Dastigar is based in Afghanistan, which means I'll have to go to Pakistan to recruit and run sources. And Dastigar travels to the UAE, so I'd need to coordinate a lure operation with the Emirates and craft a plan to snatch him."

"See, you're already strategizing. Our Dubai Country Office can handle coordination with the Emirates."

"I'll need to be there myself. I'll have to control the source in person and try to get Dastigar on tape."

"This is why I need you. I have skilled agents here, but you've done this, and there's no replacement for experience."

Trees swayed in the wind, portending the coming storm. Adam placed his hand on the window. It was cold to the touch. "It sounds interesting, but I can't travel around Southwest Asia and the Middle East while Effie is suffering at home."

"You could get a live-in nurse. You—"

"It's not just about being here for appointments and to help with her medication. I want to maximize every moment we have together. I don't know how long she has."

"Shit. I'm sorry, Adam. I didn't know things were that grim."

"It's bad."

"I won't push you anymore," Doug said. "If you need anything, I'm here for you, brother."

"Thanks, but there's nothing anyone can do. I'm working on a long shot."

"A cure?"

"It's better if you don't know what I'm doing."

Adam said goodbye and hung up. Forever Technology could preserve his love, his happiness, the thing he cared the most about. Saving Effie meant more to him than catching terrorists or solving his brother's murder. She was his life. From what he had gleaned from Bryce and Fang, the technology was almost ready. They could preserve her mind.

A nurse wheeled Effie into the room. She looked exhausted.

"How do you feel?" Adam asked.

"Awful. I'm sorry to put you through this."

"I'm not going through anything. You're the one suffering."

"I feel so guilty," Effie said.

Adam took her hand and leaned over the bed. He stared into her eyes. "I would do anything for you."

"I'm making your life miserable."

"You're not doing this. Cancer is making both of us miserable, but we're going to beat it. Together."

Tears wet Effie's cheeks, and Adam stroked her hair. A middle-aged doctor with a bowling-pin body pulled the curtain back and entered the room with his head buried in a clipboard.

"Hello, doctor," Adam said. "What did the MRI show?"

"Ms. Hope, I've called your oncologist to review the results with you."

"Has the cancer spread to my lungs?"

"Let's wait for your oncologist. He is familiar with your history and the disease's progression. He—"

"But you know if she has masses in her lungs," Adam said.

"Your oncologist will discuss that."

"When?"

"He's not on the ward, but I've put a call into his service to ask him to come in. Now, let's get you into a wheelchair so you can wait in my office. We need the bed."

"If you've called in the oncologist, you saw something on the MRI," Adam said.

The doctor fumbled with a wheelchair. "Let's see if I can figure out how to do this." He pulled the chair, but the brake was on. "There must be an elevator to get you out of here."

"This guy is making decisions about your health?" Adam whispered to Effie.

"Doctor, can you tell us anything?" Effie asked.

He stopped and looked at her. "It doesn't look good."

CHAPTER THIRTY-SIX

Edna didn't give a shit that her editor failed to see the merits of her investigation into Forever Technology. And not two shits about Harry's concerns about Bryce Hastings' power and influence. She didn't care if she ripped the lid off a can of worms and the Cape Cod Post lost funding because of it. The whole crappy newspaper industry was going to hell, anyway. If her paper shied away from real journalism, it could sink into Cape Cod Bay for all she cared.

Edna smiled when Dr. Shlomo Perlman walked into the convenience store tapping his cane on the tiled floor. She had been wandering around Chilmark, searching for Forever Technology employees to interview, like a fisherman casting a line. Hard work and a little luck had led to this nifty coincidence, but Edna preferred to think of it as destiny. She climbed out of her car and followed him inside.

"Dr. Perlman," she said. "How nice to see you."

He flinched as if she had jumped from behind a bush with a crowbar. "Do I know you?"

"Edna Cooper."

"Oh, yes." It was clear he did not know her. "I'm picking up a pack of cigarettes. Old habits, you know."

"I appreciate people bucking the trend. Everyone claims science is on their side these days, but they can't all be right."

"Science is science. A hypothesis is either proven or it isn't. Results are replicable or not. Overstating probabilities or cherry-picking data is not the scientific method."

"Still," she said, "those things will kill you."

The clerk handed Dr. Shlomo a pack of Marlboro Lights and he manipulated the pack in his hand before raising it to his nose and sniffing the plastic. "Yes, well, you must forgive me, ma'am. I'm embarrassed to admit I don't remember you."

"That's because we've never met. I'm a reporter with the Cape Cod Post. I'm writing a story about Forever Technology's employees who died under suspicious circumstances."

Shlomo straightened, his body rigid as if he panicked someone would see them together. "You're a reporter?"

"I recognized you from the press release when you joined Forever Technology," Edna said. "You were quite the catch for them. You may be the country's leading scientist in bioengineering using artificial intelligence."

Shlomo smirked. "The leading scientist in *the world*."

Edna smiled, but her expression felt more like a smirk. Had she ever been able to smile authentically? She had become so jaded, distrustful, and angry. Had she lost the ability to look happy? To be happy?

"What is Forever Technology doing behind those walls?" she asked.

"Trying to make the world a better place."

"Why Cuttyhunk? Why the secrecy?"

"Ask the Public Relations Department. I'm a scientist."

"People worry AI will steal their jobs."

"I'm not authorized to speak for the company, but people have always scoffed at innovators—Archimedes, Columbus, Galileo, Copernicus, the Wright brothers—anyone who imagines the world differently, envisions a new reality. But I can accept a little criticism. It's better than being burned at the stake."

"Aren't people's worries about a changing economic landscape valid?"

"Everything changes, but it's not my place to represent Forever Technology. They have an entire PR department for that."

"But you must have an opinion."

"My specialties are bioengineering and artificial intelligence, not economics. Besides, people always resist change. Having technology work for us frees humans to engage in more rewarding pursuits."

"What about fears that artificial intelligence will surpass human ability? What happens when the masters become the slaves?"

"Ah, yes, the robot overlords," Shlomo said. He laughed.

"More unfounded concern?"

"Critics are like natives shooting arrows at passing aircraft. Time will tell who's right. This is not on the record, correct? I don't want to be in your story."

"Do you think Dr. Smith and Thomas Locke were murdered?"

A cloud passed over Shlomo's face. "I cannot comment on that." He slapped a twenty-dollar bill on the counter. "Keep the change." He pocketed the pack of cigarettes and turned to go.

"Who had motive to kill them?" she asked.

"Excuse me," he said. The doors chimed when he passed through them and into the parking lot.

Edna followed him onto the street and caught up with him as he reached a Lincoln Town Car. "Murder can't be good for business. What do you hope to accomplish on Cuttyhunk?"

He opened the rear door and climbed into the back seat. The driver wore a Forever Technology windbreaker but looked bored and did not seem to notice her. The driver started the car, and Edna watched Shlomo as the car drove away. His face had tightened, and he looked pale. Only one thing did that.

Fear.

CHAPTER THIRTY-SEVEN

Fang passed an oxidized bell in front of the Cuttyhunk Historical Society and trudged up an incline past town hall, the schoolhouse, and a church. She left the pavement and hiked to a World War II bunker at the pinnacle of Bunker Hill. The base end station had watched for German submarines as part of New Bedford's harbor defense during World War II.

Professor Xiu Yän stood on a wooden platform perched atop the bunker. His thinning gray hair fluttered in the wind. He was portly and short, but thick in the chest and arms, signaling an underlying strength. He stared across the island and out to sea. Xiu gave no sign he had seen her, but she knew he had. He saw everything.

Yang had first met Xiu in the dean's office at Tsinghua University in Beijing. He had introduced himself as a member of the National Academy of Sciences and expressed an interest in her academic achievement. His confidence in her potential had flattered her. Tsinghua University was at the forefront of scientific research and development, and she had always hoped to make positive changes in the world. Back then, she still believed he was a professor.

She climbed the stairs and stood beside him. "People may see us together."

He did not look at her. "Can't an old friend come to say hello?"

"How did you get here?"

"I hired a boat." He smoked a Zhongnanhai cigarette, a popular Beijing brand. The toxic odor tickled her nose.

"Why do you smoke that cheap tobacco?" she asked. "Suyan cigarettes are less offensive."

"Old habits die hard. Did you know they made these for Mao Zedong in the sixties?"

"I wasn't alive then," Fang said.

"Are any of us really alive now?" Another of his damn riddles. Everything the man said had layers of meaning. What an odd profession for a philosophical mind.

"Sarah is dead," she said.

"Yes, an unfortunate accident."

A shiver danced up her spine. "Was it an accident?"

"A pity, since you were becoming so close." He took a long drag off his cigarette.

Sarah's face flashed in Fang's mind again. The wind gusted, and she rubbed her arms for warmth.

Xiu had approached Fang a second time while she pursued her graduate degree at Caltech. It had seemed like a chance meeting after a lecture about the future of artificial intelligence. Speaking with someone from home had warmed her and brought tears to her eyes. Afterward, they had met for lunch, and he encouraged her to pursue research in the field—an effortless task since AI was her passion. Not long after, she received her first living allotment subsidy from the People's Republic of China.

The wind blasted the bunker and chilled her bones. At least she thought it was the wind. "Why did you come?"

"What have you learned?" he asked, switching to Beijing Mandarin.

"I'm in the Annex," she responded in her native tongue, "but I don't have full access to Black Diamond."

"You must." His stare bore through her.

"Why is this so important? When the tech is ready, the world will have access to it."

Xiu pointed across Buzzards Bay to Woods Hole. "When English settlers landed here and looked across at the mainland, what do you think they saw?"

Another riddle.

"I don't want to play your games."

His eyes hardened. "This is not a game, little flower. It's survival. Tell me. What did they see?"

"I don't know. An unexplored land? Natural resources?"

"And?"

"A continent to support them?"

"They saw potential," Xiu said. "The future."

"What does that—"

"Do you think they foresaw the supremacy of the United States as we know it today?"

"Of course not. They—"

"Did they anticipate men landing on the moon or the invention of the internet?"

"Nobody did."

"AI won't just extend life," Xiu said. "It will alter humanity forever. It's our new frontier. Whoever controls it will control the future."

"That's why I've devoted myself to research. It will help everyone flourish."

"You're seeing the continent, but not the potential. Not the future. What happens to China when Americans have downloaded their consciousness and can live forever? What do we do after they download artificially augmented minds into military bots and control an army of cybernetic soldiers?"

"That's fantastical. Even if it's true, it's far in the future."

"Are you sure, little flower? Whoever reaches the technological singularity first will leave the rest of humanity behind. If the Americans don't need biological bodies anymore, what's stopping them from killing all life?"

She hugged herself tighter in the cold. "That's absurd."

"Is it?"

"The Americans would never do that."

"Don't be so sure. And what about the Europeans? Or the Japanese?"

"Would we?" Fang asked. "What if we reach the singularity first? What will the Party do?"

"That's not for you to decide. We're surrounded by enemies and the race to the event horizon is a race for survival."

CHAPTER THIRTY-EIGHT

Adam sat in the conference room's fishbowl and poured over binders of materials. Bryce had authorized Suggs to give Adam summary documents on Tommy's projects. Adam leafed through pages of scientific mumbo-jumbo, then glanced at the front door.

Bryce and Suggs entered the building. Adam waved and caught Bryce's attention. Bryce crossed the lobby and stuck his head in the conference room. "Find anything?"

"No clues," Adam said, "but I'm struggling to understand what most of this means."

Bryce chuckled. "You and most of the scientific community. Let me know if you need anything." Bryce turned to leave, and Suggs held the door for him.

Adam stood. "Will you be around in case I have questions?"

"I'll be in my office until late tonight," Bryce said. "I won't have time to tutor you, but I can get someone to help."

"Thanks," Adam said. "I'll power through it and make notes on what I need clarified."

They left, and Adam looked at his watch. Two o'clock. He had to raise the ante, but would he have time to execute his operation before Bryce left for the night? Adam's employment seemed tenuous, especially with Suggs looking for a reason to fire him. How long would Adam have access to

Forever Technology? A timer ticked down, and with every second, his hopes of solving Tommy's murder diminished. Things would be different if he still carried a badge and had official government resources. Luckily, he owned the gear necessary for what he had planned.

Adam had become his own quartermaster, a modern-day Q from James Bond. When he had conducted criminal investigations overseas, he had often been forced to improvise to collect evidence. DEA did not allow their most sophisticated audio and video recording devices to be given to confidential sources who would be out of their control. In places like Afghanistan, Adam had spent his own money on over-the-counter digital recorders and remote cameras. Spending his own hard-earned cash had bothered him, but he could not stomach enduring danger and hardship without collecting the evidence needed to build prosecutable cases.

He packed the binders and carried them to his new office on the second floor. He grabbed a knapsack from under his desk and returned to the lobby, where he approached Ivan. "Where can I get a bite to eat in town?"

"We discourage employees from going into Gosnold. We have food in our cafeteria."

"Noted," Adam said, "but I need fresh air. Don't worry, I won't divulge any secrets. I don't know anything yet." Adam laughed.

Ivan remained stone-faced. "Be careful."

"Maybe I'll head home to Falmouth and check on my girlfriend." Adam was not hungry, but he wanted the guard to corroborate his story about eating lunch. He exited the building, bypassed the golf carts, and walked up the long driveway. At the road, he checked to make sure he was alone, then turned south, away from town. Adam walked down the sandy path toward Bryce's residence. He forced himself not to run, despite the urgency to finish before Bryce came home.

Adam carried a black knapsack slung over his left shoulder, and he kept his gun hand free—out of habit—even though he didn't carry a handgun. He had resigned from DEA before retirement, so he did not qualify for a Law Enforcement Officers Safety Act concealed-carry license. He had applied to the Falmouth Police for a concealed permit, but Massachusetts had not yet issued it. An old police adage stated it was better to be judged by twelve than carried by six, and his chance of being arrested with a handgun was almost zero, considering there were no police on Cuttyhunk Island— but he was still a suspect in Tommy's homicide and getting caught with a handgun would make him look guilty and the minimum mandatory sentence would land him in prison.

He stretched and scanned the area. No one was visible, but the sound of the wind and waves would drown out the noise of an approaching cart. Adam walked because being saddled with a cart would prevent him from hiding if Bryce, Suggs, or anyone else from Forever Technology showed up.

The autumn sun hung low in the sky. Effie had been sleeping when he left in the morning, and she had briefly awoken when he had dug his gear out of their closet. He told her he would work late, and she had fallen back asleep before he left.

Bryce's house loomed in the distance. The windows looked dark and there were no vehicles out front. Conducting a close target reconnaissance took significant planning and time, but Adam could afford neither. He had rushed the operation, ill prepared and unsure.

He knelt, concealed from the house by the hill on one side of the path and scrub brush on the other. He dropped his knapsack on the ground and removed a miniature camera with a motion sensor. Years ago, his source had purchased the over-the-counter security device at a bazaar in Pakistan. He used black pipe cleaners to affix the camera and motion sensor to a branch on the nearest shrub. He angled it to cover the front of the house then activated it.

Concealed cameras and recording devices could be thin as paper, but battery life was always the problem, unless a device was hard-wired into a power source. Batteries did not last long, and they needed to be replaced. He buried a battery pack in the damp earth and plugged it into the camera. It should last forty-eight hours. This was not the most critical part of his plan, but it would allow him to see people coming and going. If he was lucky, he may even observe Bryce deactivating his security system.

He reached into his jacket and pressed the record button on a second camera, whose pinhole lens peeked out of his jacket buttonhole. Given time, he could have set up long-distance surveillance, but that was not an option.

Adam walked up the road, and as he approached the house, he turned his body to sweep it with his camera. He continued thirty yards past the house and stopped. He shielded the sun with his hand and pretended to look at the distant ruins of the Bartholomew Gosnold Monument. The dilapidated brick tower, a tribute to the British captain in charge of the first expedition to Cape Cod, rose above Gosnold Island in Western Pond.

Adam turned to scan the rear of the residence with his camera. He allowed himself a quick glance and noticed the black bubble of the security camera above the back door. As expected, the billionaire tech CEO had decent security. Adam wanted to get closer to the house, but Bryce probably had motion-activated sensors, and if Adam triggered them, Suggs, or maybe even Bryce himself, would get a remote notification. Many residences now possessed some sort of remote security system. Getting caught walking up to Bryce's door, even if he knocked, would be suspicious and fool no one.

Adam pretended to admire the view for a few more minutes, then walked back and filmed the house again. He kept level strides to balance the camera. He would study the footage later to identify Bryce's security measures, and hopefully, their vulnerabilities.

When he was a safe distance away, he turned off his camera and flicked his phone back to remote viewing. He checked the first camera and saw a live image of the front of the house. Would he be able to break in? At least there were no guards. Bryce must have felt confident security officers could respond from Forever Technology if needed. Or maybe he chose not to draw attention to his house. Was it worth committing a felony to get into the house when it may not contain evidence? What if he stole Bryce's key or convinced someone to hack into the security system? Both options seemed unlikely and were fraught with risk.

Adam knelt and pulled the video camera out of the inside pocket of his jacket. He rewound it and watched the video. A black bubble concealed a camera over the front door, but no other security was visible. Bryce had only recently moved in, and with only thirty people on the island, front and back cameras were probably enough to provide a sense of protection. Adam rewound the video and scanned the yard, pausing and enlarging at various points, but there were no signs of other devices. He fast-forwarded to the backyard and froze the frame again. One camera, that was all. He zoomed into the back door. The doorknob had a keyhole and above it was the silver mechanism for a deadbolt. It looked like a standard lock.

As part of Adam's overseas assignments, he had trained with a foreign intelligence service in defeating security systems. The main thing Adam had taken from that course was how difficult it was to pick a lock. He could defeat a standard lock on a gym locker with a hammer but picking even a basic residential locking mechanism took hours of study and practice. Adam should use a long-range lens to photograph and identify the make and model of the lock. He should purchase a similar lock and the schematics for it, then practice opening it with a lock picking kit over and over until he could do it quickly and in darkness. That was what he should do, but a gulf existed between should and would.

Adam returned his attention to the video. The windows were all closed. What was the chance Bryce left one unlocked? Even if he had, opening one would surely set off the security system. If activated, the response would not come from some commercial monitoring agency. It would arrive in the form of Suggs and his henchmen—armed and ready.

Adam checked at his watch. Dinner time. Bryson said he would be in the office until late, but would he go home to eat?

If what Fang had said was true, Forever Technology was more advanced than anyone outside the company knew. If they had mapped the brain and could capture synaptic connections and decode them into tangible thoughts, they were a decade ahead of the competition. The consequences of their technology were staggering to consider. Bryce's paranoia made sense. He sat on the most important scientific breakthrough since antibiotics. No, bigger than that. This technology would not just improve the health of billions of people, it would remove poor health from the equation. What did it matter if your body failed if you could replace everything with smart technology? Worst case, you would have a digital backup of your mind.

This could save Effie.

The technology was still experimental, but Effie's health declined every day. If he could get Bryce to map her brain and digitize it, maybe some part of her would continue to exist—if the unthinkable happened.

The stakes could not be higher. Adam needed Bryce to preserve the woman Adam loved more than anything. More than himself. Fang said Bryce often took papers home. If Bryce was as paranoid as he seemed, maybe he kept secrets there, things he worried would be stolen at work. There was no way to know if Bryce kept meaningful materials at his house or if they contained a clue about Tommy's death. But if Adam didn't check, he would never know.

Now that Gunn believed Tommy's death was a homicide, she would turn up the heat on Forever Technology. What would Bryce do when that happened? There was nothing stopping him from destroying evidence, moving to another state, or even leaving the country. If Adam wanted to determine if Bryce's residence contained evidence, he had to get inside.

"Fuck it."

He headed for the house.

CHAPTER THIRTY-NINE

Adam checked his remote screen, ensuring the house remained vacant, then looked at his watch. He had to hurry. He pocketed his phone and jogged back up the trail, only this time, he passed the residence and cut through the woods on the far side. Vines clung to his legs and twigs scratched his hands. He stopped, shrugged off his backpack, and removed a pair of black neoprene gloves. Adam slipped on a black balaclava that concealed everything except his eyes. He put the pack on and pushed forward.

He crouched at the edge of the yard. Not a real yard, but a sandy area cleared of vegetation. He studied the house, fifteen yards away. Windows faced the southern side of the island, half the size of the floor-to-ceiling windows in the living room. Probably making it a bedroom.

Adam unsheathed a tactical knife, which had been designed for law enforcement and first responders and included a small iron plug on the hilt. He checked his camera one more time.

All clear.

He sprinted across the yard and squatted beneath the closest window. The house hid him from everything but the pond in the distance. He stood and peeked through the window into Bryce's home office.

Adam was about to cross the line between the law and criminality, but following the law had not helped Sarah or Tommy, and Bryce's billions made a thorough investigation unlikely.

He flipped the knife, so the iron plug faced out. He struck the window with all his strength. Glass shattered, and the window spider-webbed from the point of impact. He ducked as glass showered him. Adam shook it off and used the knife to rake the glass out of the frame.

He checked his watch. How long would it take Suggs or his men to respond? If he was in his office, he would have to receive the alert, get out of the building and into a car, then drive down the path. Adam might have fifteen minutes.

Or less.

He grasped the sides of the frame, stepped on the windowsill, and propelled himself inside. He landed with a thump. The die had been cast. There was no going back.

Hurry.

He faced a contemporary desk with chrome legs and a black marble top. White-lacquered file cabinets lined the far wall opposite a couch and bar cart. Futuristic images of brains decorated the wall.

Adam moved to the MacBook computer on the desk. He tapped a key and the lock screen appeared. He raced to the file cabinets and tugged on the handle of the first cabinet. It was locked too. He wedged his knife above the hasp, and using it as a lever, pried open the cabinet.

His instinct that Forever Technology was involved with Tommy's death and Bryce had withheld information battled with his guilt over breaking into the man's office. He should have waited to see if the legal system worked, but by the time police discovered anything, Bryce could have hidden the evidence or fled.

The cabinet was packed tight with documents in green folders. Adam browsed tabs with names like building lease, sewage project, and water supply. Normal record keeping. He moved to the next cabinet and used his knife to gain access. These files had people's names, including Selectman Jones, Representative Wilcox, and Judge Barrett. Adam snatched the file for the state representative and skimmed its contents. It contained the legislator's profile, including his residence, health, and habits—deep background on the official who could support or destroy Forever Technology's business in Massachusetts.

Adam flipped through the pages, hoping to find a list of proffered bribes or other incriminating evidence, but nothing jumped out. He did the same with files for the New Bedford police chief, US representatives, and senators, and the governor. The files all appeared to be background research, characterizations of key political figures that Forever Technology needed to co-opt to do business in Cuttyhunk.

Adam looked at the time. Ten minutes left. Or less.

He cracked open the next cabinet. This one held projects named after gemstones, like Sapphire, Emerald, and Ruby. Adam rummaged through them. In the back was a file titled Black Diamond. That was the project in the annex—the one Tommy had said was their future.

Adam carried the file to the desk and laid out the contents until the pages covered the surface. He photographed them by taking a third of the desk in each picture. Adam returned the papers, then photographed the second half in the same manner. To save time, he could take the files, but part of him bristled at the thought of stealing documents, which Bryce may need for his research. It was ironic, since Adam was breaking and entering, but committing burglary was necessary to suss out Bryce's culpability, and stealing the files wasn't.

He reordered the papers in the file and replaced them.

Eight minutes.

He still had three file cabinets remaining. He broke into the next one. They had numbered the files with some kind of code. The first read 1742—2016. Adam pulled it out and looked at a photo and profile of a man named David Wilson, followed by pages of data. Adam flicked through the other files. The last one read 1899—2018. He opened it to the photo of a woman named Ellen Mejia. Similar data followed her picture. Adam photographed her profile page and several pages of data. Was he copying the woman's medical record? This level of intrusion, this invasion of privacy, tore at his conscience.

Five minutes.

Adam looked at the remaining cabinets. Did they contain more subject files, other evidence of criminality? He didn't have time to photograph them, and they were too voluminous to steal, even if he possessed the temerity to take them. He had only looked in one room in the house and security could arrive any minute.

He had to inspect the rest of the residence. He had four minutes left, maybe more. Hell, maybe the window hadn't been alarmed. Maybe nobody was coming, and he had hours until Bryce returned home. No, that was wishful thinking. Even if the window hadn't tripped the security system, there were probably motion detectors inside. He did not have time to look for them, but they must be there. No one with Bryce's level of paranoia would leave his house unguarded.

Adam hurried out of the office and down the hallway. He opened the door on his left, a bedroom. The room contained a queen-size bed, bureau, and overstuffed chair. A guest room.

He exited and checked the room across the hall. Another bedroom. He raced down the hall and into the living room, where he had met Bryce before. The windows lining the walls made him feel vulnerable, and he glanced at the driveway. No sign of a response yet. His chest tightened from the risk.

He crossed the room and entered a wing on the far side of the house. He opened the door halfway down the hall and stepped into a room covered with cardboard boxes and cabinets still fresh from the move to Massachusetts. The boxes had writing in red marker on the outside: 2014, 2013, home documents, personnel files. He had no time to break open the boxes and examine the contents. His plan seems less and less fruitful with the passing of each precious minute. He checked the time.

Two minutes.

He scrolled to the surveillance app, and the video feed from the camera he had planted outside appeared on the screen. It displayed the road and driveway leading to the house. No sign of movement, but security could arrive any time. If they came at all. He had no way to know.

Adam exited the room and moved down the hall. Two rooms left. He opened the first door and gasped. Instead of a room behind it, a stairwell led down into a basement. At the bottom of the stairs, an opaque glass door was secured with a keypad. Adam looked at the time.

Time to go.

He glanced back down the stairs. "Dammit." He bounded down the steps, tracing his neoprene gloves along the wall for balance. He reached the bottom and tried the handle. Locked.

He still needed time to get through the window and into the woods beside the road. He pulled out his phone.

Two carts careened up the road toward the driveway.

CHAPTER FORTY

Adam's heart jumped at the sight of approaching carts. Was Suggs in one of them? Or Bryce?

Adam stuffed the phone in his pocket and scampered up the basement stairs. He reached the top and ran down the hallway but stopped before entering the living room. The windows would reveal him to anyone coming up the driveway. He turned back and bolted into the first bedroom. He flung the door open and ran to the window. It overlooked the backyard and western end of the island. Adam flicked the hasp and opened the window. He punched through the screen and ripped it out.

He didn't waste time by checking his phone to see if the carts were headed toward the backyard. He grabbed the frame and hurdled out the window into the backyard.

Adam scanned the road. Nothing. By now, the carts would be at the front door. He sprinted across the backyard toward the brush, then remembered the archery range. Adam veered right and hurtled down the path he and Bryce had taken the day before. He glanced over his shoulder as he descended the hill and caught movement inside the living room.

Had they seen him?

No time to worry about it. Adam continued down the path to the archery range. He crossed it and hit the shrubbery on the far side without breaking stride. The thick vegetation clung to him as he moved through it.

He kept a steady pace to maintain his balance on the downward slope and to minimize sound. If they had not seen him run through the backyard, only his noise would reveal him. No police on the island meant Forever's security would be the only pursuers.

The angle of the slope increased, and Adam tripped. He rolled face-first through a thicket of flowers and vines. He covered his eyes as thorns tore at his skin. Adam regained his feet and listened. Nothing. At the bottom of the hill lay the pond, and somewhere down there, the road followed the western coast. He could follow it and make his way back to Gosnell. He continued down the hill. If he kept out of sight, he would make it.

CHAPTER FORTY-ONE

Fang sipped a green tea and watched Jim Wilson fiddle with a robotic arm in the P2 common area. Jim was a bioengineer and had access to Black Diamond on P3. He began his days in his lab on her floor, then descended to P3 in the late morning. Shlomo had made it clear she did not need access to that level, but maybe Jim would reveal its secrets.

She strolled across the floor and stood beside him until he felt her presence and looked up. "Good morning, Dr. Wilson."

"Ah, uh, hello."

He was socially awkward. Many other young computer scientists were hip and edgy, and the coders were mostly extroverts, but not Jim. He seemed uncomfortable talking to people, even his fellow scientists and especially women. She could use that to her advantage.

"How long have you worked on this project?" she asked.

"On this arm?"

So awkward. "I meant on Black Diamond."

"I uh, since the beginning, but I've only been on Cuttyhunk for a couple months."

"Do you live here alone?" She softened her eyes, making them welcoming.

"I live in company housing on the Vineyard."

How could some men be successful in STEM, but unable to hold a simple conversation with a woman? "Alone or are you married?"

"No, there's no one. I, uh, work too much for anything else."

Fang saddled up to the table to inspect the robotics. She brushed her arm against his and didn't move it. He stiffened from the contact.

"I am alone too," she said.

"Uh, okay."

Fang showed him her warmest smile. "What is your role in Black Diamond?"

"Bioengineering."

"I am curious about the lab downstairs. Can you take me to P3?"

Jim's Adam's apple bobbed as he swallowed. "I don't know. I don't think—"

"I am interested in what happens to my work. I have been mapping for years."

A tapping echoed across the room. Shlomo. It grew louder then stopped behind her. She watched Jim, who had returned his focus to the sanctuary of his project.

"Dr. Jin," Shlomo said.

She plastered a smile on her face and turned to face him. "Good morning."

"I heard you from my office. May I ask you what you're doing?"

Uh-oh. "I was . . . Jim, er, Dr. Wilson and I were chatting."

"About what?" Shlomo asked.

"Nothing important. There are so many unfamiliar faces here, I am trying to get to know everyone."

Shlomo scowled. "Please join me in my office. We need to have a talk." Shlomo turned and headed across the room without waiting for her to respond.

Fang followed Shlomo across the main room. The tapping of his cane had become irritating, and each tap felt as if he was poking her. She replayed her conversation with Jim. She had said nothing out of line or that would draw suspicion. Perhaps Shlomo was just in a bad mood.

They entered his office, and he slid into a leather chair behind his desk. She stood opposite him, unsure if she should sit.

"Shut the door please," he said.

Fang closed it. Her stomach balled into a fist. "What is going on?"

"I should ask you the same question."

"I am afraid I do not follow. Do you have a problem with me socializing with Dr. Wilson?"

"We discourage socializing in the lab, because it's distracting, but that's not what concerns me."

"Oh?"

"I heard you ask about his work on P3."

"I am curious," Fang said.

"Hmm. I may have dismissed your comment as human curiosity, but I also caught you down there on your first day, so I'm wondering what you're doing."

Fang's chest tightened. This was her nightmare. Had she been that sloppy? She could deny her interest in Black Diamond, but that would only make Shlomo more suspicious. He would watch her every move. He could kick her off his team. What if he told Suggs or Bryce about her snooping? She had to lean into it.

"I have concerns," Fang said. "If we have perfected technology that fixes the human substrate, we are essentially offering unlimited life. That creates ethical dilemmas."

Shlomo smacked his lips. "You're critical of our mission?"

Careful here. "This advancement should be available to everyone and not just those who can afford it."

"The right to other people's property does not exist in our economy. This isn't China."

"This product is unique."

"The same philosophy applies," he said. "Under the concept of private property, one doesn't have the right to take the fruits of another's labor. I've seen the results of utopian societies without private property. Everyone becomes equal—equally impoverished."

"So, anyone who can pay gets it?"

"Not necessarily. Despite Bryce's resistance to oversight and my distrust of government, I must admit there are national security implications. Think what would happen if our soldiers could not die? Whoever has an army of sentient robots will rule the world."

Fang remembered Xiu Yän's warning about cybernetic soldiers and shivered. There were many ethical issues attached to an unprecedented leap forward in technology. "How will we price our product?"

"How much would you pay not to die?" Shlomo said. "How much for your loved ones? Mr. Hastings can charge whatever he wants, and people will pay."

"So, the rich live forever and everyone else becomes second-class citizens with expiration dates?"

"Expiration dates are the default position," Shlomo said. "They're built into our DNA. And who's saying everyone wants to live forever. Unhappy people don't want their pain to continue. People commit suicide every day. Can you imagine how many people would kill themselves if they had no other out? Or people could end their lives but leave a digital copy in case they want to be brought back under better circumstances. If they don't like the economy today, they can upload themselves with preset conditions for being reactivated."

"Then people with mental illness or debilitating IQs will be left behind," Fang said. "They lack the ability to decide."

"Isn't that what natural selection does now?"

"You're comparing Black Diamond to evolution?" she asked.

"In a sense, yes." Shlomo said. "I'm an observer of reality. Practical matters. Both the beautiful and the ugly."

Fang wet her lips, feeling more confident. She had answered Shlomo's suspicion with reasonable ethical questions. He no longer seemed concerned, and he appeared energized by the philosophical debate.

"How will Black Diamond affect our understanding of consciousness?" she asked. "Does consciousness accompany downloaded digitized electrical impulses? Would an artificial brain impregnated with a real person's thought processes, preferences, and memories impart consciousness to the host? Would we consider a synthetic humanoid alive? What if the digital brain was completely synthetic, created with original software that mirrored our biological processes and developed through experience like a human? Would that not be life? And if we have created a life, would not basic human rights attach to a cyborg? What about God-given rights, or in this case, Bryce-given rights?"

"Ah, yes. Now we're getting to the good stuff. Your questions are reasonable and important. Unfortunately, the concepts are ethereal and hard to unpack in the abstract. Luckily, resolution is unnecessary for you to complete your work. Will these unanswered questions prevent you from continuing with our project?"

Fang suppressed her relief. He had accepted the premise that her curiosity was rooted in ethics, and he seemed willing to let her continue.

She cleared her throat. "I needed to better understand our goals here, but I feel better having expressed my reservations. Of course, I will continue. It is my honor to work on Black Diamond."

CHAPTER FORTY-TWO

Edna rode the two o'clock ferry from Gosnell back to New Bedford. The shuttle service only ran twice a day in the off-season, and after taking the morning ferry to Cuttyhunk, Forever Technology had denied her entry. She had spent hours on the pier waiting for the return boat. To make matters worse, the island's restaurants had closed, forcing her to wait on a bench in front of the abandoned Coast Guard terminal.

The ferry's engine growled as it edged against the New Bedford pier with a bump. Rope as thick as an arm, 550-cord netting, and logs strapped down with giant chains protected the dock from the floating behemoth. Young men with long hair, duck boots, and backward baseball caps unloaded the cargo. Edna crossed her arms to ward off the cold as she waited for the crew to emplace the passenger gangplank.

After a few minutes, she climbed up the ramp behind three other passengers and passed the office into the lower parking lot. She flipped through her notes as she walked.

Forever Technology stank. Something was wrong there, and she could get none of their scientists to talk to her. She would have to find another way. Maybe she could reach out to their competitors to find dirt on Bryce. If she dug deeper into the company's personnel, she may uncover skeletons she could use to pressure someone to talk. She needed a source, and this time, she needed to corroborate information before writing the story. She would not allow herself to get burned twice in a lifetime, even if the damage to her career had already been done.

Edna blew a bubble then popped it and froze.

"Son of a bitch."

The tires on the driver's side of her Volvo were flat, and the car's weight rested on its rims. She looked around, but she was alone in the lot with two unoccupied sedans and a battered pickup truck. She circled her car. The passenger-side tires had deflated too.

"This can't be happening."

Flat tires happened, especially in heavily trafficked parking lots where screws and other debris littered the ground, but four flat tires meant something else. Someone had done this. This was intentional. She leaned over and inspected the front passenger-side tire. A three-inch slash cut across the sidewall. Some asshole had cut her tires.

"Motherfu—"

"Looks like you've got a problem," a man's voice boomed behind her.

Edna jumped and spun around. A stout, bald man wearing a turtleneck and corduroys stood behind her. Where had he come from? She stepped back without thinking.

"That's what you get," he said.

"What?"

"Shit happens when you go places you shouldn't."

"They told me to park here. The attendant said this—" Edna caught the meaning of his words and stopped. He was not saying she had been careless by parking here. He was talking about her visit to Forever Technology.

"You did this," she said.

His face hardened, and he sneered. "That's a defamatory accusation. It seems you've made a habit of doing that over your career, Ms. Cooper."

He knew who she was. This son of a bitch had slashed her tires. A familiar heat rose in her neck. She grabbed her pen and clicked it several times before touching the tip to her pad. "What's your name?"

His sneer remained. People usually backed down before the power of a journalist's pen because they knew she could damage reputations and careers with the simple story. With innuendo. Even without facts, sometimes all it took was a subtle implication, association, or connection to scandal. One suggestion, and society canceled people. But this man did not seem intimidated. Not even a little.

"My name? You're the one sticking your nose where it doesn't belong."

Edna's eyes darted around the lot. Dark clouds blotted the sun and threw shadows across the pavement. The temperature dropped. She refused to back down. Fear or hesitancy of any kind invited aggression. She had not broken stories by being intimidated. "You will not get away with this. I asked for your name."

He stepped closer, and she backed against her car door. She swallowed her gum.

"Felix," he said. "Felix Suggs. That's with two Gs."

Over Suggs's shoulder, two passengers from the ferry entered the lot and approached the battered Toyota. "Excuse me," Edna called to them. "Can you help me? I seem to have flat tires."

The couple looked up then spoke to each other.

Suggs leaned in close and lowered his voice. "I understand you spoke to Dr. Perlman on the Vineyard."

How did he know that? Had Perlman told him? Were they watching their scientists? Were they watching her?

The young couple approached, emboldening her. She raised her chin and stared into Suggs's dead eyes.

"I'll talk to whomever I want. Whenever I want."

"I'd be careful, Ms. Cooper. Tires aren't the only things that can be slashed."

He turned and left. She kept her eyes on him until he was out of sight.

CHAPTER FORTY-THREE

Adam followed Fang into an office on the P2 level of the Annex. A scientist with gray stubble and a bulbous nose sat behind a desk sipping from a mug. He wore dark glasses, and a white cane leaned against the wall.

"Excuse me, Shlomo," Fang said. "Have you met Adam Locke?"

Shlomo grabbed his cane and stood. "Ah, our new security man. Mr. Locke, you have my condolences for your brother's untimely passing. Tragic, tragic. Thomas and I never saw eye to eye, but he kept the lights on here. I was sorry to hear about the accident."

"The *murder,*" Adam said.

Shlomo raised an eyebrow. "Yes, yes. We shall see. Time has a way of revealing secrets."

"Adam has come to ask a favor," Fang said.

"I'm afraid I don't have anything to add about your brother's death," Shlomo said.

"Fang is going to map my girlfriend's brain, and I want you to download it into an AI device."

Shlomo sat and drank his coffee. "That's *Meshugganah.* There are protocols."

"My girlfriend has stage four cancer. She's dying."

"Ah, I'm very sorry," Shlomo said. "This is a difficult time for you, but—"

JEFFREY JAMES HIGGINS | 173

"It's my only chance to save her. Fang told me you're a good man, a decent man. I need your help."

Shlomo nodded but seemed focused on his coffee. "Have you cleared this with Mr. Hastings?"

"I can't."

"And why is that, my friend?" Shlomo asked.

"Because I'm not supposed to know about it. Bryce told me you're still working the bugs out of the mapping process."

Shlomo looked in Fang's direction. "Then I'm afraid you may be in a bit of trouble, my dear."

"His lover is dying," Fang said. "Why should I deny him this chance? He works here. He's one of us. And this company may be the reason his brother was murdered."

"I feel this conversation has progressed beyond the realm of provable facts."

Adam had come hat in hand, but the old man grated on his nerves. "I don't need proof of murder to know my girlfriend could die any day."

Shlomo nodded. "Is her mind . . . let me rephrase this. How is her cognitive function?"

"She's sharper than I am," Adam said. "Whatever that means. It's her body that's failing, not her mind."

"We have used other test subjects," Fang said. "Please."

"It's not up to me," Shlomo said.

"Then who?" Adam asked.

"Ask Mr. Old Spice," Shlomo said. He pointed at the door.

Adam whirled around. Suggs stood in the doorway.

CHAPTER FORTY-FOUR

Adam climbed down from the cockpit of the Icon A5, his adrenaline still pumping from Bryce's radical descent into Martha's Vineyard Airport. Bryce's offer to fly Adam to the island to see Svetlana could not have come at a better time. Svetlana said she wanted to see Adam urgently and getting away from Suggs was a bonus. Shlomo had not agreed to download Effie's mind, but at least he had not informed Suggs what Fang and Adam had asked. That would have been all Suggs needed to kick Adam out of Forever Technology, and once Adam lost access, he would have no chance of saving Effie. Or discovering who killed Tommy.

"I'm taking off in two hours," Bryce said. "If you're not here, you'll have to take a boat back."

"I'll be here," Adam said. "Thanks for the loaner car."

Adam walked across the tarmac toward the hanger, as Bryce climbed into a waiting Suburban with limo tint. It was nice to be a billionaire.

The Mercedes SUV was in front of the hangar where Adam had parked it and the keys remained in the ignition. Auto theft was not a problem on the island. Where would a car thief go on Martha's Vineyard? He drove down Airport Road, turned east on Edgartown-West Tisbury Road, then onto Oyster Watcha Road. His brother's house overlooked both the Atlantic Ocean and Oyster Pond. The waves were enormous where the big-blue ocean met the island's southern coast, unlike the protected waters of Vineyard Sound.

He parked in Tommy's driveway. Svetlana's now. The two-story colonial looked like every other house on the island, only five times larger. The right wing alone was larger than Adam's and Effie's house. Before his death, Tommy had let it slip that he had ten bedrooms. He had let it slip at least five times. Tommy's classic Porsche 550 Spyder was visible through the windows of the detached eight-car garage. Tommy had loved that car.

Adam shut his car door quietly, as if disembarking at the cemetery. Svetlana had not sounded good the last time they spoke. Her voice had been tainted with stress. And probably vodka.

I'm here, he texted her, not confident she would remember his planned visit.

He climbed the marble steps and rang the bell. The door opened almost immediately. Svetlana's hair hung loosely over her shoulders, and despite her grief, she had applied mascara, eye shadow, and bright red lipstick. He had never seen her without makeup. She wore maroon yoga pants, which hugged her dancer's hips and legs, and her nipples pushed against an ivory spandex halter top.

A wave of guilt washed over him. Effie remained at home battling cancer, and his sister-in-law held onto her psychological health by a thread, yet he noticed Svetlana's beauty.

Adam averted his eyes. "How are you?"

"Better now." Her voice was sultry and a little slurred. Had she been drinking? Svetlana always seemed to have a cocktail in her hand, and an afternoon drink probably waited somewhere close.

"I don't have long," he said. "I'm flying back with Bryce in a couple hours."

"Bryce? That asshole. He's behind this."

Adam put his hands in his pockets and battled that uncomfortable physical sensation that came from cognitive dissonance. Had Bryce ordered Tommy's murder? Was he pretending to help as an excuse to monitor Adam?

"Come in," Svetlana said. She led him into the living room. "Can I get you a drink?"

Adam glanced at his watch. Eleven in the morning. "I'm fine. I need to work today. I want to interview employees at the facility."

"About Tommy?"

Adam sat on the couch. "I'm bringing them in to discuss employee security as part of my get-to-know-you interviews, but yeah, I'm looking for clues."

Svetlana nestled onto the couch beside him and curled her legs beneath her. "Thank God you're investigating this."

"I'm not technically investigating. Hell, I'm still a suspect."

Her eyes widened. "The police think you're involved?"

"They always look at the family. Don't worry, I'm fine."

She nodded. "I don't know what to do with myself. Tommy was here one minute, and then he was gone . . . forever. A few days ago, I was worried about finding a decent tennis instructor, then I blinked, and my life ended." She leaned back and covered her face with her hands.

Adam placed his hand on her knee, then quickly retracted it. She leaned against him and nuzzled her face into his neck. Her warm breath raised goosebumps. She sniffled and her body jerked with a sob. He put his arm around her.

"It's a lot to process," he said. "I'm shell-shocked too. It will take time. Don't rush yourself."

She looked up at him with red, glistening eyes. She grabbed his hand and held it. "I'm glad you're here. I couldn't get through this alone."

"You're not alone. Effie and I are here for you."

Something flashed across her face, then disappeared. She stood. "I'm going to make another Manhattan. You sure you don't want one?"

"Wish I could. I need to keep my wits today."

"I can't keep mine without one." Svetlana crossed the room to the bar cart and Adam forced himself not to watch her. She mixed a drink and returned. She sat beside him, and her perfume lingered. "I want you to promise me something."

"What's that?" he asked.

"Promise you won't stop until you prove they killed him."

Adam stared into her ice-blue eyes. "We don't know Forever Technology is involved, but I'll do everything I can to identify who did this."

She grabbed his forearm. "And when you do?"

"I'll extract justice for Tommy. I'll do it for all of us."

CHAPTER FORTY-FIVE

Edna raged across the newsroom and burst into Harry Willard's office. It had taken her four hours and a hundred dollars to have her car towed and another two hundred for a taxi back to Barnstable. She was in no mood to deal with Harry or anybody else, but the story had become personal, and she would not let it go. She slapped two pieces of paper on his desk.

Harry looked up. "What are those?"

"Receipts for a tow truck and taxi. That son of a bitch slashed my tires while I was trying to get an interview."

"Where?"

"After I left Cuttyhunk. I visited Forever Technology, but they wouldn't let me past the security guard."

"Dammit, Edna. You're not on that story. I was crystal clear when I told you to write about the antiques fair."

"You never told me to stop looking at Forever Technology. I covered the Sarah Smith and Thomas Locke deaths, and I'm doing a standard follow-up. You remember those, right? Journalism one-oh-one."

Harry stabbed a finger at her chest. "Don't lecture me about journalism. I've been in this business thirty years, and I don't need some New York hack coming in here and treating me like a high school editor. I warned you Bryce Hastings could destroy this paper if he wanted, but you didn't listen."

"Really, Harry. You're going to have a heart attack."

"Now, the voicemail I received from Richard Barrington makes sense."

"Who's that?"

"Senior counsel for Forever Technology. He left a message about an hour ago. I've got to call him back and explain why one of my reporters thinks his company is involved with murder, in two deaths the police ruled as accidents."

"My police source told me Locke's death is suspicious. They're investigating it as a homicide."

Harry raises eyebrows. "That's confirmed?"

"Off the record. For now."

Harry leaned back in his chair and massaged his forehead with his thumb and forefinger. "Dammit. Why are things never easy with you? Why can't you just cover the damn stories I assign you and make everyone happy."

"You want me to ignore a homicide investigation? Aren't those the stories that sell papers?"

"Obviously, I don't want you to ignore a homicide. If the police are investigating, report the facts. But that does not mean you can libel Bryce Hastings or his company."

"I'm not accusing—"

"They can bury us in litigation. They can scare our advertisers away. Hell, Hastings could buy our paper from Mrs. Worth, fire us, and sell our equipment at auction."

"You know something stinks here. Companies like Forever Technology don't move to Cape Cod. A scientist with a one-sixty IQ does not accidentally walk off the edge of a cliff on a sunny day. Expensive yachts don't blow up by themselves. They're up to something, and I'll find out what."

"No, you won't."

"So, you're dropping the story and pretending nothing happened?"

"I'm not dropping anything. I've been a newspaperman my entire adult life and I'm not walking away from suspicious deaths, but since you can't seem to follow directions, I'm taking you off the story."

"Like hell you are."

"You may have been one of the most famous reporters in the country, but you're not anymore. Since they debunked your VP infidelity story, you've bounced around from magazine to magazine and newspaper to newspaper. I know you're good at digging up dirt and can write a story. You know it too. So why do you think you haven't been able to hold a job? Not anywhere."

"People are afraid of the truth. They—"

"Bullshit. It's you, Edna. You have a toxic personality. You grate on people. I'm not the most warm and fuzzy human being who ever lived. My wife reminds me of that almost every day. But you can be seriously difficult to work with. Maybe you should consider that. How about acting like a team player once in a while? Take an assignment, try to get the information without pissing everybody off, then write the story I asked you to deliver. Is that so hard?"

"That son of a bitch slashed my tires."

Harry sighed. He stretched his arms and leaned back in his chair, resigned. "Who cut your tires?"

"Felix Suggs."

"And who is that?"

"Forever Technology's chief of security at their Cuttyhunk facility."

Harry leaned forward. "And how do you know he did it?"

"He confronted me in the parking lot. He all but admitted he did it."

"Let me wear my editor's hat for a minute. Did he admit it or not?"

"No, he—"

"This is what I'm talking about. This is the problem. You have—"

"I'm not giving this up," Edna said. "I'm going to find out what happened to my car, and to Dr. Smith and Thomas Locke. All of it."

The light on Harry's phone blinked with an incoming call. He sighed again. "That will be Forever Technology's legal team again. Or Mrs. Worth wanting to know what the hell I'm doing with her newsroom."

Edna held his gaze. "You know I'm right."

Harry placed his hand on the phone but did not lift the receiver. "I'll give you one more chance. Follow up on the deaths, but only report the facts.

You get sources willing to go on the record, and I'll consider publishing your stories."

"Harry, I—"

"If I hear one more allegation that you're pissing people off without evidence, you're done. And I don't mean just with this story. You'll be finished here."

CHAPTER FORTY-SIX

Adam took the stairs down to Forever Technology's lobby. Only a handful of dim lights illuminated the nearly empty building at the late hour. The guard, a husky man with more hair on his hands than on his head, stood at the entrance reading something on his phone and ignored Adam.

Adam crossed the lobby to the cafe and poured himself a cup of coffee. His pulse raced from stress over what he was about to do. Fang had agreed to walk him through the technology around data uploads, and she needed to do that in her lab. Adam had suggested they wait until most of the staff had gone home, and she had agreed.

He poured black coffee into a paper cup, then raised it to his nose and inhaled the pungent aroma. Smell was a major component of taste, and the caffeinated odor awakened him. His muscles still ached from his tumble down the hill when he escaped Bryce's residence. Security had been on alert after the break-in, but Bryce had not contacted the police. At least the State Police had not shown up at Forever Technology. Adam had asked a guard what was happening but did not get any information.

What had been behind that frosted glass door in Bryce's basement? It must be related to their work. And why had Bryce not called the police? With only a few dozen residents left on the island, Bryce had to believe the burglary was corporate espionage. After all, Adam had broken into file cabinets and not stolen anything. Had Bryce installed concealed cameras inside? Was Suggs now analyzing Adam's photo, trying to figure out the identity of the man behind the balaclava?

Bryce would probably increase whatever security he had or move any incriminating evidence. Would he bring it to Forever Technology? With Tommy's death investigation underway, Bryce could not be certain the police would get a warrant to search Tommy's place of business. He would probably keep whatever he was hiding in his basement. Or move it off the island. If he did that, Adam was screwed.

He carried his coffee back to the lobby, and the guard glanced up. Adam waved, and the guard returned his attention to his phone. Adam climbed the stairs and crossed the breezeway and into the annex. His position provided access to most of the building. He took the elevator to P2 and walked through the common area and down the hall to Fang's lab. Why had she agreed to help him find Tommy's killer and download Effie's mind? Did she think Forever Technology was responsible?

Fang looked up from her desk and waved him in. He entered, and she came around her desk. Computers and stacks of documents covered three metal tables. Cabinets lined the far wall.

"I wondered if you'd come," she said.

"I know what you're risking by helping me."

She nodded. "This technology can save humankind. It can also produce horrifying outcomes."

"Such as?" Adam asked.

"Predictive applications. Let's say the government has access to a digitized version of an individual's mind. If they entered that AI brain into a simulation and gave it external stimuli, the replicant's response could predict the individual's real-world behavior."

"A foresight machine."

"You got it. A government could run every citizen through an infinite number of models to determine who would make the best leader or come up with the next invention. Or who would become a criminal."

A sickness settled in Adam's stomach. "They could incarcerate people with a high propensity for committing crimes, like the justification for keeping sociopaths in institutions."

"I'm from China," Fang said. "What authorities call crimes can differ vastly. What would stop a regime from identifying dissidents and jailing them?"

"Scary stuff."

"They could use the same technology for objectively good reasons, like career placement, or running war games without the loss of life. But who knows how they'll apply our technology?"

"My experience tells me the government will use it to increase their power. That's the way of the world. A career in law enforcement has shown me that."

"We're assuming computer models are even accurate. Half the world bases energy policy on climate-change models which have never been accurate. The administration could imprison people based on faulty predictions."

"Not to mention discounting the notion of free will," Adam said. "Just because a simulation responded one way doesn't mean a person would do the same. Humans are complex."

"And what are we calling a real person?"

Adam sat beside her. "My head is swimming."

"Maybe just knowing what outcomes your mind created in a simulation would be enough added external pressure to adjust behavior. Like how Heisenberg's uncertainty principle states the properties of a particle cannot be measured."

"What do you mean?" he asked.

"The observer effect posits that the speed and direction of a particle can never be known because the moment you observe it, you change it. Quantum mechanics has proven this. Maybe the direction of someone's life can't be known either."

"I haven't studied physics," Adam said, "but I'm a student of human behavior, and I believe people possess the free will to change their futures."

"Even if our decisions are solely driven by chemical interactions, being informed of what you're likely to do may create enough of a chemical change to achieve different outputs and outcomes."

"If I understand you right," Adam said, "it reminds me of a corollary in criminal justice. Both genetics and environmental variables influence behavior. Some people have lower abilities to assess risk or are more prone to react physically. I've read classic monozygotic twin studies where social services separated a murderer's sons at an early age, and law-abiding foster families raised them, but both twins committed their own murders. Genes play a role in decision-making, but if we warn subjects about their genetic proclivities, they can make different choices and deviate from their destiny. The same way a victim of child abuse can choose to stop the cycle of violence with his or her own children."

"I hope that is true," Fang said, "but it doesn't mean governments will trust individuals. This technology can become a crystal ball for totalitarian regimes. Trust me. I know."

"Right now, the only things that matter to me are finding out who killed my brother and saving Effie. Show me how this works."

CHAPTER FORTY-SEVEN

Adam sat at his desk and browsed through papers Fang had given him. She had spent hours describing the process of brain mapping and downloading. He had also skimmed through the material she had recommended to learn the basics behind neuroscience, artificial intelligence, and computing. Ninety percent of what he read flew over his head, but he got the gist of it. The brain sent electrical signals through synapses when it wanted the body to do something, whether lifting a leg or remembering an event. Fang had identified these connections and linked them to specific thoughts or actions. While prior research existed, Forever Technology had taken the lead in deciphering these electrical signals. Researchers read the synaptic fireworks show and re-created what subject's saw. Then using Fang's models, they re-created memories.

Bryce's brilliance had come from merging artificial intelligence with the various sciences and technology involved in this process. By doing this, his team created a facsimile of the original frame. They made a digital shadow of not just a person's thoughts, but the unique and specific way the subject thought.

Adam leaned back and tried to remember Fang's hurried descriptions of the uploading process to the server. He pictured her maneuvering the data and plugging gigabytes of information into the digital mind.

"What a minute," he said.

Fang had mentioned downloading the digitized data into an artificially intelligent computer. That step improved their understanding of the workings of the human mind and created a backup for patients with cognitive issues. When paired with artificial intelligence, a computer implanted with the original mind's data and neural processes could theoretically think, learn, and act like the owner of the copied brain. It made sense that Fang had thought about that part of the process, even though her specialty was mapping and computerizing inner thoughts, but she had spoken about the downloading process as if it was more than theory, as if Forever Technology had the process underway. She knew things about Black Diamond, which seemed beyond her need to know. That alone did not concern him, but Fang's demeanor suggested she was hiding something. Computer theory and artificial intelligence may have been foreign concepts to Adam, but human deception was not. He had spent most of his adult life ferreting out lies and criminality, and his gut instinct told him Fang was up to something.

He conducted a thought experiment, as he often did when vetting hypotheses in criminal cases. If Fang was trying to conceal a secret, what would her behavior look like? She seemed interested in areas of the business unrelated to her work, and she knew more about what Forever Technology did than she should have. And she exhibited clusters of physical reactions indicative of deception.

She had also agreed to Adam's request for help and used it to push into areas where she did not belong. Adam liked to think his powers of persuasion were unparalleled, but this brilliant scientist's willingness to show Forever's secrets had come too easily. Was she motivated to find Tommy's killer? Had her relationship with Tommy been deeper than she let on? Tommy had always possessed a wandering eye, and the way he spoke, the way he acted around other women, all seemed automatic, too casual for a married man. Adam would have bet big money that Tommy had fooled around with other women in the six years he'd been married to Svetlana. If Fang and Tommy had an affair, it would explain her willingness to violate company policy and help Adam. But that was one theory.

The other was darker.

What if Fang was interested in the Black Diamond project for financial reasons? From the way Bryce had talked about it, Forever Technology's advancements were priceless. Did Fang want to steal it and sell to the highest bidder? Did she want to form her own company? Adam could not know the answers to these questions unless he asked her. Or he could do what he had done as a special agent and investigate?

Adam closed the files and locked them in his desk drawer. He took the elevator to the basement and followed a windowless hall to the security command center beside Suggs's office.

The sound of clacking computer keys emanated from Suggs's office. Adam typed his passcode command center's security pad and placed his palm in the biometric reader. He slipped into the room.

A heavyset security guard, wearing a white shirt and blue blazer, looked up from behind a computer console. The name tag in his jacket read, "Buck."

"Can I help you?" Buck asked.

"Adam Locke. I'm the new security consultant."

"I know who you are. What's up?"

"I want to view the computer surveillance system."

"Is there a problem?"

"Walk me through it. I want to evaluate what's covered and how it's monitored to find vulnerabilities."

"Help yourself," Buck said.

"Thanks. How many cameras are there in total?"

Buck referred to a clipboard hanging from a hook. "We have 180 cameras, including all interior and exterior units."

Adam whistled. "And they cover the entire property."

"The exterior of the buildings and the interior, except P3."

"Why is that?"

"That's Black Diamond."

"I thought the entire annex was working on Black Diamond," Adam said.

"P3 is Black Diamond Plus. It's the most sensitive part of the project."

"Why is it sensitive?" Adam asked.

"Because Mr. Hastings says so."

Adam grew tired of everyone treating Bryce like he was king. "I know who calls the shots. What's sensitive about Black Diamond Plus?"

"No idea," Buck said. "Only a handful of scientists have access."

The constant need for secrecy among the employees exhausted Adam. He had worked with sensitive compartmentalized information dealing with human sources, the highest levels of classification in the intelligence community. Forever Technology's products were valuable, but their disclosure would not destroy the United States. Buck and the other blue-jacketed Neanderthals needed to relax their super-spy attitudes.

"How do you watch 180 cameras?" Adam asked.

"The images automatically rotate, but I can lock onto one camera if I see anything suspicious."

"Is there an order to the rotation?"

"Random."

"Are you the only officer watching?"

"Mr. Suggs can watch from the monitor in his office."

"Can I access it from my desktop?"

Buck frowned. "Something wrong?"

"That's what I'm trying to figure out. How can I get permission?"

"Ask Mr. Suggs."

Adam nodded as he watched the screens rotate from camera to camera, with three angles visible at a time. The screens froze for five seconds before switching images. Adam did the math. Three screens required sixty rotations to show all the cameras. With a five-second delay, it would take five minutes to see every camera view. That meant five seconds of surveillance for any single camera over a five-minute period. An officer needed perfect focus to spot anything. It was not an effective system.

Perfect.

"Do the camera's record?" Adam asked.

"The recordings erase automatically after forty-eight hours, unless we manually save them."

"How many guards are on duty during an eight-hour shift?" Adam asked.

"One in here, one at the front door, and a rover who wanders the grounds."

"And Felix Suggs."

"That's right. He responds with the rover when anything happens."

"Like what?"

"Like yesterday's break-in at Mr. Hastings's residence. Last week we caught a local kid smoking weed in the woods near the cliffs. And a month ago, a scientist had chest pains. We had to get him a medevac."

"Was he okay?"

"He had gas."

Adam laughed. He thanked Bucky and left.

Bryce may have been paranoid, and Suggs was a hard man, but their security system depended on vigilant officers, which created a serious vulnerability. The system was decent, over the top for a research facility on a small island, but it was not foolproof.

He had a chance.

CHAPTER FORTY-EIGHT

A biting Atlantic breeze blew across the second-story deck of The Whaler restaurant in Edgartown, on Martha's Vineyard's eastern shore. Adam spotted Svetlana exiting the indoor dining room onto the deck, and he waved her to his table. He pulled her chair out and moved it closer to the heat lamp, then held it as she sat down.

"Thanks for coming," he said.

"You didn't feel comfortable at my house?" she asked. Her eyes widened with the vulnerability of a child.

"It will do you good to get out."

That was obviously not the reason he had steered the meeting to a public place after she had called and asked to see him. He wanted to help his sister-in-law through her grief, but he needed to avoid intimate surroundings and prevent a repeat of their awkward encounter on her couch.

Adam was not tempted—he would never cheat on Effie—but Svetlana was experiencing a traumatic period, and he didn't want to embarrass her by overtly rejecting her advances. Once she recovered from the shock of Tommy's death, she would regain her senses and realize how inappropriate her behavior had been. Her need for security and affection was understandable, but wrong. It would be easy to pretend the incident at her house had never happened, but not if he had to fend off her advances again. Under normal circumstances, having an alluring woman like Svetlana flirt with him would have boosted his ego, but Effie's cancer and his brother's death mitigated the flattery.

"I don't know what I'm going to do now," Svetlana said.

"Take it day by day. I know that sounds trite, but it works. Don't look too far into the future. Get up each day and do what you can to take care of yourself."

"I wish I could, but arrangements have to be made, bills need paying, and I need to know what's going to happen."

"I can do your bills and help with Tommy's funeral." Just saying *funeral* darkened Adam's soul.

"I can't impose, I—"

"You're family," Adam said.

"I'll put the bills together. Maybe you can come by tonight and pick them up."

Adam wanted to decline and tell her to drop them off at his office, but Svetlana was already resistant to accepting his help, and he needed to take care of her.

"Happy to do it. I'll swing by after work."

"And how is work going?"

"I spend most of my time looking for reasons somebody would have wanted to kill Tommy and Dr. Smith."

"Bryce murdered them."

"He may be an eccentric ideologue and ruthless, but I don't think he's evil," Adam said.

"He'll do anything to be first to market. He doesn't care who he steamrolls. Tommy's life, my life, your life—they mean nothing to him. All he cares about is that damn technology. He wants history to remember him as the man who changed the world."

"You think he has grandiose visions about his legacy?"

"He's a glory hound who takes credit for the work his scientists and people like Tommy did. Without Tommy's ability to position an unproven technology as an opportunity and excite investors, Forever Technology would never have gotten off the ground. Bryce Hastings owes everything to Tommy, but he had him killed."

Adam leaned back and let Svetlana's statement wash over him. Bryce ordered Tommy's murder? The wind picked up and ruffled the napkins beneath the silverware. "Why would you accuse Bryce?"

"I could use a drink," Svetlana said, "or do you disapprove of drinking in the middle of the day?"

Adam waved the server over and ordered two bloody Marys, the specialty of the house. When the waiter left, he leaned forward and tried again. "Why Bryce? What aren't you telling me?"

Svetlana dug in her purse and pulled out a pack of Dunhills. Her fingers trembled as she drew a long white cigarette and wrapped her lips around it. She flicked her lighter once, twice, three times, but the wind extinguished the flame.

"Allow me," Adam said.

He moved around the table and took the lighter from her. He sparked it to life and used his hand to shield it from the wind.

Svetlana clasped both of his hands in hers and dipped her head until the cigarette penetrated the flame. She inhaled, and the cigarette flared. Somehow, she made the act sensual. Was it his imagination, or was she sending signals? She probably wore over a thousand dollars in designer clothing and a multiple of that in gold jewelry. Svetlana had meticulously applied her makeup, and she looked like she had stepped off the pages of cosmopolitan or Vogue. From the first day Adam had met Svetlana, it had been obvious why Tommy married her. She radiated beauty and oozed sexuality. She held his hand for a moment too long before releasing it, then she looked up with lagoon-blue eyes.

Adam focused on the whitecaps breaking across the horizon to ignore her longing. He returned to his seat. "Do you have more than suspicions?"

She exhaled the smoke and it fragmented and disappeared in a gust. "Their research is farther along than they admit." She let her statement hang in the air between them.

"And you know this how?"

"Tommy told me a little about what was happening. He worried about Bryce's behavior."

"Worried?"

"Tommy said Bryce was acting erratic, paranoid. He said Bryce wanted to sell his technology to a foreign power."

"Sell to whom?"

"The Russians? The Chinese? Maybe the North Koreans. Tommy didn't say."

"Why would Bryce sell to another country if he was so worried about going down in history?"

"He was worried about industrial espionage," Svetlana said, "and he thought the Feds would try to control or seize his technology under the mantle of national security. If the NSA took over, he would lose everything. They would prevent him from perfecting the technology and allow his competitors to catch up. Tommy thought DARPA might make a sweetheart funding deal with another company and cut Forever Technology out completely. By selling to a foreign power, especially one out of the reach of American law enforcement, Bryce would insure himself against an administration preventing him from realizing his profit potential. Once the Russians or someone else had it, it would not matter if the US government tried to intervene."

"And what about Bryce's legacy?"

"Tommy said Bryce would attach his name to any deal. If he sold to another country, he would continue his research at Forever Technology and still be its public face."

Adam mulled that over. The threat of a governmental takeover was real. It had happened to other companies in the past. Authorities had controlled entire industries. Would life-extending technology carry enough of a national security threat to justify the complete control or seizure of private property? Probably not, but even if Bryce contested it and eventually won in court, they could delay his research for years. But would Bryce sell to a regime hostile to the US? Doing so may compromise Forever Technology's ability to market in the US. Of course, if the technology was all Bryce claimed, every country would clamor to purchase it. If Adam was CEO, he would not trust the Russians or the Chinese to keep their word. Maybe Bryce was desperate.

"Let's say that's true," Adam said. "Why kill Tommy?"

"Tommy was going to blow the whistle on him."

"About selling to a foreign entity?"

"Tommy called it treason. He and Bryce argued about it a few days before Tommy's death."

Adam rolled his neck to relieve the building tension in his shoulders. "Bryce told me Tommy was his oldest ally. Would he kill his number two?"

"He didn't do it himself," Svetlana said. "He had one of his thugs do it. Maybe Suggs. Or Bryce brought in one of his knuckle draggers from the West Coast."

"And you don't know the customer?"

"No."

"Forever employs many foreign-born scientists. Could one of them be involved?"

Svetlana took a long drag on her cigarette, then stubbed out the butt on her plate. "That's for you to figure out, Mr. Special Agent."

CHAPTER FORTY-NINE

Edna climbed out of her car on East Fourth Street in South Boston, half a block from City Point Park. At nine-thirty, the street had been dark for hours, and she scanned the sidewalk for trouble. This southeastern corner of Boston was once an impoverished and crime-ridden neighborhood, but gentrification had soared property values and created an eclectic mix of residents.

She glanced at her new tires and fumed over the expense. Harry better push her invoice through the finance office. No way she was shelling out six hundred bucks for vandalism when she had been on a story. And Harry had better not claim it was her fault because he had not approved her trip. A decade ago, when she had socialized with literati at the center of the universe, she could have expensed anything. And she had. Dinners, parties, cocktails, new clothes—all necessary. Now, she had to argue with a regional paper for tires. God, it was too depressing to think about.

It had taken almost two hours to drive to Boston for this meeting with a potential source. Hours of online research had led her to Brock Gibson, and when he had agreed to meet, she had dropped everything and raced to the city. She would expense her mileage too. No way she was paying for a tank of gas.

She popped three sticks of Trident bubblegum into her mouth and walked to the end of the block. She entered City Point Park, which abutted the Old Harbor on one side and Pleasure Bay on the other. Leaves on the trees had turned blood red and burnt orange, a canopy of autumn color.

Gibson had worked with Felix Suggs in Sudan and Afghanistan when they were both employed by Global Conflict Solutions Corporation, an international business supplying military and police mentors around the world. She had asked Gibson what he knew about Suggs, and Gibson had told her to fuck off. When she told him she would pay for information, he intimated he knew where Sugg's skeletons were buried. Literally.

She passed a square brick building containing restrooms. The doors had been padlocked. She continued past a small playground to a line of benches facing the water. Just like a mercenary to meet in a dusky park. Why did these assholes all think they were James Bond?

He waited on the last bench.

It had to be him. He was massive, with bulging shoulders and a thick neck. The kind of guy who spent his free time either in the gym or flexing his muscles in front of a mirror. She approached from his side to avoid startling him.

"Brock Gibson?"

He stood up and showed his size. If he was the wrong guy, she would probably get mugged.

"Yeah, that's right."

"Edna Cooper. Thanks for coming."

"You bring my money?"

Her stomach rippled like a waterbed. Maybe she should have met him somewhere else. She was used to pushing around fashionista and corporate types. This guy was a different animal.

"Let's hear what you have to say first. Tell me about Felix Suggs."

"What's your story about?"

She sat on the bench. He remained standing. "I'm working on a story about Suggs's employer. I want to know what kind of man Suggs is. What's he capable of doing?"

"Anything."

"Meaning?"

"He's a hard man. Dense as steel."

"Are you going to sit down?" she asked, sick of staring at his groin.

"No."

"Is Suggs capable of murder?"

Gibson guffawed. "He's a killer. As pure as any predator I've ever seen. He'd do whatever was necessary to accomplish his mission."

"Murder?"

"He enjoys killing."

Excitement effervesced through her body. When was the last time she had something this juicy? She never had a source break a murder investigation. These were not the type of stories she sought, but this had fallen into her lap. And it beat covering antique shows. "I need specifics."

"And I need cash."

Edna touched her sweater pocket where she kept an envelope containing five hundred dollars, her ATM limit. Gibson's eyes dropped to her hand. Touching her pocket had been a mistake.

"Give me a taste, so I know what I'm buying," she said.

He smirked. "I was with Suggs in Darfur. We mentored a local security force at a government facility."

"When?"

"2010, during the ceasefire. A group of a dozen Justice and Equity activists blocked our gates. Suggs ordered the guards to disperse them, and we sent the activists back into town. An hour later, two pickups arrived with twenty armed Janjaweed, and—"

"Janjaweed?"

"A militia supporting the government. Suggs and I went out and spoke with them. Suggs told them about the activists, and we drove into town with them."

"What happened?"

"The Janjaweed killed them."

"Who? The activists?"

"Everybody. The entire village. Men, women, children."

A dull throb pulsated between Edna's temples. Could she believe Gibson?

"Was Suggs involved in the massacre?"

"He shot three or four civilians, then he used his machete to lop off the head of a teenage boy."

Edna's stomach turned. "You have proof of this?"

"I watched him do it."

"Will you go on record? For attribution?"

"No."

Edna chomped on her gum. "Can I attribute it to an anonymous source with proven credentials?"

"Suggs will know it's me."

"You're a giant. You meant to tell me you're afraid of Suggs?"

His stare bore through her. "Yes."

"I guess I can use it for background." She dug into her pocket and counted out two hundred dollars from an envelope. She held out the bills.

"Two hundred?" he asked.

"That's fair for background. I need more specifics to corroborate your story."

"Give me all of it."

"Excuse me? What do you—"

He took the two hundred dollars then snatched the envelope out of her other hand.

"That's theft," she said.

"It don't matter."

"I know who you are. I could call the police."

He sneered. "I'll take my chances. You keep asking questions about Suggs, you won't be alive for long. Nice doing business with you."

He disappeared into the shadows.

CHAPTER FIFTY

Adam double-clicked the video icon on his desktop. Suggs had given him remote access to monitor Forever's surveillance cameras from the privacy of his office. He scrolled through the images of the Annex. He stopped on one and paused the camera's automatic rotation.

On the screen, Fang stood behind the computer console in her office.

Adam checked his watch. Almost lunch. Fang usually ate in the cafeteria, but sometimes she took long walks on the trail instead. Her knowledge of Forever's projects and her willingness to help Adam spy on them could be motivated by the relationship she had with Tommy, or it could be something else. If she was up to something, he wanted to know where she went on her walks.

Fang typed something then stared at the far wall for the third time in as many minutes. Adam squinted at his display. What was over there? The clock. Was she hungry or waiting for something?

At five minutes before one o'clock, Fang glanced at the time. She hung her lab coat on a hook and moved toward the exit. Adam switched monitors and watched Fang exit the lab and enter a combination into a wall locker. Forever prohibited employees from carrying cellular telephones, purses, or other personal items into the laboratory.

Fang removed a fabric purse with a red chrysanthemum stitched into the side and slung it over her shoulder. She turned and made her way toward the elevator.

Adam followed her with the cameras but had trouble keeping up. By the time he found the elevator video, the doors were closing as she entered the lobby. Adam hit the screen lock and hurried downstairs. Funny how he worked in a building full of people who followed science, yet few of them used the stairs. A sedentary lifestyle was every bit as dangerous as smoking or alcohol abuse.

He cracked open the door in the lobby and peeked out. Fang had already passed the security guard and exited the building. He caught a flash of her brown slacks moving toward the driveway, and then she was gone. He crossed the lobby and smiled at Ivan as he pushed through the front door. Three carts remained in the lot, but no sign of Fang.

The trail leading to the conservation area was on the south side of the buildings. Adam took a step in that direction then decided to check the driveway. He rushed to the bend in the driveway and looked toward West End Road.

Fang.

She hastened up the pavement and out of sight. Strange she had not taken the trail. Adam sighed, thankful he had not assumed she would follow her normal routine. DEA had trained him on multiple surveillance methods. Most DEA surveillance involved teams of agents in vehicles, and occasionally, helicopters or fixed-wing aircraft using cameras and spotters. In a vehicle surveillance, one driver would maintain an eye on the target while other cars took parallel routes. When a subject turned, the car behind the target would pass off the eye to another unit and continue straight. Adam had also trained with the British, who used a unique system, with two agents per car and a mobile dispatcher who coordinated the team's movements.

Foot surveillance was challenging because he was most visible to a target and had to appear to belong wherever he went. He had conducted foot surveillance in urban areas from New York City to Bangkok. He would blend in and stay as far behind a subject as possible, preferably on the other side of the street. If he had two or three agents with him, he would use a similar procedure as in vehicles, passing off the eye every time a target turned.

But Adam was alone on Cuttyhunk Island, and a single-man surveillance was difficult and nearly impossible if a target had countersurveillance training. Surveillance on an island with thirty residents exacerbated the problem. If Fang observed Adam behind her, he would have no reasonable explanation for his presence. Luckily, the limited size of the island would make it easier to reacquire her if she gave him the slip.

He stayed far behind her and out of sight. He opened his Google Maps app and tried to predict her route. The best trackers anticipated a target's behavior.

Fang turned right at the end of the driveway and headed toward Gosnold. Adam slowed to give her time to move down the road. If she doubled back, he would have nowhere to hide, but all surveillance entailed risk. He leaned into the street. No sign of her.

The area was deserted, as always, and shells crunched under his boots as he raced up the roadway. Surveillances could be compromised by third-party detection because it was easy to focus on a target and not pay attention to potential countersurveillance, and it only took a nosy neighbor to ruin a surveillance.

No residences were visible on this part of the road, so Adam jogged ahead. He reached the bend as Fang continued north. She did not look for a tail. He had cut the distance in half, so he stopped and waited for her to disappear around the next turn. Foot surveillance was like stretching a rubber band until a target disappeared, then racing to catch up to glimpse it before stretching the band again. This technique minimized his exposure if she checked her six.

The road forked with the ferry dock to the right and the marina to the left. The town of Gosnell sprawled across the hill beside him. Adam closed the distance as she turned onto Broadway and walked into the center of town. He paused at the intersection and watched her turn in front of the historical society and continue up the hill on Tower Road.

He walked past the Island Market and Post Office and referred to Google Maps. Tower Road led past the town hall, one-room schoolhouse, church, and farm. It led to Bunker Hill, which offered a scenic overlook of the entire island. The road continued south, and a trail continued down the other side. Adam had intended to visit the World War II bunker, but that had been before his life turned upside down.

Where was she headed? Was she on company business? China had an underground culture of Christians, so maybe she was headed to church. But scientists were prohibited, or at least dissuaded, from going downtown, so why would Fang break the rules when Suggs was on high alert?

Adam stopped at the historical society and glanced up the hill. Fang passed the church. He checked his phone and pretended to send a text in case anyone was watching. Fang continued toward the overlook on Bunker Hill. Was she circling back to Forever Technology or planning to return the same way?

The simplest surveillance maneuver would be to head down Main Street and keep an eye on the intersection, then wait for her to return. If she followed the same route back, she would not even look in his direction when she reached the bottom. That was the best technique for remaining undetected, but it would not tell him what she was doing.

He had to chance it.

Adam walked up the hill. On his left, the front door of the town hall was open, and employees milled around inside. The schoolhouse was closed. Did it even have any students left? A golf cart was parked in front of the church, and someone had parked a truck beside two more golf carts on the driveway leading to the farmhouse.

Adam kept going.

Fang had disappeared around the corner at the top of the hill. Low concrete walls lined the elevated road, and thick brush covered the ground below. If Fang turned around, she would see him. He would have to admit he had followed her, and make up an excuse, saying he wanted to talk to her about Tommy, away from the lab. She may not buy it, but how else to explain a coincidental meeting?

His pulse accelerated as he reached the midpoint of the road. Fang could reappear at any moment. He shook his hands to release his tension and practiced his friendliest smile. Fang was smart, and she would assume he had followed her.

He came within twenty yards of the top, and still no sign of her. Maybe she had decided to enjoy the view. That made sense. She spent at least ten hours a day cooped up in a windowless laboratory. He would crave sunshine too. Adam slowed near the top where the road veered left.

He edged around the corner, trying to be quiet. Fang climbed a wooden scaffold atop the World War II bunker and stared out over the bay. A short Asian man wearing an overcoat stood beside her.

CHAPTER FIFTY-ONE

Xiu Yän scowled at Fang. His teeth clenched around the end of a Zhongnanhai cigarette. She had not heard from him for months after her arrival on Cuttyhunk, and now he had signaled for a meeting twice in one week. Something was wrong.

"What is the problem?" Fang asked.

"You have something for me?" he asked in Mandarin.

"We only met two days ago," she said, switching tongues. "I haven't had time. I—"

"You've had years."

She searched his eyes—placid black pools, like the surface of a frozen Mongolian lake—except for the cloudy cataract growing over his left iris. Xiu never raised his voice to her, and he had not done so now, but his chilly demeanor felt more threatening. He spoke in a whisper. The hiss of a snake.

"I did as you asked. They gave me access to Black Diamond."

"And?"

"They are farther along than I thought. The downloads have begun."

"With tier-one subjects?" Xiu asked.

"Yes. I have seen—"

"Then where is my data? Where are my schematics? Where is my prototype?"

Hiss.

"I'm trying. I'm never alone. Dr. Perlman is watching me. I need time—"

"You're out of time. I need the data now."

"Why the rush?"

He slapped her hard across the face. Stars floated before her, and she stumbled backward. He grabbed her arm and pulled her close.

Her face stung and her eyes teared. He had never struck her before. Never threatened her. Something had happened.

"You're not in a position to question me," Xiu said. His breath reeked of tobacco. "I've been patient, but the time for patience is over. I gave you an order and I expect you to comply."

An order? She had accepted the grants from the Chinese government to allow her to travel and study in America, and she knew there would be a cost, but neither Xiu nor anyone else had explicitly spoken of it. And now he treated her as if she were what? A spy? A thief? She had always assumed he worked at the behest of Chinese intelligence. Was that true?

"I'm trying," she said, holding back tears.

"Don't try. Do it." He kept a firm grip on her arm. He was strong. The cigarette never moved from his mouth, and the putrid smoke swirled in the breeze, tickling her nose. She would have to wash her hair again tonight.

"Is Thomas Locke's death part of this?" she asked.

His face tightened, and she blinked, thinking he would strike her again. He released her and stared into her eyes. "You're a child."

"Was Sarah involved? Did you kill her?"

Xiu dropped his cigarette and crushed it against the wood under the toe of his polished wingtip. "The people under heaven need you. Your ancestors are watching. Will you have honor?"

"I'll do what you ask."

Xiu tapped another cigarette out of his pack and stopped with it halfway to his mouth. He stared over her shoulder. "Someone is there."

"Where?" She looked back at Tower Road. Nothing.

"A man. By the street."

"You're mistaken, I don't see—"

"Were you followed?"

"No, I—"

"It's time to go. Get me what I need."

CHAPTER FIFTY-TWO

Adam ducked behind a thick growth of witch hazel. Had they spotted him? The old man had struck Fang, but Adam had restrained himself from rushing to her rescue, because they had continued talking, and she did not seem to be in imminent danger. Then the man looked right at Adam.

Adam leaned into the dark shadow of the bush. He stayed still because movement drew the human eye, and the thick leaves obscured his human shape. If they came toward him, he would run. Adam glanced down Tower Road toward Town Hall. If he sprinted, he could make it. Maybe.

Or he could confront them. Who was that man? A decade with DEA had taught him not to reveal himself until he possessed the evidence he needed. Adam had interviewed many suspects, but only after he had an arrest warrant in hand. Tipping off a subject too early made them surveillance conscious and often resulted in the destruction of evidence. He should identify the old man before confronting him. Otherwise, he would not know if Fang told him the truth. If she told him anything at all.

Blurry shadows moved atop the bunker, then Fang and the man disappeared off the platform.

They were coming.

Adam barreled down the hill. He made it halfway across the raised road and stopped where part of the wall had collapsed. Seven or eight feet below, thick brush covered the ground. He looked back up the hill. No sign of them. Adam knew where to find Fang, but he needed to identify the man.

He perched on the edge of the street and dangled his legs over the side. He flipped onto his stomach and lowered himself. His feet did not reach the ground. It was farther than he had estimated. He released his grip and dropped.

Adam crashed through prickly shrubs and slammed into hard earth. His ankle twisted, and he collapsed to his knees. Branches scratched his face and hands. Something skittered through the underbrush. Adam stood and manipulated his ankle. It hurt but wasn't seriously sprained.

He watched the gap in the wall. No sign of them. He pressed against a cool pillar and stayed quiet. A bird chirped. A bead of sweat rolled into his eye, and he blinked it away.

The clip clopping of shoes echoed on the pavement; the same sound Fang's shoes had made downtown. They grew louder, then passed him and faded down Tower Road.

He strained to listen but heard nothing else. Where had the man gone? Had he seen Adam and was waiting in ambush? Had he gone in the opposite direction? If Adam climbed up too soon, he'd get burned.

"Damn it."

Be bold. Adam wedged his foot into a sturdy shrub and exploded upward. He grasped the ragged end of the wall and his knees banged against the brick column. His shoulders strained as he pulled himself up. He peeked over the edge.

The road was clear.

Adam found a toehold and thrust his chest onto the pavement. He shimmied onto the road. He stood and dusted dried leaves off his clothes. He sprinted up the hill and leaned around the witch hazel.

No sign of the man.

Adam jogged to the bunker. An electric golf cart whined from the woods to the south. It had to be the old man. Adam pulled out his phone and checked Google Maps. Tower Road joined Bayberry Hill Road and wrapped around the western shore of Cuttyhunk. It led back into town.

Adam dashed past the bunker onto an unpaved section of Tower Road, barely wide enough for a cart. The man must have parked behind the bunker. That had been cagey. Good tradecraft. If Adam had not followed her, or if she had been more surveillance conscious and forced him to keep his distance, he would never have observed their meeting.

His heart pounded as he hurtled down the wooded path. The whine of the golf cart melted away. How fast could carts go? The path intersected Bayview Drive, and he turned right and headed east. The old man could be headed to the ferry terminal. Adam glanced at his watch. The afternoon ferry departed at two. He needed to reach the ferry, get a ticket, and figure out how to follow the man out of the New Bedford terminal. Hard to do without a car. Maybe he could photograph him and his license plate. That would have to be enough.

Adam passed Broadway, which led to the marina. At the base of the hill, across Cuttyhunk Harbor, the ferry had docked beside the old Coast Guard terminal. Half a mile away. There was no sign of the cart, but the old man may have parked behind the terminal.

Adam hustled down the street. No sign of Fang either. She must have returned to Forever Technology. If she had planned to leave with the old man, they would have both taken the cart.

He jogged down the street and drew a stare from a middle-aged man driving a pickup truck, the only gas-powered vehicle he'd seen all day. Sweat moistened Adam's forehead and dripped down his back. His shoes had not been designed for running, and they rubbed his toes raw. Remember that next time. Function over form. He had not been out of DEA for long, but already his tactical sensibilities had withered.

He reached the fork and bounded past parked carts to the terminal. A quick glance at his watch confirmed the ferry would leave in two minutes.

He dashed around the terminal. A young man wearing khakis and a blue long-sleeved shirt exited the gatehouse and grabbed the gangplank.

"Hold on," Adam shouted.

The kid stopped. "Running late?"

"I need a ticket."

"Come aboard. I'll sell you a pass once we're underway."

Adam scampered up the plank as an old couple watched him with obvious amusement. "Just made it."

A dozen people milled around inside the main cabin, and a few souls braved the elements on the upper deck. The horn blew, making him jump, and the gangplank retracted. Adam walked around the lower deck and looked through the cabin's windows, but the glare made it difficult to see. The old man must have spotted him racing to the boat, so what was the point of staying outside? Adam was just another passenger, late for a meeting on the mainland. He opened the cabin door and entered. Passengers sat on plastic chairs, but the old Asian man was not among them.

Outside, the crew cast off their lines, then the captain edged the boat away from the pier. The ferry rotated and headed into the harbor. Adam exited the cabin and climbed an exterior stairwell to the second deck. More passengers reclined in chairs behind the cockpit, but not his target. Adam walked along the railing to the bow. He turned the corner and stared at the last bench. Unoccupied.

The man had not boarded the ferry.

Adam looked back at Cuttyhunk as a fifty-foot Sea Ray motorboat roared away from the marina. Adam shielded his eyes from the sun and squinted. His target stood in the yacht's bow.

The old man looked at him and smiled.

CHAPTER FIFTY-THREE

Harry rolled his eyes when Edna barged into his office.

"That son of a bitch is a killer," she said.

Harry took off his glasses and leaned back with a sigh. "Who's a killer? Bryce Hastings?"

"No. Well maybe, but I'm talking about Felix Suggs, his security chief."

Harry massaged the bridge of his nose. "We already talked about this."

"I'm writing my follow-up on Locke's death. I just met a new source—a mercenary who worked with Suggs in Sudan. He told me Suggs massacred civilians in Darfur."

Harry leaned forward and placed his elbows on the desk. "Where's the proof?"

"He witnessed Suggs kill a group of civilians and behead a teenage boy with a machete."

"Jesus. And he's willing to go on record?"

"Well, no. Not yet."

Harry groaned. "Then why is he coming forward?"

"I sought him out. It took me some time, but I identified Global Conflict Solutions employees who worked during the same time period as Suggs. I cross-referenced them with Suggs's CV that's posted on Forever's website."

"What's your source's motivation? If he's trying to blow the whistle on Suggs or Global Conflict Solutions, why not go on record?"

Edna did not want to tell Harry about the money. If she told him Brock Gibson had only spoken to her because she paid him, Harry would dismiss her source out of hand. Money was a fine motivator, but it undermined Gibson's credibility. And her journalistic integrity. A source could say anything for profit. Gibson was a scumbag, and probably a killer. He had not mentioned his role in the massacre, and as far as she knew, he had never reported it. But she believed him.

"He's afraid of Suggs," she said.

"We don't report on genocides here," Harry said. "But if you can corroborate his story, we'll do something with it. What does this have to do with Sarah Smith and Thomas Locke?"

"The state police are calling Locke's death suspicious, and Bryce Hastings employed a murderer as his chief of security. Do I have to explain the relevance to you?"

"I see you've been working on your abrasive personality," Harry said.

"If Locke was murdered, it had something to do with Forever Technology. And that makes Suggs a primary suspect."

"Listen, Edna. That's fine as a working theory, but all I'm hearing is supposition and innuendo. If you want to see a word of this in print, you must connect the dots for readers. And connect them with corroborated evidence. We won't publicly slander Bryce Hastings, Felix Suggs, or anyone else at Forever Technology. Not based on your unproven theory."

"But—"

"There is a documentary series coming to town next week. Some artist who has been following the plight of North Atlantic whales. Get the schedule and showtimes. I want seven-hundred words on the research project."

"Jesus, Harry. I just told—"

"And I want it on my desk by Friday. Or you're fired."

Edna opened her mouth and then stopped. If she lost this job, where would she go? A weekly newspaper in a tiny New England town? She could not make her mortgage with that kind of job. How had she ended up here?

"Well?" he asked.

"I'll get you the story, but I'm going to corroborate my source's information. If that's okay with you."

"Do it on your own time and only after you deliver the stories our subscribers want to read. I'm not losing a full-time staff reporter to a wild goose chase because she wants to rehabilitate her reputation."

All that Edna had ever wanted was for someone to pay attention to her. Just someone to listen to her. It had been a pipedream, and one her personality made her incapable of fulfilling.

"And if I get you the corroboration, you'll run the story?"

"You prove Forever Technology's chief security officer committed a war crime, and yes, I'll put it on the front page."

CHAPTER FIFTY-FOUR

Effie snored beside Adam in their queen-sized bed, and he watched her sleep. She was brilliant and kind, empathetic and strong, the human embodiment of man's virtues. She had worn her values like a uniform, honoring her beliefs through her behavior. Their shared morals, epistemology, and quest to excel had drawn them together since the day they met.

Effie was a contradiction. She was gorgeous and deep. Fun-loving and intellectual. Analytical and charismatic. A literary author who recited football statistics. How many women composed poetry and played fantasy football? They had met by chance at a sports bar, where Adam had stopped for a bite and Effie had come to watch the AFC Championship. Adam enjoyed watching sports, but he preferred to play them. Effie was a professional watcher. She could recite scoring records like a historian, and she had won her fantasy football league three years in a row.

Adam stared at her face, happy she could sleep and escape the psychological horror of her life-threatening disease. She was strong, but everyone had limits. Effie winced in pain and opened her eyes, wide and child-like. She took a moment to orient herself. He smiled, and she smiled back before her eyelids closed and her snoring resumed.

His phone rang. Svetlana. He glanced at the time. Eleven o'clock. Why was she calling so late? He answered.

"You okay?" he whispered.

"The house feels wrong," she said.

Adam sat up in bed. "What do you mean? Did you hear something?"

"There's nothing to hear. I'm alone."

Adam relaxed. She was grieving, not in danger. "You're not alone. You have Effie and me."

"The house is cold. Life is cold." She slurred her words. Was she drunk or just tired? Maybe it was despair.

"Do you need anything? What can I do to help?"

"What can anyone do? Tommy's gone." She *had* been drinking. Svetlana held the somber, fatalistic outlook common in Russia, and alcohol seemed to transport her onto the icy steppe.

"Maybe I can swing by tomorrow," he said.

"Please. I'm lost."

Adam had spent a decade investigating the horrors visited on the world by organized criminals, but his talent was hunting terrorists and drug traffickers, not dealing with victims. Tommy's death had brought the human suffering in the aftermath of crime to his doorstep.

"I'll come when I'm free. Investigating Tommy's death has consumed my waking hours."

"I'm worried about you. At least tell me you've learned something."

How much should he share? Adam looked at Effie. She shifted, but still appeared to be asleep. "You may be onto something," he said. "Could Bryce have been dealing with China?"

"Why do you say that?"

"After we spoke, I talked to a Chinese scientist at Forever. Something about her demeanor made me suspicious, and—"

"You've found something."

"I followed her. She met with an older Asian man."

"Who?"

"I don't know, but it looked like a covert meeting."

"How could you tell?" Svetlana seemed less intoxicated, more alert.

"She violated rules by going downtown, and his tradecraft was evident. I don't know, maybe I'm reading too much into it, but if you're right and Bryce was selling the technology, it could be relevant."

"You need to stop Bryce."

"I'm trying. I'm—"

"You'll come tomorrow?" she asked.

Adam sighed. "I'll take the Whaler in the afternoon."

"Thank you." She hung up.

Adam set the phone on the nightstand and lay down.

"Who was that?" Effie asked.

"Sorry to wake you."

She looked at the clock. "It's late."

"Svetlana is having trouble coping."

"She's calling you this late?" Effie raised up on her elbow.

"Be careful. You don't want to pull your biopsy stitches."

Effie rubbed her eyes. "Calling at eleven seems too intimate. I'm throwing a penalty flag."

"She's in shock. That's all. I don't want to abandon her."

"Hmm."

"It's fine. She just needs some hand holding. Figuratively."

"Maybe I should have married you when you asked."

"Which time?" Adam asked.

"I love you."

"I love you more."

CHAPTER FIFTY-FIVE

The shiny black box sat on the laboratory table. Fang ran her fingertips over its cool steel as it hummed and clicked. It was slightly bigger than a toaster, but the most intelligent artificial being in the world. Was that what it was? A being? It possessed general intelligence and could solve complex problems, but did that make it an entity? Was it self-aware? If it contained the experience and biases of its host brain, and it thought and reasoned almost exactly like the person she had downloaded, did it matter if it understood it was a computer? Did reasoning and learning give it life? A lab rat had a similar functionality and consciousness, depending on the definition, and a rat was alive. Not as valuable as a human, but a life, nonetheless. Even rats were not as complicated as Lazarus with an Apep processor.

"She's a beauty," Shlomo said.

Fang spun around. "How did you know I was here?"

"Your fragrance. Yves Saint Laurent, I believe. Also, the little wheeze you get when you're excited, and the faint odor of cigarette smoke on your clothes. Foreign tobacco, right? This is the second time I've smelled it on you this week."

She should have been more careful. Of all the threats she faced, Shlomo had seemed the most benign. But the blind man saw everything. "Remarkable."

"The human brain is quite amazing. It adapts. After I lost my sight, my other senses went into overdrive. Our bodies seek to survive. Did you know parts of my brain have actually grown in response to my infirmity?"

"Of course. I just didn't think—"

"What are you doing at my workstation?"

This was why she had prepared to be confronted. She assumed they would eventually catch her doing something wrong. Behavior she found abhorrent. And now Shlomo, the blind philosopher, was going to make her lie to his face. She did not believe in God, so it was not a sin, but the Party had told her lying was immoral. That's what the communists would say, if they had not been the ones asking her to do it.

"I wanted to see it with my own eyes," she said.

"Huh." Shlomo rubbed his chin.

She gazed at his sightless eyes, and a wave of guilt passed over her. "I am sorry. I did not mean . . . it was an awful choice of words."

Shlomo groped and patted her shoulder. "No need to fret. I know I'm blind."

"It is just that—"

"But my ears work. I may have lost the power of sight, but I see things clearly."

"I do not understand," she said.

"The tone of your voice tells me you do. You could have asked me to demonstrate Apep inside Lazarus, but you didn't. Instead, you came here yourself. Why?"

"Apep?" she asked, pretending not to remember.

"The great destroyer. Darkness and nonbeing, the unnatural world. He's the engine in our AI brain. Actually, he's more of a cryptographic device that allows heuristics to manipulate the blockchain-protected data. But I explained that before. Now, tell me child, what is it you seek?"

"I wanted to check data. I—"

"The truth, please."

She could not admit she had planned to download the cryptographic key. If she uttered those words, he would inform security and her world would come crashing down. What would Xiu Yän do if they arrested her?

"I had to see it myself," she said, "and decide how I feel."

"You've got *chutzpah*. But you've been working on this project for years. We've all strived for this."

"Mapping neural processes and creating digital systems, not recreating a mind," she said. "Theoretically, I understood the ramifications, but now that you have taken a major step forward . . . I do not know. It is real now."

"Maybe more real than you think."

"What do you mean?" she asked.

The phone rang on the desk, and Shlomo picked up. "Dr. Perlman. Yes, Okay. Come down. I'll wait." He hung up. "That was Mr. Suggs. He's on his way here to discuss additional security measures."

Fang's heart jumped. "Extra measures?"

"Apparently, there's been some kind of breach."

"When? How?"

"I'm afraid Mr. Suggs takes his business too seriously to share details with me. But he wants to talk about securing Lazarus and Apep."

"He is coming now?"

"Does he scare you, child?"

"He makes me uncomfortable. I will go."

"Yes, run along."

Fang hurried out of the lab, keeping her portable hard drive hidden under her lab coat. She reached the stairway as the elevator door dinged. She threw open the door and bolted upstairs.

CHAPTER FIFTY-SIX

Effie squirmed in pain on a plastic chair in the Oncology Ward. Did she ever experience a moment free of suffering or discomfort? Adam could not remember the days before her disease, before his world turned upside down.

"I'm going to get a coffee," he said. "Do you want one?"

She looked up with a pinched face and shook her head. His heart broke for her.

Adam ambled through the waiting room past a dozen people, all senior citizens. Cancer struck everyone, if they lived long enough, but Effie had just turned thirty and was too young to deal with end-of-life issues. He avoided eye contact to avoid intruding on patients' whispered conversations, and because he could not offer another ounce of empathy. Effie's illness had consumed his every moment since her diagnosis. His reservoir was empty. His terror had become a physical weight, bearing down on him, hunching his back, and bowing his head. He clung to a ledge with aching fingertips, knowing he would fall. He had nothing left.

He stopped at a beverage counter, slipped a K-cup into a coffee machine, and positioned a paper cup beneath the spigot. He pressed the brew button and waited as the machine gurgled. Liquid drizzled into the cup and the scent of caffeinated hazelnut warmed him. He closed his eyes and floated out of his body in a meditative moment, replenishing his reserves and recharging his resolve. He needed to be strong for Effie, be there for whatever she required. Stopping to consider what life would look like if the unthinkable occurred would tear his soul from his body. If that happened, Effie could not lean on him for strength.

The machine hissed and steamed. He grabbed the cup and headed back to the waiting room. He slid into the seat beside her, but she did not look up. He reached down and squeezed her knee.

I'm here for you.

Adam was not a doctor and did not understand all the science behind what was happening to his soulmate. The cancer—the malignancy—was an invader, eating away at her cells, spreading through her body and destroying everything in its path. If the chemotherapy, radiation, and surgeries could not remove all of it, she would be finished. He wanted to offer better counsel, give advice on experts and experimental procedures, but how could he make those recommendations? Should he go to medical school? Should he study on his own? Online ratings and reviews of doctors were untrustworthy, as were many medical professionals. And sometimes, a little knowledge could be dangerous. Adam did not trust himself to contradict her doctors unless their advice seemed intuitively wrong.

"Ms. Hope," a plump, brunette nurse called from an open doorway on the other side of the waiting room.

Effie looked up and sighed. She leaned forward, and Adam helped her to her feet. "This is it," she said. The doctor would give them the results from her recent high-density MRIs and biopsies of her chest and abdomen.

"Whatever the results, we will get through it together," he said.

They followed the nurse down the tiled hallway, cold and sterile, and his stomach rolled, as if he were walking to his execution. They passed tiny examination rooms with tables covered with butcher paper, and counters littered with glass vials containing swabs and cotton balls. He followed her into a microscopic office with two chairs and a desk and a view of the street. Outside, life somehow continued as if nothing was wrong.

Dr. Rosenblatt blew into the room and sank into the chair behind his desk. "Good afternoon, Ms. Hope."

"Dr. Rosenblatt," Adam said, as he assisted Effie into a chair.

"I hope you didn't wait too long," Rosenblatt said. "I'm running behind today."

Uh-oh. Dr. Rosenblatt had never engaged in small talk during their previous visits.

"Did you get my results?" Effie asked, her voice a whisper.

Dr. Rosenblatt cleared his throat.

This can't be good.

"I'm afraid it's not encouraging news," he said.

A sob escaped Effie's lips, and her body convulsed. Adam wrapped his arm around her. Her body shook.

"How bad is it?" Adam asked. His eyes burned.

"Four of the five biopsies showed malignancy. It's grade four."

Adam grit his teeth, willing away his emotion. A tear escaped and rolled down his cheek. He turned his head away from Effie. "What does that mean?" he asked, knowing exactly what it meant.

"The cancer has spread to her stomach and lungs. It—"

"Is there anything we can do?" Effie asked. Her voice was tiny and innocent, a young girl in the principal's office. But it also contained a glimmer of strength, a sign of the fighter within.

"There are experimental drugs we can try," Rosenblatt said. "More radical procedures. Unproven but promising therapies."

"What are her chances?" Adam asked.

"We don't like to give percentages. Every patient is different. Medical histories impact cancers differently. The patient's constitution—"

"But it's stage four?" Effie asked.

The doctor's eyes widened, and he resumed his normal air of superiority. "It became stage four when it spread from your liver. We removed a significant amount of your liver and lower intestine in the last surgery. I excised a large margin. I had hoped we had gotten it all."

"We left some?" she asked. "We missed some of the tumor?"

"We excised everything we saw on the high-density MRIs, and much more. This spread means the cancer metastasized. It's in your blood. Microscopic cells are everywhere."

"Surgery is no longer an option?" Adam asked.

"We can cut out the tumors we biopsied, but the cancer has affected multiple systems. It—"

"How do we kill it?" Effie asked.

Adam wanted to climb inside her body and destroy this disease. He would grab a machine-gun and slaughter anything that threatened her, but his skills were worthless against the enemy within.

"We can try stronger chemotherapy," Rosenblatt said. "I mentioned some experimental therapies. The choice is yours."

"What does that mean?" Adam asked. "Now that surgery is not an option, why wouldn't we try these options?"

"At this stage, the chance of radical intervention succeeding is unlikely, and the chemotherapies I'm considering have significant side effects. In your weakened condition, they can pose significant risks in themselves."

"Risks?" Effie asked.

"They'll wipe out whatever's left of your immune system. The hope is they will destroy the cancer too, but they leave you open for serious infection, and ironically, make your body less capable of fighting the cancer. There are other side effects as well, from seizures to heart failure. I've compiled literature explaining your options for you to review at home."

"We'll do whatever it takes," Adam said. "If giving up is the alternative we don't—"

"Ms. Hope," Rosenblatt said, "I'll support whatever course of action you choose, but I urge you to give it serious thought. If we can't stop the cancer, you may not want to further deteriorate your health for whatever time you have left."

The time she had left. Adam wanted to vomit. "What can we—"

Effie grabbed his hand. "It's okay, Adam. The clock's running out." She looked at the doctor, her tears gone. "How much time?"

"These things are hard to predict. Assuming we don't continue therapy, I'd estimate one month, maybe less."

Effie squeezed Adam's hand until he thought she would draw blood. Her body heaved beneath his arm.

"Is there anything . . . any reason to hope?" Adam asked.

"These diseases are unpredictable. I've read about cases where patients had no statistical chance of survival, and the disease disappeared on its own, but that's rare and I don't want to encourage unrealistic expectations. The prognosis I'm giving you is not good."

"You've read about those cases," Adam said, "but have you ever seen a patient with a similar diagnosis recover?"

"No."

"Put a number on it." Adam said. "What are her chances?"

"One percent."

CHAPTER FIFTY-SEVEN

Adam moved out of Bryce's way on the archery range. "Why did you enter an industry infected with backstabbing and industrial espionage?"

Bryce plucked an arrow from his quiver and threaded the bowstring into the notch. Bryce stared at the distant target—his face was a mask of stone. Something seemed to come over him when he held the bow. He seemed completely in the moment, oblivious to the world, as if his employees' deaths, the police investigation, and competitors circling like sharks had all disappeared. Had Bryce even heard Adam's question?

God, he was eccentric.

Bryce drew the waxed string back, held his breath, then released the arrow.

Thwack.

Adam squinted and looked down range. Bullseye.

"Did you hear my question?" Adam asked.

"You wanted to know what attracted me to the tech sector and why I've devoted my life to artificial intelligence?"

"That's right." Adam wanted to establish rapport, create a connection, something to motivate Bryce to save Effie. Bryce had agreed to meet at his house again, so maybe he already felt a connection. Tommy had been Bryce's closest confidante. Maybe when Bryce looked at Adam, he saw Tommy.

A drop of rain splattered on Adam's cheek. Dark storm clouds raced across the sky. The forecast predicted the late-season hurricane that had thrashed the Caribbean would sustain category-one winds by the time it struck New England.

"Early on," Bryce said, "I realized how AI could alter people's happiness. I recognized it before most, which gave me the market advantage I needed. Happiness is the key to life, isn't it?"

"Is it?" Adam asked. "I've locked up people for doing reprehensible things while chasing happiness."

"I'm not talking about short-term happiness, like sensory pleasure. Euphoria fades quickly. I mean long-term happiness that comes from satisfying cravings created through evolution, such as bettering your life, building a family, finding love. Those pursuits fulfill us and provide profound and lasting happiness, not the temporal intoxication and ecstasy we get from sex or drugs but a deep and lasting contentment."

Bryce drew another arrow and threaded it. His body stilled.

"And AI can improve that?" Adam asked.

Bryce answered without taking his eyes off the target. "In every way imaginable. We can improve every human activity with AI. That's true whether we develop predictive models, innovate technological breakthroughs, or extend life through bioengineering. AI can enhance all of it."

Bryce loosed the arrow.

Thwack.

Adam shaded his eyes and inspected the target. Another bullseye. "That's why you entered the field?"

"Studying philosophy made me feel like a historian rehashing age-old debates, questions without definitive answers. Switching to computer engineering allowed me to affect people's lives, now and in the future. Philosophers have debated the meaning of life for thousands of years, but I can use AI to answer those questions and change the way people interact with the world. Later, when I discovered the potential for eternal life, I sold my Happiness Institute and founded Forever Technology."

"But you didn't become a scientist."

"I'm smart, but my natural talents involve more emotional intelligence than classic IQ. My gift is the ability to divine the future and lead people toward my vision."

It sprinkled, and Adam scanned the darkening clouds. "I need to ask you something."

"We should get back before we get blown off this hill."

Enough with the incremental raises. It was time for Adam to lay his cards on the table. "My girlfriend is dying."

Bryce nodded. "I know."

"I need you to help her."

Bryce expelled a long breath and stared out to sea. "We're years away from using AI to destroy cancer. We—"

"But you can preserve her mind. Download her."

Bryce faced him. "We're still in the experimental stage. I understand how difficult this must be for—"

"I know you've downloaded consciousness."

"What?" Bryce's face hardened, as it had on the range. Total concentration.

"You've digitized human minds. Real people. And you've downloaded their data. I know you're creating replica brains using AI. It's what you're doing with Black Diamond."

"Whoever told you that—"

"I want you to preserve Effie's mind. Once the technology catches up, I can have her back."

Bryce snatched the last arrow out of the quiver without taking his eyes off Adam. "How did you learn about Black Diamond?"

"It doesn't matter."

"We had a break-in. Here at my house. Someone rummaged through my files."

"You have to save her."

Bryce shook his head. "It's not possible. What you think you know is wrong. We are on the pointy edge of this technology. It's too experimental. I can't take chances with it. I—"

"Please."

"Things have gone wrong. You don't understand."

"I'm willing to take that chance."

"But I'm not," Bryce said. "One public disaster and we're finished."

"But you've been doing it."

"The technology isn't ready. Not yet. And people can't know what we're doing. They won't understand. The Feds will shut us down. Our competitors will eat us alive. Only a handful of people have access to our research, out of necessity. I need scientists like Shlomo to make the science work and business minds like your brother's to fund it. We're like a football team here. Everyone has a role to play."

"Tommy's gone."

Bryce's face clouded like the oncoming storm. He threaded the arrow and turned to stone. "Tommy attracted our venture capital. I don't know how I'll replace him."

"You're worth a billion dollars and you're worried about funding?"

"I'm in big tech, which means I'm always worried about funding. Net worth is hard to calculate, and I need fluidity to bring our projects to market. And I must do it first if I want to keep the dollars flowing."

"If you can extend people's lives for thirty or forty years, or forever, you're sitting on a gold mine."

"Gold can be stolen, and we must be the first to launch life-extending tech if we want to dominate the market. We came here to protect our technology from prying eyes. I couldn't even trust my people in Palo Alto, so I only brought my most trusted and necessary staff with me—people with the skills necessary to cross the finish line. I had to go underground to escape the competition. And the press."

"There's a mole in your shop," Adam said. "Two of your people are dead."

Bryce drew the bowstring back, inhaled, and held it. He lowered the arrowhead. He became a statue, then he released the fletching. The bow sang.

The arrow whooshed through the air. It shattered the shaft of the last arrow and pierced the ten-ring.

"I know how to deal with my enemies," Bryce said.

CHAPTER FIFTY-EIGHT

Edna perched on a vintage Queen Anne chair in the anteroom to State Representative Dick Sheppard's office. She leafed through her notebook, and her body tingled with excitement. She had told no one at the Cape Cod Post about this interview, which would piss off Harry, but when he read what she had discovered, all would be forgiven.

Edna had researched Forever Technology's financial records until her eyes hurt, but the spreadsheets and voluminous entries had been far too complicated for her to decipher any wrongdoing. Forever employed world-class accountants to handle its books, and it would take a forensics team to find fraudulent activity. More likely, any criminal wrongdoing had evaded the accounting process. So, Edna had switched her focus to Forever's employees on Cuttyhunk.

"Representative Sheppard will see you now," his secretary, or intern, or staffer, or whatever title Sheppard had given the pretty girl with perky tits, said.

Edna followed her into the office. Sheppard walked around his desk and met her with a hearty two-handed shake.

"Thanks for agreeing to an interview," Edna said.

"I'm always happy to accommodate members of the press."

She'd see how happy he would be in a few minutes. "The Cape Cod Post thanks you."

He motioned to a chair in front of his desk, then returned to his seat and leaned back. The leather squeaked, and he flashed a politician's smile. "I have ten minutes, so let's jump right in, shall we?

"I'm happy to get to the point. How much money has Forever Technology given you?" The smile slid off his face. Edna let her question hang in the air, like a fart at a dinner party.

"Excuse me?"

"Forever Technology moved to Cuttyhunk, as you know. I was looking into their financial records and—"

"I'm aware of Bryce Hasting's company," Shepard said, "but far as I know, he has donated nothing to my campaign."

"Oh, he's given you three thousand dollars. He declared it, and so did your campaign, but that's not what I'm referring to. I'm talking about the money Thomas Locke used to purchase a second beach house on Martha's Vineyard."

The smile had vanished from Shepard's face, and the sides of his jaw bulged as he ground his teeth. Despite his bronze tan, the color drained from his face. "I don't—"

"You see," Edna continued, "I started by looking at the company and got nowhere. But when I investigated publicly available financial records of Forever Technology's key employees, I found Mr. Locke's real estate purchase."

"I'm not involved with that house. I—"

"I also looked in the financial records for you and Representative Charney, as well as our state senators, Duke County officials, and Cuttyhunk selectmen—just to see what I could find."

"I don't know what you're getting at, and I don't appreciate—"

"Don't get your boxers in a twist," Edna said. "And I'd be careful what you deny. Like you were careful not to declare any gifts from Mr. Hastings, Mr. Locke, or anyone else. A normal audit searching the usual filings would never have found it. But I looked at the situation differently. Mr. Hastings is a billionaire, and for his company to succeed in Massachusetts, he requires the goodwill of cronies. So, I started with people like you, and with associates of Mr. Hastings."

"This meeting is over."

"If you want to end our interview without commenting on these bribery allegations, that's fine."

"I won't sit here and listen to slanderous accusations," he said.

"Mr. Hastings is involved in some very controversial scientific research. It was only a matter of time before those in power squeezed him. But he's clever, you see. He put you in his pocket before you realized what he was doing, and he got you for cheap. A beach house is nothing. His technology is worth what, hundreds of billions? If you had held out, you could have become a ruler of the universe, but you went for the quick buck. The sure money."

"That's it," Sheppard said. "We're done here." He came around the desk.

"I'm happy to leave. I don't need your confession to write an exposé."

"There's nothing to confess, dammit."

"I wouldn't act so high and mighty before I asked my wife about the pictures she posted on Facebook."

Sheppard stopped. "What?"

"It took me less than an hour. I found her contacts on social media and sent them friend requests until someone accepted. Then I sent one to your wife. I assume she saw the mutual friend before she clicked accept. I scrolled through her pictures and was surprised and appalled," she said with a smirk, "to find pictures of you toasting with champagne flutes at the beach house on Martha's Vineyard. The same house Thomas Locke purchased."

Sheppard's eyes darted to the phone.

Edna grinned. She was a Cheshire cat toying with a mouse. "You can call her and ask her to take it down, but I've already archived the photos and taken screenshots. I'll bet Thomas Locke listed the property purchase as a tax write-off. I'm sure it won't take long for investigators to link Forever Technology's money to the house. And then to you."

"I've done nothing wrong."

"I guess that's for a grand jury to decide," Edna said. "If I choose to go public with this tidbit."

Something flashed in Sheppard's eyes. The glimmer of a way out? The return of his confidence? "What do you want?"

"Bryce Hastings. I want to know what he's doing in Cuttyhunk. What was his involvement in the deaths of Sarah Smith and Thomas Locke?"

"I don't know. I don't understand what they're doing. Not exactly."

Edna cocked her head and smiled. "But you'll find out for me, won't you?"

Sheppard glanced at the door, then back at her. "Son of a bitch." He cracked his knuckles. His eyes flared for a moment. "And you won't run the story?"

"You help me link Hastings to those murders, and I'll spend the next year writing about the takedown of the world's wealthiest man." And getting my Pulitzer. A wave of excitement welled in her belly.

"And the story about me?"

"Why would I care about the potential low-level corruption of a state official after I've broken the most sensational story of the century? By the way, what were you offering him? Tax breaks, special dispensations?"

Sheppard stared at the floor. "It doesn't matter now."

"No, it doesn't. Do we have a deal?"

"You're a real bitch."

"I get that a lot. Deal?"

"I'll get you your story."

CHAPTER FIFTY-NINE

Adam shifted uncomfortably on a leather chair in Fang's darkened living room and stared at the front door, waiting for her to come home. Effie's health had declined rapidly, and she had little time left. If Adam was going to save any part of her, he needed to act now.

Headlights flashed across the windows, briefly illuminating the room, then the shuttle bus's engine ticked as it idled, and passengers disembarked.

Breaking into Fang's residence was another felony. Adam took an enormous risk, but he needed to pressure her, shock her into doing his bidding. She had already tried to help, but now he required her to imperil her career and her freedom. If she refused and had him arrested, he could spend Effie's last days behind bars.

His eyes darted to the back hallway. He still had time to flee. Keys rattled in the front door's lock. Adam did not move. He had to do this for Effie. Nothing else mattered.

Fang entered. She locked the door behind her, then hung her coat and purse on hooks above a polished maple console. She flicked on the light.

Fang screamed.

Adam didn't speak. At DEA, he had mastered motivating his sources to take chances. Now, he needed to summon all his experience and skill because nothing he had done before was more important than this.

"What are you doing here?" Fang's eyes glowed with anger.

"I saw you on Bunker Hill."

She flinched. "What?"

"I saw your secret meeting, and I know what you're doing."

"My uncle, he—"

"Save your lies for the FBI," Adam said. He was bluffing but needed leverage.

Fang's hands shook. She clutched her abdomen. "You called the FBI?"

"Not yet."

She took half a step back. "You can't prove anything. I did nothing."

"You did. And I'll prove it, unless—"

"What do you want?" Her glare could melt plastic.

Adam backed her against the living room wall. "I need you to upload Effie and implant her mind into one of those machines."

"I can't. You know that. They said—"

"Fuck them. They have the capability, and you know it. I'm willing to do whatever is necessary to preserve Effie. I'll take Forever Technology down if I must. I'll take you down too."

"I already tried to help."

"Tell me about the man on Bunker Hill."

Fang paced. "Even if I wanted to map your girlfriend's mind, you said she's bedridden. How would we get her to the lab?"

"You'd have to do it at our home."

"Impossible. She needs MRIs, CT scans, and real-time monitoring while I do it. I need the computers and machinery at Forever. And I need assistance."

"I'll support you."

"You don't know what you're doing."

"Teach me."

Fang fingered her necklace. "Let's say we figure out a way to get your girlfriend into Forever, and we somehow manage to accurately map her synapses and download the data. Shlomo controls Lazarus and Apep."

"Apep?" Adam asked.

"The Egyptian deity of Chaos. Apep is the clever name they've given the cryptographic key inside the synthetic Lazarus brain. It's what accesses the data and heuristics that make the downloaded consciousness function. Shlomo has a sense of humor. But it doesn't matter what they call it. They haven't given me total access."

"We sneak in," Adam said.

"Suggs is on alert."

"We'll do it at night."

Fang ran her fingers through her silky hair. "Then what? Let's say we somehow pull it off. Your girlfriend's data would be on Forever's servers in Palo Alto, hidden in the blockchain. You'll need Apep to access it."

"We'll borrow it."

"Borrow it?" she asked.

"We'll sneak Apep out and you download the cryptographic key to Effie's mind onto something else. Then we return it to the lab. If the worst happens, I'll still have a piece of her. Something I can hold until the technology is ready."

"I can't," Fang said. "We'll get caught. They're planning to increase security measures."

Adrenalin jolted Adam's system. "Which measures?"

"Shlomo told me there was a break-in. They want to ensure Lazarus and Apep are safe."

"Then we need to do it soon. Tomorrow."

"I can't. I—"

"Help me save her." Adam grabbed her hands. "Please. I'll do anything."

Fang considered the floor and wrung her hands. Her fingers turned white. She raised her eyes to meet his. "You'll find out who killed them?"

"I promise."

"I'll help you," she whispered.

Adam left out the back door and hiked through the woods to his car. His heart filled with promise. With Fang, he could access the technology and preserve Effie's existence. It was a victory. The one that mattered most.

But was Fang telling the truth? If she was involved with Bryce's sale of the technology to China, would she call the police and report him? Adam needed Black Diamond to save Effie, but he also wanted to bring Tommy's killer to justice. If Bryce had murdered Tommy, would the CEO's arrest mean the end of Black Diamond and destroy Adam's chance of saving Effie? What if Adam failed to solve the murders and Bryce sold Black Diamond to Russia or China and the data disappeared behind a totalitarian wall? What would happen to Effie then?

Adam rubbed his face and stared up at the dark sky. He had to solve Tommy's murder, even if Bryce had killed him. He had to find justice for his family, and to save Effie, he also needed to protect the technology. How could he achieve both goals? Adam had been a talented agent, but this would take all his professional skills and every bit of his strength. He could not fail.

Effie's life hung in the balance.

CHAPTER SIXTY

Adam scanned the boats tied to Cuttyhunk's pier. Most belonged to residents, but even though tourist season had ended, unseasonably warm weather brought a steady stream of visitors. Beyond the docks, a dozen sailboats bobbed at their moorings. Most had not moved since he had first set foot on the island. Why did people own boats and not enjoy them?

Svetlana had asked to meet, saying she had something important to discuss. He had to make it quick, then hurry home to prepare Effie for the download. Fang had promised to have the monitoring equipment ready if Adam could get Effie into the lab after everyone left. Suggs had rejected Adam's request for a visitor pass, but a quick call to Bryce explaining that Effie wanted to see his office while she was still healthy enough had forced Suggs to approve it. Bryce had even offered to give Effie a tour himself, and Adam had stammered before explaining Effie was uncomfortable with her appearance and preferred to come when the building was empty. Adam had lied, saying he would give her a tour later in the week—because for what they had planned, they needed privacy.

Adam walked the length of the dock. Where was Svetlana?

The hum of a diesel engine caught his attention, and a forty-foot cabin cruiser roared into the harbor, leaving a two-foot wake in the no-wake zone. That had to be Svetlana. Was she drunk? She had sounded saucy on the phone, but it had been hard to tell. Svetlana had been drinking since she learned of Tommy's death.

The cabin cruiser's engines throttled back, and it coasted toward an open slip. The pier bobbed as the wake splashed against it. Svetlana emerged from the cabin and waved. He hurried across the pier to help her dock. She reversed the engine and edged against the pier until her plastic bumpers squealed against wood.

"Throw me a line and I'll tie you off," Adam yelled.

"I'm not setting foot on that island, not until Bryce is in jail. Jump onboard and we'll talk in the harbor where we have privacy."

She did not sound drunk but minimizing time alone with her was smart. "We can grab a crab roll in town," he said, "and stay away from Forever Technology."

"Get in. I prefer no one sees us together."

Adam sighed. He grabbed the gunwale and jumped onto the cruiser's deck. Svetlana climbed into the cockpit, and the engines roared to life. He ascended the ladder and stood behind her as she maneuvered the craft into the harbor.

"Can I help?" he asked.

"Go below and mix drinks. I'll take a vodka with a twist of lime."

"It's a little early in the day, and I have important business tonight."

"Don't be a wet blanket. I take mine on the rocks. If you don't want to drink, have a beer."

Only a serious drinker would classify having a beer as not drinking. He went below into the salon, a luxurious living space with the captain's desk, galley, and plush couches framing the dining table. Doors in the stern led to smaller berths, and the stateroom door stood open in the bow. The boat probably cost a million dollars. Why had Tommy needed his-and-hers yachts? Between the boats, cars, and mansion, Tommy had spent money like a Hollywood celebrity. He must have earned a fortune by tying his horse to Bryce's wagon.

Nice to be rich.

Adam peered out tinted windows as Cuttyhunk disappeared in the distance. At thirty knots, the cruiser stayed level and smooth.

He leaned into the companionway. "I thought we were staying in the harbor,"

"Out of sight, out of mind."

Adam searched the galley and located a well-stocked bar, containing everything from single-malt scotch to Russian vodka. Svetlana paid homage to her Russian heritage through her love of vodka. He poured two fingers of Baluga into a crystal glass, added ice, and jiggled it to cool the liquid. He grabbed a bottle of Sam Adams Oktoberfest from the mini fridge and took a swig. What would be better than laying on the couch, polishing off the rest of Svetlana's beer, and ignoring his troubles? He fantasized about burying his head in the sand for a moment, then dismissed it.

Ostriches were prey, and Adam was a predator.

The engine stopped, and the boat drifted to a rest. Svetlana came down the companionway backward, holding the rails as the yacht swayed in the wake. She moved gracefully, with no sign of intoxication.

He held out her drink, but she didn't take it.

"I got grease on my shirt," she said. "I'll change and be right out."

Shit. The last time she had changed clothes had resulted in an awkward moment. "Haven't we done this before?"

"No lingerie this time. I promise." She disappeared into the stateroom and shut the door.

"Why the urgency to meet?" He called after her. "And why the secrecy?"

"Get comfortable," her muffled voice came out of the cabin. "I'll be right out."

Nothing about being alone on a yacht with Svetlana made him comfortable. Adam fell back on the couch and drained a third of his beer. This has been the worst few months of his life. First Effie's cancer diagnosis, then his brother's death, then the metastasis. He'd given up a career he loved and now he worked for a man who may have murdered his brother—a man he depended upon to provide lifesaving technology to prevent Effie from disappearing forever.

Adam rested his elbows on his knees and dangled the beer from his fingertips. He stared at the floor. Could he save Effie? Would she have the strength to travel to the lab? If the cancer took her, would technology be able to recover her consciousness? Were his investigative skills enough to solve Tommy's murder? Had he ever been good enough?

He would know soon. One way or the other.

The cabin door creaked open, but he remained deep in thought. He needed a moment alone. Investigating a terrorist required one type of strength, but finding his brother's killer was different—personal and raw. He needed to succeed.

Svetlana's bare feet came into his view. He lifted his head, and his eyes followed her bare legs up. She was naked.

"See, I promised no lingerie this time." She held his shoulder for balance and slipped onto his lap.

He tried to rise, but she leaned into him and slid her arms around his neck. She kissed him on the mouth. Her tongue parted his lips.

He broke off the kiss and turned away. "Stop."

"I want you." She looked at him like a baby deer.

"Svetlana, no. This isn't right. You—"

"I want you inside me."

His manhood stirred, and he squirmed beneath her, hoping she hadn't noticed. "You don't know what you're saying. You're grieving and not thinking clearly."

She giggled. "I know you want me too. I saw the way you looked at my lingerie."

"I love Effie." He reached under her to lift her off his lap.

She grabbed him and squeezed. "You desire me, and I want you. I've lost everything, and I can't lose you too." She nuzzled his neck.

His heart raced with arousal and panic. He didn't want this. "Effie and I support you, but this is wrong. I love Effie. I'll always love Effie. You're Tommy's wife and you—"

"I *was* Tommy's wife." Her tone turned to ice. "Now what am I?"

Adam tried to rise, but she held onto him. Svetlana was gorgeous, sexy, a woman who turned every head when she entered a room. And her body. My God, her body. A lifetime of dancing had given her the perpetual figure of a nineteen-year-old woman. His body may have lusted after her, but not his mind. Not his soul. It would be easy to lie back, let this happen, release the tension that had been building within him for months.

But it was wrong.

He glanced at the Rolex Effie had given him. He would never betray her.

He removed Svetlana's hand from his lap and pulled her arm off his neck. "Listen to me. You're a beautiful woman, smart and capable of anything. I know you think your world is ending, and you're trying to find comfort, but this is not the way."

Her eyes teared. "Please."

"You're wealthy. You never need to worry about money. You'll find a way to cope with your sorrow, and once you do, you'll have the rest of your life in front of you."

"We're perfect together," she said. "I lost Tommy, and Effie is sick. Maybe we were meant to be together."

"I'm already with the woman I love. You'll find someone too. I promise—"

Her eyes brightened, and she sat upright. "Let's have a baby. Take me now, and let's start a family together."

Had she lost her mind?

Adam stood. "Dammit, Svetlana. You're not hearing me. I love you as a sister-in-law and nothing more. I'll support you, but I'm not doing this."

"I have resources—everything we need. Trust me. Hastings and Forever Technology won't survive. But I will. Be with me and you'll survive too."

"Get dressed. I'm taking us back to the pier." Adam climbed the companionway onto the deck. Clouds circled the island in the distance and a sprinkling of rain dimpled the water off the starboard side. The storm was coming.

He looked down through the hatch. Svetlana stood naked in the salon, staring at him. He entered the cockpit and fired up the engines.

How would he explain this to Effie?

CHAPTER SIXTY-ONE

It was late by the time Adam arrived home. He squeezed the keys in his hand, careful not to jingle them as he entered the house. Darkness shrouded the foyer, which meant Effie had retired before sunset. He paused and listened. The house remained still as a tomb.

The dread of telling Effie what Svetlana had done tightened his chest and threatened to explode his lungs. He had hoped to kiss Effie goodnight, but maybe a reprieve from that awkward conversation was better. He could tell her in the morning. Or maybe she didn't need to know at all. Would not telling her be a betrayal? If the roles were reversed, he would want to know. Ethical decisions that should come easily had become convoluted because of Effie's fragile emotional and physical states. Informing her that Svetlana had tried to sleep with him would increase Effie's stress, but keeping it secret also seemed wrong.

She deserved to know.

And what about Svetlana? What he had told her about grief clouding her judgment had been true. She must feel alone. Her world had crumbled, and it had happened in an instant. Violent death gave loved ones no chance to prepare. Sometimes that was better. Watching Effie suffer for months had been agonizing. Soul crushing. It had numbed him to the point where his feelings may never return. Every day brought a new level of horror.

Svetlana had not had time to say goodbye to Tommy, but in a sense, that had been merciful. What do you say to somebody before they ceased to exist?

Adam had planned to take Effie to the lab tonight, but Fang had claimed she wasn't ready. She needed to prep the machines and create a fake profile to accept Effie's data. They had to finish before everyone returned to work on Monday. One more day, she had told him. One more day to prepare.

Adam tiptoed up the stairs. He paused outside their bedroom and used both hands to unlatch the door. He peeked inside. Effie's ragged snoring echoed in the room. Her nocturnal snuffling had always been an endearing quality, but now that cancer had spread to her lungs, was her breathing difficulty caused by tissue damage? Were her coughs caused by allergies or a growing tumor? Living with cancer meant never having a calm moment. Never having a free thought. He craved a respite from the horror, but that would only come with a cure.

Or death.

Adam turned to head downstairs then stopped. His Canon EOD 80S camera perched on a tripod beside the bed. What had Effie been doing?

He snuck across the room and activated the camera. The memory card contained videos with Effie's face visible on the thumbnails. He unscrewed the camera from the tripod and carried it downstairs to the living room. Adam set it on the table and filled a tumbler with a healthy serving of McAllen twelve-year-old single-malt scotch. He usually drank it on the rocks, but this was not for pleasure. He needed it.

Adam took a long pull, and the dark liquid burned his throat and filled his sinuses with an earthy aroma. The first sip did that. He closed his eyes and breathed.

He lifted the camera and clicked the first thumbnail. The video played, and Effie's voice leaked out of the camera.

"I never wanted to make this video," she said. "But I know you'll appreciate it after I'm gone."

Adam's throat tightened, and he hit the pause button. Tears welled in his eyes. He scrolled to the next thumbnail and clicked it.

"Aunt Evelyn," Effie said, "I wanted to tell you how much you meant to me when I was a child. You—"

Adam clicked pause. These were goodbye videos to the people Effie loved. They were not his to watch. He had to return the camera and pretend he had not seen them. He would never invade her privacy like that.

Effie knew there was no hope. She knew the end was coming, yet she wore a brave mask for him. When they talked about experimental treatments, she had nodded and smiled, saying she would never give up. But she had prepared for death. She had accepted what he could not. Tears rolled down his cheeks and his body shook.

Effie was going to die.

CHAPTER SIXTY-TWO

Fang huddled beside Xiu Yän in the dark shadows behind the old Coast Guard Station. The moon flashed between storm clouds, and the wind sliced across the water and drove a mixture of rain and saltwater onto Cuttyhunk's shore.

"I assume you have the data I asked for," Xiu said.

His face was hard, without a glimmer of the man who had encouraged her to apply to college and who had helped her win her grant. Had that all been an act? A way to ingratiate himself and recruit her? His icy demeanor chilled her—too authentic to be a charade. Xiu had been a predator all along.

Fang fingered the hard drive in her pocket. "I am having trouble getting access."

He coiled like a scorpion. "What aren't you telling me?"

Did he know Adam had approached her? Should she tell him? Adam was a former federal agent. Would Xiu think they had compromised her or that she cooperated with the Americans? What a funny way to think of the people here. She had lived in the US for twenty percent of her life. These people believed in the free exchange of ideas, opportunity, and hard work. Deep inside, she was an American too. What if she didn't tell him and he found out? What would Xiu do to her? He would know she had been lying.

Maybe telling him would prove she was trustworthy. Maybe he could help her learn who had murdered Sarah and Tommy.

Unless Xiu had done it.

"Adam came to see me," she said, switching to Mandarin.

Xiu did not blink. He did not move. A wax statue. "When?"

"Yesterday. He broke into my house. He was sitting in my living room."

Xiu stayed silent. Waiting.

"He saw me talking to you," she said.

Xiu's eyes darted toward the road, as if federal agents were about to fast-rope onto the street. "What did you tell him?"

"That you were my uncle. But he didn't believe me. He said he would go to the FBI if—"

Xiu slid his hand into the pocket of his overcoat. He looked over her shoulder at the deserted street. "What does he know?"

"Nothing. He suspects."

"Tell me everything."

Fang described finding Adam in her house and their conversation. Xiu listened, but his eyes never stopped scanning.

"He wants me to download his girlfriend. She's dying. He wants to sneak Apep out of the lab."

Xiu drew a cigarette package out of his inner pocket and tapped a cylinder into his hand. He lit it and took a long drag. "He's desperate. A panicked man is dangerous."

"Don't hurt him." Why had she blurted that? Xiu had given no sign he was capable of real violence. But she knew. Deep down, she sensed his menace.

"This is not a game," he said. "Do you want to spend your remaining days in a federal prison?"

"He just wants to save his girlfriend."

"Did you agree to help him?"

"Yes."

"Then he knows you're guilty. Why else would you agree to do it?"

"To help him. To find out who killed—"

"You have forgotten why you're here. Forgotten the people who supported you. Forgotten your country."

"No, I—"

"I visited your mother and sister when I last returned home."

Fang shivered. Having this shark speak to her family chilled her. She reached for the dolphin on her necklace. "They're innocent."

"They're tools of the state. As are you."

"Please don't hurt them, don't—"

"If you fail the party, they fail the party. Do you understand?"

Fang did. All too well. "What do you need me to do?"

"Let Adam help you."

"You want me to download his girlfriend and take Apep?"

"I want you to steal it and bring it to me."

CHAPTER SIXTY-THREE

Adam held Effie's hand as they sat in the cart in Forever Technology's parking lot. She closed her eyes and waited for the Dilaudid tablets to numb her pain.

Inside, Fang prepared the equipment she would use to map Effie's mind. Once they had successfully downloaded the data into the cloud, Adam would need to take possession of Apep before Bryce sold his company to a foreign power and Adam lost access to the essence of his love.

"We need to get inside soon," he whispered.

"I need a minute. The pain . . . it's bad."

"I'm sorry the boat ride was so choppy."

"Hellish," she said. "But it's fourth and long. It's time to throw a Hail Mary."

"Thank you for doing this." He held her hand and waited.

She seemed to recover, and he helped her out of the cart. He straightened her visitor pass and escorted her into the building. The guard looked surprised at their late-night arrival, but Effie's visitor credentials were valid.

Effie took several minutes to cross the lobby to the elevator. Adam led her to his office and gave her a white lab coat. It was not much of a disguise, but if Suggs or whoever else was in the command center noticed them, it would look like Adam was accompanying a scientist into Black Diamond.

He led her toward the annex. Halfway across the elevated walkway, Effie swooned. He threw his arm around her to keep her from falling.

"I can't," she said.

"It's okay. Take your time."

"It's too much."

"We're almost there," he said. "Then you'll just lie still while she reads your brain waves."

She looked at him, her face a combination of pain and fatigue. "Brain waves?"

He almost laughed. "The science is beyond me. I admit it. But you won't have to do anything. Let Dr. Jin work her magic."

Effie nodded. She inhaled deeply, and they continued down the hall to the elevator. By the time they reached P-2, Adam was almost carrying her.

Fang met them at the door to her lab and helped Effie into a chair. "Is she alright?"

"She's in pain."

"I'll administer a battery of high-density MRIs first, then we need to bring her to the experimental lab and hook her to my electromagnetic neural network monitors for a series of scans."

"Let's hurry."

They rolled Effie's chair down the hall, and a few minutes later, the MRI clanked as it rotated around her. Adam stood beside Fang in the control room and watched her download images of Effie's brain.

"That's not good," Fang said.

"What?"

"See that white area there?"

Adam nodded. This was headed for more bad news.

"It's a mass," Fang said.

Adam sighed. That was new. It had only been a few weeks since her last cranial MRI. The cancer was spreading fast. "Will the tumor interfere with the download?"

"We won't be able to determine that until I've collected all the data."

"How will AI interpret that?" Adam asked.

"I don't know. We've never done this with a patient who had cancer. The question will be how much damage have the tumors done? If they're interfering with her synaptic connections, whatever I copy will replicate the problems. Best guess, the AI will mimic her current function, and if the cancer is interfering with cognitive processes, the heuristics will assume it's normal."

"But this will preserve her mind?"

"The data will allow us to replicate her synaptic processes. The AI should process information and learn the same way her brain works now."

"How long will this take?"

"I must administer a full battery of tests. An expert radiologist is supposed to do it, but I know enough to get what I need. In theory."

Adam's stomach turned. Even if they pulled this off, and he could keep the data safe until the technology improved, they could still make a mistake and Apep would be useless. Why hadn't Bryce agreed to use Effie as a test subject so they could do this right? Didn't he trust Adam? And why had he said the technology wasn't ready?

"Uh-oh," Fang said.

"What now?"

Fang pointed to a grainy image on the security monitor. Felix Suggs had entered the Annex.

"Close the light," Fang said. "It is time to hide."

CHAPTER SIXTY-FOUR

Edna blew a bubble and stepped into the doorway to Harry's office. Mildred Worth, the paper's owner, stood behind Harry and scowled at her. The bubble popped. The Cape Cod Daily Post had been in the Worth family for three generations, and while Mrs. Worth treated it as her birthright, she rarely appeared in the newspapers' offices.

"Come in." Harry said. He looked like he had ingested a rotten Bay scallop.

"What's this?" Edna asked. She looked from Harry to Mrs. Worth.

"Sit, please," Harry said.

Edna plopped onto the chair opposite them, and the wood creaked. Had Harry chosen the hard-backed chair to make his reporters uncomfortable? He'd probably shortened its legs too.

"Let me explain," Edna said.

"Mrs. Worth received a troubling call from the Massachusetts State House today," Harry said. "When Mrs. Worth asked me what my reporter was doing there, I didn't know what to tell her."

"I've got the goods on Bryce Hastings. I met with Representative—"

"Sheppard," Mrs. Worth said. "Yes, we know, dear. I just got off the phone with Matt Simmons, his chief of staff."

Had Sheppard told Simmons about the house Forever Technology had gifted him? Why would he have told anyone? Did he doubt she would kill the story after he provided her with information on Bryce Hastings? They had made a deal.

"I'm surprised Sheppard told him about that. It means they were in on it together. Why else would—"

"In on what?" Harry asked.

Edna looked at Mrs. Worth. "Simmons didn't tell you?"

"He said you met with Representative Sheppard and upset him. Apparently, Mr. Sheppard wouldn't tell him what was going on, so he called me to find out what kind of story we're running. I owe him a favor, but I had to say I knew nothing about a story."

"Or about your trip to Boston," Harry said. "I shouldn't have to get updates on my reporters from Mrs. Worth."

"No, you shouldn't," Mrs. Worth said in a tone as frigid as her stare.

"Enlighten me," Harry said.

Edna played with the bulbous beads on her necklace. She had planned to keep her bribery information secret, because Harry would want to run it, and that was not the point. Using Sheppard's indiscretion as leverage to take down Bryce Hastings was the best play. Murder trumped local corruption, especially when it involved a billionaire celebrity. Now, she had to come clean. She sighed.

"I've got Bryce Hastings up against the ropes," Edna said, "right where I want him. I uncovered evidence that Sheppard received a beach house from Forever Technology. He—"

"A bribe?" Harry asked.

"Yeah, that was the intent, but it may not be prosecutable."

"Dammit, Edna. When were you planning on telling me about this?"

"Thomas Locke gave Sheppard the house, probably off Forever's books, but we would have to show Sheppard did something for them in return to have him charged. It's an ethics violation for sure, but I'm not sure the DA would take action."

"You've been railing about Forever Technology and spinning unsubstantiated conspiracy theories," Harry said, "but you didn't think it was important to mention evidence that one of their executive staff had bribed a state representative?"

"I'm using it to flip Sheppard, recruit him as a source."

Harry slapped the table. "That's my call, and er, Mrs. Worth's. Not yours."

"Sheppard agreed to play ball."

"You can't make those kinds of strategic decisions without me," Harry said. "This is an enormous story."

"I knew you'd want to run something on the bribe and that would kill Sheppard's cooperation. Hastings would never talk to him after that."

"You're goddamned right I want to run that story. What's your evidence?"

"I promised Sheppard I'd bury it if he gave us the goods on Forever, and he agreed."

"What goods?"

Edna rolled her necklace in her fingers. "He, uh, he didn't say."

"You agreed to hold a story about criminal wrongdoing by a public official on the vague chance he can produce incriminating information about a tech company?"

"Hastings is up to something. They killed Thomas Locke, I'm—"

"If you think—" Harry said.

Mrs. Worth put her hand on Harry's shoulder. "I've heard quite enough. You, my dear, have become a liability. Making an enemy out of a state representative is not the way we do business. Mr. Sheppard has donated to my conservation society and has always been supportive. He—"

"I don't mean to interrupt," Harry said, "but if he's taking bribes, we need to report it."

"I'm hearing nothing but innuendo," Mrs. Worth said. "Ms. Cooper admits there is no evidence of quid pro quo. We're slandering the name of a public official to blackmail him into providing dirt on the richest man in Massachusetts."

"He basically admitted accepting a bribe," Edna said. "He's dirty."

"This is no way to run a business," Mrs. Worth said. "I don't want you talking to anyone about Representative Sheppard or Forever Technology."

"We can sue Forever to open their books," Edna said. "We can reveal what—"

"Go home," Mrs. Worth said. "You're done here."

"You're firing me?"

Harry looked at Mrs. Worth. "Mildred?"

"Let's call it a sabbatical," Mrs. Worth said. "I don't want to create the appearance we're punishing you for investigating corruption, but I won't allow you to destroy this paper with wild conspiracy theories."

"But—"

"We can make it permanent if you prefer," she said. "Go home."

Edna stood, straightened her vest, and walked out. She stopped halfway across the newsroom and looked back. Mildred picked up the telephone off Harry's desk and dialed.

CHAPTER SIXTY-FIVE

Adam met Keisha Gunn in the lobby. She wore jeans and a fluffy sweater.

"You dressed down today," he said.

Her brow furrowed. "I needed to talk to you."

"Should I call a lawyer?"

"I'm not on duty. This is off-the-record."

Adam raised an eyebrow. "I'm intrigued."

"Can we take a walk?"

"As long as we stay away from the cliffs," he said.

Adam led her outside, with a lightness he had not felt for a long time. The previous night, Fang had led Suggs away from the diagnostic laboratory. She had answered his questions about improving security, and then he had left. After Adam's heart rate had returned to normal, he and Fang had completed mapping Effie's mind. Effie's data sat on Forever Technology's remote servers. All he needed was a way to access and process it—and Apep was the key.

Outside, Gunn turned to him. "You will not like what I'm about to tell you."

"You've decided I'm the killer?"

"I don't think you had anything to do with this."

Adam stopped short. Was this a bluff to draw him out? "You've identified another suspect?"

"In the days before your brother's death, his yacht traveled back and forth between Cuttyhunk and Martha's Vineyard, while your phone stayed in Falmouth."

"You pulled my tolls?"

"Don't take it personally. Just doing my job."

"I'm not. I'm glad you investigated me. The sooner you clear me, the faster you can solve this."

"The only time you left Falmouth was to visit your girlfriend's specialists in Boston."

"How do you know I didn't give my phone to Effie and let her take it to Boston while I rigged a bomb on my brother's boat?"

"Because the doctor and his receptionist confirmed you were in Boston. It's not exculpatory, but it was enough to convince me you're not guilty. I couldn't determine your motive, but even if you had one, killing your brother while you're on the dock would have been a poorly planned crime. You don't strike me as a poor planner."

They walked along the path and entered the wildlife sanctuary. A mist blew in from the edge of the storm. The sun had not shone for days.

"Telling me I'm not a suspect is good news. Why did you say I won't like it?"

"We're calling your brother's death an accident."

"What?"

"I'm sorry."

A moment of dizziness passed through Adam. How was this happening? He stopped and took a deep breath. "You said his death was suspicious."

"I did, and it is. This order came from above. They're officially blaming a gas leak."

"But sabotaging the gas line makes it murder. What about the rubber residue inside? You thought it captured the gas to insure an explosion."

"It's a decent theory."

"And?"

"I called the marina where your brother bought the yacht, and the broker said the system was intact when they sold it. They could not explain the residue in the engine compartment."

"That proves it," Adam said. "Someone killed Tommy."

"I agree, but who's to say Tommy didn't make his own repairs. Maybe he broke the pipe."

Heat rose in Adam's neck. "That's ridiculous. Tommy was a finance guy. He wouldn't pay a million dollars for a yacht and then fiddle with the engine."

"That accident theory came down from HQ to the Cape & Islands State Police Detective Unit and then to Troop D."

"I thought this was your case. Who made that boneheaded call?"

"I called a buddy of mine in Boston," Gunn said. "They decided it in the superintendent's office."

"What an asshole."

"You slinging mud?" she asked

"I'm calling it like I see it. So, what does this mean?"

"I'm off the case, and your brother's death has been labeled an accident."

Waves broke hard against the rocks below. "Is it normal for the superintendent to weigh in on a homicide investigation?"

"Technically, it was never a homicide, but no, I've never seen it happen."

Adam walked to the edge and stared at the cliffs. "Someone got to him."

"Maybe."

"There's no maybe about it," Adam said. "Bryce paid to cover this up. Or someone did it for him."

"That's why I wanted to talk to you in person. The investigation is officially closed, but I feel bad about this."

"It's not closed for me."

"Don't do anything stupid," she said.

"Since when is bringing a killer to justice stupid?"

Gunn touched his arm. "I wish I could help."

"If you want to help me find the murderer, give me a copy of your files."

"I could get fired for that."

"You know a killer is out there," Adam said. "It will never come back to you. I promise."

"You're gonna ruin my career."

"You'll do it?"

"I'm not committing either way," Gunn said, "but check your front porch before you go to work tomorrow."

"You know something, Gunn?"

"What?"

"You're okay."

CHAPTER SIXTY-SIX

Fang had been working for hours, and her lower back ached. She locked her computer screen and stretched. She walked across her lab, cracked open her door, and leaned into the hallway. The motion-activated lights remained off, and the exit sign glowed at the distant end of the hall. She closed the door and rested her forehead against it. Out of everything she had done, this was the most dangerous.

She turned around and leaned against the door. Apep rested on the counter and wires connected it to her terminal. Shlomo had agreed to give her Black Diamond access to confirm the upload protocols had not corrupted her data. He had not, however, given her permission to move Apep into her lab. If he arrived at this late hour and discovered it missing, she would claim it was easier to work from her own terminal, but she doubted he would buy that.

It did not matter. She would steal Apep, and once she did, all hell would break loose.

She hurried to the counter. She unplugged the cables and coiled them into a clip, which was pointless, since she would never return. Old habits die hard.

She opened a cabinet and removed a black duffel bag that she had secreted under her lab coat the previous day. She spread it open on the counter and glanced at the door. There was not much she could do if anyone showed up, but she could not stop checking.

Apep was worth three quarters of a million dollars in parts alone, and it would be a priceless prize for her country. With her knowledge and a team of China's best computer scientists, they could unlock the secrets of Forever Technology's artificial mind. She would become a national hero. Unless they had killed Sarah and Tommy and planned to kill her too. Did Xiu want to eliminate the trail back to the Communist Party? She shook away the thought. They would need her expertise.

She could not indulge herself in dark fantasies. If she did not deliver Apep, her mother and sister would die.

Fang packed the device with foam cushions. If she damaged it, all this risk would be for naught. She crouched, slipped her arms into the shoulder straps, and lifted the weight of the device onto her back. She took a few tentative steps. It only weighed twenty pounds—so light for a device that replicated human behavior. So small for technology that would change the world.

This was it. She still had time to return Apep to Shlomo's department and pretend this had never happened. This was her defining moment. If she failed to deliver what Xiu demanded, her family would end up in a concentration camp or, more likely, be tortured to death. She would become the victim of a tragic accident, another example of the Forever Technology's curse.

If she stole it, the Party may decide to kill her anyway. But even if they praised her as a hero, she would hate herself. Her mother had not raised her to steal, and this technology did not belong to her. It did not belong to the Chinese Communist Party either. Bryce Hastings was a visionary, and he had entrusted her with his most valuable secrets. She was betraying him. Short and simple, and that made her a thief.

"I will never forgive myself."

She had struggled with this dilemma for days and could not find a way out. She blinked away a tear and focused on what she had to do.

She picked up the phone and dialed.

"Adam Locke," he said.

"It is me. I have it."

"Where are you?"

"I am leaving the lab now," she said. "Meet me on the beach at the base of the cliff, near the pier."

"I'll be on the water in ten minutes, but I'm coming from Falmouth, so it'll take me an hour."

"Hurry."

She would let him help her get Apep off the island and show him how they could access Effie's data. Then she would deliver it to Xiu. Once she had it in China, she would find a way to give Adam access.

She moved to the door and checked the hallway again. Clear. She hurried across the tiles and lights clicked on as she passed the sensors. She reached the main atrium and peeked around the corner. The other hallways remained dark.

She crossed to the exit, and Apep dug into her spine, just as she was about to stab Bryce in the back. She punched the exit button, and the doors whooshed open.

She took the elevator to the first floor. Her pulse pounded in her temples as the elevator door opened in the lobby. Would the guard ask to look in her bag? Had anyone in the Command Center seen her secrete the device in her duffel? She stepped into the lobby and turned toward the main entrance.

She froze with a chattering fright.

Felix Suggs stood in front of the doorway with his arms crossed against his chest. "Good evening, Dr. Jin. What do you have in the bag?"

CHAPTER SIXTY-SEVEN

Adam turned the ignition key and the Mercury engine on the Boston Whaler coughed and roared to life. He reversed away from the dock, cut the wheel hard to the right, and pushed the throttle forward. The Whaler's bow slapped against oncoming waves as it skimmed across the surface of Little Harbor. Sailboats bobbed on their moorings as he passed.

He entered the Vineyard Sound across from Nobska Lighthouse. Woods Hole disappeared behind him as he approached Nonamesset Island, the northernmost of the Elizabeth Islands. Safely away from shore, he opened the throttle, and the bow rose like the wing of an aircraft. He jumped across three-foot swells, a moderate sea for small craft but unusually rough for the Sound's protected waters.

Dark clouds blotted the moon, and Adam activated his bow and stern lights. With the storm and the cold weather, it was unlikely he would encounter another boat so late at night, but visibility was poor and a collision in these icy waters would be problematic. The wind chilled his face, and Adam closed the collar on his green tactical jacket, a shell issued to him when he first joined the FAST teams. He wore jeans and a long-sleeved cotton shirt beneath it but wished he had opted for the long underwear. The temperature hovered in the high forties, and the moisture chilled his bones.

Somewhere in the distance, a foghorn blew. A lobster boat? A Woods Hole ferry? Adam swiveled his head as he moved down the eastern shore of the islands. Martha's Vineyard lay somewhere on his left, but the fog and clouds obscured it. He motored less than four hundred yards off the Elizabeth Islands, but they remained hidden too.

Adam drew his iPhone out of his pocket, scrolled to its compass app, and took a bearing. He headed south by southwest. He flipped to Google Maps and checked his position, halfway between Martha's Vineyard and the Elizabeth Islands, far enough from land to avoid underwater rocks or obstructions. It should take another forty minutes to reach Forever Technology's private dock on Cuttyhunk's eastern shore.

Something popped behind him, followed by a sizzle, and then the engine died. The sudden deceleration almost threw him overboard. Adam grabbed the wheel as the boat canted to port and collided with an oncoming wave.

He got his feet under him as the next swell lifted the bow into the air. He grabbed the seat for balance and made his way back to the engine.

"What the hell happened?"

The boat coasted to a standstill and rocked between swells. The fog thickened. Floating out there without power created a real hazard from other ships, and the currents were notorious.

He ran his hands around the gunwale for balance and shuffled to the engine. It smelled like an electrical fire. Adam could shoot a dozen weapon systems and drive anything with wheels, but he knew next to nothing about engines. But something was burning. Adam reached for the latch to unlock the engine hood and stopped. A red insulated wire protruded from under the hood and ran along the engine and down the stern. That wire had not been there before.

Adam's pulse raced. He followed the wire with his fingers and traced it along the transom, over the gunwale, to the passenger seat, where it continued under the windshield. Adam knelt between the seats and examined the hold.

His heart stopped.

The red wire stuck out of a half-dozen sticks of dynamite tied together with black electrical tape.

A bomb.

The bow and stern lights flickered, and something snapped near the engine. Sparks flew from under the engine's hood. The bomb had failed to detonate, but something was happening. Did he have time to disconnect the wires? Adam looked over the side into the icy black water. He hadn't even brought a life preserver. Sparks popped off the smoking engine.

"To hell with this."

Adam climbed onto the bow, grabbed the bowline, and jumped feet-first into the water. The icy Atlantic took his breath away. His clothes filled with water and tugged him below the surface. Adam kicked with muscles strong from his daily runs. His head broke the surface, and he gasped.

He held the line in his stiff hands and looked back at the boat. Black smoke poured off the engine and tickled the air.

Who had planted a bomb? Whatever had gone wrong, someone had intended it to detonate when he turned the ignition. Why had he not seen the wire? He needed to be more careful. But what should he do now? If the engine burned itself out, and the bomb did not detonate, he could climb aboard and call for help.

Shit. Adam had forgotten about his phone. He tapped his pocket where his iPhone was submerged in the frigid water. He jammed his fingers inside and yanked it out. The case slipped through his fingers and out of his reach. It sank to the bottom.

So much for that.

He could wait for the fire to burn out, then climb aboard and hope the boat drifted to either the Elizabeth Islands or Martha's Vineyard. Maybe somebody would come by, and he could signal for help. Maybe—

The boat disintegrated in a fountain of flame.

CHAPTER SIXTY-EIGHT

The look on Suggs's face told Fang all she needed to know. He must have been monitoring the surveillance cameras, which meant he had seen her take the device. He knew what she was doing. Her body vibrated with panic. Fight or flight.

She ran.

She had to flee the building and escape. She raced for the stairwell.

Suggs and the security guard's footsteps echoed on the floor behind her. She pushed open the door and barreled down the steps, three at a time. Apep bounced in her backpack, thumping against her body with every step.

She grabbed the handrail and spun around the landing and onto the second flight of stairs. She jumped the last three steps and let her momentum carry her through the exit door on P-1.

The stairwell door banged open above her. Suggs and the guard were close behind.

Fang sprinted down the hall. The emergency exit sign glowed red at the end of the hall. It led to the sloping yard behind the building. A sign on the door said the alarm would sound when opened.

Please be unlocked.

Fang extended her arms and did not slow as she approached. If the door did not open, she would smash into it. Her palms hit the metal crash bar, and she burst into the cold.

She stumbled on the uneven ground behind the structure but maintained her feet. The klaxon sounded and white lights reflected off the trees. She hurtled down the incline and dove into the woods, raising her hands to swat away branches from her face. The coastal path should be somewhere up ahead.

The exit door banged open behind her.

"Get the cart," Suggs shouted.

They were coming.

Where was she going? She was on an island with nowhere to hide. She could backtrack into town and knock on some resident's door, but would she be putting some innocent family at risk? She could hide in a garage or a boat, but she would have to come out eventually, and they'd be waiting.

Fang had committed a felony, and they may call the police, but that would expose their project to scrutiny. Even if they did, it would take law enforcement at least thirty minutes to respond from Martha's Vineyard or the mainland. She could worry about that later. Her immediate problem was hiding from Suggs.

She bolted into the wildlife sanctuary.

The heavens opened, and rain stung her face. She plowed between bushes and onto the path. She turned right and followed it along the cliffs. Waves crashed into the shore far below. A seagull soared silently at eye level, just off the cliff. It turned its head and looked at her.

She glanced back down the trail. No sign of Suggs or security. A twig snapped somewhere in the tangle of brush. Was it an animal or Suggs? Should she lay down in the dense, underbrush and conceal herself among the high grass and thorny bushes? That could work if she did not mind the slithering snakes and rodent infestation, but Suggs could shine a flashlight on her, and she would have nowhere to go.

She jogged down the path, putting distance between her and Forever Technology. Her clothes soaked through and chilled her body. The leather on her flats dug into her feet. She panted from exertion. Or from terror. She tried to control her breath.

After a few minutes, the path opened, and she ran onto the grassy airfield. Sheets of rain whipped sideways across the field and wind rustled the bushes. A gust knocked her off-balance, but she sped over the open ground.

At the end of the airfield, a dirt golf-cart track bisected West Road and followed the coast around the southern end of the island. Fang dashed down it. The odor of salt, sand, and dead grass hung in the damp air. She looked east toward Martha's Vineyard. She needed to get off Cuttyhunk.

She was alone. She wanted to cry, yell for someone to help her, but the incessant wind would carry away her voice. That damn relentless wind. No one would hear her scream.

In the distance, Bryce's house stood on a small rise. She continued down the path into a low depression. She peered over high grass at the house. Tall windows wrapped around the first floor, and the interior lights were off.

She looked behind her. Even in the darkness, her footprints stood out in the soft sand, like a trail of breadcrumbs.

They led directly to her.

CHAPTER SIXTY-NINE

Adam closed his eyes as a fireball erupted high into the air above the boat. A wave of overpressure rocked him in the water. Flames singed his hair and warmed his face. He dove beneath the surface, rolled onto his back, and stared up at the orange glow. The icy water cooled his skin. His lungs burned as his oxygen depleted, and he stroked his arms to stay submerged.

The light flickering through the water diminished. Adam broke the surface and gasped. The odor of burning plastic assaulted his sinuses. Flames engulfed the Whaler, and black toxic smoke drifted into the air. Adam backstroked away from the conflagration.

If the bomb's initiator had not malfunctioned, he would be dead now. Anger swelled through him.

"Who the hell did this?"

He rode up and down on a wave, and the water stung his skin and chilled his bones. The current carried the burning boat away from him, and it was already twenty yards distant. Or was the current dragging him? The straits' violent undertows had taken lives over the years. He lifted his watch out of the water and the luminescent dial glowed.

What would Effie do if he died?

Adam spun in a circle but could not see land. Which way should he swim? Martha's Vineyard lay to the east and the Elizabeth Islands to the west. North was Woods Hole, but if he headed south, he would not hit land.

If he paddled for Martha's Vineyard, the currents could drag him out to sea. The North Atlantic was a dangerous place.

Sharks.

Predators fed at night. Hair rose on Adam's neck, and he looked behind him. He dog-paddled in a tight circle but saw nothing but dark water. His heart pounded in his chest. He submerged his face and opened his eyes in the salty water. A few feet below, his legs disappeared into the murky depths.

His worst nightmare.

He had to reach land. Naushon, Pasque, and Nashawena should be the closest Elizabeth Islands. He had traveled down the center of the Vineyard Sound for safety, but now that decision had put him equidistant from the nearest land. It was four to five miles from Martha's Vineyard to the Elizabeth Islands, so he had to swim at least two miles either way, and farther if he headed north.

Adam kicked his legs and swirled his arms in a dog paddle. His clothes had waterlogged, and their weight made it difficult to float. He could shed his clothes, but how long would he last in the chilly water? Autumn had been warmer than normal, but hypothermia would set in soon. When that happened, he would lose motor control and drown.

The Marines trained FAST in rudimentary water-survival skills, and Adam had taken the course years ago. He tried to remember his training as his breathing became labored. His hiking boots were the biggest problem. He reached down and fumbled with the wet laces. His chilled fingers groped the cloth, and he used his foot to kick one boot off. The cold of the deeper water stung his toes. He removed the other boot after a brief struggle. He swam more easily, and the pain dissipated as his body numbed, but if he did not get dry soon, he could lose toes. Or worse.

He unzipped his jacket to make it easier to swim, then remembered a swim test in the pool at the FBI's Quantico Academy. Adam zipped it all the way up and tucked his outer layer into his pants, then he tightened his belt to seal it. He buried his head into his collar and blew into his jacket until it inflated like a balloon. Air leaked out the sleeves and collar, but the added buoyancy created a jury-rigged flotation device.

Adam floated on his back and swirled his arms for balance. His imagination conjured the image of a great white exploding out of the depths and clamping onto his arm. He shook away the thought. The chance of being bitten by a shark was less than being struck by lightning. His fear was irrational—but logic did not drive his racing pulse.

He kept his arms close to his body.

The Whaler floated over one-hundred yards away, and the flames had dwindled. The air stank of diesel and fiberglass. Had anyone seen the fire? Few boats would be on the water during a storm at night, but maybe someone observed it from shore. Hope filled him.

He took a tentative stroke toward the burning boat. If the explosion drew a rescuer, he would need to be nearby.

He stopped.

The islands in the center of the Elizabeth chain were privately owned and mostly unoccupied. No one would be on shore to see the flames, and he was too far south of Woods Hole for the light to be visible. The Aquinah Cliff bordered the Gayhead shore on Martha's Vineyard and those beaches would be empty during inclement weather. Clouds and fog hung low over the water, which meant no one on the islands could see his burning boat.

What to do?

Dark clouds infused with drizzle obscured the stars. They moved fast—a portend of the coming hurricane. A cloud glowed for a moment. Was the moon behind it? During autumn, the moon hung low in the sky, and before midnight, it would rise to his southeast. If that glow had been the moon, the Elizabeth Islands would be on his right and the Vineyard on his left. Woods Hole was too far to the north. If he missed the Vineyard, he would be swept out into the North Atlantic. But if he went west and missed the Elizabeth Islands, he would enter Buzzards Bay and eventually reach either the Massachusetts or Rhode Island shores. But the mainland was too far. He would never make it. His best chance of survival was to reach one of the Elizabeth Islands and find help.

Adam stroked toward the islands. His inflated jacket made a crawl impossible, so he used the breaststroke. The water tingled his skin and numbed his hands and feet. His muscles tired. He looked over his shoulder to get a bearing, but the moon had disappeared. What if that had not been the moon?

Finding a swimmer in the water was almost impossible. And nobody was looking. Why had he not been more careful? Motoring around his childhood waters had lulled him into a sense of security, but the sea had a history of punishing those who failed to respect it.

Adam pictured Effie. Had she not suffered enough? How would she deal with his death? If Effie could fight cancer, he would not let a boating accident end him. He would never give up.

"I won't die tonight."

Adam switched to a modified elementary backstroke as he rode the swells. He moved faster, and the current strengthened. He had been near Pasque Island when his boat exploded, so the strong current could be Quick's Hole between Cuttyhunk and Nashawena Islands. It was treacherous but being close to an island would make the danger worthwhile. If he was headed out to sea, he would die.

The dark profile of an island poked through the fog. He looked over his shoulder and saw another land mass—the Elizabeth Islands. The narrow straight meant he was in Robinson's Hole.

He was going to make it.

He rolled onto his stomach and stroked toward Naushon Island, the largest in the chain and home to about thirty residents. Waves crashed against the shore. He would fight through the surf and hope.

Twenty yards offshore, something cut through the flesh over his shin. He screamed in pain.

Shark!

Terror filled him. He could not feel his lower leg. If the shark had taken it, the beast would eat him before he reached shore. He curled his legs beneath him. His mind went into the black. He flailed his arms and hyperventilated. The pain throbbed up his leg. Was he bleeding? Had a shark taken his foot?

He ran his hands down his leg. Everything remained attached. His fingers found a swollen bump on his shin. But no bite. The current had dragged him into a submerged rock.

"Thank God."

He caught his breath and swam to shore.

CHAPTER SEVENTY

Adam shook the fisherman's hand and thanked him for delivering him to Falmouth. It had taken an hour to find an occupied residence on Naushon Island and another two hours to return to the mainland. His muscles ached and he could not shake the chill, despite the sweater the man had loaned him. Adam had used the man's phone and reported the explosion to Sergeant Gunn. She had contacted the Coast Guard, and a search was on for his Boston Whaler. She had asked to meet him at his house to take a statement.

Adam wanted to tell Fang what had happened, but he did not have her number memorized, and calling Forever Technology could compromise her. Hopefully, she had secured Apep, and he could try to retrieve it tomorrow.

A taxi dropped him home. He entered the house and found Effie asleep, no doubt under the influence of sedatives. He showered, dressed, and waited for Gunn to arrive. Tommy was dead, and now someone had tried to kill him.

"I've had enough."

He borrowed Effie's cell phone and found Edna Cooper's business card. Adam wanted to talk in private, and while he should ask for an in-person meeting, he did not have time. He opened FaceTime and called.

Edna's face filled the screen and her computer reflected in her giant round glasses. She reminded him of an owl.

"I want to talk," he said.

"I'm all ears."

"Something happened. Are you alone?"

Edna sat up and leaned forward. "I live alone."

"Somebody tried to kill me."

"Hold on. I'm going to record this."

Adam bristled. "I don't want a recording of our conversation floating around."

"Bad things happen when I don't record interviews."

"I won't change my story. I want you to expose what's going on."

"At Forever Technology?" she asked.

"It's their Black Diamond project. They haven't been honest about what they're doing behind closed doors."

"I need to record this."

"Just listen to what I'm saying. You—" Something moved behind Edna. Or had the light thrown a shadow? "You're sure you're alone?"

"I've been divorced for twenty-seven years."

"I thought I saw someone."

"Honey, I wish. I haven't—"

A cord flopped over Edna's head and tightened around her throat. Her eyes bulged and her hands clawed at it.

Adam stood and gawked at the image on his phone.

Someone lifted Edna out of her seat by her neck. She kicked and flailed. Her foot knocked the computer askew. It faced the wall, where the shadows of Edna and her attacker flickered like a demonic puppet show.

Could he call the police without disconnecting? He pressed the phone icon and dialed 9-1-1.

"State police, what's your emergency?"

"Someone is murdering Edna Cooper."

CHAPTER SEVENTY-ONE

Edna dug her fingertips under the cord. Foul breath tingled her nose. The cord tightened around her throat. She could not breathe. Adrenaline filled her with strength.

The man drew her against his body. He yanked the cord and lifted her out of her seat. Her necklace snapped and large beads bounced off the desk and rattled on the floor.

She tried to scream, but it came out as a gurgle. She kicked and knocked over her chair.

Pain shot through her neck and jaw. Her eyes bulged. She could not get air. She squirmed and twisted, trying to see her attacker.

He dragged her backward onto the floor. He wrapped his legs around her waist, pinning her body to him. He tugged harder on the cord, and something cracked inside her throat.

What was happening?

She released the tightening cord and reached behind her. She groped for the man's face. He twisted away but kept his legs tight around her waist.

She opened her mouth like a fish out of water. Her vision darkened and narrowed to a tunnel. Her heart pounded in her chest. Harder, faster.

I'm going to die.

She kicked again, this time with less force. She slapped at his face, but her energy waned. The pain in her neck diminished to a numb burning. Her vision dulled until only a hazy spot remained in front of her.

Her death was imminent. Her will vanished. A sense of calm engulfed her.

The room faded to black.

CHAPTER SEVENTY-TWO

Adam leaned against Sergeant Gunn's midnight-blue Buick and watched the police activity around Edna Cooper's house. He had described to Gunn everything he had witnessed. A dozen Barnstable and State Police cruisers blocked the street. Red and blue emergency lights washed over the pavement, turning the neighborhood into a crime-scene discotheque.

Gunn exited the front door of the Cape-Cod-style house and joined him. She radiated intensity.

"Is she dead?" Adam asked, knowing the answer.

Gunn nodded. "She put up a fight. The place is a mess."

"Bryce did this. Cooper was digging into Forever Technology. She must have found something, got too close to the truth."

Gunn watched him. "This makes the third victim who knew Hastings."

"I was almost the fourth," Adam said. "How many people have to die before you bring him in?"

"You throwing shade?"

"When will it end?"

"You know the situation as well as I do," she said. "I need evidence."

"Your evidence is decomposing inside that house."

She reached into her purse and slipped a scorpion ball into her mouth. "The State Police will investigate this. Like the others."

"You mean you'll call it an accident, like you did with my brother?"

"I never said that was an accident. Maybe with this homicide, there's a chance we can reopen that one. But I don't want to get your hopes up."

"I have zero expectations," Adam said. "The past week has shaken my belief in the criminal justice system. Something must give. My brother's death may have been characterized as accidental, but we both know the truth, and Edna Cooper's murder is going to bring every news outlet in the region down on top of you."

She looked back at the house and nodded. "Good."

"You know, Gunn, you keep talking like that, and I'm going to start liking you."

"Don't judge me yet. Not until we get to the bottom of this." She rolled the hot ball in her mouth. "It thrilled me to make sergeant and then detective. Youngest woman in state history. Then they sent me out here. I don't think they wanted me investigating anything high-profile. I guess that plan backfired."

"You've been straight with me, so I'll be straight with you. I know Bryce did this, and I'm going to stop him. I—"

"Go easy. If you're planning to break the law, I'll have to stop you."

"I'll get justice for my brother. If you want to waste time trying to stop me, good luck."

"Dammit, Locke."

"Promise me you'll keep pressure on from your end."

"They can't slip this one under the rug," she said. "No matter how much money and influence Hastings spreads around. And I'll see what I can do about reopening your brother's investigation."

Adam inhaled the cool night. "Did Edna have family?"

Gunn shook her head. "Lived alone. Maybe someone out of town. I'll find out before this hits the news."

"What about her newspaper?"

"That's my next visit. You witnessed this, so I needed your account while it was still fresh in your memory. That's the only reason I'm talking to you now."

"I'll give you my FaceTime account information. Maybe there's a way they can recover what I saw from the server. Edna may have recorded it."

"I'll submit a preservation letter just in case."

His temples throbbed, and he rubbed his forehead. "Feels like the police have been doing a great job documenting these deaths and very little to find out who's responsible. While you're filling out paperwork, I plan to do something."

"Listen to me," she said. "Don't interfere. You can contaminate evidence, mess up our investigation."

"Am I free to go?"

"I've got your statement."

Adam turned, and she grabbed his arm. "I appreciate your help," she said, "but don't make me waste time throwing you in jail."

"Good luck, Sergeant."

Adam walked away. Things kept getting worse. Effie's condition deteriorated every day. Fang had downloaded some version of Effie's mind, but who knew if it would work? Hell, according to Bryce, the technology was not ready. And Bryce, the man Adam needed to preserve Effie's consciousness, was a cold-blooded killer. How could he bring the CEO to justice and save Effie at the same time?

And where was Fang? He had been headed to meet her when some asshole had tried to blow him up. Adam had checked his messages when he changed clothes at home, but she had not called. Had she changed her mind?

Tommy was gone, two women were dead, and Svetlana had disappeared into a bottle of vodka. And Adam's efforts had done nothing to save Effie or find the killer.

How many people would have to die?

CHAPTER SEVENTY-THREE

Adam's headlights illuminated the winding road as he drove back to Falmouth. Killing a reporter was a bold move, an act of desperation, and desperate people made poor decisions. His investigation had become exponentially more dangerous.

Adam's eyelids grew heavy, and the siren call of sleep washed over him. Swimming in the cool Atlantic water had drained his energy, and now that his adrenaline had gone, it took intense focus to stay awake. He had pushed his body past normal limits of endurance many times during FAST operations, climbing through the Hindu Kush mountains and hiking through the Honduran jungle. How many times had he guzzled coffee, trying to maintain focus while surveilling a target through an endless night? It would be easy to succumb to sleep now and let himself recharge, but things were happening in the case. Whatever the killer was trying to hide, he had become concerned enough to kill three people. The rhythms of a case were intangible, but they vibrated through him like music to a composer. Edna's death signaled a new chapter, a frantic race to the truth.

If Bryce had killed Dr. Sarah Smith, she must have discovered something he wanted hidden. Had Tommy been killed for the same reason? Svetlana had said Tommy and Bryce argued about selling the technology to a foreign entity. Had that been the reason Tommy burned to death? It made sense. And what about Edna? Had she discovered a pending sale? If Bryce worried the federal government would seize control of his technology and prevent him from taking it to market, it would be logical to look offshore for answers. Maybe Edna had discovered that. And if Bryce had murdered her, he wouldn't hesitate to kill Adam.

Effie's cell phone vibrated on the seat beside him. He had borrowed it before he left to meet Gunn. He hated leaving Effie without a cell phone, but she had a landline on her nightstand in case of emergency.

Adam answered.

"I left you three messages," Gunn said, "before I realized your phone was laying at the bottom of the Vineyard Sound."

"I saw you thirty minutes ago. What's so urgent?"

"Dr. Fang Jin was admitted to the hospital."

Adam's core chilled, and he closed his eyes. Had they caught Fang with the device? Had Bryce tried to kill her? "What happened?"

"She fell off a cliff. She's in surgery."

"Oh, my God—"

"The early prognosis is she'll make it. She's in stable condition, but she broke her arm and leg, and she has a concussion."

"How?"

"Unclear. Luckily, she had her phone and was able to dial 9-1-1. It went out as a medical call. They notified me because she's a Forever Technology employee."

"Someone pushed her," Adam said.

"She told the paramedics she fell. We'll learn more after surgery."

"Why was she on the trail at night?" Adam held his breath. Had they found Apep?

"I don't have those answers," Gunn said. "I'm calling because you may be in danger."

She was right. The killer had come unglued. One death may have been covered up as an accident, and maybe even Tommy's, with the right amount of influence, but Edna and now Fang? There was no way anyone could hide this. The police would be all over Forever Technology and whatever they were concealing would come out. Did Bryce think he could get away with this?

"Did you hear me?" Gunn asked, bringing Adam back from his thoughts.

"The killer is desperate," he said. "Get a search warrant for Forever before Bryce can hide the evidence. Or flee."

"I may get search warrants for the offices of Sarah Smith and your brother, but I have nothing proving Bryce or Forever Technology is involved, other than circumstantial evidence."

"That's bullshit—"

"It's a high bar, Locke. You know that. Just because a company's employees have been targeted doesn't mean the owner loses his rights against unlawful search and seizure."

"We need to act fast. Can you bring in Bryce for questioning?"

"I'll talk to him, but right now I'm more worried about you," she said. "Three Forever employees are dead. You were attacked, and Dr. Jin is in surgery. Journalists are supposed to be out of bounds, even in the criminal world. I don't know why they killed Edna, but if they did it to shut her up, you might be next."

"I can take care of myself."

"I'll send a car and have an officer sit outside your house. Maybe Falmouth PD will assign a reserve officer."

"I'll handle it," Adam said. "If Bryce wants to make a play for me at home, he'll save me the trip. I—oh, my God."

"What?"

"Effie is home alone."

CHAPTER SEVENTY-FOUR

The wide tires of Adam's Jeep Wrangler screeched as the vehicle leaned into a turn. He eased off the gas but did not touch the brake. Years of driver training and dozens of high-speed pursuits had taught him that tapping the brakes in the middle of the skid could throw the car into an uncontrollable spin.

He used both lanes to stay on the road and then eased back onto his side of the double yellow line. A pickup truck rounded the corner and passed him going the other way.

"Get there in one piece," he said. Wrecking his jeep would leave Effie alone.

He glanced at her phone on the seat. He pressed call and then speaker. It rang a half dozen times and went to voicemail. "You have reached the Lockes, please—"

He ended the call. Why wasn't she picking up? Lately, Effie spent most days sleeping or in some stage of semiconsciousness. She had probably taken painkillers and drifted off, too deep in REM sleep to hear the ringing. Or maybe she had turned the ringer off.

He stomped on the gas and accelerated down a straightaway. Gunn had promised to ask the Falmouth Police to send a patrol unit, at least until Adam arrived home, but that would not help if Bryce or his goons were already there.

Adam barreled down Main Street through Falmouth's quaint downtown. The shops had closed, but a few restaurants remained open. He slowed to avoid killing someone. Three young men stumbled away from the outdoor patio at a Mexican restaurant and stepped into the street between crosswalks. They backslapped and laughed, appearing drunk.

Adam jumped on the brake and depressed the pedal until the rhythmic thumping of the antilock braking system vibrated against his foot.

"Hey man, watch it!" the short kid yelled.

"Fuck you," his muscular friend said. He approached the Jeep and slapped the fender.

Adam wanted to drive around him, but they blocked the street. He suppressed an urge to drive over him. He raised his hands in surrender, with his palms open. "Sorry."

The man gave him the finger and stumbled back to his buddies. As soon as they cleared the bumper, Adam squealed past. In his rearview mirror, they chased after him.

Adam concentrated on the road, screeching to a halt at the intersection of Woods Hole Road. He turned left and flew down the road toward his home on Surf Drive.

His house was dark, except for the walkway light. He pulled to the side of the road thirty yards from the house, an old police tactic to avoid driving up on the suspect and being shot before assessing the situation. Adam turned off the ignition and grabbed the keys as he leapt from the car. He left the door open and sprinted to the house, scanning the yard and windows. The front door was shut and there was no sign of forced entry. He needed to hurry, but if nothing was wrong, he did not want to scare Effie by bursting inside.

He slowed as he approached and skirted the walkway. If Bryce or his thugs had come to kill him, they could be waiting inside for Adam to return home. He jogged across the yard to the side of the house. Why hadn't he taken his gun? As an agent, he had carried his gun everywhere, but not having a permit had affected his judgment.

He leaned against the house and peeked into the window. He cupped his hands to reduce the reflection and strained to see. The living room was dark. If someone had come to assassinate him, and they were not on the street, they had to be inside. Unless they had already left.

He'd kill anyone who touched her.

He slipped between the shrubbery and stopped at the rear corner. He knelt. Waves crashed against the shore, tossed by the storm. He peered around the edge into the backyard.

Nothing.

He scanned the water, but the sand dunes blocked his view of the beach. He could check that later. Adam hurried to the back door and looked through the window. The kitchen was empty. He flipped through his keys and eased one into the lock. He stopped.

Something was wrong. The house was silent, but it held a dangerous energy. Had he smelled aftershave or had a flicker of movement registered in his subconscious?

He peered through the window again. Nothing. He saw nothing, heard nothing, and smelled nothing. But the hair on his neck stood on end. He didn't need to understand the feeling to trust it. He cracked open the door and pivoted out of the threshold.

Gunfire erupted, and shards of wood exploded around him.

Adam flung himself into the bushes as rounds shattered the glass. Fragments splintered the air. Adam crouched against the clapboard siding. The muzzle flashes had come from the front hallway. The man had been waiting for him. Proper tactics would be to flee to safety and call the police.

But Effie was in that house.

"Fuck it."

Adam raked his hands beneath the bushes, looking for a stick or some kind of weapon. His fingers brushed a rock. He dug a baseball-sized hunk of granite out of the earth. He needed a wild card.

He leaned forward like a wide receiver on the line of scrimmage. He held the rock by his hip. Adam had been a pitcher in high school and his fastball had topped eighty miles an hour.

And a rock was better than nothing.

He waited, but the man did not appear. Did the killer think Adam was armed? Was he lying in ambush, anticipating Adam would enter?

The killer had concealed himself inside a fixed structure and used the stairwell for cover. Adam would be exposed as he passed through the threshold. A nightmare scenario. But Effie was in the house, and God knew what the shooter would do to her.

Adam dialed 9-1-1 and put the phone to his ear.

"Nine–one–one. What's your emergency?"

"Adam Locke, 1009 Surf Drive. Shots fired. At least one shooter inside. I'm going in."

"Was anyone—"

Adam dropped the phone in the dirt. He had to go all-in. He tightened his grip on the rock and exploded out of his crouch. Broken wood and glass crackled under his feet as he dove through the threshold and into the kitchen. He slid across the floor and collided with the island in the center of the kitchen.

He sprang to his feet. He cocked the rock behind his head, ready to throw, and focused on the corridor.

No movement. No sound.

Adam manipulated the rock with his fingers to keep his arm loose. He stayed coiled, prepared to strike.

Nothing happened.

He set the rock on the counter and unsheathed a butcher knife from its wooden block. He moved around the island, holding the knife high and ready. He scanned the living room, then stopped at the hallway wall.

He quick-peeked around the corner then yanked his head back, awaiting a fuselage of bullets. The front door stood open. Was it a trap? Adam leaned back around the corner. The hallway was vacant. No sign of the killer.

Effie.

He clutched the blade and dashed down the hall. He slowed to survey the stairwell, then pounded up the stairs to the second floor. He stopped at the top and scanned both directions. The hallway remained dark and empty. He glanced back over his shoulder into the foyer. No shooter.

He padded down the hallway toward the master bedroom, staying on the balls of his feet. The bedroom door stood ajar. He leaned against the wall, ready to thrust the knife. He eased the door open with one hand, keeping his body out of the threshold.

Moonlight illuminated the darkened bedroom. The bed was empty. His heart rose into his throat. His pulse thumped in his ears.

"Effie? Where are you?"

No answer. He bolted into the room, primed for combat. No one was there. The closet door was open. She was not in there either.

"Effie!"

Panic rose in him like water boiling in a kettle. He turned to search the guest room.

"Adam?"

He froze. "Where are you?"

The duvet moved, and Effie's head poked out from under the bed. His heart exploded with relief. He knelt and dropped the knife. He took her face in his hands.

"There's a man," she said. "He's got a gun."

A siren wailed in the distance.

"He's gone." Adam helped her up.

"I heard him break in," she said. Perspiration soaked her skin. "I tried to get your gun, but there wasn't time."

"It's okay, he's gone now." He hugged her tight.

"I heard shots. I thought—"

"He missed me by a mile," Adam lied. "Everything's okay now."

The howl of sirens filled the air.

"Don't leave me," she said. She buried her face in his chest.

"I'll never leave you again."

CHAPTER SEVENTY-FIVE

Adam finished his statement and walked Sergeant Gunn to the door. He watched the State Police cars drive away. A single Falmouth patrol car remained parked out front, a security measure he had agreed to accept. He waved to a group of neighbors who had gathered on the block, then he shut his door. He did not have the energy to explain what had happened.

He retrieved a tarp from the basement and stapled it across the broken glass of the back door. It wouldn't stop anyone from getting in, but he would hear them, and there was little chance the killer would try again so soon.

Adam climbed the stairs and paused at his bedroom door to listen for Effie's snoring. Hearing nothing, he entered and looked at the empty bed. Water ran in the bathroom where Effie was cleaning up before retiring for the night. He waited for her to finish. The odor of sanitizer hung in the air, and he pictured the doctor's office. He could smell the hospital in his sleep.

He crossed to her side of the empty bed. A dozen medicine bottles covered the bedside table—a pharmaceutical buffet. When friends or family visited, they recoiled at the billboard of serious illness, as if being close to it would invite pain and suffering into their own lives. Invite death. People were squeamish around the terminally ill.

Adam saw it differently.

Effie's collection of medicine bottles was a monument to her fight, her refusal to give up. It was a sign of courage. A medal for the living.

The doctor's report had been conclusive. The cancer had spread to her liver, pancreas, and lungs. Stage IV cancer—a death sentence. When the doctor had given them the news, Effie's face had shown pain and fear, but what had bothered him most was her resignation. She had been a warrior throughout the diagnosis, chemotherapy, radiation, and surgeries. Through it all, she had fought without complaint. There had been tears and moments of horror, but no matter how bleak the prognosis had been, she had always maintained a glint in her eye—an inextinguishable spark that signaled she would never stop trying.

The latest lab results had extinguished that spark.

Pain radiated through his chest, and the room tilted as a wave of dizziness washed over him. His life, the world as he knew it, was crumbling before his eyes, and there was nothing he could do to stop it from happening.

Almost nothing.

The bathroom door handle jiggled, and Effie came out. Adam hurried to her side and guided her back to the bed. She wore pink pajamas with daisies on them, her favorite flower. He could picture her as a child, full of curiosity and anticipation. Had her life gone the way she had expected? Did she have regrets?

He lowered her to the bed.

"Ouch," Effie said.

Her pain had been getting worse, and they had increased her dosages of Dilaudid and Codeine to her daily mix of medications. As if stage-four cancer was not bad enough, she had to poison what little time she had left on earth with heavy narcotics. Was it better to be lucid and in pain or mentally fuzzy and numb—unable to contemplate her own death?

He fluffed her pillows and helped her lean back. "What's your pain number?"

"Seven."

"I'll get you another Dilaudid."

"No, I want to feel it."

"Why?"

"I want to see you through clear eyes."

Adam's throat tightened and his eyes burned.

"Marry me," he said.

"You've asked me to marry you fifty times," she said. "You know how I feel about marriage. Living with my parents before my father left killed my desire to be a wife." She looked away. "Besides, I don't know how long I have left."

"Stop it. Don't talk like that you—"

"We can't ignore it anymore. We're inside the two-minute warning, and we need to plan. I want to make sure you'll be okay."

"Don't waste one second worrying about me. Put all your energy into fighting this thing. You need to heal."

"It won't happen—" her voice broke.

He hugged her then looked deep into her eyes. "Marry me. Please."

"You don't want to marry a woman on her deathbed."

"No one knows how long they have left, and I want to spend every minute we have being your husband."

She looked up at him. Tears wet her cheeks. "What did I do to deserve you?"

"Probably something horrible," he said.

She laughed. "Only you could make me laugh at a time like this."

"I love you."

"Okay, Mr. Locke. I'll marry you."

He hugged her tight, and his tears flowed. He had not cried since his foster parents had died.

"You make me happy," she said. "Through all of it."

"You're my life."

Effie held her chest and winced. "Maybe I'll take that Dilaudid now."

"I'll get you fresh water."

He hurried into the kitchen. Life could be hard. But Adam could be hard too. He knew what he had to do.

CHAPTER SEVENTY-SIX

Fang opened her eyes and squinted against the glare of the hospital room's fluorescent lights. She tried to sit up and winced in pain. Her head throbbed. Everything hurt. Wires suspended her leg from a Balkan frame above the bed, and her arm was wrapped in a splint. She breathed in and out until the pain subsided, then she took in her surroundings. Adam Locke slumped in a chair in the corner with his eyes closed.

What was he doing there?

She laid back and tried to remember. Her mind floated on a narcotic cloud. Images danced in her mind—Shlomo's lab, Felix Suggs, the sandy trail through the wildlife preserve. Apep.

That was it. She had taken the device, and Suggs had chased her. Fear rushed into her like a winter wind and rattled her heart. What had happened to Apep? Suggs had followed her into the conservation field. She had heard him gaining on her. Then what?

She had stashed the device in the shrubs and hidden near the edge of the cliff. She had fallen. The terror returned—the horror of plunging through the air, long seconds stretching into eternity. Her stomach flipped and vomit rose in her throat. She had been sure she would die. But she had been wrong.

She turned her head, careful not to move her arm or leg, and surveyed her body. She wore a white hospital gown with a blue checkered pattern, and starch sheets covered her. A nasal cannula pumped oxygen into her nose, and an intravenous tube ran into her left hand, which explained the burning sensation. Beside her, an IV bag of saline dripped beside an empty medicine bag.

How long had she been there? How bad were her injuries? She rolled her eyes to Adam and tried to speak, but her tongue stuck to the roof of her mouth. She smacked her lips.

"Mr. Locke." Her voice sounded meek and scratchy, and her throat ached. She tried again. "Adam." Stronger this time.

He opened his eyes and jerked upright. He saw her and smiled, then moved to the bed. "Thank God."

"How long have I been here?"

He looked at his watch. "You've been out of surgery for hours. I've been waiting for the anesthesia to wear off. They asked me not to wake you."

"Is it bad?"

"Your surgeon can give you details, but you'll make it. You fractured your arm and leg and dislocated your hip. Your doctor expects a complete recovery, but he wouldn't commit to anything. You know how they are."

She exhaled. "Am I under arrest?"

"That's why I've been waiting for you to wake up. Nobody knows what happened. You went over the cliff and somehow managed to dial 9-1-1. You told them you fell, but that was all. Sergeant Gunn is coming by to interview you. She's with the State Police."

"Does she know about the device?"

"Nobody knows anything about it," Adam said. "Not even Effie. We're the only people who knew you were smuggling data out of there. What happened?"

"Suggs did not inform the authorities?"

"What does Suggs have to do with this?" Adam asked.

"Suggs chased me. He must have seen me take Apep. He confronted me, and I ran. Suggs—"

"Did he push you?"

Fang closed her eyes and teared up, reliving the memory. She shook her head. "He chased me down the path. The device was heavy, and he was so fast. I knew I would not escape."

"He caught you?"

"I burrowed into the brush to conceal myself," she said. "It was dark and raining. I did not see the edge of the cliff. I slipped and held onto a branch. I thought I would make it," her voice cracked, "but the plant uprooted, and I dropped . . ." A tear ran down her cheek.

Adam moved closer and put his hand on her shoulder. "Take your time. I'm sorry to make you relive this, but we have to get our stories straight."

She nodded and blinked away the tears. "I remember reaching for the rocks, but everything was soaking wet. I thought . . . I knew I would be killed."

Adam brushed her hair away from her face and dried her eyes with a tissue. "But you didn't. You called for help and saved yourself. You're alive and you're going to be okay." A pained expression came over his face.

"What is it?"

"The device," he said. "What happened to Effie's data?"

"Her data is in a blockchain on the cloud, but it cannot be accessed or processed without Apep. I stashed it under a bush. Suggs may have found it by now. I am sorry."

Adam's face hardened. "I'll look for it. The important thing is, you're okay. Right now, lets focus on our stories. They may discover that I brought Effie into the lab, but no one has said anything yet. Suggs could have you on video. And Shlomo will know the device was stolen. I'm sure he discovered it missing this morning."

"Why did Suggs not report the theft?" she asked. "He knew I had it in my knapsack. Why not have me arrested?"

Adam looked out the window and rubbed his eyes. "I don't know. Maybe he wanted to wait to see if you survived. Maybe he doesn't want the world to know about Apep. It goes far beyond what Forever Technology has publicly admitted."

"You think keeping it secret is important enough to ignore its theft?"

JEFFREY JAMES HIGGINS | 295

"Suggs won't ignore anything," Adam said. "My guess is Bryce will handle this in-house. If he reports it, he'll have to explain what Apep can do. Once he does that, the Feds may get involved. I doubt Bryce will risk that."

"Handle it? How?"

"Suggs is a blunt instrument. Whatever they're planning, it won't be subtle."

"What about our deal? Your girlfriend—"

"Nobody knows anything about our plan. Let's keep it that way. This—"

"But the data."

"I'm returning to Cuttyhunk," he said. "I'll search for the device."

"And if it is not there?"

"I don't know. Maybe I can plead with Bryce. Or maybe we can download her again."

"They won't let me within a mile of that place," Fang said. "If you can't find it, I won't be able to help." Pain shot through her leg, and she grimaced.

"Take it easy," Adam said. "One step at a time."

"What do I say to the police?" Fang asked.

"Stay close to the truth. Tell Gunn you worked late and saw someone when you left. Tell her you got spooked and ran into the wildlife preserve."

"Do I tell her Suggs chased me?"

"If they planned to report what happened, they would have done it by now. Say somebody followed you, and you got scared and fled. Say you stumbled in the darkness and fell. If you tell her about Suggs, Gunn will interview him and seize the video. She'll force Bryce's hand, and he'll have to admit you took the device."

"And what if he tells them?"

"If it's captured on video, you'll have to admit it and tell them what you were doing. I'll back you up and share the blame. We were going to return it after we copied the crypto key, not steal it. I just wanted Effie's data."

"Would we go to jail?"

"It's possible, but Forever Technology is up against the ropes. Surrounded. Something happened last night. Something else." Adam rubbed his chin, as if deciding what to say. "Someone killed Edna Cooper, a reporter for the Cape Cod Daily Post."

Fang closed her eyes and pushed away the thought. Had Xiu Yän done that? Had Bryce?

"Listen, I've got to get out of here before Sergeant Gunn arrives to get your statement," Adam said. "Stick to the plan. Something spooked you and you fell. If she corners you, say you don't feel well and end the interview."

"And if she knows about the device? If she accuses me of stealing it?"

"Ask for an attorney and don't say another word."

CHAPTER SEVENTY-SEVEN

Adam skirted the nurses' station and walked to the stairwell. He needed to return to Cuttyhunk, and he did not want to bump into Gunn in the elevator and be forced to make up an excuse for visiting Fang. Conspiring with Fang to download Effie's mind and then sneaking Apep out of Forever Technology was illegal, but he would do anything to preserve Effie's life. He had planned to return the device, and while still a crime, it was in a moral gray area. Besides, Bryce was a killer who planned to sell his technology to another country.

He had to be stopped.

Ten feet away, the stairwell door opened, and a doctor stepped into the hall. Adam smiled, as if he belonged.

The doctor gave him an odd look.

"I always take the stairs," Adam said. "Good for the heart." God, he sounded like an idiot.

The doctor nodded and continued down the hall. Adam breathed a sigh of relief and caught the door before it closed. He hurried down the stairway and turned onto the landing leading to the third floor.

Adam stopped.

Why had that doctor made him uneasy? Adam was allowed in the hospital, and he had come to see Fang, Tommy's coworker. The medical staff would have no reason to mention his visit to the police. As far as they knew, Fang was a victim, not a thief. The doctor he passed would not suspect Adam of anything. Adam had spent half his days in hospitals and doctors' offices since Effie's diagnosis, and he almost always used the stairs. It made no sense to share an elevator with a bunch of sick people, and walking was better for his health.

So why had the doctor given him that look?

Something about the doctor had been off. Police existed in a different world than civilians. They lived in the same spaces but saw society's underbelly, the evil that lived in men. Cops knew what people could do when the thin veneer of civilization was stripped away. Adam spent his time dealing with monsters like Jean Laguerre, men who killed without thought—without remorse. Over years in law enforcement, Adam had developed a sixth sense for criminals, an ability to recognize others who lived in his world.

That doctor was a criminal.

It was hard to put his finger on how he knew. Maybe it had been the look in the eyes, or the way he carried himself. When the doctor had come around the corner and surprised Adam, the doctor had glanced at Adam's hands. Cops did that because hands were what killed you. Criminals did it too.

Adam headed back upstairs.

CHAPTER SEVENTY-EIGHT

Fang fought through the narcotic-induced fog and tried to rehearse the story she would tell the police. Would Sergeant Gunn believe she had been scared by someone she could not describe and had run recklessly through the wildlife preserve in the rain? Fang would invoke her pain and postpone the interview.

What would Xiu say when she told him? He had demanded she deliver Apep to him. Fang had not admitted to Adam that she had planned to give the device to Xiu. Adam had assumed they were going to download the crypto or data and return Apep to Forever. And Xiu didn't know she had intended to download Effie's data before turning over the device to him. Now it was likely both would find out.

Someone knocked at the door, and a doctor entered the room. He was tall and thick, and his green scrubs and white lab coat did not hide his physical power. He walked to the bed and read the nurse's notes on a whiteboard hanging off the wall.

He faced her. "Fang Jin?"

His question confused her for a moment. Her name was displayed in big letters on the whiteboard, and she had been in the hospital since last night. How did he not know her name?

"Yes," she said. Her voice still sounded weak and groggy. The narcotics and the trauma had fatigued her, and she had trouble piecing together her thoughts.

"From Forever Technology, right?"

Fang alerted. Her eyes darted to the door.

"What does that . . . who are you, doctor?"

"Dr. White. I'm one of your physicians. I've brought you something to help with the pain."

An icy wind tickled her back, and the hair rose on her neck. Something did not feel right. Had the drugs made her paranoid?

"Will you send in the nurse first? I must use the bathroom."

"This will only take a moment."

"What are you giving me?"

"Narcotics. Enough to put you out of your pain."

Alarm bells went off in her head. "I do not want more medicine. The pain is tolerable."

He pulled a syringe out of his pocket. That was not how doctors carried drugs, especially narcotics.

"Let me see what I'm getting," she said.

"It's fine. This will all be over in a moment."

He moved to her IV stand. Fang tried to get up and bolts of electricity traveled through her body. She grabbed the IV stand and pushed it away. "No drugs."

"It's for your own good."

"You are not my doctor," she screamed.

He leaned closer with a simper. "Be quiet or I'll hurt you."

His statement hung in the air. The pretense was gone. They both knew he was there to kill her.

"What have I done to you?" she asked. She had to keep him talking and hope a nurse arrived.

"Nothing. This is business."

"I do not understand."

"They hired me to silence you. It's a business transaction. Nothing personal, I'm a professional."

"You are a monster."

"It's what I do." He smiled. "It's who I am."

CHAPTER SEVENTY-NINE

Adam shuffled down the hallway peeking into rooms for signs of the doctor. He slowed as he rounded the nurses' station and glanced at the elevators. Sergeant Gunn would arrive at any moment.

An old woman in a wheelchair dropped a glass of juice, and a nurse leaned over to clean it up, blocking the hallway. A sense of urgency filled him. He squeezed past the hunched nurse, and the old lady scowled at him. He pressed on.

Adam hurried around the corner and slowed as he approached Fang's room. He was probably being paranoid and overprotective, but experience had taught him to listen to his instincts.

He squinted through the glass, then brushed the door open, not wanting to disturb her. The curtain concealed her bed. Had her nurse done that? Adam edged around it, feeling like a peeping Tom. He reached for the fabric.

Fang uttered a muffled cry.

Adam tore back the curtain with his heart in his throat. The muscled doctor he had passed held a syringe in one hand and struggled to hold a pillow over Fang's face with the other. She kicked and her broken leg strained against the suspension wires.

The doctor spun at the sound of the rattling curtain rings and locked eyes with Adam.

Adam exploded forward. He grabbed the doctor's arm, controlling the syringe, and drove his shoulder into the man's chest. He pinned him against the bed.

The doctor grunted and pivoted, throwing Adam over his hip. Adam fell off balance, and the man's elbow that glanced off his cheek. Stars fluttered in the corners of his vision.

The man thrust the syringe at Adam like a knife. Adam used his forearm to block the thrust. The syringe skittered across the floor and under the curtain.

The doctor twisted and threw a left jab. Adam raised his arms, partially deflecting it, but the doctor's fist crunched into his face. Pain shot through Adam's right orbital. Adam rolled with the punch and landed on Fang's leg.

"Ahh," she screamed. The pain seemed to snap her out of shock and her eyes widened. "Help. Somebody help us."

The doctor glanced at her, and Adam used the distraction to spring off the bed. Adam threw a left cross and hit the doctor square in the face.

"Ugh," he grunted and staggered back.

Adam followed with a right uppercut, his deadliest punch. The man leaned away, and Adam's knuckles grazed his hair.

The doctor stepped forward as Adam followed through. He struck Adam in the chest with the heel of his hand. The blow expelled air from Adam's lungs. He fell back against the bed, and it slid across the floor.

The doctor shook his head, then balled his fists and grinned at Adam. Adam moved away from the bed to protect Fang and spread his feet wide in a defensive stance. Round one had been a draw.

The doctor grabbed the IV stand and slung it at Adam. The metal bar crashed into him, and saline sprayed his face. Adam knocked the stand to the floor and raised his hands, ready for the next attack.

The man bolted around the curtain.

Adam tried to catch a full breath, but the blow had knocked the wind out of him. Fang's eyes widened with terror.

His breath returned. "You okay?"

"Who—?"

"Did he inject anything into your IV?"

"I don't think so."

Adam looked at the IV on the floor. The lines had pulled out of Fang's arm, leaving a trail of blood.

"Tell the nurse to test the fluid in the line. I don't know what he was trying to give you, but it wasn't a vitamin."

Adam hurried around the curtain. He dashed across the room and caught the door as it was closing.

He poked his head out in time to see the doctor run around the corner. A food cart crashed against the wall with a clang. Several nurses looked up.

"Call nine-one-one," Adam yelled. "That man tried to kill Dr. Jin. She needs help."

They gawked at him, frozen.

"Nine-one-one," he shouted again. He sprinted down the hall.

Adam rounded the corner as the stairwell door slammed shut at the end of the corridor. He barreled after him.

Adam paused at the door, then flung it open. He stayed behind the wall, because the doctor could be armed, and Adam was once again caught without his gun. There had been no obvious bulge under the doctor's lab coat, but he could have had an ankle holster.

He listened. Footsteps pounded down the stairs below.

Adam burst across the threshold and took the stairs three at a time. He needed to catch the doctor before he reached the lobby, four floors below. Adam hit the third-floor landing and paused. The closed stairwell prevented him from seeing below, but the sound of the doctor tramping down the steps continued.

Adam ran down the next two flights to the second floor. A hinge creaked far below, probably the first-floor door leading to the lobby.

A series of muffled shouts rose from beneath him. The door slammed shut, and the footsteps resumed. They grew louder, closer.

The doctor was coming back upstairs.

CHAPTER EIGHTY

Adam looked down the stairwell at the landing below as the doctor's footsteps echoed up toward him. He glanced around for anything he could use as a weapon, but the concrete walls were bare, except for red metal pipes running along the ceiling. He leaned back out of sight and peeked around the corner.

The doctor rounded the corner onto the landing and stopped. He stared up at Adam. His head bobbed with each respiration, and sweat ran down his face. He sneered.

The lobby door crashed open below them. The cackle of a radio rose into the stairwell. Security. They must have chased the doctor away from the lobby.

The doctor looked over his shoulder, then back at Adam. He turned and yanked open the door to the mezzanine level. He bolted through it.

Adam rounded the corner and descended the stairs in three jumps. He grabbed the door before it closed. He gave chase.

A coffee shop occupied one side of the mezzanine and a dozen tables covered the space in front of it. Opposite the shop, a railing opened to the lobby, thirty feet below. The sounds of classical piano music drifted up from the ground floor.

The doctor raced between tables, drawing angry shouts from patients and staff. He crossed the mezzanine to the elevator bank on the far side.

"Stop him," Adam shouted. "He tried to murder a patient."

Heads swung in the doctor's direction. Adam hustled after him.

An elevator dinged as the doctor approached and two security guards exited. They spotted him and spread out. One guard unsnapped a collapsible baton as the other spoke into his radio.

The stairwell door banged open behind Adam, and a third security guard emerged. Luckily, this urban trauma center had seen its fair share of violent patients and the security staff were prepared.

The doctor backed toward the center of the mezzanine. Patients and customers remained frozen in their seats, gawking. Adam advanced.

"Take it easy," Adam said. "There's nowhere to go. It's over."

The doctor glowered at Adam. His eyes darted to the railing. Patients and visitors milled around the marble floor below, unaware of the drama unfolding high above their heads.

"The fall will kill you," Adam said. He edged closer.

The doctor pushed away from the railing and hurtled across the floor to the closest table occupied by a woman and a tiny girl. The girl wore a hospital robe and her blonde hair poked out of a thick bandage wrapped around her head. She held a pumpkin muffin a few inches from her face as she watched the doctor approach.

The doctor grabbed the girl around her chest and jerked her out of the chair with one arm.

"Mommy," she screamed.

"Let her go," the woman shouted.

The security guards closed in. One of their radios crackled. The doctor spun around to face them. He grabbed a butter knife off the table and pressed it against the girl's throat. Her eye's rounded and her mouth opened in terror, but no sound came out.

"No," the woman screamed.

"Back off or she's dead," the doctor said. His baritone voice was measured and intentional, as if holding a knife to a girl's throat happened every day.

"Hey," Adam said, trying to distract him.

The doctor turned and swiveled his head between the two guards and Adam. He backed toward the railing.

"I'll kill her," he said.

Adam believed him. "You didn't hurt Dr. Jin. You'll be charged with simple battery, nothing more. Don't hurt the girl. It's not worth it."

"Fuck you," the doctor said. "You're not talking to an idiot."

"Don't make this worse."

The third security guard appeared in Adam's peripheral vision. Two nurses in pink scrubs sat like statues at the table beside him. Steam rose off a paper cup of fresh coffee. The air became taut, like a rubber band stretched to its limit. Adam dared not breathe and snap it.

"You're gonna back away from the elevator, and I'm gonna walk out of here." The doctor's voice stayed level, but the skin pinched around his eyes.

"Let her go," Adam said.

The doctor dragged the girl backward until he bumped against the railing. He glanced down at the lobby where a dozen people had taken notice and craned their necks to watch the drama. A police siren echoed off the hospital's facade.

Victory goes to the aggressor.

Adam sidestepped and blocked the doctor's view of the nurse's table with his body. He reached behind and wrapped his fingers around the coffee cup.

"I'm leaving now," the doctor said, "and if you try to stop me, I'll rip her throat out."

A tear rolled down the little girl's cheek. Her mother screamed something unintelligible.

Adam cocked his body like the hammer on a revolver and focused. He needed a distraction, anything to create a moment of confusion. He looked at the two guards blocking the path to the elevator.

"Don't shoot him," Adam yelled.

The doctor snapped his head toward the guards. Adam did not hesitate. He uncoiled his body like a spring and swung the coffee cup at the doctor. Steaming liquid splashed the doctor's face, and he instinctively closed his eyes and turned away from the scalding java.

Adam covered the distance in two steps and hit him like a blitzing safety.

The railing collided with the doctor's back, and his legs catapulted off the ground. He extended his arms for balance and the knife flew into the air.

Adam followed through, lowering his center of gravity, and pushed with all his strength. The force of the impact launched the doctor over backward. He toppled over the railing as Adam slammed into it.

The sharp railing dug into Adam's shoulder, and the girl fell against him.

The doctor's body disappeared off the mezzanine.

The piano shattered below with a disharmonious blare. People screamed.

Adam held the girl and inspected her neck. The dull knife had left a long scratch but had not broken the skin. She broke into tears and ran into her mother's arms.

Adam climbed to his feet and looked over the railing. The doctor had crashed through the piano, shattering it. Brass strings swayed in the air like stalks of wheat. A large pool of dark blood filled the broken instrument. The doctor stared back at him with dead eyes.

Hospital staff rushed to help, but gray matter had exploded out of the doctor's fractured skull and sprinkled the soundboard. Their efforts would be futile.

Sergeant Gunn stood beside the piano gawking at Adam.

CHAPTER EIGHTY-ONE

Adam stepped off the ferry and onto Cuttyhunk's dock. A flock of seagulls took flight. He rubbed his temples as he trudged to a line of parked golf carts owned by Forever Technology. He had only taken a short rest after his ordeal at the hospital, and his body ran on fumes. According to Gunn, the doctor who had tried to kill Fang had not been a doctor at all. The recently deceased Brock Gibson had been some kind of freelance security consultant at Global Conflict Solutions Corporation, a military and law enforcement contractor, but that was all they knew so far.

Gunn had not bought Adam's story that he had been visiting Fang out of a sense of worry over an injured colleague, but without Fang's or his admission, she could prove nothing.

Adam unlocked his cell phone and dialed Gunn.

"Good morning, Mr. Locke," she said. "I thought you would have had enough of me."

"I'm calling to see if you had any luck getting a judge to sign warrants for Forever Technology and Bryce's residence."

"I couldn't even get my lieutenant to approve the warrant applications. Nobody wants to piss off a billionaire without incontrovertible proof that he's involved in these murders. Even without Bryce Hastings' influence, a warrant would have been pretty thin. There just isn't enough probable cause."

"He's responsible."

"Forever may be engaged in unethical behavior, but it's not illegal, and I've got nothing tying them to the murders. Get me something concrete, and I'll get those warrants."

"Isn't that your job?" he asked and immediately regretted it. "Sorry, I'm tired and cranky."

"I'm sorry too. My hands are tied."

"You won't do anything?"

"I'm on Cuttyhunk now," she said.

Adam looked up with alarm and scanned the area, but only a handful of island residents milled about the parking lot. "Without a warrant?"

"I'm about to walk into Hastings' office. He's agreed to an interview without his attorney. I'll let you—" The sound muffled.

"Gunn?"

"Gotta go. He's ready for me."

Adam disconnected and climbed into a cart. At least he had tried to do it the legal way. He needed to determine if Forever Technology was behind the attacks, and more importantly, he had to access Effie's data before they fired him. Maybe if he took possession of Bryce's most protected technology, the killer would come to him. Adam would not let legality stand in the way of justice—or Effie's life.

He did not start the cart. He scrolled through his phone to the video app connected to the surveillance camera outside Bryce's house. A moment later, a golf cart parked in Bryce's driveway. He zoomed in. Suggs was driving, that was certain, and beside him on the seat was a black knapsack, like the one Fang had said she used to steal the device.

Adam switched to his second camera view and watched Suggs hurry up the sidewalk to Bryce's front door. The knapsack hung over his shoulder, and something inside pushed against the fabric. Whatever it was, it looked heavy.

The device.

If Suggs had found Apep after Fang tumbled off the cliff, why did he wait to deliver it to Bryce's residence? Was he moving it now because Gunn had come to Forever Technology? Why not take it off the island? Or did

Bryce think Cuttyhunk was the safest place? Whatever the reason, if Adam was going to recover Apep, he needed to hurry.

Suggs exited the house without the backpack. He entered his cart and drove away.

Adam ended the live feed, and his phone rang. Svetlana.

"Are you okay?" he asked.

"I'm losing my mind," she said. A seagull's caw came across the line.

"Where are you?"

"I'm sitting on my patio drinking a Manhattan. This time, the booze isn't helping. I need to know you're going to catch Bryce. You must stop him. He's a villain."

"I'm trying," Adam said. "I'm on Cuttyhunk now."

"Have you found anything?"

Adam sighed. "I'm going to Bryce's residence now. If he's hiding anything, it's there."

"Be careful."

Adam promised he would and stuffed his phone in his pocket. It was time to push all his chips into the center of the table. He started the cart and raced up the path. He took the long way around to avoid Suggs, who probably headed back to work.

Ten minutes later, he parked in Bryce's driveway and leapt from the cart. What was his plan? The device belonged to Forever Technology, but if Bryce sold it to the Chinese, he would damage national security. Taking Apep and informing the feds seemed like a good idea, though he had no legal authority to seize it. He could tell Bryce he only wanted the data, but then Fang would be fired and arrested, and if Bryce declined to help, Adam would lose access to Apep. Effie's data would be worthless without the cryptographic key needed to unlock the block-chain-protected data so Forever's heuristics could process it. Without Apep, Effie's digital mind would be lost forever.

He had to steal it.

Once he had Apep in his possession, Effie would be safe—at least her mind would be—and he could decide whether to turn the device over to authorities or negotiate its return to Bryce. But if he failed to find it, and

Bryce disappeared, Effie's last hope would be gone. Stealing was wrong, but Forever had killed three people and attempted to murder two more. They operated outside the law and protected themselves with political cronies, legal defense teams, and extralegal force. He would take the device, secure her data, then figure out how to use it.

Effie was his life.

Adam climbed out of the cart and walked up the path. He tried the door. Locked.

He stepped back and kicked the wood beneath the handle. The frame splinted, and the door flew open. A red light flickered on the panel beside the door.

He had fifteen minutes.

CHAPTER EIGHTY-TWO

Adam dashed across the living room into the kitchen, grabbed a stool, and dragged it down the hall. There was no need to search the first floor— Bryce's treasure would be in the basement.

He opened the stairwell door and carried the stool down the steps. He stopped in front of the frosted-glass door. Adam held the stool over his shoulder and turned his head. He smashed the stool into the glass and hundreds of fragments rained on him.

Fluorescent lights illuminated as he stepped across the threshold into a square room with linoleum flooring. Stainless steel desks lined the walls, and another glass door was closed on the far side of the room.

The backpack Suggs had been carrying sat on the far desk.

Adam smiled. He strode across the room and pieces of tempered glass fell off him and clacked against the floor. The odor of Old Spice hung in the air. He unzipped the knapsack and noted the damp fabric. It must have sat in the bushes all night. He removed the device and placed it on the counter.

"I have to know," he said.

Apep was a solid black cube with ports for wiring, and a dozen buttons on the front. The power cord was still attached, so he plugged it into a wall socket and stared at the controls. The top left button was larger than the rest and had a red circle with a dot in the center, a universal power symbol. He pressed it.

Nothing happened.

The device may have been damaged by water. Could they salvage the data? He stuffed Apep back into his knapsack and slung it over his shoulder. He headed toward the steps, then stopped. Adam looked over his shoulder at the second glass door. It looked like the entrance to an airlock, like those in the Black Diamond project laboratories. What was Bryce doing here? Adam had risked too much not to know. He checked his watch. He had ten minutes, maybe more, before security arrived to check the alarm.

He dashed across the room. A single backlit button glowed red beside the door. He pressed it. The light turned to green, and the door slid open with a sucking sound.

Adam stepped in the airlock, and the door snapped shut behind him. Being underground and inside an airtight compartment made his skin crawl. He moved to the other door, which was constructed of opaque plastic. He slapped the button, and it turned green.

The door opened, revealing a large laboratory room with stainless steel tables in the center and tall lockers flush against the walls. He entered and the overhead lights illuminated.

From behind a pane in each locker, a human face stared back at him.

Adam gasped. He wanted to run, but he stayed. Their eyes were open, but none moved.

He approached the first locker and peered through the window. The face was human, so real, but below the sternum, the body was steel and polymer. It rested on a shelf, and wires protruded from the bottom like roots.

Robots.

What the hell was Bryce doing? Adam moved to the next closet. It contained a robot with a complete male body. The detail was amazing, right down to the genitals. If it had been lying on a beach, people would easily mistake it for human. Except for colored wires hanging from ports in the head, chest, and waist.

How far had Bryce's research come?

Adam continued down the length of lockers. Each contained a unique-looking machine, including male and female, young and old. Why the diversity? Did each match the appearance of the patients Bryce had downloaded? Bryce had claimed his research had not perfected mapping, but that had been a lie. This was another level.

His bots were lifelike, but to what extent did they function?

Adam moved to the table in the center of the room. Robotic parts, including hands and feet, intermingled with devices similar to Apep. A female head and torso, without arms or legs, rested on the end of the table facing him. It resembled a blond-haired girl, no more than ten years old. Like the models in closets, wires hung from sealed ports, but it also had a thick bundle of cables running from its torso into a port in the floor. Adam leaned in and examined her. Her features were so lifelike. So real. Her skin appeared natural. Human. What materials had they used? He pressed a finger against her cheek.

Her eyes opened.

Adam yelped and fell backward. "What the fuck?"

He stood and dusted his trousers off. Her eyes were crystal blue, with natural lashes. That had scared him shitless.

"What is a fuck?" she asked.

Adam backed away. "Oh, my God."

"Are you praying?" she asked.

Adam's eyes darted around the room, and gooseflesh rose on his skin. He glanced at the lockers, ready for the other robots to come to life. They remained dormant.

Adam shook away his fear. This was amazing. The robot had reacted to his speech and responded appropriately. That meant it comprehended his words, analyzed the meaning behind them, determined a proper response, and created a verbal action. Lifelike. He had to test it.

He looked at his watch. Seven minutes.

"What's your name?" he asked.

"Olivia. What's yours?"

"Adam," he stammered. "How old are you?"

"I just turned nine, but my Forever date is six months and three days."

"Forever date?"

She smiled. "The date they gave me a new body."

New body? Was she a shadow copy of a real person's brain? "What happened to your body?"

She looked down at the table and curled her lip. "It broke."

Her face moved with complete realism. How did they manage that?

"Broke?" he asked.

"I had an accident. My doctor said my body wouldn't work anymore, so they gave me a new one."

The implications were too horrific to imagine. Or were they too wonderful? Had Bryce uploaded the mind of a dying child into this thing? Was it a robot, a cyborg, or a human? What did this say about humanity? Adam had always resisted religion, because he did not trust institutions to frame the concept of God. Churches, temples, mosques, and synagogues had created myths and fairytales to make people believe. To make them obey. That had made him dismiss their ideas as childish notions designed to persuade the masses.

What if he had been wrong?

What if religious doctrine described phenomenon rooted in science? Were stories a way to explain physics and interpret a world we did not fully understand? Recent discoveries, like quantum entanglement, the God particle, and dark matter, proved humanity did not comprehend the physical world. Most physicists believed in a multi-verse and a dozen dimensions, so what made the idea of God unbelievable? The physical world and consciousness remained mysteries.

"What are you?" he asked.

"I'm Olivia."

"I didn't ask your name. I asked what you are."

"I'm a girl."

"How long—?"

Something crashed upstairs. Someone was in the house.

CHAPTER EIGHTY-THREE

Adam took a last look at Oliva then raced through the airlock carrying Apep. Smoke filled the outer room.

Fire.

He looked back at the lab. Should we go back and rescue Olivia? What about the other cyborgs? He could not carry them all. His only hope was to find the source of the fire and extinguish it.

He covered his mouth and climbed the stairs.

Smoke thickened as he rose, and the taste of charcoal filled his mouth. He gagged. He coughed and spat tarry saliva. The air warmed at the top of the stairwell. Fire crackled in the hallway.

He pushed through the door and covered his eyes with the crook of his arm. Fire licked the walls and washed across the ceiling like waves crashing against the shore. It was too late.

Adam stepped toward the living room, but a wall of fire bubbled over the floor. He retreated down the hallway. Heat stung his back and flames crawled along the ceiling. The last door was closed. Adam lowered his shoulder and did not break stride.

He crashed into it.

The door buckled, and the wood frame broke free. He fell onto the carpet inside a bedroom. Fire rolled across the ceiling into the room. Thick smoke cloaked the space in darkness. Adam coughed and clutched the backpack. He bent at the waist to stay low and ran to the window. He kicked out the screen and dropped his knapsack into the yard. Toxic fumes burned his nostrils. The bedspread burst into flames.

He dove headfirst through the window.

Adam landed hard on his elbows and rolled onto his back. Tendrils of fire tickled the window frame and blackened the siding. He crawled away from the window.

The conflagration fully engulfed the house. Would the airlock protect Oliva and the other cyborgs? Flames flickered out the window. Black smoke formed a cloud over the island. Someone must have activated the volunteer fire company by now. Adam turned to leave.

Suggs stood in front of him, holding a Glock at his side.

"Good afternoon, Mr. Lock. I thought I'd find you here. This feels . . . inevitable."

"Fuck you."

"When the alarm went off, I knew it would be you. You burglarized Bryce's office too. You wouldn't leave it alone. You had to keep digging."

"You bastards killed my brother."

Suggs grinned like a sociopath. "An unavoidable complication."

"You piece of shit." Heat rose in Adam's neck.

Suggs pointed the gun at him, holding it at his waist like a gunslinger. "I told you to stop. I gave you many opportunities to walk away."

Adam coughed and spit. Behind him, the fire sounded like a freeway. "Why did you murder Tommy? What did he find?"

Suggs laughed. "You've got it all wrong."

"Did he discover your cyborgs?"

"Tommy knew everything. He had total access to Black Diamond. He pushed the project from the beginning."

Tommy was behind Black Diamond? It didn't make sense. Adam's head ached from the smoke. "Then why did he have to die?"

"Your brother had second thoughts about our plan to sell the technology."

"You're lying."

"Your brother was no saint. He got cold feet and needed to be dealt with."

"And Edna Cooper."

"Also unavoidable."

Adam balled his fists. "You won't get away with this."

"I already have."

"You sent Gibson to kill Fang too?"

"Her loyalties were always murky. When she tried to steal the device, I knew she had to go."

Pain stabbed Adam's chest. His decision to pressure Fang into helping him had signed her death warrant. It had been pure luck Adam had been there to stop her. Now, nothing would prevent Suggs from finishing the job. "What did Sarah Smith do to deserve this?"

"That's the irony," Suggs said. "I didn't kill Sarah Smith."

"Who did?"

"I think she went over the cliff on her own."

"Suicide?"

"An accident. It gave us the idea to kill Thomas."

"You and Bryce?"

"You still haven't figured out the angles, have you, hotshot? I thought you'd work it out, but I guess now you'll never know."

Suggs extended the gun toward Adam's chest.

A siren blared in Gosnold. The fire department would arrive soon. Adam had to stall Suggs for as long as possible. "What you're doing here is inhuman."

"That's the question, isn't it?"

"What do you mean?"

"What is human?" Suggs asked.

"Don't play word games. You developed technology that will change the definition of human. And you're selling it to China."

His smile disappeared. "How do you know that?"

"I know everything," Adam bluffed.

Suggs took a step closer and aimed the Glock at Adam's head. "Tell me who told you that. Tell me what you know."

Suggs remained fifteen feet away. Still too far. "I found evidence you were selling Black Diamond to China to prevent the federal government from controlling it under the guise of national security."

Suggs's shoulders relaxed and his eyes gleamed. Adam had it wrong.

"You're guessing."

"Fang set up the deal for you," Adam said. "You and Bryce would make billions and then disappear."

"You had me worried for a moment."

"I have the evidence," Adam lied. "I can prove it."

"Not if you're dead."

"If I die, my attorney will turn everything over to the FBI."

"You're bluffing. You don't have shit."

"Why take that chance?"

"I can give you five hundred million reasons," Suggs said. "I don't suppose you'd be interested in a share of it."

"I'd never take your blood money. You killed my brother."

Suggs smirked. "That was a test. I wouldn't have believed you even if you had agreed. You'd turn me in. This sale will change my life, and I'm not letting you stop me. Step away from the knapsack."

Adam glanced at the knapsack. The device inside belonged to Forever Technology, but if Suggs took it, he may never have access again. "All I want is the data."

"Move away or I'll shoot you and take it."

"No need for that." Adam stepped away and stopped with his left foot forward in a partial fighting stance. When Suggs bent over to pick up the knapsack, he would attack with a snap kick.

"I'm not an amateur, Mr. Locke. Farther away, please."

Adam complied and moved away from the house, increasing the distance between them.

Suggs picked up the knapsack without taking his eyes, or the Glock, off Adam. He held the bag between his knees, unzipped it, and peeked at the device. He flashed a dominant smile. "That's grand theft."

"You know my situation. I just want to preserve Effie's data. I was going to return the—"

Suggs tossed the pack through the open window and into the fire. Flames and smoke poured out the opening in response. The conflagration devoured Apep.

"No," Adam screamed. He moved toward the window.

"That's far enough, Mr. Locke."

Adam stopped. His heart pounded in his chest and his breath came fast. "Why?"

Suggs flashed a dominant smile. "Because I can."

"You destroyed the evidence of theft. Let me go and I'll give you time to get away. Time to—"

Brakes squealed from out front. Someone had arrived. The fire department? Suggs frowned and stepped to the corner of the building to look. He kept his gun pointed in Adam's direction, but his attention focused on the new arrival.

This was Adam's chance. He bolted across the yard toward the shrubs.

A gunshot shattered the silence.

CHAPTER EIGHTY-FOUR

Bullets sliced through the air, inches from Adam's head. He ducked and juked. Rounds zipped through the underbrush as he neared the end of the yard.

He stumbled the last three paces and dove headfirst into the bushes. Thorns and branches scratched his skin as he plowed through the brambles. He landed on hard-packed earth. His lacerated hands stung, but his adrenaline dulled the pain.

Adam pushed off the ground and knelt, keeping his head low. Another bullet snapped twigs off to his left. He squatted and shuffled through the brush, pushing branches away from his face as he moved down the slope.

The shooting stopped, and he pictured Suggs running across the lawn. He was no match for a man with the gun—especially against Suggs's combat experience. Retreat was the only option.

He stayed hunched and fought through the vegetation. Suggs would hear him, but he had stopped shooting, which meant he was either out of ammunition or angling for a better shot.

The incline reached thirty degrees, making it difficult to maintain his footing, but at least the hill provided cover and concealment. The southern end of Cuttyhunk twisted before him, like a hooked finger, with Westend Pond in the center. His best option was to put as much space between him and Suggs as possible. He headed for the southern tip.

Adam tripped and toppled forward, unable to keep his feet beneath him. He fell headfirst into the brush and covered his face before he hit the ground. He rolled and tumbled down the hill. He came to a rest near the bottom. Suggs must have heard him.

Adam rose to his feet and hacked through the brush until the terrain leveled and he reached Westend Pond. Beyond Gosnold Island, the peninsula hooked like a scorpion's tail. The Bartholomew Gosnold Monument towered over the tiny isle, and behind it, remnants of the light station's oil house poked out of the ground.

Adam stopped and listened.

Far above him, Suggs barreled through the brush like a charging bull. Adam peeked over the shrubs. Suggs held his Glock high as he fought his way through the underbrush.

Hurry.

He could try to slip past Suggs, but if Suggs heard him or saw the movement in the underbrush, he could easily cut Adam off. Suggs had the high ground and the only weapon, which gave him a superior tactical advantage. The other option was to hide. But where?

All that remained of the oil house was its foundation, and the monument must be locked. Ankle-deep flora and fauna covered the island's southern claw, providing little concealment. Maybe he would get lucky and spot a boat, or if he stayed out of sight, he could wait for Suggs to move, and then sprint to the opposite coast and run into town.

He had to warn Gunn that Suggs was behind this. If the state police launched soon, they could be in Gosnold by the time he arrived. Maybe they could send a helicopter to the southern claw. If Suggs heard it, he would likely flee. Adam reached for his phone.

His pocket was empty.

Effie's phone must have fallen out when he had plummeted down the hill. Adam peeked over the shrubbery again. Suggs was closer and coming hard. If Adam moved to his right, Suggs would have a clear line of sight and spot him for sure. Adam had to run around the pond, then take West End Road toward Forever Technology and Gosnold. That was his best play.

Adam bolted from cover and scampered across the pond's sandy shore. Thirty feet from West End Road, a bullet cracked over his head as it broke the sound barrier.

Adam spun around. Suggs was twenty yards from the bottom of the hill, moving to the east. He would reach West End Road before Adam did. Adam's only choice was to follow the peninsula around the other side of the pond. A small channel had been dug through the narrow shoreline to allow seawater to flow into the pond. He could wade through and head up the western shore. By committing to the road, Suggs had left the other route unguarded.

Another round zipped over his head.

Adam dashed toward the southern tip.

Suggs fired again, and the bullet splashed into the water nearby. Only Fifty yards separated them, but still a tough shot at a moving target.

Lactic acid burned in Adam's thighs. He peeked behind him as he approached the oil house ruins. Suggs had closed the distance. He stopped and took the shooter's stance. Adam juked right as Suggs fired again. The bullet kicked up sand at Adam's feet. Adam dove onto the beach as another round snapped overhead.

The small strip of land separating the pond from Buzzards Bay was too open. Eventually, one of Suggs's rounds would find their mark. He must have brought extra ammunition. Damn Suggs for being prepared.

Adam scurried across the beach on his hands and knees. His palms and shoes dug into ground still wet from days of rain, and he slowed to a crawl. The more he pushed, the deeper he sank. He was living his childhood nightmare of being chased by a monster and unable to move.

He reached a low dune and his soles grabbed traction in the grass. He glanced behind him. Suggs hurried along the beach.

Thirty yards away.

Adam braced a foot beneath him and exploded like a sprinter out of the starting blocks. He hurtled across the uneven ground.

One, two, three . . .

He dodged right. The retort of Suggs's gun echoed off the hill, and a tuft of sand peppered the air in front of him. Adam juked as the gun fired again.

A bullet ricocheted off something in the ruins. He lost his footing and fell. He rolled onto his back and looked back. Suggs was not yet visible on the beach below.

The oil house's foundation was no bigger than a cottage. The lighthouse had been gone since a hurricane knocked it down in 1944. Adam stood and surveyed the beach. Suggs kept coming.

Twenty yards.

To the west, the beach narrowed to a few feet across where the berm separated Buzzards Bay from the pond. Adam could run along it, splash across the narrow outlet, then continue north until he reached the road that led to Gosnold. But he would be without cover for more than a hundred yards, and Suggs could take his time aiming. Adam would never make it, which limited his options to either charging Suggs or fleeing into the pond.

Adam dashed into the foundation and leapt onto the bricks on the far side. He hoisted himself up and over the top. He landed in the sand and let his momentum carry him toward the pond.

Suggs had probably reached the foundation and was edging through the grassy dunes to avoid being ambushed. Suggs could not be sure Adam was unarmed. Who in their right mind would not have brought a gun?

Adam did not stop. Gosnell island lay twenty yards offshore—a tiny mound of earth with the decrepit monument poking out like a chimney. Adam dove into the icy water and it took away his breath.

He pushed off the sandy bottom, and his face broke the surface. He tasted the crisp saltwater. Adam stroked for the island with everything he had. Suggs would have heard the splash, but Adam had committed. He dug hard for the island, angling toward the eastern edge. He had to put the rounded mound of earth between him and the shoreline, because if Suggs shot enough bullets, he'd eventually get lucky.

Despite his waterlogged clothes, he reached the island faster than expected. Suggs's first shot splashed the water a few feet away. Adam inhaled and dove below the surface, using his hands to guide him around the island and out of Suggs's view.

Another bullet tunneled through the water, trailing a line of bubbles behind it. It dislodged a rock near Adam's face. Adam dug his toes into the bottom and burst out of the pond. He clawed at the grass and pulled himself onto the island.

Rounds kicked up dirt at his feet. Adam dove behind the monument. He curled his legs and concealed himself behind the brick structure. He leaned against it to catch his breath.

The shooting stopped.

Suggs would have two choices. Either climb into the water and forge across the pond or move along the shore to find a better shooting angle. The entrance to the seventy-foot tower had been sealed with bricks. There was no way inside. Adam had to keep the tower between him and Suggs until help arrived. Hopefully, someone had heard the shooting. But an unarmed civilian would not come to his rescue, so he had to hope the State Police were en route. How long would they take? If they came at all.

The tower was a few feet wide, which meant Suggs had to travel a much greater distance on shore to get the proper angle. All Adam had to do was spot him and take a step right or left to remain behind cover. He peeked around the monument. Suggs stood up to his knees in the water and seemed to be debating what to do.

"Give it up, Suggs. I've called the police and they're on their way."

"Have you?"

"I told Sergeant Gunn what you've done. She's sending a helicopter."

"Oh, really?"

"It's over. Why don't you escape while you still can?"

Silence. Adam waited. Had Suggs bought his bluff?

"One question," Suggs shouted across the channel.

"What?"

"How did you call the police without your phone?"

Adam's stomach knotted. Suggs held his cell phone in the air.

Shit.

"I picked it up outside the window," Suggs said.

"That's my work phone," Adam lied. "I called from my personal cell." It was a weak bluff, but could Suggs take the chance?

"No one's coming," Suggs said. "You can't stay there forever. Swim back across, and I promise to make this quick and painless."

"You'll never get an angle on me," Adam said. Once darkness fell, Adam would have a better chance of escaping across the pond or risking a run down the causeway. Suggs had to know it was hopeless. Unless . . .

"You think you'll survive that long? There are only a handful of residents on this island, and nobody close enough to hear the gunfire. Not over the waves crashing against the rocks. This is Massachusetts. Nobody out here is armed."

"The State Police will come," Adam said.

"This isn't my first rodeo, Locke. My backup will arrive long before the police. You may dance around that tower, but you can't escape shooters on both sides. I called Forever Technology and told them you stole the device and set the fire. They're responding to an armed burglary. Once we get you in a crossfire, it's over."

Adam looked up at the hill. Somebody moved along the path halfway down the hill, and two more heads bobbed above the brush near the top. Ivan and Buck. Suggs had been telling the truth. Adam had maybe ten minutes before they positioned themselves along the northern shore and opened up. He had to act now, while he had a chance.

Adam scrounged on the ground and dug a rock out of the earth. He hefted it in his hand. Adam had a powerful arm, but at this distance, a rock would be useless as a weapon. He dropped it and watched the guards weave their way down the hill.

Adam leaned around the tower again. Suggs smiled at him. Bastard. Adam rolled out of sight and slipped into the water on the opposite side of the monument. He submerged up to his chest, trying to make as little noise as possible. He breast-stroked into the middle of the pond. If he could cross without being noticed, he could flee up the western coast.

Halfway across the pond, he glanced over his shoulder. Suggs ran along the western causeway. He had seen Adam. It was too far to swim the rest of the distance underwater, and Adam could not return to the tower. He was finished.

But he would never stop trying.

He turned onto his stomach and used the crawl stroke to cross the surface. He aimed for the far shore. Five strokes, ten strokes—he dared another look behind him.

Suggs waited for him on the distant shore. He spread his legs in an isosceles shooting stance and aimed.

Adam dove under the water as bullets pierced the water and sizzled toward the sandy bottom. Adam turned underwater and headed back to the island. His lungs burned. He needed oxygen. But first, he scooped a rock off the bottom. A lucky throw could save him.

Adam broke the surface and got a bead on Suggs, who had moved halfway down the causeway and stood only fifteen yards away. He grinned at Adam and raised his Glock.

Adam cocked his arm.

The air above rustled with a flap, and something flashed past. Adam glanced up, but nothing was there. He looked back at Suggs and gaped.

Suggs had dropped his handgun. He clawed at a feathered arrow protruding out of his chest.

CHAPTER EIGHTY-FIVE

Suggs fell to his knees, his face a mask of pain and surprise. A crimson stain spread across his shirt. His face paled. He clutched the arrow and his body arched in agony. He swayed and then pitched forward. The fletching dug into the dirt, and the shaft plowed through him until the arrowhead punched out his back. Blood dripped off the tip and curled down the shaft.

Suggs convulsed, and then his body lay still.

Adam faced the direction from which the arrow came. Bryce stood on the causeway holding his compound bow.

Bryce lowered the bow and made his way along the causeway. He knelt beside Suggs and placed two fingers on the security chief's neck. Bryce looked at Adam and shook his head.

Why had Bryce killed Suggs? Adam's mind reeled. He swam to the causeway and climbed out of the water.

"Suggs is gone," Bryce said.

"He tried to kill me."

"I know."

"He wanted to shut me up," Adam said. "Why didn't you let him?"

Bryce cocked his head, as if Adam's question had shocked him. "Let him? When I saw him chasing you, I grabbed my bow and took a path to beat the security team. I came to save you."

"But Suggs—"

"He was with me for a long time, but I couldn't let him commit murder."

"He killed for you before."

Bryce's brow furrowed. "Never."

"It was Suggs all along, doing your dirty work."

"I never told him to hurt anyone," Bryce said. "I knew he could be heavy-handed. He was a hammer. But I could not have predicted he would go this far."

"You knew."

Bryce stared across the water. "Maybe I turned a blind eye to his excesses. I never thought he would do more than threaten anyone. I would have stopped him if I'd known. He didn't tell me he'd hurt anyone, and I never imagined he'd do this."

"But he did."

Bryce scratched his head. "Why? Did he think this would help the company?"

"I saw the girl, Bryce. Olivia. You've been lying to the world. You've perfected the technology."

Bryce snorted. "We're years away from perfection."

"But you're closer than you've admitted."

"Closer, yes, but we're still not there."

"You're selling your technology to the highest bidder. To China. Suggs killed Tommy because Tommy figured it out."

Bryce's face hardened. "I'm not selling anything to China."

"You are."

"They would steal my technology the second they laid their hands on it, and there would be nothing I could do to stop them. Black Diamond is my child. My legacy. I'll never give it up."

Was he telling the truth?

"Suggs didn't share your vision," Adam said. "If he wasn't doing it for you, then he was stealing your technology."

Bryce looked at the body and shook his head. "Suggs."

"Tommy found out what he was doing, and Suggs murdered him to keep him quiet."

"You think he was involved in Sarah's accident?" Bryce asked.

"He said he didn't do it. Called it an accident. But I think he threw her off the cliff because she knew too much. Sarah was sleeping with Tommy, and Suggs probably assumed Tommy had confided in her."

Bryce exhaled and walked to the water's edge. The two security guards had reached the bottom of the hill. Bryce seemed genuinely upset. But sociopaths could mimic human behavior. Was he behind this?

"What was Suggs's endgame?" Bryce asked.

"He planned to sell Black Diamond to China, then disappear. I thought he was implementing your plan."

Bryce shook his head. He looked hurt. "I'd have charged him. He would have been a fugitive."

"You would never have found him. China offered him five hundred million dollars to deliver. Someone with Suggs's skills could become a ghost with that kind of money."

"How did you discover this?"

"Suggs told me," Adam said. "He offered me a piece of the pie."

Bryce searched Adam's eyes. "Why didn't you take it? That money would have changed everything. You would never have had to risk your life again."

"Because stealing is wrong."

"That's it? You turned down half a billion dollars because it's *wrong?*" Bryce's mouth hung open.

"Following my conscience is the only thing that matters. My honor and morality are not for sale. Not for any price. Fighting evil has been my life's work."

"You're an interesting person, Mr. Locke."

Two security guards rounded the pond and jogged down the causeway. Bryce waved to signal he was okay. A frigid wind blew off the water. It carried the odor of blood. Adam shivered.

"If you weren't working with Suggs to sell Apep to China, how did you know where to find me?"

"Security informed me after Suggs called for the boys. He told them you stole Apep and burned down my house. He said you tried to shoot him."

"If I had wanted to shoot Suggs," Adam said, "he would have been dead long before this."

"I didn't believe it, so I called the police and asked Sergeant Gunn to turn her boat around. Then I grabbed my bow."

Adam stared into Bryce's eyes, looking for a flicker of deception. "You're telling me you had nothing to do with any of these murders?"

"Your life's work may be combating evil, but mine is extending life. Killing to protect that would betray everything I've sought to achieve."

It was plausible Suggs had kept Bryce in the dark and orchestrated everything behind his back. Suggs had claimed Bryce was not his partner. Why would he lie if he planned to kill Adam?

"I didn't set your house on fire," Adam said, "but I broke in to retrieve Effie's downloaded data."

"If you didn't burn it down, who did?"

"Suggs, I guess."

Bryce nodded to himself. "I think I know how you managed to download Effie. Did you recover everything?"

"Suggs threw Apep into the fire." Adam's chest tightened, and he bit his lip to hold back his emotion. Maybe he could persuade Bryce to download her again. "What will you tell the police?"

"I'll tell them whatever's necessary to separate Forever from Suggs's crimes. A scandal is inevitable. This will set us back, especially with my most advanced models destroyed."

Rotors beat overhead. A Massachusetts State Police helicopter crested the hill and headed toward them.

"The government may stop you," Adam said.

"We'll see."

"May I ask you for a favor?"

"You mean besides saving your life?"

"Download Effie's mind again. You can give her a chance."

Bryce looked at the ground. "The technology is still experimental—"

"Please."

"Bring her into Black Diamond after the dust settles, and I'll capture her data the right way. It's the least I can do."

CHAPTER EIGHTY-SIX

The sun sunk below the horizon and cast long cloudy fingers over Buzzards Bay. Adam stared at it with a gnawing sense of cognitive dissonance, which added to his already heightened sense of disquiet.

The evidence pointed to Suggs masterminding the theft, not Bryce. Suggs had basically confessed outside Bryce's burning house, and he had laughed off Adam's suggestion that Bryce had orchestrated everything. What words had he used? Something about Adam not understanding. Suggs had admitted he had worked with someone. But who?

Fang had to be the link. She was a Chinese national with access to Black Diamond and she had been digging into their latest technology. But then why had Suggs sent Gibson to murder her? Adam rubbed the bridge of his nose. He was missing something.

He could not wait to tell Effie the good news that Bryce had agreed to download her mind again and upload it into an earlier model Apep unit stored in the annex. Despite all Adam's failures, they would preserve a part of her, and if the worst happened, she would not disappear.

His house was dark, so he opened the front door and closed it without a sound. If Effie was awake, they may have a chance to catch up before her mind fatigued too much. Even before her diagnosis, her energy levels had waned. He had noticed her lack of desire to socialize and her disinterest in after-dinner walks. There had been so many subtle signs she was sick, but he had attributed her fatigue to her author's sedentary lifestyle.

He had missed so much. Maybe if he had worked less and been home more, he would have been more aware and insisted she visit a doctor. If only they had diagnosed her sooner.

If only.

His life had become one of solitude, like a prisoner sentenced to live within his own mind. Except for the past week's chaos, he had done little but care for Effie's medical needs. They shared deep affection, but not the companionship of lovers experiencing life. He had put his life on hold as she traveled toward the end of hers.

His legs grew heavy as he climbed the stairs to their bedroom. The events on Cuttyhunk had physically worn him out, but his exhaustion came from a deeper place—a psychological hell. Unending torment.

He paused at their bedroom door and summoned the strength to smile. She could never know he was suffering. His pain meant nothing compared to the valiant battle she waged against the cancer. Whenever he wanted to complain about his problems, he thought about the tumors eating away at her organs and the way she persevered without complaint.

Not all heroes wore medals.

He turned the handle and eased open the door.

Effie sprawled on the bed, her skin pal and waxen, her face twisted in pain.

"Effie."

He rushed to her side. Her eyes passed over him without recognition. He pulled her into a hug and her head rolled back. Her body went limp as if her life force had already left.

"Effie, can you hear me?"

Her eyes focused on him. "It's time."

Tears blurred his vision. "I'm calling an ambulance."

"Stop," she said. "It won't help."

"Effie—"

"Talk to me."

"Baby, hang in there." He grabbed the landline off the nightstand. "I'm getting help."

"I . . ."

"What is it?" he asked.

"I'm so sorry."

"I love you, and there's nothing to be sorry about. I should have been here with you. I should never have left your side."

Her eyes unfocused.

"Effie."

Her eyes found his again. "Promise me something."

"Anything."

"Go on living. Have a good life."

"Effie, my darling, hang on. Please don't leave me."

"Promise me you'll be happy, Rufus."

"I can't. Not without you. Don't go."

"Promise me."

Adam's throat tightened and tears rolled down his cheeks. "I love you more than anything."

"Please . . ."

"I promise."

Her face softened, and the wrinkles in her forehead disappeared. The pain seemed to leave her, and the corners of her mouth turned up in a smile. She held it until her eyes rolled back.

She was gone.

CHAPTER EIGHTY-SEVEN

Svetlana met Adam at her door wearing a little black dress, pearls, and stiletto shoes. Her mourning shroud had lifted after Effie's funeral, and she appeared to have rediscovered the fire within her.

"How are you?" she asked.

"Surviving."

She kissed him on both cheeks and led him through the house and out onto her back deck. An open bottle of Chateau Margaux breathed between two place settings. He held out her chair then sat across from her.

"You didn't have to go to all this trouble," Adam said.

"I need to talk to you about something."

His shoulders tensed. Did she want to revisit their relationship? Svetlana was gorgeous, but she was not right for him. Not the person with whom he could build a relationship. Even if she had been perfect, Effie had just died, and he could not think about dating again. He would need time to recover. A very long time.

"I'm not ready for anything new right now," he said. "I'm still struggling to find reasons to get out of bed every morning. Making it through the day is all I can handle. I—"

"Take a breath. I'm not hitting on you. Not yet anyway. I know you need time. I know it better than anyone."

"It's been rough. Hard to—"

"I need you to steal Lazarus and Apep and bring them to me."

Adam blinked. "What did you say?"

"It's Sunday, so few people will be at work. Use your access, take the devices out of the lab, and bring them here."

"What the hell are you talking about?"

Svetlana turned to stone. "I may as well confide in you. It's the only play left. I've tried everything else."

The pieces came together. "It was you."

She smirked. "Took you long enough, Mr. Special Agent. I wondered when you'd figure it out."

"You were helping Suggs steal the technology and sell it to China."

"Bingo. Now, you're my last chance. Get Lazarus and Apep for us and we'll become millionaires."

Adam shook his head. This was too horrible to be true. "The fire destroyed them."

"But there are other models. Older units."

"Why did you tell me about the sale to China if you were behind it?"

"I needed you to take down Bryce and sow dissension. If the police arrested or detained him, the technology would have been easier to steal and deliver to China."

"Tommy tried to stop you."

"Tommy was an idiot," Svetlana said. "He was in on the plan from the beginning, but he got cold feet. He felt guilty about betraying Bryce and was going to confess. Tommy was always weak."

"You killed him."

"I didn't have to. I told Suggs about the problem, and he took care of it for me."

"Suggs was in on your plan?"

"It would have been hard to walk out of Forever Technology with the devices and software without him. Tommy didn't have your clandestine skills. We needed Suggs."

Every muscle in Adam's body fired. He wanted to jump across the table and beat her to death. She had killed Tommy in cold blood. And for what?

Money? He flexed his fingers and rolled his neck. He had to suppress his emotions and get Svetlana to tell him everything.

"You and Tommy took an enormous risk by revealing your plan to Suggs," he said. "What if he had decided not to play ball? What if he had told Bryce or gone to the police?"

"That's why I didn't let Tommy approach him."

"Then how?"

"I fucked Suggs and recorded the whole thing."

"You blackmailed him?"

"I didn't have to. The simpleton fell in love with me. All men think with their dicks. I never told him about the recording. I got him talking about the project to make him look guilty on tape, but I didn't need it to persuade him. He was lovesick and bitter that Bryce had never given him a share of the company. He thought Bryce belittled him. It was easy to get him onboard."

"You're a sociopath."

"I'm practical."

"You mean immoral. You caused the death of three people."

"Don't forget Dr. Smith."

"She fell."

"I helped her."

Icy fingers tickled Adam's spine. "Was she on to you?"

Svetlana's eyes hardened to stone. "Tommy was fucking her. That idiot thought he could have another affair without me knowing."

Infidelity, theft, treason, murder. Adam tried to process the layers of evil swirling around a quaint little island. "I don't understand why you're confessing. Why now?"

"I need you. Without your help, all of it will have been for nothing. That fire set Bryce back a bit, but he'll recover and be ready to launch soon. The Chinese need it before he does. I want—"

"You set the fire."

"To buy time. I was on Cuttyhunk when you told me you were going to Bryce's house. I gave you time to get inside, then I followed."

Svetlana was psycho. "Why burn the technology?"

"That State Police whore was digging into everything. I had to stall Bryce's research and create a diversion to give Suggs an opportunity to steal Apep. I didn't know he had moved it to Bryce's basement, and I didn't know you would kill Suggs."

She was evil to the core. Irredeemable.

"Bryce killed Suggs, not me."

"Either way, he's dead. Useless to me. You're my only chance. China will pay five hundred million. We can buy a mansion in Macao, live like royalty. We'll be able to purchase our own village."

"*We?*"

"Effie and Tommy are gone. We only have each other. We'll be fugitives, but we can buy new identities. It's time to start our lives together."

"I would never—"

"Never what?" She spat the words. "What do we have left here? You're broke. Tommy's money will only last a few years. Then what? Let's be filthy rich."

"You don't know me at all."

She came around the table and slid into his lap. "I'm offering you *everything*. Come with me and become a king."

"I would never betray my oath."

"This is the biggest decision in your life. It's time to seize your future." She took his hand and placed it on her breast. "You can have it all."

"I won't betray my country, and I won't betray the memory of my wife by sleeping with you."

A hurricane raged in Svetlana's eyes. She grabbed a steak knife off the table and swung it at his neck.

Adam blocked her thrust with his forearm. He punched her in the face. Svetlana dropped the knife and fell off the chair onto her bottom. A dribble of blood trickled from her nose. She looked stunned.

Adam pulled his phone out of his pocket and dialed 9-1-1.

CHAPTER EIGHTY-EIGHT

One week after Sugg's death, Fang nodded to the security guard and hobbled out of Forever Technology on her crutches. In the days following the incident, Cuttyhunk had been a beehive of police activity. State Police investigators and FBI agents had jockeyed for position as they served search warrants and dug through company records for evidence of homicide and espionage. Federal forensics teams combed through communication devices and servers under the authority of a FISA warrant seeking links to Suggs's Chinese customer.

Fang had been as surprised as anyone to hear China had negotiated a deal with Suggs, especially since Xiu Yän had ordered her to steal the technology. Had they been trying to save money or had the sale been a backup plan in case she failed?

She laid her crutches in the back of a cart and motored south on West End Road. A few minutes later, she turned into the Allen P. Spaulding Memorial Solar Field. Solar energy defrayed the island's exorbitant energy costs. She continued down the driveway to the base of the hill where black tiled solar panels ascended the slope like bleachers in a stadium. Machinery hummed inside an electrical building.

She climbed out and used her crutches to shuffle down the row of solar panels. Getting away from the machinery would help her hear Xiu approach. He had a knack for sneaking up on her. She reached the middle of the row, and a familiar scent tingled her sinuses, but she could not place it. She eyed the driveway and waited. He would arrive soon.

The past week had been a whirlwind, with every day bringing another critical decision. Had she made the correct choices?

She looked down at her shoes, lost in her thoughts. She snapped back to the present.

Two cigarette butts lay in the dirt. She recognized the blue writing on the paper—Zhongnanhai cigarettes. Xiu had been there.

"You're early," Xiu said from behind her. "That's new."

She whirled around and faced him. How had she not heard him approach? Where had he been hiding? Did he know what she had done?

"I did not see you," she said.

"In my business, arriving first promotes longevity." He wore a heavy trench coat and kept his hands in his pockets.

"You heard what happened?"

"I read what was in the media," he said in Beijing Mandarin. "Unfortunately, they sealed the search warrant affidavits. What about the device?"

"Lazarus and Apep were destroyed in the fire," she responded in Mandarin.

Xiu lit another cigarette. He took a long drag, held it, then blew the smoke into her face. "But you told me you stole it before your accident."

"Mr. Suggs found it and returned it to Mr. Hastings' private lab. Adam Locke rescued it from the house, but it is gone now. Suggs threw it into the fire, probably out of spite."

"Why didn't he report the theft to the police?"

"The police said Mr. Suggs was planning to sell Lazarus to China." She tried to keep her face passive, but her eyes flared. They had not trusted her. Xiu had not trusted her.

"A backup, my little flower. In case you failed."

"Why—?"

"A wise decision by our Party leaders . . . considering you did fail."

"I can still retrieve the technology for you. Most of the data and software still exist. The fire only took the most advanced cyborgs, and they still have earlier models of Apep."

"The police must know you stole it."

"Apparently, Suggs deleted the video recordings before he died," she said. "I heard the police found nothing on the security system."

"You're Chinese. You will be under suspicion, even if they didn't record you stealing the device. They'll be watching."

"I'll accuse them of racism and xenophobia if they press me." Fang took a deep breath and tried to remember everything she needed to say. "I can deliver an older unit to you, but if the Party needs the latest technology, I'll have to wait for new units to be constructed."

Xiu narrowed his eyes. "How could you possibly get a unit out of that building now?"

"Things are hectic, but in a week or two, once the police have left, I may be able—"

"They'll change their security procedures. You'll never walk out the door with technology."

"I can download pieces of the software and bring it out a little at a time. Do you want me to do that?"

"Hmm." Xiu finished his cigarette and ground it into the dirt.

"Tell me what you want."

"You must be anxious about your mother and sister," he said. "They're depending on you to succeed."

Fang knew they were out of his reach, but a shiver passed through her. "Have you spoken to them?"

"Not since I left."

"If I steal the technology, you'll leave them alone?"

"We'll celebrate them as heroes of the state."

"Then I'll do it."

"Wait two weeks, no longer, then copy as much of the newest technology as possible."

"I was hoping you would say that." Fang said in English. She smiled and a massive weight lifted off her.

Xiu cocked his head and his eyes hardened. "What do you—"

"FBI, freeze," an agent yelled from the woods.

Other agents wearing blue windbreakers emerged from the trees, their guns pointed at him. Xiu did not turn to look. He stared at Fang. "Your family is finished."

"They left China yesterday. You won't be able to touch them. Or me."

Fang stepped back as an agent tackled Xiu. Her heart pounded as they handcuffed him. It was done. There was no going back.

Someone placed a hand on her shoulder, and she turned.

Adam smiled at her. "Your mother and sister landed in Los Angeles an hour ago. They're safe."

She hugged him and wept.

CHAPTER EIGHTY-NINE

Adam sat on his porch, his mind and body numb. Effie and Tommy were gone, and Svetlana would spend the rest of her days in a prison cell. Waves lapped the shore, and the rhythmic sound caressed him like a mother humming to her child. Before Effie's illness, Adam's career had been the source of his passion, his identity. Now, his job was gone, along with the love of his life.

At least he had solved the mystery of the calls between Effie and Tommy. Old emails between them made it clear Tommy had been planning to use his company's technology to help Effie, once it was perfected, but she had kept it a secret because she thought asking Tommy for help would have made Adam uncomfortable.

He dragged himself out of the chair and wandered down the flagstone path to the beach. His heels sunk into the gritty sand and shells crunched beneath his feet as he rambled along the shore. The sea air smelled alive.

"What will I do now?"

Doug Barnstable had suggested he reapply to DEA. Adam could probably get rehired, but returning to the Special Operations Division was not guaranteed, and he did not want to go back to investigating domestic narcotics cases. Could he resume the life he had before, or did he need something new?

He had always been self-conscious about being an agent while his brother shined as a tech start-up star. But scientists and techies did not always use their math skills and intellectual abilities to help people. Sometimes great thinkers used their brains to control others and seize power. Evil affected geniuses too. Maybe fighting terrorism had a more positive influence on society than Tommy's entrepreneurial pursuits. Law enforcement did not allow him to discover the true nature of matter, but it had shown him something equally important.

The true nature of man.

Maybe it was time to be proud of his accomplishments. Although he had violated the law to do it. Sometimes, following the rules did not lead to justice. He had learned that over these past weeks. And maybe he had not finished writing his story. Monsters inhabited the world, and Adam had the ability and courage to stop them.

His phone vibrated, and he pulled it from his pocket. Doug Barnstable's number displayed on the screen. He had called every day for a week, ostensibly to comfort Adam through a hard time, but Doug had an ulterior motive. He wanted Adam back.

Adam let the call go to voicemail.

Adam had devoted his professional life to fighting for justice. But what did finding justice really mean? He had been willing to break laws to save Effie. Was he still righteous? Forever Technology had covered up Sarah Smith's death and inhibited the investigation of Tommy's murder to protect their business. Justified or not, they had perverted the system, lied to authorities, withheld information from their stockholders. Bryce's billions had manipulated the legal process, but did that justify Adam's lawbreaking?

Whatever the answer, evil existed and had to be stopped. Adam had seen it in the mountains of Afghanistan, the jungles of Honduras, and on the streets of New York City. Good and evil battled for supremacy and people needed to choose sides. Finding out who killed Tommy had been important because he was family, but it also meant something to the broader idea of justice. Adam's quest to protect virtue had etched itself into his DNA. He had needed to help Effie, and prioritize her healthcare, but he could not turn his back on the mission that had driven him for his adult life. Adam needed to be a force for the good.

He called Doug back.

"You doing okay, Bud?" Doug asked.

"I'm a train wreck."

"Maybe you need to get back to work. Take your mind off everything." Doug forced a chuckle.

"I'm not sure I want to rejoin the bureaucratic beast."

"I had something else in mind."

Adam stopped and stared across the Vineyard Sound. The haze had cleared after the storm, and Martha's Vineyard appeared crisp on the horizon. "Okay, I'll bite. Tell me."

"We've been meeting with Jean Laguerre since you arrested him," Doug said. "We just had another proffer at the US Attorney's Office in New York, and Laguerre finally agreed to cooperate."

Excitement rumbled in Adam's stomach, a flash of his former self. "And?"

"Laguerre's organization has been assisting radical Islamic extremists to sneak into the US."

"That's a new endeavor for him."

"Laguerre used his drug transportation routes to facilitate human trafficking, weapons shipments, counterfeiting, and other illicit business, but yeah, this is the first we heard about his trafficking terrorists."

"Who was he dealing with?"

"ISIS."

Adam's pulse raced. Doug had set the hook, and they both knew it. "If you're not asking me to reapply to DEA, how can I help?"

"It would take time to get rehired, and they'd assign you where the agency needed bodies, not back with the narco-terrorism group. God knows how long it would take to get you back here. We don't even have an opening right now."

"Then what?" Adam asked.

"I need you on this now. I arranged to bring you back as a contractor. You can work on a case-by-case basis."

The sun broke through the clouds and sunlight shimmered off the water. The blanket of grief lifted off him. "Contracting takes years. There are bids, competition—"

"I'm not suggesting you start your own firm," Doug said. "I spoke with Sam Baxter at Global Criminal Threat Solutions, and he agreed to hire you. They already have a contract with DEA. You'll be assigned to work with my group on the Laguerre case."

"And do what?"

"What you always do—investigate. Work your magic. Develop and run sources, collect evidence, put a prosecutable case together. And once we get indictments, lure your targets to a country with an extradition treaty and help us arrest them."

"You want me to be a special agent, but without the badge."

"I want you to do what you've always done—without the government bureaucracy. Without the rules."

Adam ran his fingers over his Rolex. Being a contractor would give him the freedom he never had as an agent. Sometimes protocols needed to be broken. What would Effie want him to do?

"It's tempting."

"Help us stop these animals."

Adam raised his face to the sky and let the sun warm him. The heat filled him, opened his soul.

"It's time to get back in the game. Tell Sam I'll take the job."

CHAPTER NINETY

A new security guard escorted Adam into the Black Diamond annex and led him to the laboratory once used by Fang. She had made a deal to cooperate with the Feds, which would keep her out of jail, and she had entered the Witness Security Program. Adam had not been back to her office since before Effie's death, and he had only returned at the insistence of Sergeant Gunn. She rose from behind a desk where two white-coated forensic techs huddled over Fang's computer.

"Adam," Gunn said. "I was so sorry to hear about your loss."

"What's this about?" his voice sounded dead, devoid of humanity. He had had enough sympathy. Virtue signaling and condolences would not bring Effie back.

"I appreciate your coming," she said. "I'm sure this is the last place you want to be."

"True."

"As you know, we've been scouring Felix Suggs's files. We finally got around to digging into Dr. Jin's files to corroborate her story. Her cooperation has helped."

"And?"

"We found an encrypted file with your name on it."

"Why not ask Fang about it?"

"We did. She said the file isn't hers. We traced the code back to Suggs. He uploaded it the day after Fang fell off the cliff."

"What's on it?"

"We were hoping you could tell us."

"I have no idea."

"You don't know the access code?"

"I didn't know Suggs had a file on me. Is this why I came all this way? I could have told you this over the phone."

"For obvious reasons, the FBI has prohibited us from discussing the details of our joint investigation over the phone. But that's not the only reason I asked you here. Bryce Hastings flew back from Washington this morning, and he should join us any minute. He claims he has an override code, a backdoor that gets him into any file on the system."

As if on cue, Bryce entered the lab. "A basic safety precaution."

"Mr. Hastings," Gunn said. "Thank you for coming."

He nodded and smiled at Adam. "How's life back at the DEA?"

"I haven't started yet. I've been preoccupied."

"Yes, of course," Bryce said. "You're always welcome back here. I promise you it will be more lucrative."

"I have to follow my calling."

Bryce smiled and spread his hands out in surrender. "You can't blame me for trying."

"I hate to interrupt," Gunn said, "but if you can access this file, our analysts can get started. It may be the last piece of the puzzle."

"I'll need some privacy."

Gunn nodded and ushered the forensic techs to the other side of the room. The keyboard clacked as Bryce entered his password into his secret digital tunnel. His eyes moved back and forth across the screen, then he blinked and leaned forward.

"I'm in," Bryce said. "This is a massive file. What the hell was Suggs doing?"

Adam followed Gunn and stood behind Bryce.

"What is it?" Gunn asked.

"He may have stored the data here that he planned to sell," Bryce said.

"He hid it on your own servers, right under your nose?" Gunn asked.

"Maybe . . . no. Here's the summary file."

"Why is it under my name?" Adam asked.

Bryce clicked through a series of screens and read code that looked like gibberish. A smile spread across his face.

"It's here."

"What?" Adam asked.

"Effie."

"A file on his girlfriend?" Gunn asked.

"Not a file on her," Bryce said.

"What then?" Adam asked.

"It's her." Bryce said.

Adam's heart swelled. "You mean . . .?"

"It's a copy of the cryptographic device to access her data, her full download," Bryce said. "Suggs must have dumped it from Apep before he took it to my residence."

"Maybe he wanted to use it as leverage," Gunn said.

"Can you," Adam's throat tightened, "implant it in a cyborg?"

"Not until I rebuild the machines," Bryce said. "But once I do, yes."

"What the hell does that mean?" Gunn asked.

Adam opened his mouth to answer but could not speak.

"It means," Bryce said, "Effie's consciousness is here."

"It means," Adam said, "she's not gone forever."

Bryce grinned. Behind him, a server came to life. Its light blinked green.

ACKNOWLEDGEMENTS

I write all my books for my brilliant, caring, and courageous wife—Cynthia Farahat Higgins. She has supported me from the moment I told her I wanted to write novels, despite the dismal economic outlook for authors. Hang in there, our breakout novel is coming.

Objective criticism is crucial to editing a manuscript, and with that in mind, I wish to thank my beta readers. Nadya and James Higgins, Bryan Talebi, Stephen Cone, and David Holtzman were the brave souls who suffered through early drafts of my book. Your notes vastly improved this work.

I'm a proud member of International Thriller Writers and Sisters in Crime, two wonderful organizations who support authors in so many ways. They've made me a better writer. Thanks to the Royal Writers Secret Society for their insightful critiques.

Finally, thanks to Reagan Rothe and everyone at Black Rose Writing.

ABOUT THE AUTHOR

Jeffrey James Higgins is a retired supervisory special agent who writes thrillers, short stories, scripts, creative nonfiction, and essays. He has wrestled a suicide bomber, fought the Taliban in combat, and chased terrorists across five continents. He received the Attorney General's Award for Exceptional Heroism and the DEA Award of Valor. Jeffrey has been interviewed by CNN, National Geographic, and The New York Times. He's a #1 Amazon bestselling author with eighteen literary awards, including the Claymore Award, PenCraft's Best Fiction Book of 2022, and a Reader's Favorite Gold Medal. Black Rose Writing published his first two novels, *Furious* and *Unseen*.

Discover his writing at https:// JeffreyJamesHiggins.com.

OTHER TITLES BY JEFFREY JAMES HIGGINS

NOTE FROM JEFFREY JAMES HIGGINS

Word-of-mouth is crucial for any author to succeed. If you enjoyed *The Forever Game*, please leave a review online—anywhere you are able. Even if it's just a sentence or two. It would make all the difference and would be very much appreciated.

Thanks!
Jeffrey James Higgins

We hope you enjoyed reading this title from:

www.blackrosewriting.com

Subscribe to our mailing list – *The Rosevine* – and receive **FREE** books, daily deals, and stay current with news about upcoming releases and our hottest authors.
Scan the QR code below to sign up.

Already a subscriber? Please accept a sincere thank you for being a fan of Black Rose Writing authors.

View other Black Rose Writing titles at www.blackrosewriting.com/books and use promo code **PRINT** to receive a **20% discount** when purchasing.